BREAKAWAY

Breakaway

GRACE REILLY

2

**BEYOND
THE
PLAY
SERIES**

Published by Moonedge Press, LLC

Cover Design and Illustration by Melody Jeffries Design

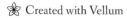 Created with Vellum

For Moira, who loved Cooper from the start.

AUTHOR'S NOTE

While I have tried to stay truthful to the realities of college hockey and college sports in general throughout this book when possible, there may be inaccuracies within, both intentional and unintentional.

Please visit my website for full content warnings.

1

COOPER

AFTER A LIFETIME of waking up at random times to head to the rink, plus two full seasons of McKee hockey, you'd think I wouldn't mess up something as stupid as the time of the season-opener exhibition.

Yet here I am, running at a full tilt to Markley Center, my duffel bag slung over my shoulder like it's full of cash and I'm trying to get to the getaway car before the cops. I dash across a crosswalk, ignoring the outraged honk of a car as the driver brakes to avoid me, and almost fall on my ass as I hustle past a group of students pre-gaming on their way to a party.

I smack into a girl's shoulder, and she wheels on me, shouting, "Watch out, asshole!"

I'm not fast enough to dodge the cup of beer she throws at me.

Fantastic. I wipe the drip away as best as I can while running. When I finally reach the doors, I yank them open and skid inside.

I make it into the locker room at the exact moment Coach Ryder wraps up his pre-game chat. All my teammates are wearing our home purple, pads on, skates on, sticks and helmets in hand. This game against the University of Connecticut won't count for the standings, but it signals that it's time to get serious. After weeks of preparation for the season, it's our first chance to show Coach how much we've absorbed the new playbook—and a chance for me to make my case for captain.

Right now, though? He gives me a hard look with those pale blue eyes that can cut through you like a knife. They remind me of my father's, and not in a good way. "Go on," he says. "Show me what you've got, gentlemen."

"Where were you?" Evan, my defensive partner, asks me. He shakes out his braids before he puts his helmet on. "And why do you smell like a frat house?"

"I got stuck in class." That's not technically a lie; I just thought I had more time for office hours with Professor Morgenstern. I needed to beg her for an extension on my *Macbeth* essay for her Shakespeare seminar, and when she gets going, it's hard to wrap up the conversation. The semester has been underway for a month now, but I still don't have my shit together, especially for the three seminars I'm taking. Shakespeare. The Feminist Gothic. Fucking *Milton*. I haven't done my readings in a week.

I pull my sweatshirt over my head and shove it into my locker along with my lucky Yankees cap. "I'll see you on the ice."

"Callahan," Coach Ryder calls. "A word."

My stomach sinks even though I expected as much. I keep undressing, throwing on my pads as quickly as I can while doing it right, but look up when I hear his footsteps.

I've had a lot of coaches in my life, but no one screams "hockey coach" like Lawrence Ryder. He always wears a collared shirt, not just for games but for practices too, and while he hasn't played since his senior year at Harvard—when he led his team to a Frozen Four victory—he has the crooked nose and hard-ass attitude to prove he did his time on the ice. He's improved my game so much in our first two seasons together, and we've spoken about the future—the only future I'll accept for myself—in a way I can't with my actual father.

I know Dad will never admit it, probably because Mom won't let him, but I'm sure he still wishes that I fell in love with football like him and my older brother James. Instead, I traded cleats for skates and never looked back.

"Why were you late?" Coach asks.

I bend to lace up my skates. "I lost track of time, sir."

"Is that why you smell like cheap beer?"

"A girl spilled a beer on me. Outside the rink." I look up at him as I stand, balancing on the blades of my skates. "It won't happen again."

"What did you lose track of time doing?" The unspoken question hangs in reserve. Not that I've ever spoken to Coach about my personal life, but it's not exactly a secret that under normal circumstances, I spend my free time getting tours of the campus dorms, one Daddy's little girl at a time.

"I was in office hours with a professor."

He nods. "Fine. But I don't want you coming in late again, Callahan. Especially not for an actual game. Preparation—"

"—Makes the game," I finish. I've heard it from him many times. He expects the best from all of us, but especially from players like me, the ones with a shot at a future in hockey.

Coach Ryder is a college coach; we're students, not his employees. McKee University isn't paying us to play. We're here for an education, however important sports are to the overall profile of the college. Academics are supposed to come first—but he's known since freshman year that if I could, I would have declared for the NHL Draft the moment I turned eighteen. I'm getting my degree for my parents; my dad has always urged us to consider past our athletic careers to the rest of our lives. Originally, I wanted to play in a junior league, get drafted, and work on an online degree in between, but that wasn't enough for him and Mom. The only consolation? I've had great preparation for the NHL so far at McKee, so hopefully I'll be able to go straight into the league, rather than start at a farm team, as soon as I graduate.

I just need to get through two more years. Two more seasons. Now that I'm an upperclassman, the pressure has ratcheted up even higher. The crop of seniors who graduated left the team in a precarious position, and if there's anything that would help solidify my post-grad plans, it would be two full seasons as team captain, proving that I can lead as well as play. I don't know if he's considering me for it yet, but I hope like hell that he is.

"Yes," Coach says, those serious eyes still studying me closely. "And I thought we cleared up your issues last season."

I hold my chin up, despite the hurt that hooks into my belly and tugs, like a fish caught on a line. We fell just short of Regionals last season for lots of reasons, but I won't pretend that the fighting penalty that led to my suspension from the last game of the season didn't play a big factor. I should have been on the ice for that game, and I wasn't. "We did."

"All right," he says. He claps me on the shoulder. "Warm up quickly. Show me what you've got."

After the quickest stretch I can get away with, I head to the ice. Even though it's only an exhibition game, there are a bunch of students here, and even some supporters for UConn. While the football program is the jewel of the school, McKee hockey games turn out a good crowd.

Evan and I are first shift defenders now, so when Coach Ryder stops his chat with UConn's head coach and the referee signals the first faceoff, we're already on the ice, in position to protect our goalie, Remmy—Aaron Rembeau—and our zone. I settle into the game quickly, relishing in the pace, however low stakes, of a game. When the season officially starts this Friday, it'll really feel like I've moved on. Since the spring, I've stewed over the failure of last season and everything that came along with it, but I'm finally close to wiping the slate clean.

The puck rockets down the ice, followed by one of the UConn players. I meet him at the edge of the defensive zone and try to jostle him for it, but misread his pass. The puck ends up on our side of the rink, deftly brought in by another player on UConn's offense. He slaps it straight between Remmy's legs into the net.

Shit. I don't usually make mistakes like that.

I skate off the ice when my shift ends and watch the second shift take over. Settling on the bench, I gulp down some water. Despite all the conditioning to stay in shape in the off-season, I'm heaving from the near two-minute sprint. I rub at my chest guard. There's a knot of pressure building behind it, making it hard to swallow. It's not just about being late and missing the opportunity to screw my head on straight before the game, or about letting that goal through. It goes deeper than that, running like a fissure down my breastbone.

The pressure of performing well so the NHL will come calling when I graduate.

The pressure of helping the team make it to the Frozen Four this season, rather than sabotaging the whole effort.

The pressure of taking care of my little sister Izzy, a freshman at McKee this year, like my parents are expecting from me now that James has graduated and gone on to the NFL.

Usually, the ice is where I want to be. I'm focused there. Calm. But during practice for the last few weeks, and now during this game, and last spring when I punched Nikolai

Abney-Volkov in the mouth and got us both ejected from the game, I've been losing my grip on that focus, along with everything else.

If I'm being perfectly honest with myself, there's another reason, too. Something I haven't wanted to name, because it sounds stupid, even in my head. It's one thing to like sex, and another to feel like I'm on edge because I haven't had it.

But I haven't gotten laid in months.

Months.

The last time I saw a pair of tits, it was spring. Now it's almost fucking October, and I'm striking out with every girl I try to chat up. Usually, my status as a star hockey player on campus leads to my choice of puck bunnies, but now, I'm not getting their attention. I don't know what's wrong with me; why it feels like I have cooties or some grade school shit like that. I look the same, act the same, talk the same—and the charm that used to lead to me fielding multiple offers a night is giving me a big fat nothing.

Sex wouldn't solve anything, but getting off inside a girl instead of my fist would be a start, however embarrassing that sounds.

We're only playing a few ten-minute periods, since this game's just for practice, so time flies by, and soon we're in the last few minutes, knotted at 1-1.

"Callahan," Coach says. "You and Bell are back in."

Evan and I hop over the boards and settle in. Not thirty seconds go by before one of our freshmen, Lars Halvorsen, sends a beauty of a shot into the UConn net. We skate over to congratulate him. It's not a real game goal, but he's talented, so I'm sure he'll have his first one soon enough. Plus, it breaks the tie, and we won't have overtime for a game like this. Another minute, and we'll be able to hit the showers and go home.

We win the faceoff, but we're quickly forced back into our

own defensive zone thanks to good pressure. A UConn player shoves Evan into the boards behind the net. I rush over to see if I can jostle the puck free and smack it away, forcing a chase until time runs out.

"—Mom was a hot lay," the UConn player is chirping as he pins Evan with his shoulder. "When did she have you, when she was fifteen?"

Evan freezes. For a heart-stopping moment I think he's hurt, but then I realize that he's working back tears. My whole body locks up, my heart pounding so hard I can hear the rush of blood in my ears.

Evan's not just my teammate, he's one of my best friends.

And his mother died of cancer over the summer.

My fist connects with the UConn player's jaw with a satisfying jolt.

2

COOPER

DISTANTLY, I hear the referee's whistle. Feel the arms of someone pulling me back. The UConn guy gets in a shot, knocking my helmet askew as he connects with my mouth, before we're hauled away from each other. I poke my tongue at the corner of my mouth and taste copper.

Guys chirp at each other all the time, and there's no way he could have known he was touching such a sore subject.

But I know, and I won't fucking stand for it. Even if it means dealing with Coach Ryder's anger.

His eyes are blazing when I make it to the bench. He scrubs his hand over his clean-shaven jaw. The buttons on his shirt look like they're about to pop off. For half a second, I'm convinced he's going to chew me out right here, but then he shakes his head. "I want you in my office."

I nod. "Yes, sir."

I hold my head up as I walk to the locker room. I even keep my shit together as I unlace my skates and take off my gear, piece by sweaty piece. The team files in around me, hushed in their talking even though we got the win. A bunch of the guys hit the showers, but I know Coach means he wants to see me now, not after I've washed the grime of the game away.

I catch sight of myself in a mirror. I look like a wreck, my hair flopping into my eyes, blood dripping down from my lip into my beard. I pick up my stick and crack it in half right over my knee, then throw the pieces onto the floor. Behind me, someone coughs.

Fuck.

I don't regret defending Evan, but I hate that Mr. "Yo Mama" Douchebag baited me into taking a real swing.

I knock on Coach's door out of habit, even though he's still out with the team, and sink into the chair in front of the desk.

When the door opens, I don't look up. Coach's disappointed face is just like my dad's, and I see that often enough.

I hear him settle into his chair. He leans back, and the chair creaks in the silence. He clears his throat.

"Callahan," he says.

That makes me look at him. That's a difference. Dad says my first name, Cooper, but here, I'm Callahan. I'm the name stitched on the back of my purple-and-white McKee sweater. It's my family's name, but at least on the ice, it's only mine. Dad and James can have it on the football field, but I've never been comfortable there. My adopted brother and best friend, Sebastian, can choose to wear it on his baseball jersey. The ice is all mine.

He sighs. "Late, sloppy, and short-tempered. You promised me different."

I swallow. I deserve to hear what he's saying, but it still stings. "I know, sir."

"Want to explain what happened?" he says. "Because Bell won't stop babbling, and I love that kid, but he doesn't make a lick of sense when he's all worked up."

I bite my lip, accidentally digging my teeth into the cut. I hold back a wince as I look at Coach. "That guy was talking shit about his mother."

Coach's mouth twists. "Fuck."

"I know we agreed no fighting—"

"We didn't agree," he interrupts. "I gave you an order, which you were supposed to follow. And you didn't."

"I couldn't let him get away with it."

"So you retaliate in a way that won't lead to penalties." He pinches his nose, shaking his head as his eyes close. "You're lucky it happened in a game like this, because I managed to keep you eligible for the season opener."

He looks at me, working his jaw. When he raises one eyebrow, I just stare back at him. I know he's expecting an apology, but I'm not about to give it. Not for defending my teammate. Truthfully, I didn't even think about whether the fight would lead to a suspension until this very moment.

Another mistake. Another slip in the opposite direction; down the mountain rather than up to the summit.

"Someone needed to shut him up," I say eventually.

He stands, turning to look at a photo on the wall behind his desk. The photographer captured the exact moment his team realized they won the Frozen Four—the excitement, the joy, the sheer fucking relief to have made it to the top of that mountain. I want that to be me, just in royal McKee purple instead of crimson, waving the cup up high.

And that's before I get to the NHL and I'm raising the Stanley Cup, of course.

"I want you to be captain," he says.

Of all the things I was expecting him to say right now, that wasn't at the top of the list. I wasn't sure it would even be *on* the list anymore.

"Sir," I say, smoothing out my sweatshirt and sitting up straighter. "I..."

"Of course, I can't do that if you're going to get yourself thrown out thanks to fighting penalties," he says. "Or if you're going to play like crap. You have the potential to be the leader of this team, Callahan. I want you to be. You have the hunger." He points to the photograph. He's right in the middle of the huddle of Harvard players, recognizable even over twenty years in the past, the 'C' on his jersey shining like a beacon. "If we go anywhere this season, it'll be thanks to you."

I swallow down the emotion threatening to show on my face. It's one thing to know you're talented and another to hear it put so plainly. Captain. I've been trying to make my case, of course, but I didn't really think it would happen this year. When last year's group of seniors graduated, it really weakened the team, but there are still a few talented upperclassmen.

"But I'm just a junior," I say. "What about one of the seniors? Brandon or Mickey? Brandon's the center."

He shakes his head. "If it's going to be anyone, it'll be you. But you need to earn it. Do you understand? No more fighting. Keep your head down and focus on your game."

I nod. "Got it."

Anything for that 'C' on my sweater. James was the de facto captain of the football team last year, and now he's leading the offense for the Philadelphia Eagles. It's not a direct comparison, considering how different football and hockey are, but two seasons as captain—hopefully of a Frozen Four finalist team—will help build my case for the NHL and the nice rookie deal I'm hoping to scoop up.

"I have an idea that I think will help," he says. "You know the rink in town?"

It takes me a moment, but then I picture it in my mind. Moorbridge Skating Center. It's downtown, near the arcade.

James and I went there last year with his girlfriend, Bex—now his fiancée—to teach her how to skate. "Yeah."

"The owner, Nikki Rodriguez, is looking for help. They have skating lessons, that sort of thing."

My excitement sours; I can see where this is going. Everything costs something when it comes to Coach Ryder. "And?"

"And I think you'd be a perfect volunteer. You'll go, starting on Wednesday, to help with the lessons. There's a junior ice sports class that meets every week."

I bite back the urge to tell him that honestly, getting laid would probably be a better route to stress relief. "To help... the kids?"

"You were their age once, finding your passion for skating and hockey. Help teach them how to unlock that. I think it'll help you find some patience." He claps my shoulder. "Which you'll need if you're going to be my captain."

"I can't," I say. "I don't even—"

"Son, listen." He leans back against the edge of his desk, crossing his arms over his chest. His gaze is sympathetic, but that does nothing to undercut the intensity in them. "Not to use the obvious metaphor, but the ice? It's thin. Either you do this and get your head on straight, or the next time you lose your temper, however justified, you'll leave me no choice but to bench you."

3

PENNY

I WORK the toy even deeper, my toes curling against the sheets as my knees fall open. I let out a little gasp as it hits the right angle. It might not be a warm cock, but it's at least as thick, making it easier to coax along my fantasy. I drag it in and out, turning my head into my pillow as my mind fills with the right images. Strong, tattooed arms hooking my legs around his trim waist. Biting my neck before he turns me over, spanking my ass as he spreads my legs. His rough voice in my ear, whispering about how good I'm being, smelling like —

No. Not that. Anything but that.

I shake my head as the fantasy falters. I arch my back, searching for enough sensation to keep it going, but it's useless. My eyes fly open, the fantasy fleeing as images—the bad kind—flood my mind. I dig down against my lip, panting. Half an hour spent working myself up, only to hit a wall again. I scrub my hand over my face.

Three times in a row now. I've worked hard for years to keep Preston—and any future Prestons—out of my life, but lately, he's found a way into my fantasies. My happy place.

There are two things he's never been able to touch, my fantasies and the stories I scribble into my notebooks, but after this? It's safe to say that the former just broke.

I used to be able to whip up a good fantasy scenario without a problem. Some girls don't like to masturbate, but I've enjoyed it ever since I realized how good I could make myself feel. A couple minutes thinking about Mat Barzal or Tyler Seguin, or if I was in more of a supernatural mood, a sexy werewolf or orc, and I'd be ready to go. Lately? I get as far as my fantasy guy thrusting inside me, and no matter what I imagine, whether it be the position, the setting, or the specific type of boning we're doing, my orgasm dissolves like a rock hitting the center of a lake, never to be recovered. The spicy romance novels haven't helped. Neither have the hockey highlights. Not even revisiting the sexiest parts of my half-written novel has led anywhere. Something reminds me of that February night, of him, and a hint of panic poisons it all.

As I press my hand to my chest, trying to ease my racing heart, I swallow down that spoonful of poison, willing it to neutralize. I've worked with Dr. Faber for years on how to pull myself back from the edge before I spiral. It's okay to be frustrated. I don't have to let it control me.

Except three times now, it has.

Just like that, my arousal is gone completely, replaced by a dangerous, brief flicker of unease that makes my stomach roll. I swallow as I try to relax my tight shoulders. I stare down at the dildo in my hand and fight a wave of revulsion. "Fuck!"

I throw it across the room.

My roommate bursts in, wrapped in a towel, her dark hair hanging over one shoulder, eyes wild with panic. Is that a razor in her hand?

"What's going on?" she demands—at the exact second my bright blue dildo hits her in the face.

You know when you see something horrible happen in real time, and it feels like slow-motion? Yeah. That's my dildo hitting Mia like a freakin' puck to the face guard. It smacks her cheek, the fake balls bouncing, before landing on the floor with a wet smack.

We stare at each other for a moment that stretches out for approximately a million years. Her grip tightens on the razor as she wipes at her cheek.

I remember something very terrifying. My best friend used to play softball, and she was a pitcher.

"Penny!" she shrieks, slicing through the air with the razor wildly. I duck, but it doesn't leave her hand. "I thought you were dying or something! What was that?"

I throw the blanket over my head. The mortification of this moment hits me like an avalanche, and if I look at Mia for even half a second longer, I might throw up. My cheeks must be redder than my hair. "I'm so sorry!"

"Fucking Christ. You threw *Igor* at me? I'm going to murder you!"

This stops my would-be anxiety attack in its tracks. I make myself into a tiny ball, torn between screaming again in frustration and laughing. If I laugh, though, Mia might slice me open with that razor. She names all my sex toys, and I forgot the big blue dildo's name until now. Igor.

She snatches the blanket off my head. I grab it back and use it to cover my boobs. Why did I have to get myself totally naked for this? The murderous expression should make me want to flee, but it bursts open the floodgates instead; I double over in laughter that feels dangerously close to tears. I feel her pull my hair, but I just snort.

"Igor," I say in between wheezes. "He went *flying*."

"And now I'm traumatized for life." I peek at Mia; she's wiping at her face again. I don't blame her. I might not have gotten off, but that doesn't mean I wasn't feeling it. I've held back her hair while she threw up in the gutter, but that doesn't mean she wants my... stuff... all over her face.

"You should probably go back into the shower."

"You're lucky I don't kill you right here." She smirks, but then her expression softens. "You couldn't do it? Still?"

"No. And now I can't stop thinking about... him. Ugh." I press the heels of my hands over my eyes as my amusement fades. "Fuck this. I'm so tired of being stuck."

Mia sits on the edge of my bed, her hazel eyes big as she looks at me. She rubs her hand over my shin. "He's just a memory."

I take a deep breath and nod. She's right. I haven't seen Preston in years, and even if it means never setting foot in Arizona again, I never will. But this isn't even about him. This is about me. I might be good with my fantasies and stories most of the time, but they can only get a girl so far. While everyone around me has been having the college experiences of their dreams, I've been stuck in neutral, unable to make my desires my reality. When getting off used to be easy, I could pretend I didn't care, but now?

Now I think I'm going to scream if I don't orgasm. Fuck Preston Biller. Fuck the love I thought we shared. I draw my legs up, hugging them to my chest through the blanket. "I hate being broken. I can't do this anymore."

"Don't say that." Mia takes my hand. Our manicures match. We went to the fancy nail salon at the Moorbridge mall yesterday. Hers are bright green with black tips and little ghost stickers, and mine are white with orange tips and pumpkin stickers. Perfect for October, which starts in a few days. She squeezes reassuringly. "Maybe you just need to spice it up a little."

"I've expanded my hot fantasy creature roster to include orcs," I say helpfully.

She rolls her eyes. "You know what I mean. Maybe it's time."

A pit opens in my stomach and my heart jumps straight through. "I don't know."

"You're at a huge university. Surely there's someone here on campus who you'd like to hook up with."

She's not wrong; technically speaking, there are potential hookups everywhere. We go to McKee University, which has thousands of undergraduate students alone, and it's not like guys haven't tried to hook up with me. Usually, it's some gross flirting that involves asking if my carpet matches the drapes, since I'm a ginger, but still. College guys don't need a lot of encouragement with hookups; throw a wink their way and they'll chase you all evening.

"You know it's not about that."

"I know," she says gently. "But you can't go on like this."

She looks through my nightstand, pulling out my journal and waving it around.

"Hey," I say, snatching it away from her. I hug the bright pink cover to my chest. "Treat her gently."

When I first started going to Dr. Faber, she wanted me to keep a journal, and while I have three years of notebooks now, I always start it with the same list. It's a list of everything I wish I could do with someone else in bed; everything I want—desperately—but haven't had. Preston took away my biggest first and ruined it, so I wanted to reclaim whatever I could, to make it mine to control. Since I first wrote it, I've refined it, taken away some things and added others. When I started college last year, I updated The List and decided I was going to make it happen. I'd find a fuck buddy, or maybe a couple of guys, and go through

The List item by item. But every time I got close, I just couldn't pull the trigger. I retreated into my books and fantasies, no matter how hot the guy was or how nice he was acting. How could I trust a stranger? He might have been nice then, but who knows what he'd really be like, alone and in control of me.

Now, I'm well into the first semester of sophomore year, and I still have done nothing with The List. I look down at it now, running my finger over the page, full of items like oral sex, orgasm denial, and bondage. The last item on the list, vaginal sex, has always remained the same. If I do this, that'll be the biggest hurdle. The biggest show of trust.

I glance at Mia. "What if things get fucked up all over again?"

Mia raises an eyebrow. "If you keep waiting, you'll just make excuses."

"You're right, you're right. I know you're right."

"Well, you must be okay, if you're quoting *When Harry Met Sally*."

We smile at each other. Mia would rather watch almost anything than a romcom, but she indulges me from time to time. Even she can't deny Nora Ephron's talent.

"And if you didn't actually want to do it, I wouldn't push." She gets up, tightening the towel underneath her arms, and picks up her razor. "But I know you do, Pen. You deserve to have sex. Or a relationship. Or both. But it won't happen if you keep hiding in your room with Igor. Use The List."

"I guess I should give up thinking I'm going to get a Bella Swan situation, huh?" I try to joke.

Mia's face stays stone-cold serious. She's been my best friend ever since the school assigned us to be roommates last year. Dad was nervous about me being in the dorms, but I had a good feeling about it, and it has paid off in spades. Mia's more of a friend than the people I knew in high school ever were, even before everything went down with Preston. While sometimes I resent her honesty, usually I admire it. She says what she's thinking, regardless of who she's talking to or where she is. If we switched places, she'd go to a party, find a guy, and cross number one off The List within an hour.

"You deserve this," she says. "Don't let him keep ruining your life. He's not worth it."

I take a deep breath.

I can go around and around in circles forever, or I can try to break the pattern. I can keep letting Preston into my life, or I can bury his memory with new experiences. I glance back down at The List. The first item, *Oral Sex (Receiving)*, stands out in my neat handwriting.

I started it to give myself some sense of control. But what's the use of control if I never do anything with it? What's the use of desire if I don't honor my own?

One item at a time. One experience at a time. I can do this.

I nod, pressing the heels of my hands against my eyes to stop the tears that are threatening to fall. "Okay."

She lurches forward and hugs me. "Okay?"

"Okay." I take in a big, gulping breath. My heart is racing, and my body feels all tingly, but I feel good. Steadier already. I never want to be that girl again, splayed out on the ice, caught like a butterfly pinned underneath glass. Beautiful and broken. Scrutinized by everyone I knew. My entire school and half the town saw the birthmark I have next to my bellybutton, and whenever I think about that for more than half a second, I need to work hard at staying in the moment.

I'm sick of it being the end of the story. I'm not sixteen anymore. I'm an adult, and I deserve to be in control. The fantasies I have and the stories I write only go so far. Mia's right. If I'm going to have the future I want, I need to take the risk.

I pull away from her embrace and sit up straighter. "I don't want to be scared anymore."

Mia gives me her biggest, rarest smile as she tucks her hair behind her ear. "You're so badass. Think of it as research for your book."

When she goes, shutting the door behind her, I dart off the bed and scoop Igor up. I don't feel badass, but I definitely feel better, and that's going to have to do for the moment. I need to clean him, and it's not like I'm going to get off now, so I just shimmy into clothes and run a comb through my hair, then shove my laptop and chemistry notebook into my bag.

I check my phone for the time. I'd planned to go to The Purple Kettle early to write for a few minutes before Dad meets me for our weekly coffee date; since the semester kicked into gear, my half-written novel has been languishing on my laptop like a forgotten houseplant. Now, though, I'll be lucky if I make it on time. Listening to him grouse about his hockey team will be a distraction, at least. I'm the reason he works here instead of Arizona State, and since going to the games gives me hives, this is the best I can do.

4

_____

PENNY

I PICK up my drinks from the counter and thank the barista, Will, who nods at me before moving on to the next patron. I don't know all of Mia's coworkers, but he's one of the few she talks about without distaste. Usually, the boyish vibe bothers her—she prefers a partner whose hand won't shake when it goes up her shirt—but I think he reminds her of her many siblings and cousins.

I take a fortifying sip of my drink, a pumpkin chai, as I walk out of the student center and into the chilly air. I might've grown up on the ice, being a former figure skater with a hockey coach for a father, but I still prefer the warmth to the cold. When I'm skating, at least my blood is pumping. Standing at the edge of the quad, looking at the maples with leaves just beginning to turn, means that the cold is running straight through my jacket.

"Penelope."

I turn with a smile as my dad approaches. He pulls me into a hug, careful not to spill the drinks, then takes his black coffee. "Thanks, bug."

His nickname for me, which hasn't changed since I was four, makes my smile widen. Maybe some people wouldn't want to go to college at the same place their dad works, but I'm grateful to be able to see him like this whenever I want. It's been the two of us ever since Mom passed, so I try not to take his presence for granted. The fact we even have a weekly coffee date is a miracle, considering the mess I made of things at sixteen and how distant we were before that. Our relationship isn't the same as it was when I was younger, even years after Mom's death and everything that happened with Preston, but he's trying, so I'm trying.

I just wish this was happening at Arizona State instead of McKee.

"How are you?" he asks as we walk along the edge of the quad. The cold has never bothered him; he's in a lightweight jacket with McKee's logo over the chest, although his nose, broken when he played hockey and crooked as a result, is bright red. "Did you do well on that microbiology exam?"

"Um, okay?" I fiddle with the lid of my cup. What I'd like to say is that I don't give a crap about becoming a physical therapist like he thinks I should, but I don't, because that will just lead to a conversation that I'm not ready to have. You don't come to my dad with wishes—just with plans, with concrete steps. Telling him I want to change my major, and oh, maybe write smutty romance novels for a living, would lead nowhere. "I mean, I thought I did well. Mia helped me study."

"And how's Mia?"

I think of the Igor situation and hold back a wince. I need to make it up to her. "She's good."

"Good." He takes a sip of his coffee. "Hey, bug. I'm sending one of the guys to help you out at the rink."

A couple of afternoons a week, I work at the skating rink in town, helping with the lessons. Since I can't skate competitively anymore, it's a way to keep myself on the ice—and not McKee's, because I'd rather give up my favorite pair of Riedells than run into Dad's players. I make a face at him as I sip my chai. The guys stay away because they know I'm their coach's daughter, but I've heard enough about them to be able to picture each one in my mind. Like most of the male athletes on campus, they think their athletic prowess means every girl should count herself lucky to have even half a second of their attention. Hopefully it's not Callahan. I'm surprised the ice doesn't crack from the weight of his ego every time he steps on it.

"Someone from the team? Who?"

He scratches at the back of his neck, shaking his head slightly. "Callahan."

Crap.

"Cooper Callahan? Seriously?"

Cooper is the most talented player on McKee's men's hockey team, and if Mia's sources are correct, at yesterday's exhibition game against UConn, he got into a fight. From the highlights I haven't been able to avoid, I've seen that he practically flies down the ice when he skates, throwing himself in front of the puck to defend the net, gritting it out every single game. He's almost ready for the NHL, but according to my dad, he didn't enter the draft when he was eligible, which means he's at McKee for the duration of his college career.

It also means he's not supposed to fight. They don't do that in college the way they do in the NHL, and he should know better. It's laughable to think of such a rough guy trying to teach little kids how to ice skate.

"He needs to curb his frustrations," Dad says. "I don't know what's wrong with him, but he's letting himself get distracted. I thought last season was in the past, but now... Maybe if he spends some time with these kids, remembering why he fell in love with the game in the first place, he'll refocus."

"You know him, right? He's an arrogant player, Dad."

He just raises an eyebrow. "He's helping you, Pen. He'll be at the rink tomorrow, so make him feel welcome."

When my father decides something, it's nearly impossible to change his mind, so I just sigh. "Fine. But if it doesn't work out, it's not on me."

"No," he agrees. "It's on him. He knows it's this or getting benched the next time he can't control himself."

My heart twinges slightly. Just a teeny bit. Say what you want about hockey players—and believe me, I have plenty to say—but their whole lives revolve around the game. Cooper might have a lot of fun off the ice, if the stories are to be believed, but being benched would be an immense blow.

When I skated competitively for the last time, I felt my heart break, and even years later, it hasn't completely healed.

"That's harsh."

Dad rubs at his nose. "He needs to stay focused on his future. Just like you, bug. Tell me how the microbiology exam really went."

5

COOPER

THE NEXT MORNING, I drag myself out of bed before daybreak and get ready for my workout. When James moved out, Izzy moved in, and because we can be nice big brothers when we want to be, Sebastian and I gave her the room with an ensuite. That means I'm still sharing a bathroom with Seb, who graciously ignores when I leave towels on the floor, so in return, I try not to grumble too much about his extra-long showers. We're used to it; even though we're not actually twins, our parents act like we are. We've been attached at the hip ever since Seb's parents—his dad was my dad's best friend growing up—passed in a car accident. Seb came into our family when we were both eleven. James and I defended him in a fight his first week at his new school, and the rest was history.

I don't bother knocking on the bathroom door. It's barely 5 in the morning and Izzy is on her own schedule with her volleyball teammates; she has an away game today. Seb sometimes joins me at the gym, but he's on a lighter workout schedule because it's his off-season, so I'll be heading out alone. I yawn as I try to will away my headache. Why did I choose to get into Izzy's wine stash last night? Wine always makes my fucking head pound. I should have sulked with a six-pack instead.

The moment I push open the door, rubbing the sleep from my eyes, a shriek fills my ears.

"What are you doing?" someone demands.

I hit the light switch, squinting as the overhead light illuminates the small room. There's a girl in my bathroom. A very naked girl in my bathroom. She shrieks again, grabbing the nearest towel off a hook. I clap my hand over my eyes, backing away.

"Who are you?" I demand.

"Sebastian said no one else would be up!"

I groan. "You hooked up with him?"

"I'm wearing the towel," she says, sounding much more collected. "You don't have to cover your eyes anymore."

I slowly drop my hand. Now that I can look at her without being an accidental pervert, I see that she's smoking hot, even halfway through washing away the remnants of last night's makeup. There are pink streaks running through her dark hair, and tattoos cover half of her right arm. I wouldn't have taken her for Sebby's type, but he's been on a hot streak since the summer. So annoying. Sure, he went out last night, probably to Red's or a dorm party, and I was stuck at home stewing over my new role as pee wee skating instructor. "Sorry. I just wasn't expecting anyone to be up."

Seb appears at my shoulder, a sleepy expression on his face and, to my satisfaction, some dried drool next to his mouth. "Is everything okay?"

I scowl. "Dude. You're supposed to tell me when you have a girl over."

He has the decency to blush. "You were already asleep when we came in. I texted."

Crap. My phone is still on my nightstand, charging because I forgot to plug it in last night. After Coach let me go, I went straight home and played *Dark Souls* until I passed out. "Still. Knock on my door or something next time."

"Nice tattoo," the girl says, gesturing to the piece on my upper arm. "Is that Andúril?"

"*Lord of the Rings* fan?"

"I was obsessed with it as a kid."

Sebastian pokes me in the back and says, "Coop, Vanessa is a huge Zeppelin fan. She has a classic rock show at McKee's radio station."

I lean against the frame of the door more firmly, crossing my arms over my chest so she's drawn to my pecs. The tattoo over my heart isn't *Lord of the Rings* related; it's the Celtic knot, same as my brothers, but if she likes tattoos, maybe we can keep this conversation going. She's not my type, but at this point, I'll take anything. "Clearly you have good taste."

She laughs shortly, running her hand through her hair. "Um, yeah. Well, I should go."

"Why don't you stay for breakfast?" Seb says. "I know it's early, but I can run out for coffee while you and Cooper exchange tattoo stories."

She looks me over, but unfortunately, without an ounce of heat in her expression. "Sorry, but I don't get involved with brothers. Or athletes, usually. You were a fun exception, Sebastian." She brushes past me and gives Seb a kiss on the cheek. "See you around, Callahan boys."

She disappears into Seb's room. He shrugs, giving me an apologetic look.

"Sorry. I tried my best."

Annoyance rumbles through me. "I don't need you to find hookups for me."

"That wasn't it," he says. "I thought you might actually get along."

"After you fucked her? Gee, thanks." I go to the sink and splash water on my face. "I wasn't in the mood for your sloppy seconds, anyway."

"What's the matter?" he asks. "She's a nice girl."

I huff out a breath. "Sorry. I've just been so—fuck, I don't know."

Seb's voice is as dry as the desert. "In need of a lay?"

"I swear, Izzy cursed me last spring. My hookup game hasn't been the same since Bex's gallery show." Or my hockey game. Maybe my mistakes on the ice are throwing me off-balance when it comes to my sex life. Or maybe my nonexistent sex life has led to the sloppy play. Whatever it is, I need to figure it out, especially since I have the chance to become team captain. Even if I play along with Coach's demands, if I'm playing like shit, he's not going to put me in charge of the team.

He just raises an eyebrow. "Tell me you don't actually believe that."

"You're the least superstitious baseball player I've ever met," I grumble. "I'll talk to you later; I need to go work out."

He looks like he wants to keep talking, but I clap him on the shoulder before pushing him into the hallway. "Tell Izzy I said good luck on her game today."

I WIPE a towel over my sweaty face as I lean against the gym wall. Throughout my workout, I've been struggling not to hurl all over the floor. Depressingly, I look better than Evan, who has gone through the motions of his routine with all the energy of a zombie. When he saw me earlier, he tried to apologize, but it's not his fault I punched that guy. Coach is right, I should have just put pressure on him next game, tried to get him to make a mistake on the ice, instead of going after him directly. There are ways to make a message clear in hockey that don't involve fists, but I just couldn't remember any of them. Maybe I didn't want to. Letting my temper boil over into violence felt like a great idea at the time.

I pause my music and cross the gym. He's just settling in at the bench press, but he needs a spotter. "Hey, Evan."

He pulls out one of his ear buds. "Hey."

"Need a spotter?"

His voice is thick as he responds. "Yeah, thanks."

I get into position, watching as he adjusts the weight before settling on his back and planting his feet firmly on the floor. He's a little on the small side for a defenseman, so he's been trying to bulk up. We've been a defensive pair since our first season together. He deserves for hockey to be a happy distraction for him right now, rather than a burden.

I clear my throat after he gets a couple of reps in. "Look, man. You don't have to worry about what happened yesterday. I deserved it."

His brown eyes are swimming in tears. Fuck. His mother had been sick for as long as I've known him, but I know that just makes it worse in some ways. "At least you didn't get suspended."

I take the bar from him as he rests for a few beats, wiping the sweat from his face. "That dude's an ass. He needed someone to shut him up."

He sits up, looking around before ducking in closer. "Jean said that Coach wants to make you captain, but last night might've fucked it up."

I bite the inside of my cheek. "I'm figuring out a way to make it happen."

"You know Brandon wants it too."

"Yeah, well, Brandon's not a leader. Coach will see that."

Evan settles back into position. "He's a senior."

I look across the room, where Brandon and a couple of other seniors on the team stand around talking. Brandon's a good hockey player, but he's not great. There's a reason he didn't declare for the draft, and why his post-graduate plans include working at his father's investment firm instead of continuing to pursue hockey. Making it a profession isn't for everyone, but it's all I want. All I've dreamt about since I was a little kid is playing for the NHL. Being part of a rare brotherhood, no matter what team I'm on. I want to feel the rush of the game for as long as my body will let me. He shouldn't be captain. I should. I'm talented, the guys listen to me, and I work my ass off to get better each game.

I force myself to pay attention to Evan instead, in case he slips, but my mind is going in a million different directions. It's ironic, because losing my cool on the ice led to this mess in the first place, but I wish I had the game to sharpen my focus and release some of the pressure I can't seem to dislodge from my chest. The workout hasn't helped; maybe I should go for a run. What I'd really like to do is find a hookup. Nothing gets me out of my head faster than a pretty girl wrapping her hand—or even better, her lips—around my dick.

"Yeah, well, I worked out something with Coach," I say. "I'm doing some volunteer work for him, to help prove I'm ready to be captain."

"That's great."

"Yeah." I don't bother explaining that it's basically glorified babysitting.

When Evan wraps up, I check my phone. There's a missed video call from my father, so I call him back, slipping out of the gym to the hallway.

When he picks up the call, his face is as red as mine must

be. He swipes his forearm across his face, pushing back the dark, silver-threaded hair sticking to his forehead. Even through my phone screen, I can see the coloring of his eyes. A clear blue, the same shade as mine and my siblings', minus Sebastian.

I'm not looking forward to seeing them cloud with disappointment, but whatever. I'm used to it. If he's calling, it's because he knows what happened yesterday.

"What's up?" he asks.

"Where are you?"

"At James'. Bex needed help with something in her studio, and he's already in London for the game against the Saints. Glad that when I played, we didn't have games on other continents."

"You drove all the way to Philly?"

"Hey, Coop!" I hear Bex call in the background.

"Your mother came too, but you just missed her. She ran out to get breakfast. You okay, son?"

I resist the urge to shake my head. Last spring, Dad didn't even want James and Bex to be together. Now, apparently, he loves her enough to help her set up her photography studio? Of course. Even when James messes up, Dad can never stay mad for long. James lost his championship game for Bex, and now he and Mom are already calling her their daughter-in-law, even though they're just engaged and aren't planning the wedding yet.

"Fine." I clear my throat, forcing back the wave of emotion rushing through me. "I, um, had an exhibition game yesterday."

Dad sits down in what looks like an armchair, heaving a sigh. "Did you get suspended from the next game?"

I was right; he knows about it. I'm not sure how, but he always knows about my fuckups before I have a chance to tell him myself.

"He deserved it, sir. I was defending a teammate."

He just raises an eyebrow, leaving me to either deal with the awkward silence or babble on about the details. I choose to endure the silence, waiting for him to break first. He doesn't agree with the NCAA's no-fighting rule, but that doesn't mean he's not pissed that I fucked up in the same way twice now. To Richard Callahan, mistakes are a one-time thing, and making the same one twice is stupidity.

"That's a shame," he says eventually. He doesn't sound angry, just resigned. Like even this conversation is a burden he's not interested in continuing. "The team will suffer without you on the ice."

"Coach managed to keep me eligible for the season opener, actually." I drag my teeth over my lower lip. "But he's making me do this volunteer thing. He thinks it's going to help me focus."

He raises an eyebrow. "I've always admired Coach Ryder."

I drop my gaze to the floor, rubbing the toe of my sneaker over a scuff mark. "He says if I can clean up my act and get back to playing well... he might make me captain." I lift my head at the last part; I can't help it.

I don't know what I'm expecting. Congratulations? Pride? An "atta boy," like I'm a freakin' golden retriever?

Instead, I get a frown. "Interesting." He sighs again. "I can't say I'm surprised this happened again, Cooper. It's not the first time you've let your temper get the best of you. I've always wondered if hockey brings out the worst of your personality."

"Says the man who played a tackle sport professionally." My voice sharpens like an ice pick as frustration floods through me. "It's not hockey. I'm not—"

"Please," he interrupts, his voice just as pointed.

I should hang up; I know I should—but I can't make myself do it. I'm not expecting an apology from him, but maybe he feels a little bad, and I'll be able to see it in his eyes.

"What are you doing?" he asks, eventually. "For the volunteering?"

"Teaching local kids to skate."

"That doesn't sound too bad. How old are they?"

"Seven? Eight? I don't even know."

"You were that age once, learning how to handle yourself on the ice."

I wait for him to go on, but of course he doesn't. He doesn't like to skirt too close to the topic of Uncle Blake, even casually. Uncle Blake might be my father's younger brother and the one who introduced me to hockey, but because he's been in and out of our lives for years, struggling with addiction, Dad keeps him at arm's length. It's shitty, but fighting with him about it leads nowhere. "I guess."

"This seems like a good thing. Maybe it'll help you learn some patience."

"I'm sure that's his plan."

He surprises me by laughing. "You don't need to sound so put out about it. He's just being a good coach."

"I guess."

"You know how you got here, and you need to deal with it."

I barely resist the urge to tell him that if he was talking to James, he'd at least try to be helpful. He got him to McKee after everything that went down at LSU, after all. "I know that."

"Let me know how it goes. We're still planning on coming up for the UMass game."

"The one we're hosting, I hope."

"Of course." I hear a door open and close. My mom, probably, back with breakfast. "I've got to run, but keep your nose clean, son."

He hangs up before I can manage a goodbye.

I didn't really expect anything else from that conversation, but it still makes my heart sink in my chest like I dropped it in quicksand. I shove my phone into my pocket, dragging my hand over my face. It's not that I wanted him to get me out of the volunteering or expected him to celebrate me losing my temper, but having his support in something would be nice.

Maybe by the time we have the UMass game, he'll see the 'C' on my jersey. That would be proof of my commitment to the sport that he can't ignore. Proof that even if he wishes I chose to carry on the family legacy like James, instead of following in the footsteps of the brother he gave up on long ago, I'm building the future I want for myself.

6

PENNY

"AND REMEMBER that your exam will be next Wednesday," my chemistry professor says as she erases the whiteboard. "I'm hoping to see an improvement from the last exam for many of you."

I shove my books into my tote bag and sling it over my shoulder, hiding the face I make behind my scarf. Words cannot express how little I care about this class. It barely makes sense, even though I go to all the extra tutoring offered by the TA, and the exams are brutal. I'd rather pull my own fingernails out than sit through another 100-question exam, knowing that the result will be the same no matter how hard I study. Dad got on me about microbiology, but I'm doing even worse in chemistry.

Maybe if I fail everything this semester, it will be enough of a signal to him that I can't do this. I've tried because it's what he wants for me—even if he's holding onto a half-formed dream I had when I was sixteen, trying to make sense of the demise of my figure skating career—but if I can't make it through undergraduate science classes, how in the world will I be able to do this for work?

I walk out of the building, tugging my scarf around my neck tightly. Leaves crunch underneath my ankle boots as I walk back to the center of campus. There are so many hills on campus—a sick design flaw, if you ask me—that my knee is aching by the time I reach the student center. I reach down, rubbing it through my jeans, feeling the surgery-smooth scar. Like every figure skater, I had my fair share of injuries, but my last one, my knee, never quite healed as neatly as the doctors hoped. When it's cold like this, the air seeping through my clothes, it makes my body even stiffer.

I spot Mia waiting at a bench outside The Purple Kettle. I'm not sure how, but she pulls off black matte lipstick like it's casual. Throw in the leather jacket and thigh-high boots, and it's no wonder nearly every guy who walks by glances at her twice. When she sees me, she hurries over and wraps me up in a hug; our cold cheeks press together. She pulls back, studying the pout on my face. Mia's got the gift of a resting bitch face, but I've never been able to mask my emotions.

"How was chemistry?" she asks.

"Terrible," I whine.

We loop our arms together as we walk inside. I take a deep breath, enjoying the coffee and sugar smell.

"Worse than attacking your roommate with a sex toy?" she asks.

The girl in front of us turns around, her eyebrows raised. We try to hold back our laughter, but it comes out anyway. At least Mia's not actually all that mad about the flying dildo. Last night, we scrolled through Tinder to look for potential hookups, and when we stumbled upon a guy named Igor, she laughed so hard she slid right off my bed.

"Yes. Horribly worse." I rummage around in my bag for my

wallet. "Hang on, I'll buy. It's the least I can do after the trauma you endured yesterday."

We shuffle forward in line. "We'll use my employee discount," she says. "But I'm ordering a huge caramel macchiato. Get ready."

"You're never going to guess what my dad is doing." I peer at the counter to see what baked goods they have. It looks like there's coffee cake, my favorite. At least one thing is going my way today. "Also, do you want to split a coffee cake?"

"Always. And what?"

I look at the menu hanging on the wall, even though I already know I'm going to have the pumpkin chai. It's the only thing that is going to make my boring science classwork bearable. "He's sending someone to volunteer at one of my classes."

"Who?"

The girl in front of us finishes paying and moves to the side to wait for her drink, so I order next, throwing in a sandwich for us to split too; it's lunch, after all. When we made this plan earlier, we hoped to get in a little studying before work. She waves to her coworkers as we claim a table by the window and each take a seat, pulling out our notebooks and laptops.

I break off a piece of coffee cake, savoring it before leaning in. I swear, you can't say the guy's name without at least three girls looking up, in case just speaking it aloud is some sort of spell to summon him. I get it, he's handsome, but a lot of hockey players are. A lot of them are jerks, too, but that doesn't stop the interest from girls who'd like to see if someone like Cooper can handle them as well as he can a hockey stick. "Cooper Callahan."

The girl at the table next to us looks over for half a second before burying her face back in her phone.

Typical.

Mia raises an eyebrow. "Why?"

"He thinks volunteering will help him get his game back on track, I guess. I don't know. I'm sure he doesn't want to do it, least of all with me."

I hear my name, so I hop up to get our drinks. I breathe in the smell of pumpkin-y goodness wafting from my chai, taking a sip before walking back to our little corner by the window. When I settle our drinks and the panini down on the table, Mia has an expression on her face that makes the back of my neck prickle. That's her scheming face.

Usually, her schemes involve whatever person she's into at the moment, but she doesn't like guys like Cooper any more than I do, so I doubt she's looking for me to make an introduction. Which means... she's thinking of something involving me.

"Mia," I start.

"Penny," she says, serenely taking a sip of coffee. "This is an excellent opportunity."

"To hear one of my dad's arrogant players mansplain ice skating to me?"

She just smiles. "The universe is giving you a gift. It's telling you to seize the dick, if you will."

I choke on my next sip of chai. "No way."

"This is perfect! He doesn't do relationships, and you need someone guaranteed to give you a good time. His reputation in that regard is delicious."

I blush, stuffing my mouth full of hot panini instead of responding. The melted cheese burns my tongue, but I force myself to swallow. Anything to avoid thinking too hard about Cooper Callahan's good-time reputation. And seizing his, er, dick.

"It's true," the girl who looked at us before says. "Sorry to butt in, but my friend slept with him last year and he made her come three times. She says it was life changing."

Mia gestures to me. "See?"

"You're ridiculous. I can't hook up with one of my dad's players."

"Why not? It makes it even more perfect, honestly, because you know you can't fall for him."

"Or would even want to, more like," I mutter. I already fell for one self-important hockey player, and it ruined my life. There's no way in hell I'm doing that twice. "Dad basically forbade me from getting involved with another hockey player. I can't go trawling his roster for potential options."

"He said not to *date* another hotshot hockey player," Mia says, rolling her eyes. "Which, I agree, jocks are the worst. But this would be a hookup, which is totally different."

"I'm not tainting The List with him."

"What's The List?" the girl asks.

Mia glances over and says, "Sorry, but this conversation is officially closed. There's an open table near the door. If you want to continue to get your lattes without fear that I spit in them first, you'll move."

The girl practically trips over herself as she switches tables.

I sigh as I look over at Mia. "Really?"

"The personal space bubble around a café table is sacred," she says. "And you're missing the point. You don't have to like him; you just have to invite him to stick his head up your skirt. He'd be a great way to jumpstart The List."

I pick at the coffee cake. It makes a certain amount of sense. Cooper Callahan is casual all the way. I doubt he's ever used the word "girlfriend" in his life, so there's no risk of messy feelings. And I'd rather wither away than give Dad even a whiff of what I'm planning to do with The List, so it's not like he'd find out.

Despite all that, I raise my eyebrows. "I think you're forgetting the fact that he'd run in the other direction the moment he realizes who's asking."

She just shrugs. "It's not like you're proposing to the guy. You heard the girl; she made her friend come three times. If anything, he'd fix your little problem, ah, arriving."

My blush darkens. I can't believe she's talking about this so casually in public. "Mia!"

"What? It's not like you can stay orgasm-less forever."

I shudder. That's not an option. "It can't be him. It's too complicated."

Mia glances to the counter, where Will is currently fighting with the espresso machine. "Want me to get Will's number for you? I know he's just a baby, but he's reasonably cute."

"No!" I smack my hand over Mia's wrist to prevent her from getting up. "No. I'll find someone else on my own."

She settles back in her chair, taking a sip of her coffee before opening her laptop. "And that's a promise? No chickening out?"

I meant what I said yesterday; it's time to take control of my own experiences. But that's easier said than done, even with therapy and finally finding an anti-anxiety medication that doesn't make me experience life like a zombie. I can't promise it won't be a disaster, but I know I owe it to myself to try. And while I'm not about to admit that Mia's right, Cooper Callahan could be the perfect option—if I can woman up enough to ask him.

I stick out my pinkie as I reach across the table. "Promise."

7

COOPER

THE INSTANT I walk through the doors of Moorbridge Skating Center, I'm hit with a wave of nostalgia. The air is frosty, even outside the rink itself, and the ugly red carpet underneath my feet needs replacing. The faded banners hanging from the ceiling, the long rows of skates behind the front counter, the smell of popcorn and slightly burnt hot chocolate wafting over from the concessions stand... it's exactly like every other skating rink, which means it feels like home. I might not want to be there—and trust me, the entire drive over I was mentally dragging my feet—but at least it's comfortable. I'll bet the benches are rickety and the Zamboni breaks down on occasion.

"Hello?" I call as I walk to the counter. I don't see anyone around, but there were a couple of cars in the lot.

"One moment!" A woman hurries out of a door labeled "Office," tossing her long hair over her shoulder. She's in skinny jeans and a pink sweater that says, "Lutz do this!" on it in script. I'm terrible at guessing ages, but if I had to, I'd say she's in her mid-thirties; her brown eyes crinkle at the corners as she smiles, holding out her hand for me to shake. "Hi, I'm Nikki Rodriguez. Cooper, right?"

"Yeah. Lawrence Ryder sent me over?"

She smiles warmly. "And how's Larry?"

I'm sure that Coach Ryder didn't go into the details about why he wanted me to volunteer. She probably thinks I've been itching for something to add to my resume, instead of being forced to help her out so I won't lose my cool the next time a guy chirps in my vicinity. "He's good."

"Good, good. Today's lesson starts in just a couple of minutes, so want to get on your skates? Penny's down there already."

"It's just ice skating, right?" I ask. I scratch at the back of my neck in embarrassment. I probably should have done some research on the website before I came over. I want to ask who Penny is, too, but I don't want to sound like a total idiot.

"This class teaches ice skating and introduces the kids to ice sports," she says. "Most of them are six or seven years old. This session just started, so they're pretty much all beginners. Don't worry, you'll be great. Just help them keep their balance and learn to find their way on the ice."

"I'll try."

"Larry said you were the best on the team." She gives me a grateful smile. "I'll be in the office if you need anything. Thanks, Cooper."

This is the way to keep myself on the ice where it counts, so despite the squirming in my belly, I head down the stairs to the rink itself. The ice looks fresh and glossy, which is a good sign. I park myself on a bench and lace up my skates.

"There you are."

I look up at the sound of the voice—and find myself staring at a girl my age.

Scratch that. A beautiful girl my age.

I must be pretty fucking hard up, because I can feel my face redden and blood going to another, more embarrassing place as well. She's a redhead, her long, light orange hair tossed over one shoulder. Freckles cover every inch of her face like a universe of tiny stars on her skin. Her eyes are blue like mine, but paler, like ice on a winter morning. She's swimming in an oversized gray knit sweater, but her leggings cling to her thighs and calves enticingly. She has a pair of well cared-for white Riedells dangling from her hands. As we stare at each other, she licks her lower lip, and my stomach tightens.

This is bad. Terrible. I'm about to be around kids. I can't be thinking about how much I want to peel off her sweater to see what her tits look like.

She cocks her head at me. "Cooper, right? Cooper Callahan?"

I clear my throat. "Yeah."

She crosses her arms over her chest. She's skinny, barely any curves to speak of, but that realization just makes me want to get my hands on her, see how big they look on her soft, fair skin. Do the freckles continue all over her body? God, I hope so.

"Cool. Are you going to just stare at me, or are you going to help?"

I stand up. "Sorry. I wasn't sure who to expect."

She gives me a look, almost like she's offended, which is weird, because I've never seen this girl in my life. I wouldn't forget a girl with hair like fire and eyes like the sky in early spring.

"The kids are coming in soon," she says. "This is a beginner class, so nothing too intense. They're still learning how to balance on the ice."

"Gotcha."

She gestures to a bag leaning against the boards. "Set up some cones. Couple yards apart, enough to skate between."

I salute her. "Aye, m'lady."

She keeps on giving me that weird look, but after a moment, she just shakes her head slightly. "Whatever. See you out on the ice."

Fucking hell. It's no wonder I haven't been getting laid recently. M'lady? If Sebastian heard that, he'd piss himself from laughing so hard.

I pick up the bag and skate onto the ice, the cool, crisp air hitting my cheeks above my beard. I give my head a shake. I need to focus. Why didn't Coach mention I'd be working with someone so fucking gorgeous? That sort of shit needs to come with a warning label.

I put out all the cones, and not a moment too soon, because then about ten kids come charging onto the ice.

Maybe this won't be completely terrible. At least I get to check out Little Miss Red for the entire hour.

"Hi," she says to the kids, hugging them one by one as they skate over to her on wobbly legs. I was around their age when I first got on the ice; after only knowing football fields, thanks to Dad, it was intoxicating. Uncle Blake helped give me a crash course in the basics, but pretty soon I was flying from end to end on my own.

"Penny," one kid says, pointing to me. "Who's that?"

"This is Cooper," she says. "He's going to be helping us out. He's the right defenseman on McKee's hockey team. Where I go to school, remember?"

I glance at her sideways, but she doesn't look over. It shouldn't make my stomach tighten pleasantly to hear she knows the position I play, but I can't stop myself.

"Is he your boyfriend?" another kid asks.

I snort. That makes her look at me; she's biting her lip like she's on the verge of laughing. For a second, it feels like maybe there's something sparking in the air between us; a camaraderie borne out of being the two adults in this situation, which is ironic considering we're just a couple of college kids. But then she straightens, shaking her head slightly.

"No," she says. "What do you know about boyfriends anyway, Madison?"

"Lots," Madison says, crossing her arms over her chest.

I stifle my laughter as Red—well, I suppose her name is Penny, but with hair like that, I can't resist—deftly brings the subject back around to the lesson. Coach might've been right about this. There's something nice about seeing a bunch of kids be really into the same thing I am. Their eyes are round as saucers, and they keep whispering to each other as Red explains the lesson. They're still working on skating without holding onto the railing, and I see apprehension in the way they're crowded against the boards. At the very least, I can keep playing nice.

"Okay!" she says cheerfully. "We'll do this exercise together, and then you'll get to practice on your own. Remember, keep your knees bent. We want to keep ourselves low and use our arms for balance. How do we fall again?"

"Not backwards," a boy says. He's wearing a hockey sweater, Ovechkin's. His long blond hair nearly falls into his eyes.

"Right," she says. "We want to protect our head. We also don't want to use our hands to break our fall because we could hurt our wrists. When you keep your knees bent, you can fall onto your side more easily."

She skates in a circle around me. "Want to show us, Cooper?"

"Falling?"

She nods. "Even hockey players fall sometimes, right?"

"We do." I skate to the middle of the rink. "You're going to fall, and that's okay. She's right, I fall a lot still."

Usually because of a hit, but I don't add that. I demonstrate how to fall, letting my shoulder take the impact instead of my head or wrists. After that, Red makes me show the kids how to do the little cone exercise. I do that twice, weaving from one side to the next, then watch as the kids line up and give it a shot themselves.

I thought this would drag on, but I get into the groove quickly. I save one boy from crashing into the boards and give extra feedback to a girl who keeps buckling her knees. They're like newborn colts trying to figure out how to stand on their own, but to their credit, most of them get right back up after they fall.

When it's time for practice, I skate over to the boy wearing the Alex Ovechkin jersey. His chubby cheeks are red from the cold. He's fallen three times in a row now, unable to make it from the edge all the way to the cones.

I crouch down so we're at about eye level. He's holding on so tightly that the blood has drained from his fingertips. I pry them off one by one, holding him steady myself.

"I've met him, you know."

He wipes his nose with the back of his hand. "Who?"

"Ovechkin. He's nice as f—he's a nice guy. Really cool."

The kid brightens. "He's my favorite player."

"Just him, or do you root for the Caps?"

"Caps," he says.

"Good stuff." I point at the cones. "You know, Ovechkin had to learn how to skate when he was a kid. I had to, too."

"I want to play hockey." He bites his lip, looking over to where Red is showing a couple of kids how to spin. I follow his gaze, momentarily distracted by the look of concentration on her face. We lock eyes for half a second as she brushes her hair away from her face.

I swallow and turn back to the kid. "What's your name?"

"Ryan."

"Ryan what? What's the back of your sweater going to say?"

"McNamara."

I clap him on the shoulder. "That's a good name. It's going to look nice on you one day. But you need to learn to skate first, buddy."

He nods, rubbing his nose again. "I know."

"I'm going to skate over here," I say, gesturing to the nearest cone. "I'll be waiting for you."

I stay crouched down, arms open, looking at Ryan with what I hope is an encouraging expression. I'm sure in a few weeks he'll be learning to skate backwards; he just needs to take the leap and gain some confidence. After a few seconds, he pushes off the railing and skates over to me slowly.

When I steady him, I give him a high-five. "Nice job. Let's do it again."

When the lesson ends, Ryan hugs me, which definitely doesn't suck. He asks if I'm coming to the next lesson, and because I doubt Coach will buy that I'm cured of what my dad apparently thinks are violent tendencies after one session—and fine, because I enjoyed myself—I nod and tell him I'll see him next week.

When we're alone on the ice, Red skates over to me, her cheeks flushed from the cool air and exertion. Her hair is messy, swept up around her like a ginger halo. She scrunches up her cute little nose. Something about her feels familiar, but I don't know where I'd have seen her. Maybe she's on McKee's figure skating team? We have one, but I don't know much about it. Our paths could have crossed on campus half a dozen times, although if that's the case, I have no idea why I wouldn't have introduced myself. I scrub my hand over my face, letting a scowl replace the smile I wore throughout the lesson.

"That bad, huh?"

I work my jaw, my frustration at the whole situation rushing back now that I don't have something else to focus on. "No, it's just... it's not like I asked for this."

"You were good at it." She nudges her shoulder against my arm. "I thought you'd be terrible."

"You know I know how to skate."

"Not at the skating, at interacting with the kids." She grins, and fuck, it's cute. I work to hold back a groan. During the lesson, I managed to ignore the zing that would race from my scalp to my toes whenever I felt her near me, but now my body is doing its hardest to remind me I haven't gotten laid in way, way too long for a guy my age. "It was really sweet."

I scrape at the ice with my toe pick. "Yeah, well, tell that to my coach. He thinks this is going to help my game, but honestly..."

I trail off, because it's one thing to complain about my dry spell with my brother, and another entirely to announce it to a stranger.

"Honestly what?" she asks.

I look at her. Maybe it's her eyes that look familiar? Did we have a class together freshman year or something? Fuck it, I don't know her anyway, and it's not like I can get any *more* pathetic. "Honestly, I just need to get laid. It's been months and I'm wound too tight."

She raises an eyebrow. "Don't you hockey players have an entourage of puck bunnies following you around?"

I shrug. "I don't hook up with the same girl twice."

"Why not?"

"Do you always have so many questions about other people's sex lives?"

She looks up; she's not the shortest girl in the world, but I still have several inches and nearly a hundred pounds on her. She must have a figure skating background; her poise on the ice has a presence of its own, and quality skates like that don't come cheap. She reaches out, her delicate fingers a mere inch from my chest. Her nails are perfect little ovals, white with orange tips. I have the absurd urge to take her hand in mine and examine the differences, the places where my palms are rough and hers are as smooth as the inside of a seashell.

If I didn't know better, I'd say she was about to kiss me.

My breath stutters.

We lock eyes, and she seems to make some sort of decision.

And then she actually kisses me—on the cheek, I mean. Her lips are feather light against my beard. When she speaks, it's in a whisper against my ear. She's trembling, but I've got it worse. I'm frozen in place while my mind and body scramble to keep up with her.

"Hook up with me."

8

PENNY

THE MOMENT the words leave my mouth, I steel myself for the rebuff.

Cooper is staring. I force myself to keep meeting his gaze. I have enough self-respect for that. Just not enough to keep from propositioning one of my dad's players because something about him makes my insides twist, apparently. As soon as he said he was hard-up, I felt a twinge of sympathy. Having an itch that you can't scratch seriously sucks. I know that all too well.

It's not like I arrived at the rink knowing I was going to ask. The entire bus ride from campus to Moorbridge Skating Center, I replayed the conversation with Mia in my mind. What she suggested made a twisted amount of sense, but there's a big difference between agreeing with something in theory and wanting to put it into practice.

Yet the moment I saw Cooper, the wheels began to turn. Throughout the lesson, I couldn't stop looking at him. Every cut he made across the ice, every word of encouragement or bit of advice he gave one of the students, every time I realized he was looking at me—it drew out the ache I usually keep tamped down with success.

I knew what he looked like before today, of course, but up close and in person, he's even more handsome, with deep blue eyes and thick, almost wild, dark hair. His beard is a touch too long, but I still have a weird urge to feel it under my palm. He's an athlete, so of course he's built, but his broad shoulders matched with his trim waist—especially when he was in motion on the ice earlier—have turned my insides to a warm, bubbly liquid. There's a scar underneath his ear, a ragged half-moon, and even though I don't know him, I want to ask him how he got it. When one kid made a joke as he said goodbye, he threw back his head and laughed, and it was like the sound took on a physical form, scraping over my skin.

Cooper Callahan is everything I'm not—confident, cocky, and unafraid of intimacy. Mia's right. If there's anyone to jumpstart The List with, it's him. The fact he's one of my father's players—and a hockey player at all, ugh—is less than ideal, but from everything I've heard about him, it won't make him hesitate. Maybe if I cross one item off the list, the rest will come easier.

He's still staring at me like I spoke in Klingon instead of English. I cross my arms over my chest. I'm not the shortest girl ever, but he towers over me. I can feel the blush coloring my cheeks, but I hold my ground. My words are out in the open, and it's not like I can take them back now. Especially not when they had a kiss attached to them.

"Hook up?" he repeats finally. He scratches at his beard.

My stomach tightens at the thought of that beard rubbing against my sensitive skin. Even that kiss on the cheek made my heart rate spike. I've imagined it, but I've never truly experienced it before. If the stories are to be believed and he really is generous in bed, not a hotshot player who takes his own pleasure and leaves the woman hanging, that already gives him a leg up on half the guys I was considering on Tinder last night. "Sounds like you need it."

His mouth twists. "I don't need a pity fuck."

"It's been way too long for me too." Several years long, but I don't mention that last part. "I noticed you looking at me."

"And I noticed you noticing me." He looks me over, from my skates all the way to my frizzy hair. Under normal circumstances, this level of attention from a guy would send me running, but even though my heart is pounding like it's an entire freakin' drumline, I don't hate it. I'm not sure why he's acting like he doesn't know I'm his coach's daughter, but if he wants to pretend, I'm content to let him. It makes things easier.

I skate backwards, biting my lip to keep from grinning when he follows me. I could still bail, pretend I was joking, and maybe that would be the smarter thing to do, but the thought of going back to my dorm room and trying to get off again on my own is depressing as fuck, and I'm turned on by the way he's looking at me, and even though it's hard to remember, I know I deserve this.

He catches up to me easily. His hand splays out on my waist, drawing me closer. He has a bright look in his eyes, almost boyish with excitement. He probably thinks I'm a total vixen who does this all the time. The truth couldn't be further from that, but what's the harm in pretending? He just said that he never gets with the same girl twice. He'd never talk about it because I'm his coach's daughter. This is as safe as a hookup can get.

"Your place or mine?" he asks.

"Now." I gesture across the ice; we're alone, with no one to interrupt us. "There's a supply closet down the hall."

I've surprised him; I can tell. He blinks, a smile growing on his face.

"Didn't take you for a rule breaker, Red."

The nickname makes warmth bloom in my chest. "There's a lot you don't know about me."

He glances around to check we're alone before leaning in, his mouth a mere inch from mine. So close to a kiss, yet so far. "Come on, sweetheart. Show me."

———

WHEN WE REACH the supply closet, I ease the door open and flick on the light. It's not exactly a prime location, but it is private. I check my gut one more time, but despite my nerves, I don't feel any hesitation. I know I could be smarter about this than choosing a guy on my dad's team for my first hookup, but it's not like he's ever going to find out. And well... hockey players have always been my type.

Cooper shuts the door behind us. He looks bigger in an enclosed space like this; his chest is deliciously broad, his arms thick with muscle. There's a tattoo on his arm, some sort of sword, but I'm too busy looking him over to make out the details. I know that if he took off his shirt, I'd see the hard lines of his abs. He's staring at me with languid interest, like a panther lounging in a tree branch, observing prey. I reach out and drag my nails down his shirt.

He catches my palm in his, squeezing. "This is your show, Red," he says. "What do you want to do?"

I gather all my courage and lean up to press a kiss to his lips.

For half a second, he doesn't respond, but then he wraps his arms around me, dragging me closer, his mouth hungrily exploring mine. I gasp at the scratch of his beard against my skin. He bites my lower lip, sucking gently. When I need air, I barely take in a full breath before kissing him again. It's been

years since someone has kissed me, and I knew I missed it, but
not quite how much, until now. I like having a guy pressed up
against me, his big hands on my waist, feeling him breathe.

When we break away, he puts his chin on the top of my
head. "Come on," he coaxes. "There's something you want, I
can tell. But I'm not a mind reader."

I laugh, squeezing his arm. Being so near him is already
making my body burn with want. He's right, I do have
something on my mind—the first item on The List. Something
I've wanted for ages but haven't had the courage to seek until
now. I adore kissing him, so I can't even imagine what it would
be like to feel his beard against my sensitive inner thighs.

He gives me a moment, not pushing or getting impatient,
but continuing to touch me, his fingers teasingly tracing down
my back, his lips brushing against mine from time to time.
Something about him puts me at ease. Maybe it's that he hasn't
laughed at me about any of this, even if I am doing something
slightly ridiculous. Maybe it's his reputation for being a player;
I can't be the first girl to proposition him with an agenda in
mind. Whatever it is, I know, instinctively, that he's going to
give me a good time, and I hope I can do the same for him.

I look up. His eyes are blue like mine, but so much deeper.
The sky instead of a sheet of pale ice. I swallow down the rush
of anxiety and say, "I want you to go down on me."

He grins crookedly, brushing my hair behind my ear. "You
want me on my knees?"

"I've heard you're generous."

He strokes my cheek with his thumb, then presses it right
against my lips. I bite down gently, pleased to see the heat in his
gaze. "So I've been told."

Keeping his eyes on me, he sinks down to the floor. His
hands settle low on my waist, gripping tightly enough I feel it.
That self-assured smile is still on his face, and I'm sure it's

because the moment he switched our positions, I started shivering with anticipation.

"Show me your panties, Red," he says.

I do as he says, inching my leggings down. My breath catches in my throat as he rubs his thumbs against my bare skin. He licks his lips, sending a spike of heat straight to my core, and tugs my leggings to my ankles. He glances at my panties—and then presses a kiss to the bow at the top.

"Cute," he says. "Blue looks good on you."

I swallow down a whimper. "You can take them off."

He doesn't, though, instead running his finger down the middle, parting my folds through the fabric. My toes curl in my boots against the dirty floor. Part of me wants to pull up my pants and flee before he sees me, but the larger part wants to stay rooted to the spot just like this, allowing Cooper Callahan to explore my body. Eventually, he inches down my panties bit by bit, like he's unwrapping a gift he knows is going to be good. I can feel my wetness, know he'll be able to see it the moment my panties are off all the way. When they join my leggings around my ankles, he kisses me again, this time against my bare skin. I dig my nails into his shoulder, surprised to feel his beard against such a sensitive place.

His gaze flicks upward. "Are you going to be a good girl and give yourself to me?"

A strangled whimper escapes my mouth.

"Because I can tell," he continues. "You need it bad. I need it bad too, sweetheart. My cock is fucking aching just looking at your gorgeous pussy. But I work best when I know my girl trusts me to take care of her."

As he talks, he strokes my thighs. He's close enough I can feel his breath against my skin, and it makes my belly tighten with want. I find his hair, gripping a handful and tugging; I wish he'd just press right up against my folds and suck my clit until the slick coats my thighs.

Do I trust him? Not with my life, but right here, like this? Maybe I shouldn't, maybe it's stupid, but I do. He doesn't even know how much I'm trusting him right now. I'm on the edge of a cliff, balancing as best I can, while rock crumbles beneath me.

He presses a kiss to my belly button. "Freckles here too," he murmurs. "Adorable."

"Cooper."

"Yes?"

"I want..." My voice fades before I can force out the words.

"Go on," he prompts. "Tell me you want to be my good girl. Let me give you what you asked for."

My face burns as red as my hair. I've fantasized for years about someone calling me their good girl, and now it's finally happening. He has no idea what he's giving me right now. How much this moment means to me.

I tug on his hair harder. "Yes. I want... I want to be your good girl."

He spreads my legs wide, his hands stroking my inner thighs, where my skin is softest. "Atta girl."

He starts at the top of my folds, pressing light kisses to my skin, dragging his beard against it. I'm moaning softly all the while; even that relatively innocent touch is winding me up. He drags his mouth down, exploratory, trading off kisses and small licks. But then he winds his arms around my legs and spreads me even wider, licking right over my hole, and he drags a gasp out of me. He finds my clit next, lapping at it before sucking it, sending a wave of pleasure through me. He clearly knows what he's doing, teasing the little bud until I'm moving against his face, desperate for more contact. He breaks away, laughing, pressing a kiss to the inside of my thigh.

"You taste delicious," he says. "Fuck, I could stay just like this for hours."

That must be a line he uses on every girl, but it works. I grind against him, aching for more contact.

"Don't stop," I whisper.

"'Course not," he says. "I said I'd take care of you, didn't I?"

He fucks into me with his tongue, no doubt getting his mouth and beard messy with slick, and uses a finger on my clit instead, making me rock my hips forward, hoping for more friction. His other hand goes to my ass, squeezing firmly, drawing out a moan that has me throwing my head back against the wall. Each lick, each touch, brings me closer to the peak of pleasure, but even moving against him, I'm not there. I need something more. I grip his hair so tightly it must hurt, pressing his face against my folds.

"That's it," he says right against me. The vibrations of his voice have me gasping. "Ride my face, needy girl."

Needy girl.

Is that me? In this moment, yes. I haven't allowed myself to do anything like this since I was sixteen, hoping for a deeper connection and leaving my life in ruins instead. Cooper has coaxed out the side of me that I keep locked down tight. Maybe I was more desperate for a change than I realized. Needier than I thought.

The thought just makes me press against him more firmly, tugging his hair to move his head where I want it. He goes along, licking and sucking everywhere he can reach. My stomach tightens like it's caught in a vise. I moan aloud, the sounds pouring from me without a thought as he pays attention to my clit again. His nails dig into my bottom hard enough to hurt, and I gasp, almost losing my balance. He runs his hand down my leg—and then props it up on his shoulder, spreading me out so wide I feel the cool air on my pussy. I feel ridiculous for half a second, with my tangled leggings stretched almost to the point of tearing, but then I see the look on his face.

Maybe he's got a thing for stick-thin girls with hair the color of carrots. Maybe he just really likes eating pussy. Maybe he'd be looking at any girl like this, worshipful, almost gentle in the way he blinks his storm-blue eyes.

"Cooper," I whimper, curling and uncurling my toes. I dig my shoe into his shoulder. He steadies me with his firm hands, rubbing down my sides.

"You're almost there," he says; his mouth is wet with my slick, his beard soaking. He licks his lips. "Be good and let me finish my meal."

He doesn't stop, or tease, or even come up for air; he breathes right against my cunt, letting his nose bump my clit as he laps at my skin.

The moment his finger pushes into me, agonizingly slow, a stark contrast to the way he's licking my clit, I come apart. I muffle my cry against my shoulder, curling in on myself, almost falling as I yank my leg down. There's slick all over my thighs; when I press my legs together, I feel sticky. He rises to his feet, pulling me into a crushing kiss. I taste the salt on his lips and lick into his mouth without thinking.

When we eventually break away from each other, he just presses his forehead to mine.

And even though I'm the one with stars swimming in my vision, he thanks *me*.

9

COOPER

THIS GIRL IS A GODDESS.

I've loved sex ever since my first time, a fumbled hookup in a closet not unlike this one. I felt accomplished as fuck, hearing Emma Cotham's moans as I moved inside her. It's been a long time since I've had a proper hookup, but I wasn't prepared for how satisfied this would leave me. As I kiss Red, I can feel my almost painful hard-on straining against my jeans, sure, but I can't stop smiling. She made the sweetest little noises. I know I don't really know her, but at least right now, she seems like the kind of woman I like best—adorable and easy to overwhelm, yet fiery and full of spirit. The moment she dangled the offer of a hookup in front of me, I had the feeling it would lead somewhere good.

"Thank you," I murmur. I don't even know if she believed me when I said I was in a dry spell. Even if she did, she doesn't know quite how much I've needed this. I'm grateful anyway. This was better than a hard workout or meditation or getting off to my favorite porno. She strokes my hair—way more gently than before, when she was pulling me against her just the way she wanted—as we press our foreheads together. I bite the inside of my cheek as she runs her hand down my side, settling on my waistband.

"I should be thanking you," she says. She worries her lower lip with her teeth as she looks up at me. "That was..."

"Hot as fuck?"

Her lips quirk into a smile—right before she cups my crotch over the fabric of my jeans. "Yes."

I duck in for another kiss. "I don't have a condom."

She strokes me through my jeans. "I can think of other ways to thank you back."

I groan as she unbuttons my jeans and pushes them down far enough to free my cock; she holds it almost delicately, rubbing her thumb against the head, smearing around the beads of pre-come. I kiss her again, happy to hear her sharp intake of breath.

She kisses me back, but then she pulls away. She gives my cock an experimental tug that has my stomach clenching, but doesn't take it further.

"I have a confession," she says abruptly. "I haven't... done this... in a long time."

"You don't have to," I say, even though I very much want her to keep going. "I can just take care of it quickly."

She shakes her head. "No, I want to." She cocks her head to the side, giving me another little stroke.

I take pity on her and wrap my hand around hers. I press a kiss to her forehead. I move our hands together, thumbing at the head of my cock, twisting slightly in the way that never fails to make my breath hitch. She follows along, using her other hand to cup my balls. They're aching already, and her touch sparks another, deeper level of desire. We're quiet except for our breathing, still pressed up against the wall of this tiny space. I've never minded getting dirty in the name of sex, especially when it holds a hint of the forbidden. Despite the dusty, cramped surroundings, I'd rather be here than anywhere else. Tasting Red on my tongue, watching her brow furrow as she learns what movements make me moan. When I get close, feeling that familiar tug in my gut, I drop my head to her shoulder and murmur a warning.

We jerk me the rest of the way together. I come groaning her name. Not Red, but her real name, Penny. Our hands get sticky with my seed, and before I can offer my shirt as a wipe, she lifts her hand to her mouth and licks it clean.

I think my brain short-circuits, seeing her cute pink tongue working over her delicate fingers, and then it absolutely fries when she moves on to my hand, taking each of my fingers into her mouth and licking away the rest of the come. She ends with kissing me, the same as I did for her when I got up from my knees. When she pulls away, I just keep staring at her, even as I pull my pants back up and tuck myself away. She tugs up her leggings, then runs both her hands through her hair, tossing it over her shoulder.

"You do know my name," she teases. "I was getting worried."

I grin. "Can I have your number? Do you have a Snap?"

I take out my phone and start a new contact, typing in "Penny" and handing it to her so she can put in her last name and number.

I shouldn't, but I can't help myself. I wasn't lying earlier when I said I don't do repeat hookups; I've only done it a few times, over the years, and they almost always edged into complicated before I could break things off. Once I almost broke poor Sebby's heart. But if we're going to be teaching this class together, it can't hurt to have her contact information.

For some reason, she scowls as she takes my phone. "Is this how we're going to do it?"

"Do what?"

She puts her number into my phone but doesn't hold it out. "Callahan. You know who I am."

I'm shaking my head before she even finishes her sentence. "I wouldn't forget you."

"Oh, spare me," she snaps. She slaps the phone into my palm. "I'm not planning on telling my father, in case you're worried about that."

I glance down at my phone as her words hit me. Penny *Ryder*, it says.

Ryder. As in...

"Oh, fucking hell," I say. The words come out strangled. I kept thinking that she looked familiar because I've seen the photograph of her on her father's desk dozens of times. The red hair might be all hers, but the eyes sure as hell aren't. He's mentioned before that his daughter goes to McKee, and why wouldn't the daughter of a hockey coach know her way around a rink?

She reaches out and squeezes my arm, but I jerk away. "Callahan," she says. "I'm sorry, I just assumed that you knew. I thought you were pretending."

"Why would I pretend about that?"

"I don't know! I knew who you were, I just thought..."

"He's going to fucking murder me."

She rolls her eyes. "He's not going to find out. And I wanted it just as much as you."

I yank open the door. "I need to go."

"Wait—"

"I don't know what kind of game you're playing, but I don't like being used," I interrupt. Her face falls, and I feel a twinge of sympathy. I don't know her, but she wears her emotions on her face like a brand. It's a pretty face, too, one I can't stop staring at, even now. It's clear that she really thought I knew her, but I don't like what that implies either. Why would she want to hook up with one of her father's guys, anyway? And why me? She said she knew about my reputation. I've never been ashamed about being a player; I'm upfront with everyone I hook up with and who the hell cares that I love sex, but now? It's like she chose me because she knows I'm easy, and whatever her motives, this could fuck up everything for me. Nothing screams serious captain material like hooking up with the coach's daughter in a goddamn storage closet.

And if *my* dad gets wind of this? I'll never hear the end of it.

"I wasn't trying to use you," she says. "I thought I was helping. I needed it, and you did too. You said so."

"I'm trying to make captain." I can't help it, I take a step closer, although my hand is still curled around the doorframe. "If your daddy dearest finds out, I'm screwed. I'm already stuck doing this stupid volunteer thing with you. He'll bury me so far down the roster I'll never make the NHL."

"He wouldn't do that," she says. "And it's not like I want him to know either. So quit looking at me like I forced you into something."

I take a deep breath. She's right; she asked, but I could have easily said no. I wanted it, and we had a good time together, and although I can feel my blood pressure rising the longer this conversation goes on, it helped. Tasting her, kissing her, coming thanks to a pretty girl—it loosened some of the pressure that's been building in me for months.

"Sorry," I mutter. I need to escape before I make a real ass of myself. Like argue with her a bit more, or even worse, kiss her. I still very much want to do that; the fact she's Ryder's daughter hasn't magically erased the attraction I'm feeling. I peer into the hallway to make sure the coast is clear. "I'll see you around."

"You're coming next week, right?"

I glance back at her. "I'll come as long as your dad thinks I need to. But this" — I gesture between us — "isn't happening again."

"Cooper?"

"Yeah?"

She fiddles with a piece of her hair. "Good luck on your games this weekend."

I huff out a breath. "Thanks, Red."

10

COOPER

I BLAST Red Hot Chili Peppers the entire way home, singing along. Either I bellow the words to "Suck My Kiss" off-key or think about Penny Ryder, and the latter isn't an option. Not now, and not ever.

When I pass by Red's, my favorite bar—which just makes me think of her, go figure—I almost head inside for a drink. It sounds ridiculous even in my head, but I'm almost certain that hooking up with Penny brought back my game. I have the feeling that if I tried to chat up a girl right now, she'd be more than willing to entertain my proposition. It's like I had a lock on my junk, and Penny helped me jimmy it open. But instead of stopping off at the bar, I keep driving.

When I get back to the house, I find Izzy vacuuming while she plays a Sheryl Crow album at top volume. She doesn't notice me at first, thanks to the competing loud noises, so I just lean against the banister, taking in the rare sight of my sister acting domestic. She's dressed in her nice pajamas, a silk nightgown and matching robe, and she's pushed her hair back with a headband that, somehow, also matches. Did she buy the entire set at Pink or something? Unless she's going to a sleepover, I'd bet that she has company on the way.

She notices me eventually and startles so badly she drops the vacuum handle. "Cooper! You scared me!"

"Sorry." I walk over and tug on her headband. "Why are you cleaning?"

"Victoria is coming over."

"Oh?"

She bats my hand away from her headband. "Just her. We're going to watch *Legally Blonde* and drink margaritas."

"Victoria is the girl you knew before McKee, right?"

"Volleyball camp, yeah. We're on the team together." She squints at me. "Why are you so interested?"

"I'm not." Which is not a lie; I'm still thinking about Red—Penny—and what the fuck just happened. It was incredible, but now that I know it was Penny *Ryder* I ate out in a fucking storage closet... I just need to trust she has no interest in her father finding out. He'd chain me to the ice and make me the first official death-by-Zamboni murder victim.

The only reason it felt so good was because it had been ages since I kissed a girl, much less tasted pussy. Now that my game is back, soon she'll be a distant memory. Working alongside her is less than ideal, but it's only once a week, and hopefully Coach will free me of the obligation soon.

Izzy is still looking at me a little too closely. "How was the volunteer thing?"

"Great, actually."

She raises an eyebrow. She's good at that, the single eyebrow thing. It reminds me of Mom. "You were convinced it was going to suck. I thought you didn't even like kids."

"It was fine. You know I enjoy being on the ice." I'm not about to get into the whole Penny thing with my little sister, so

I start up the stairs. "I'll get out of your hair. Enjoy your movie night."

"There's something you're not telling me." She crosses her arms over her chest. "I'm not a little kid anymore, Coop. I'm in college just like you. Talk to me."

"It's nothing." I run my hand through my hair. Hair that less than an hour ago, Penny held onto tightly as she rode my face. I can't stop thinking about her Halloween-themed manicure and stacks of thin rings. It was clear by the way she reacted, how I had to walk her through jerking me off, that she's not very experienced, so why the hell did she decide to have a hookup in a closet in the first place? I know I'm good looking, but even my ego isn't big enough to think I thrust her into some sort of heat, like a cat. "I'll see you later."

I've only been in my bedroom for two seconds, feeling shitty about leaving Izzy hanging, when Sebastian comes in.

"Hey," he says. "Looks like Izzy is having a friend over, so I'm heading to the batting cages. Come along?"

I look at my bed. The plan had been to order in and continue my *Star Wars* rewatch, but while I can't confide in Izzy, Sebastian is a good bet. "Sure. I just had the weirdest experience."

"Weird how?" he asks as I grab my jacket and throw it back on.

"I hooked up with someone."

"Finally," he says with a grin.

"Yeah, well, she's Ryder's daughter. I didn't realize until after."

He stumbles on the last step of the stairs. "Dude."

"I know, I know," I say with a groan. "I didn't recognize her."

As we make the short drive over to the athletic facilities, I fill Sebastian in on what happened. He's a good person to vent

to because he just lets you talk without interrupting. The
moment he parks the car, though, he turns and looks at me.

"You need to forget her."

"I know."

"It's her business what she does with her body, but you
don't want her father to get involved. He's already watching
you like a fucking hawk."

I scowl as I open the door. "Got it."

Seb grabs his bag from the back and slings it over his
shoulder. "What? You know I'm right. I'm glad you finally
broke the dry spell—"

"—The fucking curse," I interrupt.

"—Whatever. I just mean—"

"—Aren't baseball players supposed to be the most
superstitious, too?"

He rolls his eyes. "Just keep your eyes on the prize. Being
captain is a big deal. It would be dumb to lose it over something
like this."

"Thanks for the lecture, Dad." I push the door to the
building open and lead the way down the hallway. This isn't
Markley, but I can still find my way around easily; I've been
here with Seb often enough. He ruffles my hair in retaliation
for the jab, which leads to me kicking him in the shin; we play-
wrestle for a moment before bursting into laughter.

"Was it good?" he asks when we finally keep walking.

"Really fucking good." I groan at the thought of all that
long, orange-red hair. Not to mention the freckles. Penny even
has freckles on her legs, which turned me on an unfair amount.
Pretty soon, I'm going to need to put a gag order on myself: no
thinking about Penelope Ryder. "Remember that lady at
Tiffany's? When we helped James pick out Bex's engagement
ring?"

"She was hot."

"They could be cousins or something. But Penny is even hotter," I say as I help Seb get set up with a bucket of balls in his favorite cage, the one at the end with the machine that hardly ever glitches. I sit down on the bench, watching as he gets out his gear. I've never gotten used to the feel of a baseball bat in my hands, even though my general athleticism extends to most sports. I know how to throw a football in a tight spiral—thanks, Dad—and I can muscle out a line drive here and there. I'm even good at volleyball, thanks to years spent helping Izzy perfect her serve.

Seb raises his eyebrows as he puts on his batting gloves. "You do have a weakness for redheads."

"She has the freckles and everything."

"Whatever, Gilbert Blythe."

I chuck a baseball at his head. He ducks, snorting with laughter; the ball hits the other side of the cage with a rattle. He steps into the box, bat set against his shoulder. "Just saying."

I roll my eyes. The tragedy here isn't that he just compared me to that little snot-nosed kid pining after Anne in *Anne of Green Gables*, it's that he unwittingly reminded me of the mountain of reading I'm still avoiding. "Ready?"

He adjusts his helmet. "Yep."

I press the button, and the first ball comes out. He swings, connecting with a satisfying crack. I watch as he hits a few in a row, adjusting his feet from time to time. It's the equivalent of a shooting drill, something to run over and over until the motion is instinctual. I'm not a baseball expert, but I know as well as anyone that Sebastian has always been a beast with a bat in his hands. His dad was like that too, in his prime, and I know Seb has heard the comparisons on more than one occasion.

This kind of silence is perfect. We don't talk; I just watch as he works. It's like when he comes with me to the rink and hangs over the boards, his gaze intent upon me as I attack different skills.

But the whole time, I'm fighting to get Penny out of my mind. I've never seen her at a game before, which now that I think of it is sort of odd, considering her father is our coach. It's possible that I just haven't noticed her, but she's so striking that I don't know why I wouldn't. Even though she wished me good luck on tomorrow's game, I don't think I'm going to see her there.

When Seb finishes the whole bucket, he holds out his bat. "Take a turn," he says. "Looks like you could use it."

11

PENNY

I'M A MONUMENTAL IDIOT, but I can't bring myself to care.

I'm behind on my homework and laundry and studying for that chemistry test. My stomach is rumbling, and I feel sticky; I'm in desperate need of a shower. Above all, I need to put Cooper Callahan and his wicked, talented tongue out of my mind. But instead of going to my dorm and treating myself to an extra-hot shower before buckling down with my books, I head to The Purple Kettle.

I dash to the building, relieved when I see Mia at the counter, handing a guy a pair of steaming-hot drinks. Her hair is up in a ponytail, and she's got the distinctive purple apron— the same color as our home jerseys—tied tightly around her waist. She notices me and waves, and my expression must alarm her, because she hurries out from behind the counter as soon as the guy moves on.

She pulls me into a tight hug. "Are you okay? You look freaked out."

I pull back, running nervous hands through my hair. That's

one way to put it, I guess. I also feel fantastic, yet incredibly guilty; a million emotions crowding in on each other. If I'd known that Cooper had no clue who I was, I never would have put him in such an awkward position. In the end, he didn't seem too angry, but that doesn't erase the fact it was shitty.

"I did it," I blurt.

Her eyes go as wide as the chocolate chip cookies in the bin next to the register. "Oh my *God*. Tell me everything!"

I glance around. We're basically alone; the guy with the coffees just left, and whoever is working this shift with Mia is in the back room. Strangled laughter bubbles up. Back room, storage closet. There's basically no difference. What the hell was I thinking? I didn't want to lose my nerve by waiting until we got to the dorms, but we're lucky that no one walked by, least of all my boss, Nikki.

Mia stalks to the back room. "Pete, take over at the register for a few minutes," I hear her saying. "I need the room."

When we're tucked away, I slump against a bag of coffee beans and cover my face with my hands. "I can't believe I actually did it."

"It, as in..."

I look at her, my face instantly red hot. The last thing I need to think about is Cooper's cock. If he felt big in my hand, how big would he feel inside me? "No, not *that*. The first thing on The List."

She grins. "Okay, nice. Some oral action."

"He's as good as advertised," I admit. "Apparently, he was going through a dry spell, and before I could stop myself, I just..."

Mia hits my shoulder lightly. Her smile is wider than it has any right to be. "Look at you, being a total bad bitch. You came, right?"

"Yes." And it was the best orgasm I've ever had in my life,

although I don't add that part. I haven't had anything but a toy inside me since Preston. While I'm nowhere near ready for penetrative sex, the feeling of Cooper's thick finger tipped me over the edge. "But, um... he didn't know who I was."

She cocks her head to the side. "What?"

"He didn't recognize me. I guess it's fair since I never come to the games, but we didn't talk about it until after. I thought he was just pretending, and meanwhile he thought I was some random girl who was good at ice skating."

"Was he upset?"

"Sort of. But he knows my dad isn't going to find out." I snort. "That would be a disaster."

She shrugs, leaning back against a row of shelves filled with unopened bottles of flavored syrups. "No harm, no foul. Sounds like a success to me. As long as you feel good about it. You do, right?"

The memory crashes over me like a wave. It's like I can still feel his hands on my thighs, the way his beard scratched my skin, the vibrations of his voice as he teased me. After fantasizing about having a guy go down on me for years, it was incredible to experience it for real. It blew every single one of my daydreams out of the water, and if I could have it all over again right now, I would sign up in a heartbeat.

"Yes," I say. "Remarkably, he wasn't the douchebag I thought he would be. He was almost... sweet. During the lesson and after, with me."

Not to mention the fact that he wasn't *just* sweet. I may have sent the first domino falling when I asked him to hook up in the first place, but he deftly took over. He knew exactly what he was doing and wanted to give it to me—if I was a good girl for him. I have no idea if he's like that with every girl he hooks up with, but it pushed my buttons in just the right way. If it wasn't for how it ended, it would have been perfect.

I hope that when I see him next week, we can put any lingering weirdness aside and teach the class as well as we did before I went around throwing in complications. Or who knows, maybe he'll have a pair of incredible games this weekend and my dad will just name him the captain. I don't know who else is in the running, but there's no doubt, after watching Cooper on the ice, that hockey is the chief love in his life.

"Cooper Callahan, a secret sweetheart," Mia muses. "Who would have guessed?"

I pull out my phone to check the time and see a text waiting from my dad, asking about how the class went. Honestly, he could have mentioned to Cooper that I was going to be there.

"I'll see you later," I say. "I just couldn't wait until you came home to tell you."

"Wait," she says. "This is great. There's a party tomorrow at Haverhill. You can scope out your next hookup."

I've only gone to a couple of parties in my time at McKee. When I was with Preston, I went to them all the time, but they lost their luster—if it ever existed—after the one at Jordan Feinstein's. "You know I don't really do parties."

Mia clasps her hands together. "Come on, it'll be fun. Haverhill parties have cocktails, not just cheap beer. It's way better than a frat party. Those are always disasters."

Haverhill House is the best off-campus housing option for seniors. It's a couple of houses grouped together around a sprawling lawn north of campus, so I guess it should be called Haverhill *Houses*, but Haverhill was the first one built, and even though the other houses have names, none of them stuck. It's relatively new—built in the '90s instead of the '60s, or even older—so it's not a crumbling relic. It's the best chance a McKee student has of experiencing a big party that's not attached to a fraternity or sorority, and thanks to the people who snag rooms there—take this as a hint at their income bracket—the alcohol is top-shelf. One of Mia's hookups invited her last year, and if she shows up looking like eye candy, she gets in without fuss.

The next item on the list isn't anything especially crazy—I want to experience giving a blowjob. I have no idea if I'll feel ready to try that with a guy who catches my eye, but it can't hurt to put on one of my nice dresses and dance before it gets so cold, I resent the idea of stepping out to a party in anything less than jeans and a thick sweater. At the very least, it'll be a way to get Cooper out of my mind. The faster I move on, the faster I'll forget about him.

"Okay, fine. But we're not doing anything weird that might get back to my dad. You know he'd flip out."

Mia kisses my cheek. "Hell. Yes. Let's keep getting you laid."

12

COOPER

THE REFEREE'S whistle cuts through the air, stopping play. I glance at Evan, who gestures to the other end of the rink; Mickey's getting to his feet with help from Brandon.

"Two-minute penalty for tripping," the referee says. The player from the Boston College side, a forward, skates to the penalty box, and we set up for the power play, the first of the game. It's the third period, and our defense has been flawless, but unfortunately, so has Boston's. With only a couple minutes left, I have a feeling that whichever team gets a goal will end up winning. A power play is a perfect chance to make that goal belong to us.

A home victory for the first game of the season would be sweet.

With Boston down a defender, we're able to penetrate their territory and stay there. Brandon and Mickey and the other forward, Jean, pass the puck back and forth as they look for an opening, and Evan and I shore up the line. All game, I've been sharp. Focused. When Brandon shoots and the Boston goalie sends it right back, I stop it from heading into our zone, passing it back to him between the legs of the remaining Boston defender. The goalie denies his second try too. Mickey tries to send in the rebound, but the goalie slaps it all the way to our end. I chase after it, protecting it against the Boston forwards as I look for an opening. I finally see one and send it to Jean, who slaps it to Evan, who loops back around and passes it off to me again. I'm back in Boston's territory now—and the goalie isn't protecting his right side well enough.

I take the shot. It squeaks by the goalie into the back of the net. The crowd erupts with cheers as the band starts up the McKee victory song.

Evan practically skates into me as he pulls me into a hug. Mickey and Jean crowd around me, patting my helmet and congratulating me. The first goal of the season? Mine, with an assist from Evan. I'm a defenseman and don't get many scoring chances, thanks to my position, so each goal means even more. I can't control my grin as we resume play. I can't wait to hear what Coach has to say when the game ends.

We hold on to the defensive end of things after the power play ends, and the crowd—the stands absolutely filled with students and fans from Moorbridge and other nearby towns alike—cheer so loudly we can barely hear the buzzer when time runs out. I pull Evan into another hug, breathing in the cold air and the sweat on our skin. The team skates onto the ice, raising our sticks, bellowing the lyrics to the victory song. The lyrics aren't actually "Go McFucking McKee," of course, but no one cares. When we finally make our way over to the bench, I look for Coach Ryder, but something else catches my eye. A flash of orange hair.

Penny?

No, some other girl. I shake my head, willing the disappointment away. The less I think about her, the faster I'll forget her.

Someone slams into my shoulder. "Watch yourself," Brandon snarls.

I whirl around. "What the hell was that for?"

"I know you think you're getting the captain position," he says, "but I'm a senior. It's my year. I'm the center."

"It's based on merit."

He snorts. "One power play goal doesn't make you better than the rest of us, Callahan."

While I can admire his ability to get under our opponents' skin, he turns it on his own teammates too often for my taste. I grind my teeth. He's a douchebag, but that's nothing new.

I lean in. "Maybe, but actually leading in something other than taunting counts, too."

"And you're a saint?" He laughs shortly. "Say what you will about me, but I'm not the one who pulls my gloves off at the slightest provocation."

Brandon is the kind of player I can't stand; he chirps his head off, but at the end of the day, he won't throw an elbow when necessary. I know the college rules, but it's still hockey; it's a physical game, and hits are part of the game.

Before I can reply, Remmy skates over, throwing his arms around us. We get caught up in the celebration, and it's for the best, anyway; Brandon and I have never been best buddies. If Coach ends up making him captain, it'll be a bitter pill to swallow. I can only hope that games like this one, as well as the volunteering, show him I'm willing to play by the rules. Whatever the hell allowed me to get into the zone—Ryder's lecture, or the skating class, or even my hookup with Penny— I'm grateful for it. I haven't felt this good about my play since early last season.

Coach Ryder gathers us around for a post-game debrief while we're still in our skates and pads. When his hand comes down on my shoulder, clapping firmly, I drop my gaze, so the guys don't see the flush on my face. "Great effort, men," he says. "All of you played your hearts out and got us a great win to take into tomorrow's game. Callahan, excellent job taking advantage of the power play, and great assist by Bell. Enjoy the win, gentlemen, but make sure you stay focused on tomorrow, too."

Evan grins at me. I knock our shoulders together.

"McFucking McKee!" Jean shouts in his hoarse French-Canadian accent. We all join in, putting our fists together and cheering before breaking away to hit the showers and change. I catch Coach's eye once more; he nods before disappearing into his office.

I bite the inside of my cheek to keep from smiling too hard and shoot off a text to the family group chat:

1st W.

Then I head for the showers. There's a game tomorrow, sure, but tonight? I'm using the end of my hookup curse to huddle up with a puck bunny or two... and to get Little Miss Red Ryder-hood out of my head.

WHEN I STEP out of the locker room, however, it's Seb waiting for me instead of a hopeful puck bunny.

"If you want him, he'll be at Haverhill House," he says to a girl who pouts as he grabs my arm.

"Haverhill House?" I repeat, raising my eyebrows. I've only been to a couple of parties there. I fit in better with the frat crowd, even though, despite repeated attempts at recruiting, I'm not a member of any of them. "We didn't have plans."

"Yes, we did," he says, dragging me through the knot of

bodies; my teammates and their partners and hookups—current and hopeful—are crowding the hallway. "Important plans."

I shake him off and stop walking. "What?"

"Jesus," he says. "Stop being so dense. I'll tell you in the car."

"You're acting weird, you know," I grumble as I follow him out of the building. "What's going on, you chasing a chick at that party? It's not our usual crowd."

"Not yours, maybe," he says. "But guess who got an invite and is currently in everyone's Snap stories?"

My eyes widen. "No."

"We need to find her. The last thing I saw, she was—"

"No," I interrupt. "Don't even."

"There were body shots involved."

I scrub my hand over my face. "I thought the Haverhill parties were supposed to be exclusive."

"Someone invited a bunch of freshmen. It's been a mess since the doors opened, apparently."

"Shit." I yank open the passenger door of Seb's Jeep and hop in. "Doesn't she have a game tomorrow?"

"It's not until the evening." Seb lowers the radio as he turns out of the parking lot. I'm still full of adrenaline from the game, so I can't sit still; the entire drive, I'm tapping my feet, drumming my fingers over my knees. Izzy is probably fine, but she's a party girl, and sometimes she's not as careful as she should be. You never know what kinds of assholes you might run into at a big university. When she was in high school, our parents had to bail her out on more than one occasion, and those were just high school parties. Now that she's here at McKee, they're counting on me to keep an eye on her. I'll need to deliver her to Long Island in one piece come Thanksgiving.

When we get to the row of houses, light spills out of the one in the center, along with the thump of music. Seb finds a patch of grass to park on. I barely wait until he turns off the car before I'm slamming the door shut and stalking across the lawn. It's a chilly night, the start of October turning from golden days to autumn, but I suppose it's hoping against hope that my sister came to this party dressed in a parka.

At the door, a bored looking kid wearing glasses and a tweed jacket glances at us. "Names?" he asks.

"Fuck off," I say as I shoulder past him. I'd rather go to a frat with an open keg than beg for a watered-down rum coke from a philosophy major high on shrooms. This first room must be the dance floor, because we walk straight into a knot of sweaty bodies.

"Want to split up?" Seb calls over the beat.

I jerk my head to the right. "I'll go down this hallway. You check the dance floor."

I wriggle past a couple getting handsy and slink down the hallway, peering into each room. There's a group of people sitting in a circle around what looks like a Ouija board, the makings of a threesome, a couple of guys passing around a joint. One of them holds it out to me, but I shake my head. I'm not strict about not drinking during the season like James is, but I only touch weed when I'm off duty in the summer.

"Hey," I say, "you see a girl here? Tall, dark hair, blue eyes? She's probably wearing a necklace with the letter 'I' on it?"

"You're the hockey player," one of them says, blinking at me with all the urgency of a sloth.

"Yes," I say impatiently. "Have you seen that girl?"

"Upstairs," another says, coughing dryly. "You sure you don't want a hit, man? It's primo shit."

"Nah, thanks." I fight back the little hook of panic trying to reel me in. Upstairs at a house party usually means one thing. I'm not naïve, I know my sister has probably had sex before and that it's not my business to forbid her from it, but what if she does something she regrets? She's a relationship girl. She's been heartbroken ever since some jerk at the club down at Kitty Hawk stood her up for the date they planned in Manhattan. If she found someone new to date, I would have heard about it by now.

I take the stairs two at a time, calling her name. The lights are dim up here, the music muffled, the air filled with the sour smell of weed, undercut with incense. My eyes water as I push past someone at the exact moment they blow out a smoke ring. I start opening doors, which is a dangerous proposition, but I'd rather walk in on her than miss her entirely.

At the end of the hallway, I finally spot her. She's on a bed, thankfully fully clothed, laughing as a girl—Victoria, I think— whispers something in her ear. Sparkles cover her midnight blue dress, and the gold-and-diamond initial necklace Mom and Dad gave her during one of her middle school era Izzy Days glitters as well. When she spots me, she shrieks, jumping up from the bed and wrapping me into a hug. She smells like booze and weed, but it's not like I give a shit about that. Her eyes are clear enough, which means she's not roofied.

"Hi," she says. "You're here! This is so cool! Where's Sebby?"

"Downstairs." I pull away and look at her. "What are you even doing here?"

"Victoria's cousin invited us."

"You're only a freshman."

"I know, right?" She reaches up and pets her hands through my hair, like I'm a fluffy dog instead of her older, taller brother. "Sooooo cool!"

"Iz, we saw you on Snap. That sort of stuff can't get back to Mom and Dad."

She just waves her hand. "They went to college too."

"Let's go home."

"What? No way, you just got here! Let's go find Sebby and dance!"

I pull her hands out of my hair. "You're drunk. Don't you have a game tomorrow?"

"Not until the evening," Victoria says. She hangs over Izzy, swaying them both slightly.

"Oh my God, you had a game," Izzy says. She reaches up again, but I block her hands. "How did it go? Did you win?"

"Yes," I say shortly. I wish I could go find Seb for backup, but I'm afraid if I leave, she'll disappear into the crowd again. I check my pockets, but of course I left my phone in the car. "Now let's..." I trail off as I see a flash of red hair out of the corner of my eye.

Penny.

This time it really is her; she's looking hot as fuck in a tight sweater dress and tall boots, her hair half-up, half-down, braids framing her face like a crown. She's hanging on the arm of some random fucking guy, letting him push her up against the wall as she laughs with a cute snort.

I can't breathe for a second. I thought I was on edge before, but now I'm on the verge of fucking losing it. I wish I could rip the image of her in that dress out of my mind. Or save it for later, but without that prick in the picture. Her eyes widen as she notices me, and something shifts in her expression as she takes in the scene; Victoria hanging over Izzy, and Izzy hanging over me.

She definitely doesn't know that Izzy's my sister.

I don't recognize the guy, but my guess is he's a senior, maybe even lives here in Haverhill House. I got the sense, given the hand job walk-through, that Penny isn't all that experienced. Does he know that? Did she tell him? Is she planning on hooking up with him?

I have no claim to her. In fact, I actively try to avoid having a claim over any girls at all, especially when their last names are Ryder. But something about seeing her with another guy makes my chest hurt, and when I swallow, it's like I have a bone stuck in my throat.

She murmurs something to the guy, pushing him away. "Callahan," she starts, her voice trailing off.

Before she can collect her thoughts, Izzy heaves—and hurls all over me.

13

PENNY

THIS GUY—ALFRED, I only learned his name after about ten minutes of conversation—is pretentious as hell.

The moment he spotted me at the party, he walked over and started to flirt. A drink in, I haven't done much but nod along as he drones on and on about himself. He might be attractive, with long blond hair pulled into a bun and wire-framed glasses perched on his strong nose, but he's self-centered, and if I was looking for more than a hookup, I would have wriggled my way out of the conversation ages ago.

"What do you think?" he asks. I'm so taken aback by the fact he's asking me a question that I don't answer right away. "We could go together; it's playing at the theater in town."

I blink. When the conversation veered into date territory, I have no idea, but there's nothing I'd like less. I muster a smile and say, "Sorry, what?"

"It's too damn loud in here," he says, leaning down so he can talk into my ear. "I said, do you want to go to see the newest A24? It's a psycho-erotic thriller about—"

I grab his arm and yank him even closer. At least he smells

nice. I can appreciate a man who knows that Axe isn't a suitable body spray past sophomore year of high school as long as he's using any cologne but Tropic Blue.

"Want to go upstairs?" I interrupt.

He raises an eyebrow with a lazy sort of interest. "What do you have in mind?"

I lean up and press a kiss to his lips. "Less talking, more... other things."

It's not the smoothest way I could put it, but right now, I don't need smooth; I have the advantages of a sexy outfit and the inhibitions of the party. He flicks his gaze down to my cleavage. There's not much to see, but my push-up bra helps, and my plum-colored sweater dress clings to my hips nicely. Paired with sheer tights and my thigh-high leather boots, I know I look like a snack. He strokes the hair back from my neck, and I shiver. It's not him that's turning me on so much as the thought of finally crossing another item off The List. Taking back another piece of power. The experience with Cooper was intoxicating. I have no idea if it was him, or the fact we were in a closet where technically anyone could walk in, or just that I finally did something with a real guy after years and diminishing returns on orgasms, but I feel more confident. More like the girl I always wanted to be, and maybe who I was on the way to becoming back before Preston shattered everything.

I grip Alfred's hand in mine and lead him through the crowd, nodding to Mia as we pass. She's making out with some girl I don't recognize, but she winks at me. I fight my blush as we head upstairs. It's probably hoping against hope that there's total privacy to be found, but if we take this out of the party, I know I won't want to go through with it. It's either happening here, or not at all.

I open the first door, hoping to find a dark corner, but

Alfred takes us to the end of the hall. "Might have a better chance here." He squeezes my hand as he opens the door. "You're feistier than I thought you'd be, Penelope."

I fake a laugh even though I want to poke him in the ribs, hard, for calling me by my full name when I very clearly introduced myself as Penny. He pushes me back against the door, his hands on my waist.

Before he can kiss me, I notice who else is in the room.

Cooper Callahan. With not one, but *two* girls.

It shouldn't surprise me. He told me himself that he only hooks up with girls once—to him, we're Kleenex. He makes it worth your while, but the price of admission is the acknowledgement that it won't be anything more than a fleeting moment. Seeing him with two brand-new puck bunnies shouldn't hurt. It's not *allowed* to hurt. Here I am with a guy of my own, after all, and an agenda just like him.

But it does hurt, and that realization is enough to push Alfred away.

"Callahan," I say. I have no idea where I'm going with this. What do I even want? All I know is that if he kisses either of those girls in front of me, it'll hurt worse than wiping out while attempting a triple axel.

He looks at me, his expression unreadable. I know they won the game thanks to his goal, and maybe the smart thing to do would just be to congratulate him and find a different room to go to, but before I can make myself say anything else, the dark-haired girl throws up all over him.

He staggers back, cursing up a storm. I snort with genuine laughter at the sight of him covered in vomit. The girl is fluttering around him, apologizing in a high, distressed voice. Alfred heaves, clapping his hand over his mouth.

"I've got to go," he says, his voice cracking. He books it out of the room without so much as a glance over his shoulder.

I sigh. It's not like I wanted to suck his dick all that much, anyway.

"Izzy," Cooper says, his voice somewhat more level now. "Stop crying, it's fine."

"It's not fine, you're going to hate me!" she says. "I ruined your shirt!"

"Not everyone cares all that much about clothes," he says, but he grimaces, looking down at the shirt. It's a vintage-style band tee advertising Nirvana, and the stain is, unfortunately, electric blue. He looks over at me and adds, "Does your date have an overactive gag reflex or something, Red?"

I ignore the nickname and stalk over to the closet. Maybe there's something in here we can use to clean him up. "He wasn't my date."

"Looked like you were about to get something going."

I pull out a towel and toss it to him. "Not your business."

"He looked like a prick." He makes a face as he mops at his shirt. "Izzy, what were you even drinking? This is *blue*."

"Tequila something," she says with a hiccup. Her friend, who had disappeared into the bathroom, comes back with a wet washcloth. She helps Izzy wipe at her face without ruining her makeup, although they need to sacrifice the lipstick.

"No, he was..." I sigh, unable to fake any interest. "Fine, yes, he was a bit of an ass. But whatever, I just wanted to blow him."

He blinks. "We're going to unpack that later."

"We?"

"Yeah, come on, I need you. Help me get my sister out of here."

I ignore the little tendril of relief that pokes its head up at his words. His sister, not his latest hookup. "Sure, okay."

"Unless you want to go track down that weasel."

"You're terrible," I say, even as I take Izzy's arm. "You don't even know him."

"And you do?"

I flush. He cocks his head to the side, like he's witnessing an interesting reaction in chemistry lab.

"I have questions, Red," he declares. "And as soon as I don't smell like tequila and my sister's stomach acid, you're answering."

"Is this your idea of flirting?" Izzy mumbles to her brother as we head out of the room, her friend on our heels. "You're terrible at it."

"We're not flirting," I say with a scowl. "Cooper doesn't know how to flirt."

"Neither do you," he shoots back.

That hurts more than it should, so I keep my mouth shut and focus on not falling down the stairs in my heels. When we're back on the main floor, we wind through the crowd to the entrance. Cooper's scowl is even more pronounced, the black energy coming off him in waves as he cuts through the mob of drunk college kids with ease. At the door, he allows Izzy to lean on him, stroking a hand through her hair in a tender gesture that makes my breath stick in my throat. "Give me your phone, Iz."

She plunges her hand down her front and pulls it out of her bra. Cooper stares at it like it's a scorpion, which makes me double over with laughter; he snatches it out of his sister's hand and glares at me. "Not another word, Red."

"I didn't even say anything!"

He turns his back as he presses the phone against his ear. Izzy giggles, poking me in the stomach. "He likes you."

Cooper puts up his middle finger without looking back at us. I'm not sure if he's telling off Izzy or denying that he likes me. I push down the warmth that wants to spread through me;

a drip of happiness that could easily settle low in my belly. Izzy's just doing what drunk people do: talk.

Izzy hugs her friend, who promises to check in later. She disappears into the knot of people on the dance floor as a guy I vaguely recognize as Sebastian Callahan walks over. Even though he's not related to Cooper by blood, which I remember Mia telling me ages ago, there's something similar about them; they both have a determined set to their mouths and commanding energy.

"Oh, good," he says. "You found her."

"Only cost me my favorite t-shirt," Cooper says. "Let's go, I'm getting a fucking headache."

"Doesn't care about clothes, my ass," Izzy mutters to me as we head out into the night. I bite my lip to keep from laughing again.

Sebastian throws me a look when he realizes I'm tagging along, and I stop on the porch, unsure if I should continue or if I should go back to the party and find Mia, but then Cooper says, irritably, "Penny, come on," so I loop my arm through Izzy's again and let her lean on me as we troop across the half-frozen lawn.

In the car, a nice new Jeep which must be Seb's, because there's no question that he's driving, Cooper gives me the front seat and sits in the back with his sister, who is petting his hair again. I text Mia to let her know I'm leaving. Sebastian turns on the radio to cut through the semi-awkward silence, and when "King of my Heart" by Taylor Swift comes on, Izzy hollers along. I sing along too, catching the look in Cooper's eyes through the windshield. He's still scowling, but really, he's fighting a smile.

After a couple minutes, we pull up to a house in town that's close to my father's. It's cheerful looking, with pumpkins on the porch steps and a fall wreath on the door. Seb helps Cooper get

Izzy to the door. I follow along, somewhat hesitantly. I thought
we'd be heading to the dorms. I'd rather not walk all the way to
my dorm from here, especially past midnight, or try to catch
the bus.

"She doesn't live in the dorms?"

"Nope," Cooper says. "We all live here."

I step into the entryway. "That's cute."

"It would have been better with James," Izzy says with a
pout. "I miss him."

I look around the house. The entryway has a staircase to
the left, and to the right, it opens to a living room. There's a big
leather couch, a matching loveseat, and an armchair with a
plaid blanket folded neatly over the back, grouped around a
wall-mounted television. It's easy to tell what belongs to
Cooper and his brother, and what touches their sister has
added; the bottle-opener in the shape of a skull must be theirs,
but the tapered pink candles on the coffee table, hers. "He lives
in Philadelphia, right?"

"With his fiancée," Izzy says with a sigh as she flops down
on the couch. "We haven't seen them since the summer. He
abandoned us to go play *football*."

Sebastian ruffles her hair as he walks past, heading into the
kitchen. "You can call him whenever."

Izzy brightens at that. "Coop, where's my phone?"

Cooper shakes his head. "Not now, he'll have my ass for
letting you go wild at a senior party."

Izzy rolls her eyes. "You didn't let me do anything. Besides,
I won't tell him."

"Iz, I love you, but secrets aren't your strong suit." He sighs,
looking down at his shirt again. "Come on, let's get changed.
You should have some water and go to bed, so you're good to go
for your game tomorrow. I'll drive you home in a minute,
Penny."

When they troop upstairs, Sebastian gives me a narrow-eyed look, clearly unwilling to let go of the fact that Cooper brought a girl he's already been with—because I don't believe for a second he wouldn't tell his brother about the indignity of accidentally sleeping with his coach's daughter—to their house, and apparently is going to drive me home himself instead of offering to pay for an Uber like a normal guy. I shuffle my feet, unsure what to do with myself. There's a slamming sound from upstairs, and then a high-pitched giggle.

"Sebastian!" Cooper roars.

Sebastian's gaze flickers to the stairs before settling on me once more. "You should have told him who you were beforehand."

I swallow. He doesn't even sound all that upset, but the words chastise me all the same. "I didn't know."

"When the consequences only go one way, you make sure." He nods once, like he's pleased with himself for that cryptic, metaphorical slap, and then bounds up the stairs two at a time.

Of course, he doesn't know that the consequences wouldn't just go one way; if my father finds out, it could ruin the relationship I've fought carefully to repair. What better way to remind my father of the version of me who forced us out of Arizona than recklessly getting involved with another hockey player? *His* hockey player? I'll lose the little respect of his that I've built back up, and it wasn't until I did something as monumentally stupid as asking Cooper Callahan to go down on me that I realized how much I treasure it. If I tried to explain The List to him, on top of being mortifying, he wouldn't understand. It wouldn't be growth to him; it'd be regression.

Yet despite knowing that, I know something else, too: I'm about to ask Cooper to do it again.

14

COOPER

"THANKS again for helping me with Izzy," I say as we climb the stairs to Penny's dorm room. "I still can't believe she threw up on me."

"It happens," she says, looking at me over her shoulder. I've tried not to stare at her too much, but it's hard with that dress she's wearing. It clings to her ass deliciously, and the neckline, combined with her bra, is doing its best to remind me that when we hooked up, I didn't even get to see her tits.

She clearly went to that party with fun on her mind, and I can't stop stewing over it. She obviously didn't know the guy she was with, and she made no effort to go after him when he ran away to blow chunks in private. There's something up with her, and maybe it's not my business, but I'm curious anyway.

At the right landing, she leads the way to the room at the end of the hallway. This is one of the older dorms, so she pulls out an actual key to unlock the door. When we parked in front of the dorm and sat for half a second in awkwardness, I nearly stopped myself from offering to walk her to her door, but I couldn't quite manage it. Now we're here, and weirdly, I'd rather be standing in this hallway with her than back at the party with any number of girls, and that odd ache in my chest still won't kick the bucket.

She blushes as she opens the door. "Do you... want to come in for a few?"

"Only if you want me to."

When she replies, there's some of that teasing back in her tone. "I thought we had something to unpack. What are you studying, anyway? That's an academic word if I've ever heard one."

"English." I step into the room. It's actually a small suite, two separate bedrooms instead of one. I suppose being a staff member's daughter has advantages beyond free tuition. "I've spent most of my college career *unpacking*."

Her pretty lips curve into a smile. "I'd rather unpack than analyze, especially when there's math involved. I'm studying biology."

"You sound thrilled."

"I know, right?" she says dryly. "I can hardly contain my excitement."

"I know we don't really know each other," I say abruptly. "But what are you doing, hooking up with random guys?"

She just raises her eyebrows as she crosses her arms over her chest. "Why do you care? Ours was a one-time deal, as I remember. And he wasn't random."

"What's his name?"

"Alfred."

"Alfred what?"

"Alfred Something." She glares at me, a defiant look in her eyes. "Not that it's your business who I hook up with."

"You called him an ass, Red."

She laughs shortly. "I'm sure the trail of girls you've left behind would throw around worse about you."

I ignore that. "Two days ago, I had to walk you through your first hand job, and now, you're..."

"What?" she asks as I trail off. "A slut? Don't you fucking dare."

"Christ, no." I scrub my hand over my face. Maybe it's the fact she's Coach Ryder's daughter, but I can't help wanting to be protective. "I'm not saying you shouldn't do what you want to do, and I'd never call a girl that. I'm just worried, okay? I don't know, you seem pretty inexperienced. I don't want you to get hurt."

Her cheeks are flushed dark red. "Fuck you, Callahan."

She whirls around and throws open one of the doors. I don't exactly expect her to come back out, after the mess I've made in approximately two seconds, but she does a moment later, holding a bright pink journal. She rifles through the pages until she finds the one that she wants and hands it to me.

I stare down at it. It's a list, clearly, simply labeled *The List*, but instead of a list of normal fucking things like groceries or movies or hockey stats, I see words like *spanking* and *public sex* and *anal*. For some reason, regular old vaginal sex is last on the list. The first item, *oral sex (receiving)*, is crossed off.

"What is this?"

She swallows, but even with blush all over her speckled cheeks, she holds her head up high. "It's what I'm doing. You asked, so I'm showing you."

"What is this, a sex bucket list or something?" She tries to snatch the notebook, but I hold it over her head. She jumps for it, so I step back, taking another peek at the list. I nearly choke when I see *orgasm denial* and *double penetration*. "This is kinky, Red."

She huffs. "It's not like I'm *dying*."

"Then what is it? Have you even done any of this? Besides the first, of course."

She stomps on my foot, and she's still wearing her boots, so it hurts enough it startles me. She grabs the notebook, slams it shut, and holds it close to her chest like she's giving it a hug. "I thought you might understand, but never mind."

Her genuinely hurt tone gives me pause. "Understand what?"

She drags her teeth over her bottom lip. "You were right. I don't have a lot of experience, but I'm trying to change that. These are all things I've wanted to do for years now."

"Why don't you get a boyfriend to do them with?"

She's shaking her head before I even get the whole question out. "This isn't about getting a boyfriend. This is about me. It's about being in control of my own life." She looks up at me, that fierce light in her eyes, like she's daring me to laugh in her face. "And I'm not planning on doing all this with anyone I'd ever consider dating."

I sidestep the implication that I'm someone she'd never catch feelings for to say, "So you're giving yourself a crash course in sex? You know, most people are content with regular old boning. Maybe a few fun positions thrown in."

She sets the journal on the little table next to the loveseat in the common area between the two rooms and reaches down to unzip her boots. She pulls them off and throws them, one after the other, into her bedroom. Why would she need to cling to control over her own experiences so tightly? Something about this whole situation is making the back of my neck prickle uncomfortably, but I doubt she'll choose to confide in me. She just said that she'd never consider dating me, after all. Combined with the arousal I'm feeling low in my stomach—I swear, I can still taste the salt of her on my tongue—I'm halfway to bolting out the door. That would be the smart thing, right? Shut this conversation down and keep things firmly in co-volunteer territory.

Her assessment of the situation shouldn't hurt, but it does. If I wanted to be in a relationship with someone, I totally could, I just haven't wanted to tie myself down. I'm not James, who took his fucking fifth grade girlfriend seriously. My priority has been fun, but there's a difference between not *wanting* to be in a relationship and not being boyfriend material. I'd be a fantastic fucking boyfriend if I wanted that.

Without her boots on, she's a couple inches shorter, but no less formidable. Even though she doesn't look like her father beyond those light blue eyes, I can see a bit of him in the way she juts up her chin, like she's expecting a challenge. Something tells me he taught her how to get physical when necessary. "I know," she says. "But *I* want it."

I don't think I've ever had a conversation with a girl about sex that got this detailed without ending in us doing the nasty, but I try to push past the awkwardness for her sake. "All of that stuff is fun," I admit. "You have good taste."

"I knew it," she says, and her eyes are gleaming like she's just gotten me to admit a secret. "You're not most people."

"True." If we're talking kinks, then fine, I'll be honest. She saw a taste of it when we hooked up in the closet, after all. I like sex, so I'm not always all that particular, but nothing gets my dick harder than seeing a girl trust me with her pleasure, even if it's only for a night. Praising her, rewarding her, pushing her until she goes somewhere she's never gone before—Penny doesn't know this, but I've introduced a fair number of girls to anal—is when I'm in my element the most. Ironically, I'd be a good choice of partner for her list if she wanted to stick with one guy all the way through, but that can't happen. Even if I can't rid myself of the memory of the soft noises she made, or if I want nothing more than to cross the slight gap between us and kiss her again. "But it's not like I'm one of a kind. I would pick better than Asshole Something—"

"Alfred," she corrects, her lips twitching as she fights a smile.

"—but I understand that it's hard to follow up after me." I grin, so she knows I'm mostly joking, and she rolls her eyes.

"You know," she says, "for a second, I forgot how arrogant you are."

"Not arrogant. Just confident."

She cocks her head to the side. "Callahan."

"What?"

Now she smiles, and it's distracting and suspicious all at once. "You played well at your game, right?"

"Yeah," I say. "Why?"

"And you said that you just needed a hookup to relax. Which it clearly helped you do."

"Is that how correlations work?"

"Shut up, you know where I'm going with this." She runs her fingers through the ends of her hair, her head still cocked to the side. She takes a step forward, the ghost of a smile on her face. "Take me through the list. I'll get what I want, and it'll help your game. Playing like that, you'll be captain in no time."

Tempting, but impossible. There's a litany of reasons it wouldn't work, and at the very top of the list is one Lawrence Ryder. If he ever finds out about our seven minutes in heaven-style hookup, I'm toast, but if he learns that I've been sneaking around with his daughter repeatedly, I'll find myself selling skates in Dick's Sporting Goods for a living after graduation. And that's if I'm still breathing.

"Your father," I start.

"Doesn't decide who I sleep with," she interrupts. "He won't find out. Trust me, it's not like I want him to know about this either."

"Except he will, and he'll forgive you because you're his daughter, but me? I'll be lucky if I stay on the team."

"He wouldn't do that."

"Don't underestimate what a pissed off father will do."

She huffs out an annoyed breath. "Look, I'm not going to beg."

"As tempting as it would be to see you on your knees," I can't help but say, because apparently, I'm an idiot; now the image is in my brain and I want to see that more than anything, "you already know I don't do repeats."

It's physically painful to open the door. I can't make myself take the first step into the hallway. Even though it's ridiculous, she has a point; I played better than I had in ages. I look over my shoulder. Part of me desperately wants to say yes, if only for the chance to kiss her again, but I'd be playing a dangerous game. When a hookup goes on for too long, feelings inevitably get involved. I don't know what happened to Penny to get her to this place, but I don't want to have to break her heart. "Don't do it like this, Penny. Find a nice guy to take you out."

She gives me a light shove. "Thanks for the unsolicited advice, but if it's not you, I'm sure I'll find better matches than Alfred."

Then she shuts the door in my face.

15

PENNY

IS it masochism if you offer sex to a guy and he turns you down, but then the next time you get yourself off, you think about him?

When Cooper left last night, I knew I should have done yoga or something to calm myself down, re-center, whatever, but I was so wet I could barely hold it together. We didn't even do anything, and he made it clear that he doesn't want to do anything with me ever again, but my body was gleefully traitorous. From the moment we were alone in his car, a truck that he told me he bought with his own money and restored to glory when he was seventeen, to when I slammed the door in his face, I struggled not to jump him. Whenever he called me Red, my pussy literally throbbed.

And so, instead of doing the smart thing, the moment I was alone, I took out Igor and fucked myself with it. I didn't even pretend to conjure up a fantasy; I just replayed what we did in the closet together, and when I ran through that, I imagined what it would be like to go down The List with him. I didn't stop until I came three times, trembling and sweating, and now, in the light of day, I know I should muster up some regret, or at the very least embarrassment, but I can't. Cooper is in a class all his own, and nothing made that realization starker than seeing him in the same room as Alfred.

Ugh, Alfred. I can't believe I was ever going to blow him. This whole "seize the dick" plan is getting shakier by the day.

I really ought to re-focus on the chemistry textbook in front of me, since next week's test is looming and all I've done so far is add a new spicy scene to my book. It's been over an hour since I dragged myself out of bed. I'm in the library, nestled in my favorite chair. My bag of gummy bears and upbeat studying playlist would help in any other scenario, but I've been staring at this one page for the better part of my time here.

I give in to the urge to take out my phone and send Mia a Snap. She replies almost immediately, so she's finally awake. When I left earlier, she didn't even stir. I have no idea what time it was when she came in last night, but it was a lot later than me. She says she'll head to the library with coffees, which is a draw on the productivity front—I could use more caffeine, but she'll want to know about last night. I'm about to accept defeat and move on to my Spanish homework when my dad calls.

On either Fridays or Saturdays, or with this weekend, both days, we usually don't see each other, because he's busy with work and I've never gone to see a game. Ironically, Mia has; we have some other friends who go regularly, and we have standing invitations. I also have a standing invitation from my father, courtesy of two seats right behind the McKee bench that are permanently reserved for me. The last time I watched him coach was at his final game at Arizona State, and that happened three years ago.

"Hey," I say cautiously. "Everything okay?"

"You went to Haverhill last night?"

My stomach drops. "How did you hear?"

"That's for upperclassmen, bug."

"I can handle an off-campus party."

"You don't know who goes to those things."

I swallow as I twirl my hair. "Just other students. Who told you, Dad? You promised not to look at my social media anymore."

"I know," he says. "I didn't, one of the guys mentioned to me you were there."

"So now you have your players spying on me?"

He sighs deeply. "Penelope, I just wanted to make sure that everything is okay. That you're focused on the right things. You need to be dialed in on school, not running around off-campus parties. I thought we were past that."

"Going to one party doesn't mean I'm not working hard, Dad."

"I just don't want you falling into old patterns."

"No," I say. "That's unfair and you know it. How many of your guys went out to celebrate the win last night? If that's fine for them but terrible for me, you're no better than Preston's parents and everyone else."

I hang up. The moment the call ends, I shove my phone back into my bag and burrow my head in my arms. This is the exact reason it's better if he doesn't get involved in my life outside of academics; we always end up arguing. He's not as bad as Traci Biller, because as far as I know, he's never called me a "manipulative slut," but I couldn't help letting the words slip out. I hate when he brings up my past, especially since I've tried so hard to move on. He keeps telling me he knows I've changed, but how can I believe him when things like this happen?

For what feels like the millionth time, my chest aches like someone just stuck a rusty knife right into the center. I miss my mother. I miss the family I used to have. When she died, my dad retreated so far into his grief that I barely saw him. It had been the three of us, and then suddenly the glue holding us together was gone, and he couldn't handle it. Going to parties and getting drunk, blowing off school and my training to hang out with Preston and his friends, acting like nothing mattered—it was better than coming home to an empty house because Dad slept in his office yet again. I paid the price for it, in the end, and I guess in some ways I'm still paying it.

Someone puts their hand on my shoulder. I look up, startled; it's just Mia, holding out a coffee.

"Thanks," I say, wiping at my eyes quickly.

"Chemistry going that badly?" she teases as she pulls over another armchair. "Or wait—I don't have to go beat up Cooper Callahan, do I?"

I shake my head, a smile on my face despite myself. "Pretty sure he'd win that one."

"Absolutely not. I could take him. I'd jump on his back and claw out his eyes."

"As much fun as you'd have," I say, "it was just something stupid with my dad."

She pulls her laptop out of her bag, along with a highlighter and a bunch of articles that no doubt need annotating. "Everything okay?"

I bite my lip. Talking about Cooper, even though he rejected me, sounds a lot better than getting into the thing with Dad, so I say, "I saw him last night. I helped him get his sister home, and then... he escorted me home."

Mia raises her eyebrows. Even though I'm sure she's hungover, she's wearing makeup; I opted for my usual mascara but couldn't muster up anything beyond that. "What happened to that other guy I saw you with?"

I explain the whole thing, from the vomit situation to the

moment I shoved Cooper out of our room. By the end of the story, I'm blushing. It wasn't like I asked Cooper on a date. I offered him sex—repeated sex, no strings attached—and he turned me down. What's wrong with me that I couldn't entice a guy whose middle name is practically "casual" to agree to that? It's pathetic.

"Interesting," Mia says.

I glare at her. "That's all you've got? I tell you this whole thing and you Mr. Spock me?"

"Doesn't he say, 'fascinating?' Like, what a fascinating observation, Captain Kirk?"

"Whatever."

She taps the highlighter against her laptop. "Did you really say you'd never date him?"

"Not in so many words." I sigh. "Besides, it's not like he'd ever date me. He doesn't even want to fuck me again."

"So? That probably stung, Pen. I mean, good for you for being clear about what you want, but you can't blame him if he's a little hurt. Guys are always defensive when they feel slighted."

"You're the one who encouraged me to do this," I say. "You told me I should go through The List."

"Yeah, but if you're going to use someone, don't tell them that to their face." She leans back, setting her feet on the table with her ankles crossed. At least we're not at one of the antique walnut tables in the center of the Reading Room; the librarian at the circulation desk glares at anyone who even so much as puts a book bag on top of one. "If he doesn't want to be a living sex toy, you can't blame him."

"That's not what I said," I mutter. "Besides, I didn't want to use him, he'd get something out of it too. He plays better when he's getting regular sex, and he needs to perform well if my dad is going to make him captain."

"Fascinating," Mia says gravely.

I lean over and poke her cheek. She sticks her tongue out at me, and we collapse into giggles. After a long pause, I say, "Do you really think I insulted his manhood or whatever?"

"Maybe. Maybe he's been wanting a girlfriend. Who knows, really."

"He told me I should find a boyfriend. Or, rather, a nice guy to take me out. Even though I explained—"

"Oh," she interrupts, her eyes widening. "Wait, that changes everything."

"...Why?"

"He doesn't want to say yes because he thinks you're too good for it. He's not annoyed, Pen, he's being protective."

I snort. "What?"

"He's protecting you from *him*. He doesn't want to be the big bad wolf sullying Little Red Riding Hood."

"First of all, ew. Second, that's the stupidest thing I've ever heard."

She shrugs as she takes a sip of her coffee. "Boys have that tendency, yes. You need to make it clearer that you don't need protection, you need to get dicked down. If you're set on him, that is."

I sigh, risking another look at my phone. Today's game, the second in a pair against Boston College, is starting in under an hour. The smarter thing to do would be to forget him, aside from when we're forced to work together, and be more discerning about choosing guys to hook up with as I try to tackle The List. There are plenty of guys out there that aren't pretentious like Alfred or connected to my father like Cooper.

But judging by the way my body reacts to even the mere thought of him, none of them would give me the experience I'm craving. Is it possible to be kindred spirits in sex alone?

If I go to the game, I can kill two birds with one stone.

Smooth things over with my dad and make it clearer to Cooper that I know what I want. Not to use him at his expense, but for us to be real friends-with-benefits. Both of us reaping the rewards of this arrangement. He might laugh in my face, but I can at least try.

"Fine," I say. "Want to come with me to the game?"

16

COOPER

WE'VE BEEN SUCKING for two periods straight.

I hop off the bench and skate onto the ice for what will be my last shift of the period. Down by two goals—and it should have been more, but Remmy has stepped up with the saves—we've been chasing Boston College the whole game. Pissed off from yesterday's loss, I'm sure, they came out faster, grinding harder. We've been stuck playing catch up, and the longer the game has gone on, the worse I've been playing. The last goal we let in happened because I totally misread a pass. A stupid mistake, and a costly one.

We execute a neat forecheck and get the puck back; Evan passes to Mickey, who passes to Brandon. He attempts a wrist shot, but the BC goalie snuffs it with his mitt. The seconds trickle down, and before we can try to go for the goal again, the period ends. I shake my head, wiping my sleeve across my face. Whatever boost I had during yesterday's game has completely dissipated. I need to regain my focus for one more period. Not just to wrestle the game back, but to keep everyone's energy high. My play on the ice matters, but an excellent captain doesn't just lead by example. He inspires the guys to give their all, too. If I come into the locker room full of frustration, it will influence other guys on the team, especially the freshmen. The clearer we are mentally, the better we'll play.

The cheers and chanting of the crowd echo around the arena as we skate to the bench. Even though there's a football game this afternoon, there are plenty of students and fans in the stands. The football team isn't nearly as good as it was when James was here, anyway, and there's always a lot of excitement around the beginning of the hockey season.

In the locker room, I take advantage of the break to cool down, rehydrate, and breathe. Coach Ryder and his assistants lead a quick meeting to go over adjustments we can make in the third period to gain an edge. To my grim satisfaction, Brandon throws his gloves and snaps at a freshman over a turnover, which means Coach looks to me, not him, to say a few words from the player's perspective before we head back on the ice.

"It's not over until it's over," I say, looking at the group. They're as sweaty and winded as I am, but we have another twenty to play, and part of hockey is endurance. Can your legs go the entire game? Can you outlast your opponent? Can you grind until you have nothing left in the tank, and then can you grind a little more? I straighten up further, tapping my stick against the floor. "We need to focus and execute. It feels like a tall order, but we're only down by two goals, and we can make up that difference. I know that every single one of you has another period left in you, so let's fucking get it done."

When we come back out of the tunnel, Coach Ryder is standing off to the side—with his daughter. I freeze in place, nearly colliding with Remmy. Coach has his arm around Penny, who's wearing a purple McKee knit cap with a pom-pom on top. My mouth feels parched, suddenly. The royal purple looks good with her hair, and the pom-pom adds an almost unspeakable level of cuteness. Until now, I've tried to keep her out of my mind, but now every second of last night comes flooding back.

"Thanks, Dad," Penny is saying. "Sorry, I just couldn't wait until the end of the game."

"I'm just glad you're finally here," he replies. He gestures for me to come over. "Callahan, look who joined us for the game."

"Hi," I say. "Um, that's cool."

"Penny is confident we'll come back," Coach says. "Right, bug?"

She attempts a wink, but it's more like an exaggerated blink in my general direction. I bite my lip to keep from laughing. Why that's so endearing, I have no idea, but it makes my lingering frustration at the game melt away.

"Score a goal for me, Callahan," she says. She leans up and kisses her dad on the cheek—and then *hugs* me before heading back to the stands.

Coach must not notice that I'm as stunned as a bear with a tranquilizer in the ass, because he just claps my shoulder and says, "You heard her."

I manage a smile that I'm hoping looks semi-normal. A hug. What the fuck does a hug mean?

"Doesn't matter who scores as long as we get it done."

———————

THE PERIOD PASSES IN A BLINK, and soon we're at the five-minute marker.

As a team, we've rallied, but we're still coming up short.

Individually, though?

I'm locked the fuck in.

The energy that I played with during yesterday's game

came flooding back the moment the period started. It's like I'm a racehorse with blinders on. The crowd becomes background noise, no more noticeable than a car motor. I force BC into making mistakes and playing sloppily, rather than the other way around. Evan and I are like a pair of magnets, circling around each other, perfectly in sync, and BC has a hard time even making it past the neutral zone, much less reaching Remmy for a shot. I don't score, but a pass to Brandon helps lead to our second goal, and when we celebrate together, he doesn't even sound that put upon when he credits me with the assist.

And throughout it all, I'm aware of one thing.

Penny.

I don't even know how I didn't notice her before this, because now that I know she's here, she's the only person in the stands that I see. She's cheering and clapping and shooting to her feet to yell whenever the whistle blows. If there was any doubt that she's Coach Ryder's daughter—and knows her hockey—that's laid to rest five minutes into the period. She's sitting with a couple of friends across from the benches, so whenever I get a breather, my gaze goes right to her.

I give it my all for my last shift of the game, forcing another turnover, but we can't convert it into a goal. The game ends 3-2, but somehow, I'm feeling even better than after yesterday's win.

When I finish up in the locker room, I swing my bag over my shoulder and hustle out into the corridor.

Penny is waiting, like I'd hoped she would be, her hands tucked into her pockets as she leans against the wall. I glance around to make sure her dad isn't anywhere near us before tugging her into an alcove. When she hugs me again, I smell lavender. She steps back, adjusting her hat as she smiles at me.

"Two hugs, Red? I'm starting to think you like me."

There's a determined sort of gleam in her eyes. It's like last night all over again, and like last night, my body can't help but react. There's nothing especially sexy about her outfit, and I'm sore as all hell from the game and should get myself into an ice bath, but my cock is twitching with interest.

Why did I say no to her proposition again? Clearly, past me is a massive idiot.

"Look, we need to talk," she says. "This is your territory; do you know another closet we can go to?"

17

PENNY

COOPER DOESN'T TAKE me to a closet. Instead, we duck out the back and settle in his car. When he sees me shiver, he turns on the heat, leaning back in the driver's seat and fixing me with a look that clearly says I need to start talking, because his patience is already thin.

I lace my fingers together. "I don't need you to protect me."

He blinks. "What's that supposed to mean?"

"Especially from you. You're not going to break my heart, Callahan." I lean in. Being in the cab of an old truck with him, it's more apparent than ever just how big he is—even underneath his sweatshirt, his shoulders look nearly as broad as they do when he's wearing his pads, and his dark wash jeans show off his muscular thighs. The column of his neck looks downright lickable. If he rejects me again, aside from living with the embarrassment, I'm going to spend a lot of time trying —and likely failing—to get him out of my fantasies. "I know what I want."

He raises his eyebrows. "I don't know, Red. I think you're underestimating my charm."

"Or perhaps you're overestimating it," I shoot back. "Look, if you don't want me, just say so. I'll get over it. But if you said no last night just because you want to protect me against whatever you think is going to happen, you're not listening to me. I don't want a relationship right now. I just want to explore a little."

"Which is fine, but that doesn't change the fact your father is my coach." He takes off his backwards baseball cap and sets it on the dashboard, running a hand through his hair.

I wet my lips; his hands are so big. When I became so desperate that a nice pair of hands does me in, I have no idea. "He's not going to find out." I laugh shortly. "And trust me, if he does, he'll have no trouble believing it was all my idea, and you just went along with it."

"Why?"

I smile wryly. "Doesn't matter. So, which is it? Was I really such a bad hookup?"

The bark of laughter he lets out startles me. "Sweetheart, nothing about that was bad except the fact it had to end," he says; there's a low note in his voice that makes my belly quiver. "I'd have spent forever with you in that closet, dust bunnies and all."

It's taking a massive amount of effort to ignore the butterflies in my stomach. "Then take me through my list." I lean closer, putting my hand on his thigh. His gaze darts down, taking in the gesture. I swallow my nerves and press my lips to his jaw. Near his mouth, but not quite close enough to count as a proper kiss. "Keep yourself relaxed and playing well with me. Let me be good for you."

He fists his hand in my hair, pulling me into a kiss—the kind that leaves me breathless, my toes curling. He bites on my lower lip, dragging out the friction before pulling away. "Quid pro quo?"

"Friends." I kiss him again; he fumbles for the seat control and shoves it back, giving me enough space to slide into his lap. "Friends who fuck."

"Dangerous," he murmurs. "You're playing with fire, Red."

"You like it, don't you?"

"Can't deny it." He takes my hand in his, pressing it against the bulge in his jeans to emphasize his answer. He's hard as a rock. I grin, pressing another kiss to his lips as I massage his cock through the fabric. His breath hitches, making my core clench. It feels good to know I can affect him too; that even though he has all the experience, I have my own kind of power.

"What do you say?"

He brushes his thumb across my cheek. "Okay," he says. "Friends with benefits."

"Friends with an agenda."

"You are rather organized."

I bite my lip deliberately as I continue to work my hand over his pants. "You know what's next."

He strokes across my bottom lip. I open my mouth, biting down on his thumb. First a closet, now a truck cab. It's not a picture-perfect moment, but it's exactly how I want it.

"Here?" he says.

I play with the button on his jeans. Someone could walk by and see, but we're in a quiet corner of the lot. "Why not?"

He grips my wrist, stilling my hand. When he speaks, his voice is rougher. I nearly tremble from the intensity of his gaze; even though I'm still bundled up, I feel exposed, like he just ripped my clothes off. "Back seat. I want to see your tits."

I climb into the back and pull off my hat and sweater, tossing both aside, and kick off my boots. I'm wearing one of my nicest bralettes underneath; it's light blue like the panties that he complimented last time. Now, I shiver for real. Even with the heat on, it's not exactly toasty in here. He joins me in the backseat, shirtless too, and stops me when I reach around to unhook the bralette.

"Fuck," he breathes. He plucks at my hardened nipples through the lace, dragging a moan from my throat. "Such pretty little tits. I've been imagining these, Red."

I lean into him, reaching out my hand to trace down his chest. He has a couple of tattoos; the detailed sword I noticed earlier, plus an artful rendering of a Celtic knot over his heart. I want to trace over the thick black lines with my tongue. He continues to tease me through the fabric for a moment before he just pulls my tits out of the bralette, rather than taking it off; I moan as his big, rough hands each cup one and squeeze. He kisses me, running his tongue over mine.

"Do your panties match?" he says as he pulls back. "You strike me as that sort of girl."

I unbutton my jeans and tug them down my thighs. He helps me get them off completely, so I'm sitting on the leather seat in a tiny, wet scrap of fabric. Dark blue this time. He rubs his knuckles over the front of my panties. "Pretty."

I gasp out a breath as I try to manage a flirtatious smile. "You said blue looked good on me."

"It does." He kisses me hard. "You really want to blow me, gorgeous?"

I rake my nails down his stomach. "Show me how you like it."

He pulls down his jeans and black boxer-briefs, freeing his cock. It looks even bigger than I remember, framed by neat, dark hair, the tip reddened and covered in pre-come. I lick my lips, which wrestles a groan from his chest; he pulls me close, into another kiss, his hand palming my bottom.

"Take off my panties," I whisper. "They're ruined already."

He drags them down my ass. "So needy," he says. "Does the thought of tasting me get you that hot and bothered?"

The words tumble from my lips as I take his cock in hand, giving it the sensual stroke that I remember from last time. "Want to drink your come."

"Fuck." He tugs on my hair until I slide down, so my face is right near his cock. "Explore a little, Red. Take your time."

I mouth at the tip, shuddering as he scratches his nails over my scalp. Even the head feels big in my mouth, velvet-soft and tasting of salt. I lick away the pre-come, then move my tongue over the vein running down his cock. His hand tightens in my hair. "Good," he says. "Keep going."

I use my hand to steady the base as I move my mouth on him, alternating between kissing and licking. I flick my gaze upward; his eyes are half-shut, his Adam's apple moving as he swallows. I accidentally get him with my teeth, and he jolts, but half a second later he's back to moving against me.

"Use your lips more," he murmurs as he pets my hair. "If you want to suck me, take me into your mouth nice and slow. Breathe through your nose."

I want that; I want to feel him in my throat. Even the thought has me pressing my thighs together, desperate for at least a little contact. The moment I get real friction, I know I'll come. Our positions, his rough, quiet voice, the way he has my hair wrapped around his fist—it's all coming together to bring me as close to the edge as I've ever come without direct contact.

I squeeze his balls gently; they're tight and clearly aching because he groans. His hips jerk slightly, pushing the first inch of his cock into my mouth. I suck on it, relishing in the taste. He's trembling with the effort of holding still, I realize with a jolt. He could easily push right into my mouth and make me take it, but he's holding back, letting me set the pace. I reward him by taking another inch, and then another, sucking lightly as I breathe through my nose. I haven't even taken him halfway yet and I feel him deeply.

"Red," he says, his voice breaking. I bob my head, moving slightly as I suck. He can't help but push into my mouth more, but I take it the way I've always imagined I would, the way I've fantasized about for years, the way I've practiced with my own toys. Before long, he's cupping my jaw, murmuring that he's close. I pull off, but not all the way; just enough that I taste his come on my tongue when he tips over the edge. I swallow it down, continuing to lick at him softly, closing my eyes for a long moment as I breathe. His hand continues to work through my hair.

Eventually, he pulls me up. Saliva covers my mouth and chin, but he kisses me anyway as he runs his hands down my breasts and belly, settling on my hips. When he pulls back, I feel shy suddenly, unable to meet his gaze. He tilts my chin up and presses a softer kiss to my lips.

"Was I good?" I ask. My voice breaks slightly. My whole body feels like a spark plug, ready to come alive.

"So fucking good," he says. Warmth blooms in my chest at his words, but it heads straight between my legs when he spreads me, rubbing my clit until I cry out softly against his shoulder. I feel him press a kiss to my head as he works me over. The sensations are exquisite, but his words leave me so close I can hardly stand it. "Come for me, baby."

I shake apart. If I thought I came hard when he went down on me, this is ten times more intense; stars burst at the edges of my vision as my cunt clenches almost painfully. I'm so sensitive I try to twist away from his touch, but he just switches to stroking my inner thigh instead. Slick coats my skin. I'm panting, and so is he; it feels like we're in a sweat lodge instead of a barely warm truck cab.

It's almost strange to look at him and see the evidence of what we did together. I can see the lingering hunger in his eyes. The still-rapid rise and fall of his chest. I can feel the burn of his beard on my mouth and jaw. I was expecting awkwardness, but I feel completely relaxed, and judging by the looseness of his body, he feels the same way.

I know this won't lead anywhere real, but for a moment—half a second, really—I let myself pretend.

18

COOPER

I FINISH SCRAWLING the last few sentences of my essay, close the blue booklet, and sit back in my chair. After a frantic hour spent writing about the gothic in *Jane Eyre*, I'm beat, and even though I have a million other things to focus on—like schoolwork and practice—I just want to think about Penny.

Again.

Does everyone think about their hookups this much? I'm not used to having a girl stick in my mind. We've been texting nonstop, which is almost weirder than knowing exactly who I'm going to for sex. She's adorably chatty, sending me links to *Buzzfeed* quizzes she wants me to take and informing me of every time she pets a dog and telling me what's happening in *The Americans*, which she's watching with her roommate, Mia. I'd say that she's working overtime to make sure we stay firmly on the "friends" side of this arrangement, if not for how she acts when we get in the same room. In the past week and a half, we've hooked up half a dozen times; memorably, I ate her out in an old basement-level classroom when we ran into each other after class, and she blew me again—while on her knees, looking like an angel in her white nightgown—when I came to her dorm last night.

I tried sexting, in the beginning, but it doesn't seem to be her style; if she's in the mood and wants to meet up, she just sends me an interrobang. It's gotten to the point where when I see that little ?!, or send it myself, my heart quickens. That was what led to me coming over last night, and as soon as I shut the door to her room, she was on me, murmuring, "Wanna wear your hand like a necklace." I let her set the pace, but by the end, she was begging me to fuck her face, pressing down on her throat with enough pressure that tears pricked in her eyes.

The rough-and-tumble stress relief has been helping. I've been sharp during practice, and at one of last weekend's away games, we won in overtime. In a twist that should have felt horribly awkward but has left me decidedly unrepentant, Coach told me yesterday that he's been noticing my improvements and restraint on the ice.

If only he knew where my newfound focus was coming from.

I hand in my essay, then head out of the building, pulling my phone from my pocket. There's a text waiting from Pen, and before I even open it, I'm smiling. Tomorrow, I'll see her for the skating class, and I've already invited her back to my place. Pizza, some studying, abandoning our books for my bed... it sounds like a good fucking evening.

> **RED PENNY**
> I pet a cat on a leash!!!

> Pics or it didn't happen

To my slight surprise, she immediately sends back a picture of herself crouching on the sidewalk, petting a cat wearing a harness. The cat is cute, black with big yellow eyes, but I barely glance at it before focusing on Penny. Her hair is in a thick braid, and she has a knit cap on her head. Underneath her coat, I can see she's wearing a fuzzy black turtleneck. She looks so good in a New York autumn, it's hard to imagine her as an Arizona native, but when we chatted on the phone a couple of days ago, she had me in tears laughing about the time a lizard snuck into her skate and hitched a ride from Tempe to Salt Lake for a figure skating competition.

> I underestimated you, Red

I don't mess around where cute animals are involved

Speaking of pussy... ?!

> You're incorrigible

I did terribly on my chemistry test. Take my mind off it?

> Wish I could, but your dad is making us show up for an extra practice

Boo

Tell him hi

Jk jk

> As previously stated: Incorrigible

Even though I could use some time to catch up on my readings for my Milton seminar, I head to the rink. We usually don't practice on Tuesdays, but Coach Ryder and his staff have put together some new formations, and we have another away game, this time all the way up in New Hampshire, to prepare for. I'm a little early, so I change into athletic shorts and a throwaway t-shirt and hit the treadmill for a run.

After a couple minutes, Brandon steps onto the treadmill next to me. I give him a nod, but he just responds with a stony look before getting started on his warmup. We spend a long time in silence, running side by side. If Evan was with me, this would be a fun competition as we sang along to Foo Fighters. If it was Jean, it would be companionable silence while we listened to Led Zeppelin. This is torture, with no music to save me.

Although I've done nothing but try to be a good teammate and leader, Brandon seems determined to hate my guts. Before this, we weren't close friends or anything, but we'd chat during team parties, play some beer pong together, that sort of thing. Last New Year's Eve, I spent the weekend at his parents' lake house in Michigan, and I even hooked up with his older cousin, this hot chick named Amanda who wanted a memorable experience before a stint with Doctors Without Borders. We don't have to be best buddies, but getting the cold shoulder is exhausting.

"Look," I say eventually, because we're about to be on the ice anyway, and there won't be much opportunity for chatting then, "just tell me what I can do to get you to cut the shit."

He wipes a towel across his forehead. "You know what."

I do know what, but it's surprising to hear him be so bold. "Besides that."

He shrugs. "Then I don't owe you anything off the ice. You want friends, stick with your crew and I'll stick with mine."

"I'm not going to tell Coach not to make me captain so I don't hurt your fragile fucking feelings."

He stops the treadmill suddenly, his chest heaving. He's flushed, a bead of sweat running from the sweaty blond hair plastered to his temple to his cheek. "You have another year. You're only a junior, Callahan. And you'll have a chance in the league for all the validation you're seeking from your daddy."

I just stare back; I don't want to give him the satisfaction of knowing he hit me somewhere real. "So?"

"This is my last season playing hockey. It's been my life for as long as I can remember, and this time next year, where am I going to be?" He laughs shortly, wrapping the towel over his shoulders. "I'll be stuck in a fucking office, managing stocks."

"You could have entered the draft. Or you could try to get in somewhere after graduation. The AHL, or somewhere in Europe."

"You're not the only one with a hardass dad." He gathers his things. "I'm not going to stop fighting for this. It's my year. I'm the senior center. You're just a junior defenseman who makes a fist whenever you hear something you don't like."

"Seriously, Finau?"

He leans in close enough I want to flinch, but I hold my ground. "Tell Coach you're backing off," he says, his voice deceptively quiet.

"Oh, there you are," Evan says from the doorway. "Come on, Coop, we need to get started. How's it going, Fins?"

"Fine," he says, still looking at me. I just glare back, because there's no way in hell that I'm doing that for him in the name of fairness or whatever the fuck he thinks it is, and after a moment, he stalks off.

Evan watches him leave the gym before turning back to me. "Still annoyed about the captain thing?"

"Nothing's even been decided yet." I grab my water bottle and take a long gulp. "He's just being a massive douchecanoe."

"He can tell that Ryder is close to deciding."

I grab my bag and follow him to the doors. "Maybe. Or maybe he'll just tell both of us to fuck off."

Evan is a great friend for lots of reasons, but at the very top is his ability to switch topics tactfully when it seems like the conversation is about to veer into the pits. He claps my shoulder. "Want to come to my place later? We can get takeout from that Thai restaurant on Westbrook; Remmy's been wanting to challenge Hunter to a new mission in *Call of Duty*."

Hunter is one of Seb's teammates, and thanks to the two of us, the hockey and baseball teams have become tight. Last year, we were friendly with the football guys, thanks to James, but not so much this year. I should work on homework before tomorrow, since I doubt much will get done when I'm with Penny, best intentions aside, but the thought of an evening spent unwinding with my crew sounds too good to pass up. Milton, or *Call of Duty*? While my teammates are getting some shuteye on the drive to New Hampshire, I'll be puzzling over passages of *Areopagitica*, but it'll be worth it.

"Hell yes, let's do it."

19

PENNY

October 5th

> Would you rather live in the Star Trek world or the Star Wars world?

CALLAHAN

Good morning to you too, Red

> Idk I was just thinking about it last night

Take a guess

> Star Trek?

Nope. I'm more of a fantasy guy

> But they're basically the same thing

...Red

No

> ???

Star Trek is science fiction. Star Wars is space opera. Totally different

Well, I choose Star Wars because I wish I could hug Chewie

And make out with Han Solo

You'd look good with Leia braids

My Halloween costume?

October 6th

CALLAHAN

Wait, so you've written a whole book?

Not quite

More like half. But I've written shorter things before, like fanfiction

That's seriously cool, Red

Yeah, well, it'll be cool if I ever finish

That's what she said

No

:)

What's it about?

You're going to laugh

I'm really not

?!

...Fine

Yay <3

But I'm going to wrangle it out of you eventually

You babble post O

I do NOT

October 7th

CALLAHAN

?!

Ugh, fine

Pretend all you want, but you were about to ask. I can sense it

...I may or may not be on the bus into town

Ha, knew it

You have New Hampshire this weekend, I was being proactive

October 10th

I have a question

CALLAHAN

Yeah?

Our ?! is exclusive, right?

I realized I assumed

It's okay if not

Hell yes it is

How else can I stay focused on your sexperiences?

Callahan, please

Aw, come on. I was proud of that

You're a secret dork, you know

Definitely not a secret, sweetheart

But obviously you're into it, so who's the real dork?

20

PENNY

I CIRCLE around as my students practice skating on their own again, in the middle of the ice this time so they're pushing off with the power in their own bodies, rather than using the boards for momentum. Aside from a couple of spills, they've been balancing well, giggling as they skate from one orange cone to the other. It reminds me of learning to ice skate with my mother. My parents had a very typical boy-meets-girl love story, and it all started at an ice rink just like this. They bumped into each other during a free skate at The Boston Common Frog Pond. She was with her friends; he was with his, and they ditched both groups to get hot chocolates. The way my mom used to tell it, she knew right away that he was a hockey player and didn't want to get involved, and he could tell that she was a figure skater and assumed she'd be stuck up, but by the time the hot chocolates had cooled, they'd made plans for a real date, and never looked back.

I meet Cooper's gaze. He's on the other end of the ice, talking to Ryan. Ryan is wearing a Capitals sweater again, along with a knit cap that covers most of his forehead. He's waving his arms around as he talks to Cooper, and Cooper's laughter booms across the echoey space in reply. I don't bother hiding my smile. Here I am with my own hockey player, although love isn't on the table.

Since we hooked up in his car, I've been floating on air. I haven't felt this good since Dr. Faber finally got me situated with Lexapro after trying three other anti-anxiety medications. I might've failed my chemistry test and have a pile of work to finish, but I have a new friend, and this arrangement—casual, sexy, fun—is exactly what I needed. Cooper knows how to push my buttons, and judging by his relaxed attitude, I'm not doing a bad job of keeping up with him.

Before him, I never felt truly sexy. When I've had a guy's attention, it's been about objectification, not desire. With Cooper, though? He's ten yards away and I can feel the heat in his eyes. I took care putting on my makeup and picking out a cute skating outfit before heading to the rink; I'm in pink leg warmers, black leggings, and a tight pink sweater. Combined with the scrunchie holding my thick braid in place and my little gold hoops and necklace with the butterfly charm? I look like a hockey player's wet dream. The second we wrap up class, I'm going to skate over there and kiss him.

He beats me to it, nearly colliding with me in his eagerness. "Ryan's mom is signing him up for hockey," he says, wrapping his arms around my waist and squeezing. "I'm going to talk to her about it super quick, okay? Then we can get out of here."

He raises his hand as he skates to the exit. "Ms. McNamara!"

I bite the inside of my cheek as I follow, watching him ruffle Ryan's hair as he talks to his mom, who is wearing scrubs; she told us last week that she's a nurse. I unlace my skates, saying goodbye to a couple of the kids as they pass with their guardians, and rub my aching knee.

Nikki gives me a smile as she walks by. She's dressed for coaching and has a clipboard tucked under her arm; her junior figure skaters are coming on after this. "Good class?"

"They're getting the hang of it."

"Wonderful." She glances at Cooper. "It seems like he's a natural with kids. He should work with a hockey team, don't you think?"

The thought is adorable, and Cooper would probably enjoy it, but I doubt he has the time. I think he's roughly as behind on his schoolwork as I am. Still, when he walks over, I say, "You'd make a great hockey coach."

"Ryan's mother asked if I was going to be working with the team," he says as he settles down next to me and pulls at the laces on his skates. "Don't tell your dad this, but I wish I could."

"He knows you like the lessons."

"Which he's thrilled about, I'm sure."

I put my skates into my bag and trade them for street shoes, a pair of boots with nice fuzzy insides. Uggs used to be the special shoes I would only wear at the rink; otherwise, I'd stick to a pair of Birkenstocks, but here I have more uses for them. "He's used to his plans working out. He's an evil genius that way."

He sidesteps that to say, "Pizza?"

"God, yes, I'm starving. Let's order from Annie's."

We walk to the exit together. "No way," he says as he holds the door open for me. "Annabelle's is the way to go."

I stop in my tracks, even though it's raining lightly and I'm already shivering. When Cooper offers me his jacket, I take it without argument and sling it over my shoulders. I should have worn my winter coat, even though it makes me look like a lumpy cloud. "That's slander, and I won't stand for it. Annabelle's has crust like a communion wafer."

"And *that's* not slander? Annie's sauce tastes like it's from a dusty old can."

I make a face. "Rude. We're ordering from Annie's, and we're getting it with tons of veggies, plus the Caesar salad."

"Veggie pizza? Come on, you've got to be kidding me. You need to go meatball and sausage or bust."

I flounce ahead of him. "If you're such a meathead, order two pizzas, but don't forget the garlic knots."

21

PENNY

WHEN WE GET to Cooper's place, it becomes apparent immediately that we made the right call by getting two pizzas. Izzy disappears upstairs with a couple slices of veggie and a glass of wine, muttering something about her English paper, and Cooper and Sebastian split the meat pizza in two. I nibble on a slice, watching them devour the food. Apparently, I'm hanging out with a pair of starved wild animals, not boys. We're in a surprisingly modern kitchen; the gold-plated hardware on the cabinets feels like Izzy's doing, since in the short time I've known her, I've gotten the sense that glamour is her middle name. It opens into an area big enough for the table we're sitting at. The layout is like my dad's house, only a couple blocks over, but work-related paraphernalia perpetually covers his kitchen table, whereas a vase of drooping flowers and a painted bong that, according to Sebastian, came with the house, decorate Cooper's.

I know our plan includes doing homework first, and that we really should, but I can't stop thinking about how much I'd like to slide into his lap and kiss him, pizza breath and all. We haven't gotten any further down The List, despite hooking up right and left, but I'd like to get going on it. I'm not going to magically feel safe having vaginal sex again if I don't try anything else first.

"I'm just saying," Sebastian says as he sets down his now-empty beer; they've been chatting about football while I've been staring, "if they can get past Dallas, they'll be golden."

Cooper snorts. "You say that like it's easy. They're chasing the Cowboys and James knows it, however fast he's been improving." He grabs another slice of pizza, looking at me. "You watch football, Red?"

"Not really. My dad and I are diehard Lightning fans, though."

He makes a face. "Not the Coyotes? I thought you were from Arizona."

"Dad worked on the Lightning staff before focusing on college coaching."

"Or maybe you just like those back-to-back Stanley Cups."

"Maybe it's that I like the players. Pat Maroon has a spectacular beard."

Cooper's mouth drops open. "And I don't?"

I just smile, pretending to ponder it deeply as I tap my nail against my chin. "Let's see. Do you root for the Islanders or Rangers? You're from Long Island, it can't be the Sabres."

"Choose wisely, Red. Our next hookup depends upon it."

"Oh yeah?" I lean over the table, getting close enough we could kiss, but stopping just before our lips brush. It's fun to flirt when it means nothing; there's no pressure when I know we're just friends. It's good practice in seduction, anyway. "What are you going to do?"

"Think about that list of yours," he murmurs into my ear. I shiver at the feel of his warm breath on my skin. "Keep teasing and I'll have to punish you. I can think of two things that would be suitable for slander."

Sebastian clears his throat. "I'm right fucking here."

Cooper pecks me on the mouth before leaning back. His eyes are dark, like he really would pull me over his lap and spank me here in the kitchen. I press my thighs together, trying and failing not to feel the swoop of desire low in my belly. He glances at his brother. "Sorry, Sebby. We're engaging in some serious sex coaching here."

"Because that's such a smart idea," Sebastian says dryly.

"Don't worry, she already promised not to fall in love with me."

I roll my eyes as I hit his shoulder. "As if."

"Can't imagine it, anyway." Sebastian grabs another beer from the fridge. "Have fun, kids. Use protection."

As he leaves, Cooper calls, "Be glad I'm like this instead of a raging bitch! I've been cured!"

"Did he call you that?"

"Pretty much." He leans back in his chair, draping his arm over the back. "So, what'll it be?"

"Islanders," I say. "Isn't Mat Barzal so dreamy?" I know it's wrong; I noticed the Rangers sticker on his truck. But it's too fun not to tease, especially when he drags me into his lap—and then over his shoulder, like he's hauling a sack of flour.

"Cooper!" I shriek, kicking at him. He steadies me by palming my ass, then pinching it, making me squeal. His laughter rumbles in his chest as he carries me upstairs. I'm flushing for half a dozen reasons, but at the top of the list is the fact that both his siblings are home, and while I only saw Izzy for five seconds, Sebastian knows what we're about to be up to. Cooper is clearly unrepentant, calling down to his brother to save him some pizza for later, and I think Sebastian yells something back, but I'm too distracted to listen.

He pushes one of the upstairs doors open, then flicks a light switch. I crane my neck around, wanting to see what his bedroom looks like, but instead of setting me on my feet like a normal person so I can check out the surroundings, he strides to the bed and throws me down. I bounce, laughing, as he joins me, and then we're kissing, and maybe this ought to feel weird or awkward, but I don't register a thing except that delicious tingle between my legs and the weight of Cooper's body over mine.

Eventually, he pulls back. His eyes are dancing, and a smirk plays across his lips. "You noticed the sticker on my truck."

"Obviously."

"You're such a little brat."

"So punish me," I say. I undo my braid, shaking my long hair over my shoulders. "You promised me lessons. I'm ready for a new assignment."

"I'm impressed, Red," he says as he drags me close, running his hand down my back and squeezing my bottom. "You're bold."

I gasp as his fingernails dig into my ass through my leggings. I've imagined being spanked before, and it's always turned me on; I hope it does the same for me in real life. He pulls down the neckline of my sweater and sucks a hickey into my skin low enough no one will know about it but us. I grind against his lap in return, pleased when it makes him groan and kiss my mouth again. We go at it until we're both breathless, gasping for air. He tugs on my loose hair, pressing another hard kiss to my lips before pulling back. He looks me in the eye, and, apparently liking what he sees, tugs off my sweater entirely. I take off my bralette, just pulling it over my head and tossing it onto the floor, and he abruptly buries his face in my tits as he drags down my leggings and panties. Between his rough fingers pinching one of my nipples and his mouth nearly engulfing my other breast, I feel overwhelmed—but that pales in comparison to the heat that courses through me when he puts me over his lap, naked, my bottom in the air.

I whine, burying my face against his still-clothed thigh. All his clothes are on, even his belt, and I'm completely bare, laid out for him like a buffet. He strokes a hand down my bare back, all the way to my ass, and squeezes.

"Freckles here, too," he says, a note of amusement in his tone.

I bite down on his thigh in recompense. He doesn't even do me the solid of pretending it hurts. "How about ten, Penny? That ought to be enough. Don't want to overwhelm you too much."

He uses my real name so infrequently that I'm distracted for a moment, but then he digs his fingers into my ass. "Sweetheart?"

"Yes. Cooper..." I swallow down the lump in my throat. I don't use his first name very often either.

"I'm going to take care of you," he says, somehow catching the drift of my unspoken question; I'm so turned on I know I'm probably staining his jeans, but I don't care. I'm shaking with anticipation. "Count for me. If I take it too far, tell me and I'll stop right away."

His voice has taken on a low, soothing tone. He strokes my skin for a moment more before issuing the first slap. It's not hard enough to really hurt, but enough to sting. I gasp, kicking my feet a little; he holds me in place with a strong hand on my back. "Count," he prompts.

My voice wobbles with unexpected emotion. "One."

"Good girl." He smacks me again, his open palm hitting the other cheek this time. I get out the count faster, so he moves back to the other side, and we go on like that all the way to seven, him murmuring praise all the while.

I knew it would turn me on, both the sharp little blooms of pain and the position, the knowledge that he has me caught and put on display for his eyes alone, but I'm riding a tidal wave of emotion, too, my eyes burning as I struggle to keep my breathing even. He smacks me lower, at the crease of my thigh, and I cry out before I can tamp my tongue.

"You're looking so pretty and pink like this," he says, bending to kiss the top of my spine as I stutter out the count. "Giving yourself to me, being my good fucking girl."

"Cooper," I say, my voice strangled; it's that or call him something that I'm terrified would ruin the mood entirely.

He spreads my cheeks, no doubt giving him a glimpse of my hole, and slaps right over it. The tips of his fingers catch my cunt, and I moan, mouthing at his thigh again. He presses his hand there, getting his fingers slick, and finishes the last three smacks that way: his hand wet, marking my skin in more ways than one. Half of me wants him to keep going, to push me until I'm nothing but trembling goo, but I'm pressing down against his lap like the slightest bit of friction will help ease my aching core, and I nearly sob with relief when he drags me into a kiss, one hand tangled in my hair, the other patting my reddened, stinging bottom. He presses a fast kiss to my cheek.

"Gorgeous girl," he murmurs. "So good and perfect for me."

He moves his hand between my legs, running his fingers over my pussy. I moan aloud at even that slight brush, wishing he would just press down on my clit until I see stars, but he uses his wet fingertips to play with my nipples, each a stiff little bud. "I'd ask if you enjoyed it, but I have my answer right here."

"I need more," I say, arching into his grip. "Please, anything."

He nips at my lip as he kisses me. "My cock is going to fill you up so perfectly."

22

COOPER

THE MOMENT the words leave my mouth, I know I did something wrong.

Penny stiffens, and not in the way she did unconsciously just before my hand landed on her cute-as-hell bottom. Something about my suggestion has taken her far away from me mentally; already she's shutting her eyes, shaking her head. She rubs her eyes with her fists and shudders out a breath. "No. Not that. Something else on the list."

"I'm sorry," I say quickly, even though I don't know yet what I'm apologizing for. "I didn't mean to push you."

She shakes her head, opening her eyes. They're glossy with tears, and her small smile is rueful. "It's just—it's last on the list for a reason. I'm not there yet. I shouldn't have said *anything*."

I kiss her cheek softly, more out of compulsion than anything. At least she hasn't scrambled off my lap. I think I startled her, not scared her. Still, I'm an asshole; of course there's a reason regular old dick-in-vagina is last on her list. I don't know all the details, and I'm not owed them, but that doesn't mean I have to be a massive idiot about the whole thing. "Take a deep breath for me."

She blinks, nodding, her throat moving as she forces herself to swallow. "I'm okay."

"You still want to do something? Whatever you want, I want to give you. You were so fucking good for me just now."

She keeps her gorgeous eyes on me as she reaches between her legs and rubs her clit, panting softly. The small curves of her body, the tits I can suck on whole, if I'm so inclined, the fucking birthmark right next to her bellybutton that looks like a starburst—a real star, I mean, not the candy—it all adds up to a picture that has left me so hard up for it I can barely think. My cock is straining against my jeans, and I'm loathing my bright idea to wear a belt today. I can't quite fight back the possessiveness running through me as I look at her. I know she's not really mine, that this is just an arrangement, but I'm not going to anyone else for this right now, and neither is she. We've made that clear. It's my name she said just now while I spanked her bottom red, and it's going to be my name on her lips as she comes.

Her delicate fingers keep working between her legs. "Make me wait," she says.

"More teasing?"

"As much as I can take." She gasps as she hits a particularly good angle. "It'll keep me focused on now."

Focused instead of thinking about what, is the question, but I'm not her boyfriend, so I don't try. Instead, I gather her up and set her against my pillows. She looks extra pretty like this, flushed all over as she settles against the slate gray sheets. I take off my belt, an inch at a time.

Fucking hell, she's gorgeous. She's a brat, but she's a good girl, and right now, she's mine.

"Hold out your wrists, sweetheart."

Her eyes go wide, and she swallows visibly. That's another item on her list, but why not do two at once? Bondage and orgasm denial. She'll be at my mercy completely if she can't use her own fingers to tease her swollen clit, and I'll be able to edge her as long as I can handle. I've had some practice with this, so I get her wrists over her head, the belt holding her hands together against the headboard, tight but not tight enough she wouldn't be able to get it off in an emergency. Just enough that the control tips in my favor once more. It's how I like it best, and guessing by her labored breathing, she's finding this hot as fuck, too.

She drags her front teeth over her bottom lip—and then spreads her legs wide, anchoring her feet flat on the bed. I groan aloud, pulling my t-shirt over my head and tossing it away. I fumble with the button on my jeans, unable to take my eyes away for even a moment. The red curls between her legs are dark and wet, her silky-soft core just as deliciously slick. I'm a goddam lucky bastard. My mouth floods with saliva at the memory of her salty taste.

"Everything good?" I ask. "If you need to stop, tell me and we'll stop."

"I have a vibrator in my bag," she replies, in a tone that clearly says, *I'm fine, don't be an idiot.*

I raise an eyebrow. "What, you carried it around all day?"

She gives me the defiant tilt of her chin that I adore. "Are you going to use it to help, or are you one of those jerks who thinks it's cheating?"

I'm already rooting around in her bag for it. "Please. Toys and I have a special understanding. What's good for you is good for me."

She snorts. "You're so weird."

I hold up the bullet vibe. It's a truly atrocious shade of fuchsia, but ends in a pair of cute rabbit-style ears. When I click quickly through the different speeds, her breathing stutters, and her hips jerk up like she's dying to get closer. I grin as I settle on the bed. "Should I put on some music to cover up your screaming? Metallica could work nicely."

She glares at me. "I'm not coming to Metallica. And I'm not a screamer."

"Who said anything about coming? This is about denial, sweetheart." I turn on the vibe, dragging it down her stomach as I kiss her breasts. I take one into my mouth, lavishing her nipple with attention; she lets out a soft little cry. I let go slowly, looking her in the eyes all the while. "A brat like you could use some more discipline."

The words do exactly what I intend; she blinks rapidly, her chest heaving, and lets her legs fall open even wider. I reward her by pressing the tip of the vibrator right against her hole, using her slick for lube. She stutters out my name, but before she can beg, I give her a taste of what she's after, using the tips of the vibe to massage on either side of her clit.

My cock is straining for attention, pressed up against her thigh, but I ignore it in favor of continuing to tease her. I scratch my blunt fingernails down her soft skin as I rub her clit with the vibe. She rewards me with sweet, quiet moans, as if aggressively trying not to make noise, which I'm sure is true, because if there's anything I've learned about Penny, it's that she's stubborn. I hold the vibrator against her clit as I stroke down her folds, and little by little, the way she's rocking up against me gets desperate; enough pressure and she'll gush. Instead, I ease off, kissing her on the mouth; she bites down on my lip, hard. When I gasp, the sharp half-second of pain pulsing straight through my hard-as-granite dick, she smirks.

"You're a menace," I tell her. "Do you want to come at all?"

"You'll let me eventually."

"Oh?"

"You like watching me come too much not to." She tugs at the belt, but her wrists stay bound. I give my cock a long stroke, considering just getting myself off and leaving her there to sulk, but she's right, I want to see her eventual orgasm too badly for that. I settle between her thighs again, using the vibe on her clit as I lick at her hole, taking in each of her moans with greed. She's so slick it drips down my chin; she arches her back, trying to get more contact. I bury my face between her thighs even more deeply, tracing patterns into her skin, nipping at the soft parts of her thighs. She cries out, louder this time, which is music to my ears; she might not be a screamer, but I can get her to lose her inhibitions.

When she's shaking hard enough that I know she's on the edge of coming, I ease off again, leaving her right at the peak without the extra push she desperately wants. She continues to tremble as I suck hickeys into the skin of her inner thighs. I give my cock another jerk, thumbing at the head. My balls are tight and aching, but I ignore the urge to keep going until I come into my fist.

Her betrayed expression tugs at my heart. "Cooper," she whines. "Please..."

Her voice breaks. I take pity on her and switch the vibrator to a higher setting as I work her clit again. "Get louder for me, baby," I say. "I want to hear you."

She obliges me with a moan loud enough I need to swallow it with a kiss, grinning against her mouth as I do. As I pull back, she smiles too, soft and just for me, and I swear, I almost come from that. From a fucking smile. It's like she just gave me a present, and it's one I never have to share with anyone.

"I've got you," I say as I put pressure directly on her clit. I angle it just right while I wet the fingers of my other hand with her warm, slippery slick. I'll bet her ass is still aching, marked red from my palm. I press my fingers against her asshole with enough pressure to make her cry out. Next time, I'm going to spank her harder, and then I'll keep her on her hands and knees to fuck her sweet little bottom. The thought alone is enough to make me wobble on the edge of climaxing, but then she seizes and comes with an honest-to-God sob, wetness flooding over my hand, and if I wasn't about to blow my load then, I do now, right on her belly.

She's crying. For half a second, caught between the wave of pleasure reverberating between us both, my heart thuds with fear. I undo the belt, rubbing her wrists. "Pen. Good tears or bad tears?"

"Good," she says. She laughs wetly as I wipe the tears from her face. "God, Cooper, I've never squirted without penetration before."

I crush her lips to mine, tangling my wet hand in her hair as I rub my come into her skin. The vibrator gets swept onto the floor somehow, landing on the hardwood with a loud buzz that reminds me of the indignant squawk of a bird. We burst out laughing, kissing in between bouts; I wheeze so hard my chest aches. Penny is a trembling mess against me. We hold on to each other for a long moment, catching our breath. I'd be willing to bet that's the most intense she's ever been in bed with someone else, so I'm going to need to lay on the aftercare especially thick.

"How do you feel?" I ask as I stroke her hair.

She tugs my arm around her. "Good."

I take the hint and hug her even tighter. As I press a kiss to her head, I breathe in her lavender scent. "My good girl."

We're still for a moment, but then she digs her nails into my taut back and kisses my Andúril tattoo—and bites down. I pull her hair in retaliation, and as I expect, it makes her grin.

"What is this?" she asks.

"The Flame of the West, baby."

She squints at me. "It's not just a random sword?"

"Absolutely not. It's the sword re-forged from the shards of Narsil in Rivendell. Aragorn renames it Andúril. Flame of the West."

"Aragorn?"

My mouth drops open. "Come on. If you haven't read it, you've at least watched the *Lord of the Rings* movies."

She just shakes her head. "No, never."

I reach over and switch off the vibrator. It's covered in dust, which is a gross reminder that I need to clean my room, so I set it on my nightstand before she can notice and grab my computer from my bag. "Okay, let's start right now."

"We have homework," she reminds me. "And aren't they like, a million years long?"

"We can multitask. Plus, that was intense. I was going to cuddle you either way, so if I were you, I'd just surrender."

She smiles. "What makes you think I'd even like it?"

"I saw the book you were reading while you waited for class to start. It's fantasy, right?"

"Fantasy romance," she says, a touch of defiance in her tone. Like she's waiting for me to make fun of her. As if I'd do that; I'm fully aware I'm a nerd where media is concerned. I'm happy to play *Call of Duty* with my bros, but I prefer *Legend of Zelda*. I'll read Fitzgerald and Sontag and Baldwin and enjoy it, but I'd still rather read George R.R. Martin. It makes perfect sense to me that Penny enjoys a good romance novel. Judging by the couple of paperbacks I've noticed in her dorm room and the stickers on her Kindle, she likes 'em sexy. I wonder if that's what she writes, too. I haven't gotten her to admit what the book she's writing is about, but it's cool as hell that she's doing it in the first place.

"Hey, I like romance in my fantasy too. You'll like the love story in these movies."

"Okay, fine. But I'm using your shower first."

I tuck my hand under her chin, looking her in the eyes. "You sure you're good? Can I get you anything?"

She nods, biting her lip. "More pizza?"

She looks so pretty I can't help but kiss her. I put my palm against the Celtic knot tattoo on my chest. "Ah, a woman after my own heart."

She rolls her eyes, trying and failing to hide a smile, as she picks up her clothes. She makes a face, looking down; my come still streaks her stomach, and her inner thighs must be getting stickier by the moment. I still can't believe she squirted; that was hot as fuck. While she's in the bathroom, I'll change my sheets, so she doesn't get embarrassed about the wet spot. She grabs my t-shirt and throws it on.

"This doesn't mean anything," she says, poking me in the chest with her index finger. "I just don't want to get my clothes dirty."

I salute her. "Yes, ma'am."

"What, no m'lady?"

I grin at her. "Turn around so I can see my handiwork."

Right before she opens the door, she pulls the shirt up, giving me a view of her cotton candy-pink ass. I whistle, and she gives me a faux outraged look, but I just wink.

Then I get down to the serious business of queuing up *The Fellowship of the Ring*.

23

PENNY

"I JUST CAN'T BELIEVE he's gone," I tell Mia.

We shuffle forward in line. Halloween is coming up soon, so the theater in town is showing *The Silence of the Lambs*. I don't really like horror, but Mia is obsessed with Jodie Foster, so the plan is to eat a bunch of popcorn and cover my eyes whenever anything particularly creepy happens. I'd rather watch the next *Lord of the Rings* movie, but I haven't seen Cooper in a few days.

Mia glances at me. She's wearing an enormous black scarf wrapped around her neck twice, giving the impression that her head is detached from her body. "I guess it was his time."

"He was fine just yesterday!"

The girl ahead of us in line turns around and says, "I am *so* sorry for your loss."

I glance at Mia, who says, "We should hold a funeral. Although I'm not sure how, it's not like you can flush him down the toilet."

The girl gets a confused look on her face and turns back

around. I try to control my laughter. "We could have a ceremony over the garbage can down in the laundry room."

"Or maybe we should nick a spade from the greenhouse and dig him a grave."

"Here lies Igor," I start. "A loyal servant."

"Devoted to the pursuit of pleasure until the end," Mia continues.

I bow my head gravely. "A true hero. He will be missed."

"What the fuck," the girl mutters with a glance back at us.

We just giggle. It really is sad that Igor kicked the bucket while I was trying to spin a really hot fantasy about a werewolf who kidnapped me and—I haven't admitted this part to Mia— had eyes just like Cooper's. I *may* have been working on my book before I abandoned it for my bed. I tried to revive him with fresh batteries and a recharge, but neither worked. Maybe his flight across my room was his swan song, and I didn't even realize it.

I have my rabbit vibrator, the one last used when Cooper teased me out of my mind, but it's not the same. You'd think that hooking up with someone on the regular would mean I wouldn't care, but I've been hornier than ever. It's like getting a taste of the real thing has just supercharged my fantasies; I had a wet dream the other day that involved another blue-eyed hottie spanking me *with* his belt instead of just using it as a restraint. Damn that dark mafia romance reading binge I went on over the summer.

"I just can't believe he would abandon me in my time of need," I say. "I need something to distract me from the fact I'm actually going to fail chemistry."

We step up to the ticket booth, so Mia has to wait to answer until we're on the concessions line. "Are you serious? I thought you passed your midterm."

I nod glumly. "I went to office hours to talk about it and the professor all but said that she didn't fail me so I have a chance to scrape by with an overall pass in the course, but I should have failed. Without the curve, she couldn't even have fudged it enough to be a pass. There's the next test, and the final, but still."

"Shit, Pen, I'm sorry."

I give a little shrug. "Maybe Dad will finally realize this is a terrible idea."

Mia gives me a surprisingly serious look. "Or you could just tell him. Say you're going to declare a different major and be done with it."

"Doesn't your family think you're studying to be a teacher?"

"Ugh. Don't remind me." She scowls, but it turns into a smile a moment later. "Hey, it's your hockey player."

I turn around. Cooper and Sebastian and a third guy I vaguely recognize from the hockey team are walking to the concessions line, cutting through the crowd of college students and Moorbridge locals with ease. They blend into the line right behind us, and when someone protests, Cooper says, "Sorry, man, just joining my girl."

I glare at him. You let a guy spank you and then watch his favorite movie after, and he acts like it means something. He shouldn't be talking like that in public, anyway, you never know who my dad might know.

He winds his arm around my waist. Despite the windy, miserable weather outside, he's just wearing a sweatshirt, his Yankees cap backward like usual. What is it with boys and acting like the weather doesn't affect them?

"Didn't peg you for a horror fan," he says.

"I'm just here for Mia." I should shrug away, but I can't quite make myself. I glance at his friend. "You're on the team too, right?"

"Yeah," he says, nodding. He's handsome, with a sharp jawline and a medium-brown complexion, his dark hair twisted into braids. "I'm Evan."

"Oh, right, Evan Bell." I smile. The way Dad talks about him, he has a nice skill set and impressive speed on the ice. "Nice to meet you."

"Don't worry," Cooper says in a loud whisper. "He knows I'm your sexperience tour guide. Your spice coach, if you will."

Mia bursts into laughter. "No fucking way."

I try to stomp on Cooper's sneakers, but he steps out of the way in time. "I regret teaching you that word. Is he always this insufferable?"

"Yes," Sebastian and Evan say at the same time.

"Game days are the worst," Evan adds.

Cooper sulks, looking to me for backup, but I just grin, as unrepentant as he is when he drags a really good orgasm out of me. It's been harder than I thought, not letting feelings get tangled up in any of this. I'm not falling for Cooper—that's not what I want right now—but we're friends, and that means I like him. He's a better guy than I thought, unexpectedly sweet and genuinely funny, and I have to admit that since we began this whole thing, my life has improved for the better. It's fun to tease him with his friends, because I know he's going to find a way to get revenge when we're in the dark of the theater.

We order popcorn and sodas, and Cooper pays for the whole thing, which should annoy me but doesn't, really—at least, not as much as it should. When we walk into the theater, Cooper—and therefore Sebastian and Evan—follows us, and of course I end up sitting next to him. I just heave a sigh and open the packet of gummy bears I added in once I realized he was determined to treat us.

"Can I have some?" he asks.

I shake a couple into his palm. "They're my favorite."

"Noted."

"Igor died."

I'm not sure why I tell him, exactly. When he discovered Igor—after snooping around my room while I went to go pee, mind you—he thought it was hilarious that we gave him a gender and named him and everything. But then he watched me use him in what had to be the hottest mutual-masturbation session to ever take place in Lamott Hall, and he gained a new appreciation for him.

"What happened?" he asks. He waggles his eyebrows. "Did you ride him too hard?"

"Don't make me regret telling you."

His face softens. "I'm sorry. That sucks. Did you get to finish, at least?"

"No," I admit.

"Ah, no wonder you're so grumpy."

"I'm only grumpy because you're acting way too familiar in *public*. What if someone sees us?"

The lights dim at that exact moment, of course, so Cooper says, "I think we're in the clear," and then I feel his hand on my thigh, and my breath stutters in my throat.

"Come to the city with me tomorrow," he says. "I'll buy you new toys. As many as you want."

"I have class."

"So do I. Play hooky with me. I'm meeting my brother for lunch; you can meet him and then we can go to my favorite sex toy shop."

I wish I could see his face better, because I can't tell if he seriously has a favorite sex toy shop or if he's teasing. His hand slides to my waistband, his fingertips stroking my bare belly. He traces my birthmark, a part of me that always seems to fascinate him. The first time he did it, I tensed, and he asked if I didn't want him to touch me there—and of course the consideration made me want him to do it again.

"I don't know."

"It'll be fun." He shifts closer; I can feel his breath against my skin. The trailers have started, so it's loud in the theater, but I can still hear him when he whispers, directly in my ear, "Whatever you want, Red. And then we'll try them out."

24

PENNY

THE NEXT MORNING, instead of hurrying to my microbiology lecture, I sip on a chai latte at the Moorbridge Metro-North station, scanning the parking lot for Cooper. I've been here for ten minutes, and the train comes in two. If he doesn't hustle, he's not going to make it on time, which would be a bummer because—putting aside the fact this is a bad idea—I'm excited to get away from campus for the day. I love McKee, but sometimes it's easy to forget that there's a world beyond the postcard-perfect campus and equally cute town. When Dad and I first moved, I couldn't get over all the ivy-covered bricks, maples and evergreens, and tiny one or two-lane roads. I've only been to New York City a couple of times, but I think the city environment will do me good, even if it's way bigger than Phoenix.

I finally spot Cooper's truck, and a moment later him, dashing to the platform as the train slows to a stop. His cheeks are red from the cold and the exertion; he grins at me as he pushes his hand through his hair.

"I got tickets on my phone already," he says, guiding me

onto the train with a hand on the small of my back. "Let's find somewhere quiet to sit."

There aren't very many people on the train on a random mid-morning during the week, since the commuters have traveled already, but Cooper still leads the way to a smaller seating area, one where the seats face each other with room in the middle. I see why when he flops into a seat and stretches out his long legs. I sit in the window seat, crossing my ankles as I smooth down my denim skirt.

He rummages around in his jacket and pulls out a crumpled white paper bag. "Glad I went for these instead of coffees."

I smile as I peek into the bag; there are a couple of apple cider donuts nestled between sheets of wax paper. I give one to him and take another out for myself. "Thanks. Where'd you get them?"

"The coffee shop in town. Not the campus one."

"Ah." I take a bite. It's still warm, the sugar around the outside competing with the tartness of the cider. "Mia works at The Purple Kettle, so I don't usually go to the one in town."

"Oh, that's funny. My brother's fiancée used to work there."

"James, right?"

"Yep. He made us reservations at Bryant Park Grill. We can walk there from Grand Central."

I just shrug. "That means nothing to me."

"It's right near the New York Public Library," he says around a bite.

"Oh, that's cool."

"And the place I want to take you is just a couple of subway stops away from there. It's called Dark Allure."

I raise my eyebrows as I polish off the rest of my donut. "Should I be scared?"

He laughs a bit, reaching into the bag for another donut. "Don't pretend you don't like it."

I glance out at the window. It looks like we're passing a residential neighborhood, the fences tall to keep out the view of the train tracks. "Tell me more about your brother."

We chat comfortably for the hour-long train ride. After sharing a bit about James, the football player, and his fiancée Bex, who just started a photography business, Cooper runs a thesis for a paper by me. He's taking a class on feminist gothic literature, which sounds so cool I can't help but be a little jealous. He tries to help me with the microbiology homework I brought along in my bag, but after a couple of minutes, we give up and talk about books again instead.

When we pull into Grand Central Station—which just makes me think about Serena coming back home at the start of *Gossip Girl*—Cooper grabs my hand, holding on tightly. I follow along as he leads the way out onto the platform. "Cooper?"

"Just want to make sure you stay with me, sweetheart," he says distractedly as he finds the right set of stairs for us to go up.

I fight to ignore the little scrap of warmth that settles in my belly. I told him I've only been to New York a handful of times, so that's probably why he's being protective. He doesn't have to go around calling me sweetheart, though, it's not like we're in bed.

We walk through the station, and while Cooper is naturally a fast walker, he's forced to slow down so I can look at the gilded ceiling, because he refuses to let go of my hand. Eventually, we leave the warmth of the station for the sidewalk. I shiver immediately; it's windier here. He tuts, knotting my scarf around my neck and tucking it down the front of my jacket.

"Can't have you turning into an icicle," he says. "Do you want to get an Uber instead?"

"Isn't it really nearby?"

"It's not far, but I don't want you to freeze," he says with a frown.

I reach up and kiss his cheek. "I'll be fine."

I'm not sure why I do it. Maybe it's because he's being weirdly sweet, or maybe it's because we're anonymous here. Just a couple of kids on the sidewalk. He smiles at me, and I swear he's blushing, but I can't quite tell because of his beard. He takes my hand again and practically drags me to the crosswalk.

We arrive at the park after just a couple minutes of walking. Even in autumn, it's pretty, with gold-and-brown leaves covering the sidewalk. People dot the lawn; an older couple walks arm-in-arm, a woman with a shopping cart feeds the birds, a man watches as his toddler plays in the leaves. At one end, there's a restaurant with a rooftop patio. I'm sure it's packed during the summer, but right now, the tables and chairs are stacked against the wall, hidden underneath tarps. The host leads us to a table by a window overlooking the park, where a guy who looks just like Cooper, minus the beard, sits with a blonde woman wearing a pair of dangly earrings with charms shaped like tiny strawberries. When she sees us, her eyes light up, and her smile is so warm I'm immediately set at ease.

"Coop!" James says, standing to clap Cooper on the back. "So glad you're here."

I can't stop staring at Cooper and his brother. Their eyes are the same shade of deep blue, their hair the same thick, almost-black brown. Cooper's nose went crooked because of a hockey injury in high school, but otherwise they're the same shape, and so are their strong jawlines. I wonder if Cooper has facial hair not just because it's common for hockey players, but because it helps to distinguish him a bit. And Bex? Maybe it's impossible to be unattractive when you're engaged to the hottest new quarterback in the NFL, because she's stunning.

"Cooper," she says, standing too and hugging him tightly. "I've missed you."

He smiles at them both as he steps back. "I missed you too. This is Penny."

"James mentioned you'd be bringing someone," Bex says. "It's nice to meet you."

"It's nice to meet you too," I say with a little wave as we sit. I get a peek at her engagement ring and my mouth almost drops open. I manage to stop myself, but holy crap. I'd be too scared of losing it to wear something that expensive on my finger all day. The diamond is huge, and it's framed on either side with sapphires. "I'm Cooper's... we're friends."

"And co-volunteers," Cooper says. "Also, there's a friends-with-benefits thing going on. Really, I'm her sex coach—"

He cuts off as I stomp his foot underneath the table, but not before the server arrives to take our drink orders. She pretends to ignore us, but I think she's mostly caught up staring at James, who she clearly recognizes. She stutters a bit as she reads out the specials.

The moment she's gone—with as much venom as I can muster while Cooper is grinning at me like the unrepentant lettucehead he is—I say, "You're a menace, Callahan."

James laughs. "I like this girl."

25

COOPER

I GIVE Penny a sideways look as she steals yet another fry off my plate. "If you want my fries, just ask."

"I thought the swoop-and-steal method would be more effective," she says, her hand darting in to grab another one. She dips it in ketchup—ew—before popping it into her mouth. "I'm regretting everything about my life right now."

"Cooper is usually a lot stingier about sharing his food," James says. "You must rate, Penny."

She smiles at me with her mouth full. I roll my eyes as I angle my plate away from her. It's her fault for ordering a salad when the burger was right there at the top of the menu. "You ought to know by now that if life offers you French fries, you take them."

"That's a good motto," she says after she takes a sip of her iced tea. "You should make that into a sticker. I'd put it on my Kindle."

"Right next to the 'smut goddess' one?"

She nearly chokes on her drink, giving me an outraged look. "I showed you my Kindle in confidence!"

Bex looks between us with her eyebrows arched. I busy myself with my food. This lunch hasn't been excessively awkward or anything, but it's clear that Bex—and probably James, let's be real—thinks something more is going on here, and that's not the case. Sure, Penny is possibly the best girl I've ever met, but it's my job to help her get more comfortable with sex, not fall for her.

"That hit at the game last weekend looked rough," I blurt to change the subject.

James sighs heavily as he sets down his water glass. "Yeah. That wasn't fun."

"I was so scared he got hurt," Bex says. "Longest minute of my life."

"Shoulder is still aching," he says. "But it's not my throwing arm, so we're just dealing with it. Not the first time I've played banged up."

I nod in commiseration. I've been fairly lucky on the injury front. Throughout my hockey career, I've dealt with relatively mild things like broken noses and pulled hamstrings, but I've never snapped a bone or tore anything.

"I used to figure skate competitively," Penny says. "That ended when I tore my ACL."

James and I both shudder. If there's any phrase you never want to hear when you're an athlete, it's 'torn ACL.' That's a bitch to rehab and come back from. My first year at McKee, a senior went down with it, and he never got back on the ice for his last season.

"Shit," he says. "When did that happen?"

"I was sixteen," she says. "I wiped out during my short program at Desert West and had to have knee surgery."

"Jesus," James says. "That's terrible."

"I didn't know that," I say.

"You know I used to skate," she says. "You see me do it every week."

"Yeah, but you never mentioned having a career-ending injury." It must be why I see her rubbing her knee sometimes after we finish a lesson.

She laughs shortly. "It was hardly a career. It wasn't like I was going to make Team USA or anything." She wipes her mouth quickly and sets her cloth napkin on the table. "That was my mom."

I feel the urge to take her hand, but stop myself in time. "Are you okay now?"

"Fine. My knee still hurts sometimes, the rehab didn't go that great," she says. "It's a long story."

"Penny, will you come to the ladies' with me?" Bex asks.

As they wind their way through the tables away from us, James leans in. "Friends, huh?"

I polish off the rest of my burger before answering. The moment Bex asked Penny to go to the bathroom with her, I figured that something like this was in my future. James and Bex have been sharing knowing, couple-ish looks all lunch. It would be disgusting if I wasn't so happy for my brother. "Yeah. She's Coach Ryder's daughter."

"Interesting."

I scowl at him. "Why are you looking at me like that?"

He huffs out a laugh and leans back in his chair. "Coop, you like her."

"I do," I say defensively as I stab a French fry with my fork. "She's a cool person."

"Come on, don't bullshit me. You like this girl."

"Not like that. We're friends."

"Do friends look at each other like that?"

My scowl deepens. "*Yes.*"

"Uh-huh."

"I'm helping her out with something."

"Something that happens to involve sleeping together?"

"It's just sex."

He just ignores that, pressing on. "And how many times did you get on my case about how I looked at Bex before we made things official?"

He looks so smug I have the urge to tackle him to the floor, but that wouldn't be appropriate restaurant behavior, so I settle for kicking his shin. The tablecloth hides it well enough that the couple having lunch next to us doesn't even glance over. "I'm not lying. She's my friend. You know how I do things."

"I recall the rules including no repeats," he says. "So, what do you call this?"

"A favor. One that happens to be fun."

"Fine, keep lying to yourself." He shrugs, like he's unbothered. "Or man up and do something about it, either way."

He doesn't know the whole situation—such as the very important fact that Penny has specifically said she wants nothing romantic—but I can't quite make myself ignore his words.

I don't like Penny Ryder like that. She's not my schoolboy crush. She's my friend and we're kindred spirits in the sack, but that doesn't make me want to be her boyfriend.

Even if all my wet dreams lately have involved her.

Even if her laughter is so adorable, it makes my chest hurt.

Even if I've never enjoyed sex more, and I haven't even gotten my dick inside her anywhere but her mouth.

Even if my favorite recent memory is cuddling with her in my bed while watching *Lord of the Rings*.

"It's not happening," I tell him. "Even if I wanted it, which I don't, she doesn't."

26

COOPER

"WHY IS this your favorite sex toy shop?" Penny asks as we climb the stairs from the subway to the sidewalk. Someone shoulders in between us to hustle down the stairs. I grab her hand again and pull her closer.

"It's where I lost my virginity," I say as I lead the way around the corner.

She narrows her eyes. "Seriously?"

I laugh at her expression. "Just teasing. That was at Emma Cotham's pool party. They have a nice massage oil here."

"Only the best for your dick?"

"You're starting to get me." At the right storefront, I pull open the door. Dark Allure is tiny, a scrap of a shop sandwiched between an Indian restaurant and a nail salon. I could get the oil I like to use when I jerk off somewhere more convenient, but I enjoy browsing the aisles. People get up to some seriously freaky shit. The first display is tame, just a row of nicely sized butt plugs, but around the corner, I know there are some metal chastity devices. "Why don't we make it into a game? Cheesy or cringe?"

She gets my drift right away, a smile breaking out on her face. "You're on."

"Sweetheart?" I say just before I lose her in the aisles.

She looks over her shoulder. "Yeah?"

"And pick out whatever you want. But choose wisely, because whatever you get, I'm using on you later."

She flushes, but holds my gaze for a moment before hurrying down the aisle.

I poke around the front of the store, which has some costumes for roleplaying, and grab the jasmine-and-bergamot scented oil off the shelf. I need to introduce Penny to it sometime soon. I spot her looking through a bin of cock rings and grab a fox tail butt plug before heading in her direction. She's so engrossed in looking at the different options that she doesn't notice me until I dangle the tail in front of her face.

"Cooper!" she says, giggling. "What even is that?"

"It's almost Halloween. You could be a fox; you have the hair for it."

"Ugh, no. That is the literal definition of cringe."

I gesture to the cock ring in her hand. It's hot pink, and the tag says it's made by a company called The Big O. "That vibrates, nice. Cheesy?"

"I can imagine someone buying it for their husband because things have gotten stale." She spots a pair of fluffy handcuffs and holds them out. "Wait, this is even cheesier. Whenever I think about porn, this is what comes to mind."

"Never watched any?"

She shakes her head. "I'll stick to my spicy romance novels, thanks."

"Weird."

"I'd rather imagine the guys looking exactly like I want them to."

"Oh yeah? And what's that?"

She smiles sweetly. "Don't you wish you knew. Where are all the dildos?"

"Wall in the back."

She goes to look, but I hang back, distracted by a mannequin wearing a leather corset. That would look hot as fuck on Penny. If she added heels and put her hair up? I think I might have a heart attack.

I notice a rack of videotapes—the old-fashioned kind, not even DVDs—filled with vintage porn, and rifle through the bunch. Some of the ladies on the covers are hot enough to make me wish I had a way to play them. The one redhead in the bunch doesn't hold a candle to my Red, though. There's a tripod on the shelf above them, a little one that could sit atop a dresser to facilitate a homemade sex tape. I grin as I grab it. Does this count as cheesy or just cringe? I've never given much thought to how many bad homemade sex tapes there must be in the world, but I'm sure the answer is way too many.

I hold up the tripod as I make my way to the wall of dildos in the back. Penny has a pink box tucked underneath her arm, and she's peering at the vibrators with a serious expression on her face.

"Hey, Pen. Sex tape? Cheesy or cringe?"

She glances over. I wiggle it, but instead of laughing like she did with the fox tail butt plug, her expression shutters. "Put that down."

"I think it's cringe, but I guess if—"

"Put it down," she says again, cutting me off.

"You okay?" I say as I set the tripod back on its display table.

She bites her lip. Her whole body looks stiff, like someone just gave her an electric shock. I'm not sure what the hell I did, but clearly it was something, because she's wound tight. She holds up the pink box. "I'm going to get this."

"Penny."

She shoulders past me, heading for the register.

I catch up in a hurry, pulling my wallet out. "I've got it."

She looks up at me. "This is the expensive one."

"Good." I hand the credit card to the cashier, who glances at me with interest before scanning the bar code.

"You have excellent taste," she says. "I wish I had a boyfriend to buy me fancy vibrators."

"He's not my boyfriend," Penny says automatically. "He's my…"

"Sexual educator," I say as I put the oil on the counter too.

She rolls her eyes. "No."

"What? It's apt. I have more experience than you and I'm showing you the ropes. Like a teacher."

She covers her face with her hand. "I can't bring you anywhere." She peeks at the cashier. "He almost said the same thing to his brother at lunch."

"Wow," the cashier says, glancing between the two of us. "That's kind of freaky."

"And now apparently I can't shut up, because I'm telling you," Penny adds. She glares at me. "Why do you make me so chatty?"

"I guess you're just comfortable with me," I say. I think it's the truth, but unfortunately, that makes her wrinkle her nose. What about the tripod made her so jumpy? Did she ever try to film something? That doesn't sound like her; she just admitted she's never watched porn. She's a freak in the sheets, sure, but she doesn't strike me as the type to want people besides her partner to see her pleasure. This is supposed to be a fun day, though, so when I spot a little remote-controlled vibrator, I snag it from the shelf and slide it over to the cashier too. The least I can do is make it up to her by crossing another item off her list.

"Does this come charged?"

27

PENNY

THE MOMENT we're on the train, Cooper leads the way to a car like the one we were in last time. There's a look in his eyes that is making my stomach twist up pleasantly; I don't know what he has planned, but it's not another hour of talking. Thank God, because I don't want to think about, much less discuss, what happened in the store with the tripod.

He kisses me as we sit down—on the same side this time—and puts his hand on my thigh, underneath my skirt. Past Penny knew what she was doing when she opted for the skirt and tights today.

"Callahan," I murmur as he traces a nonsense pattern into the tights. "What are you doing?"

"What number is public sex?"

The blush practically erupts on my face. This is perfect; we're not the only ones on the train, but it's not so crowded that we're likely to be interrupted. An edge of danger, but not enough risk to make me hesitate. "Semi-public. And six."

"Skipping ahead a little," he says as he kisses my neck. "Still need to fuck your ass sometime soon, sweetheart. But not here." He digs his nails into my tights—and then rips them to get at my panties.

"Those were my good tights," I protest, my voice fading as he rubs his knuckles over the front of my thong.

"I'll buy you new ones." He keeps kissing my neck, unwinding my scarf and flinging it onto the seat across from us. "I'll buy you ten new pairs. Whatever you want."

He certainly didn't bat an eye at buying me a hundred-and-fifty-dollar dildo, so I don't doubt he'd take me to the mall to buy new tights. It's easy to forget because he doesn't seem like a rich boy—certainly nothing like Preston's type of rich boy—but his family is loaded. He keeps teasing me over my panties as he rummages around in the bag from Dark Allure, and the underlying level of arousal I've been feeling whenever I'm around him gains steam. When he finds the remote-controlled vibrator, he curses at the packaging; I take it from his hands and rip it open at the exact moment he ruins my panties, too.

"Cooper!" I say, scandalized. The tights are one thing, but my underwear? He *definitely* owes me new ones. "You're acting like a barbarian."

"I've had a fucking hard on since the store," he says against my ear. "Fuck, you're wet too. You're such a little slut."

The words make me moan, tipping my head back against the seat. The train starts to move, the lights dimming as we head through the tunnel. For a couple of long minutes, I can't see anything but the lamplights streaking by us in blurs of orange—and I can't fucking focus on a thing but Cooper's fingers teasing my clit.

"Wanna put my fingers in," he murmurs against my ear. "Can I finger-fuck you right here, where anyone could see us the moment we're out of the tunnel?"

I nod against his shoulder; I don't trust myself with words right now. He presses in one of his long, thick fingers, deliciously slow, and I moan again, grabbing the air until I settle my hand on his arm. He kisses the side of my head as he adds another finger, scissoring them roughly. I cry out, but fortunately the sound gets swallowed up by the train whistle.

The world around us explodes into light again. Cooper keeps fingering me, angling his body so I'm hidden as much as possible. It's like he doesn't want anyone to see not only because it would be mortifying, but because he wants me all to himself. Right when I start rocking against him, squeezing tightly to keep his fingers inside, he eases out.

I look at him pleadingly, a protest already on my lips, but he grabs the little vibrator—which I now see is shaped, abstractly but still recognizably, like a fox, complete with a pointed nose perfect for nudging against a clit—and tucks it against my folds. He tugs my skirt down. I smooth out my wrinkled sweater. You'd be able to glance at us without finding anything out of the ordinary—other than the bulge in his pants and my flush, that is.

He grins as he holds up the remote. "Gotta be quiet for me, baby girl."

I bite my lip as he turns on the vibrator. The sudden burst of motion has me gasping, but he kisses me to tamp down the noise, his hand stroking over my skirt. The remote is hidden in his palm; he presses another button and the rhythm changes. The tail part of the vibrator, just barely pushed into me, vibrates rapidly, while the head—and that nubby nose, bumping right up against my clit—pulses in long, slow strokes. I'm thinking it's going to be hard not to come in approximately thirty seconds, never mind how loud I am, when the door to the car slides open.

I bite my lip so hard it hurts. Cooper doesn't even blink; he just crosses his ankle over his knee and pulls out his phone as the conductor, an older woman with curly hair, approaches. We're the only two in the car, so she makes a beeline right for us, smiling all the while.

"Tickets?" she asks.

"Here you go," Cooper says, holding out his phone.

"Perfect," she says as she scans the tickets. "What were you up to today? Something fun, I hope?"

"We're McKee students," Cooper says. He puts his arm around me casually—and then he must press the button on the remote again, because the vibrations ratchet up higher on both ends of the toy. It's all I can do not to moan aloud, aching for relief. "We just had lunch with my brother and his fiancée."

"Oh, how nice," she says. "Are you familiar with the city?"

Cooper, the bastard, chats with the conductor for a few minutes as he changes the speeds and rhythms of the toy. I just smile tightly, trying desperately to avoid making it clear what's going on through an ill-timed gasp or whimper. Not that I want him to stop—I don't want that. I just want to come, and then get on my knees and suck his cock until he calls me a slut again.

When she finally moves on, he abruptly switches off the vibrator. My mouth drops open; I'm about ready to give him hell for being such a fucking tease—but before I can, he pulls the vibrator away, tosses it into the plastic bag from the store, and hauls me into the bathroom at the end of the car.

"What—"

"Need to taste you so fucking bad," he says as he presses me against the door and slides the lock into place. The train rocks, and I nearly fall, but he holds me up. He looks as desperate as I feel, licking his lips, his backward baseball cap knocked askew. I swear his irises are several shades darker. He drops to his knees, onto a floor that has to be filthier than the closet we first hooked up in, and sticks his head right up my skirt.

Stars burst in my vision as his tongue swipes over my clit. He groans like he's the one being pleasured, nuzzling his beard against my folds. "You're my favorite taste in the whole goddamn world."

I knock his baseball cap off his head so I can grab his hair, pushing his face right where I want it. The train sways again, and I nearly go with it; my legs are like jelly, but he saves me before I ruin the whole thing by concussing myself on the metal sink built into the wall. My pleasure reaches the peak it had been hovering at throughout the conversation with the conductor. If he pushes just a little harder, gives me a finger or a bite, I'll come all over his face. Yet he continues to tease me, and his words echo in my mind like a pinball.

That's just what boys say, right? Pleasure makes them ramble. You can never trust what a guy says in bed. Or a train bathroom, apparently.

The door rattles loudly. I freeze, but Cooper just keeps going. I stuff my fist into my mouth to keep from making noise, and good thing, because he works two fingers into me at once. I clench around him, and he moans, turning his face into my thigh and biting down. I dig my fingers into his hair in retaliation, tugging hard.

Whoever is on the other side tries the door again. I stifle a hysterical giggle. If the lock breaks and we're banned from Metro-North forever, I'm making Cooper drive me into the city whenever I want.

"Fantastic," a voice says. I listen hard for the sound of footsteps, and when it's clear we're not on the verge of being walked in on, I relax, but only for a moment, because Cooper seems determined to make me lose any scrap of decency I have left. As he pushes in a third finger, I plummet over the edge, dropping my fist so I can cry out.

He's on his feet in an instant, cupping my face in his hands and leaning in to kiss me. I taste myself on his tongue as I work my hand into his pants, gripping him tightly. He moans into my mouth, pressing me against the door with enough of his weight that I feel deliciously trapped. The train slows to a stop, which I'm grateful for because I still feel wobbly but would very much like to be on my knees to return the favor. When he sees where I'm going with this, he braces himself against the wall with his hand, dropping the other to my hair.

When I went to the bathroom with Bex, she asked me if we were dating. I told her the truth—a big fat no—but now I imagine it more concretely. Would it look just like this? Day trips into the city, double dates with his brother? Mind-blowing sex and deep conversations about literature? Maybe a label would change the whole thing. Maybe it would force us into territory that neither of us is equipped to handle.

As I take him into my mouth, he sighs, like I really am offering him much needed, much anticipated relief, and strokes his hand through my hair. I look up at him through my lashes; his eyes are screwed shut, his mouth slack. He's so beautiful it hurts. I'm too scared to name, even in my mind, the tendril of emotion running through me.

It would shift things inexorably. I could lose whatever relationship I've rebuilt with my father. I doubt I could handle it, anyway. Following The List gives us structure. We're friends, but there are strings attached. An invisible expiration date. I need the strings to tether me down, and once he's captain, this whole thing will probably fizzle out. The friendship and the hookups both.

But I can't deny that I haven't felt this happy or settled in a long time. Here, specifically, on my knees in a bathroom on a moving train, hoping that I can drink down the come of the guy who just told me I'm his favorite taste of all.

Am I everything Preston's family said I am?

It didn't hurt when Cooper called me a slut. I felt treasured. Special. I know he meant it the same way he calls me Red. But I've been called that before, and back then, it hurt worse than almost anything.

Maybe in between the two, there's a way forward.

It just can't be Cooper by my side when I figure it out.

28

PENNY

October 23rd

MIA

He did what????

I know

Holy shit

I KNOW

This is even more wild than the bondage thing

Good for you

I can't even. He's like a gigantic puppy one second, and a wolf the next

Sounds like good inspiration for your book

I may have changed the dude's name

To Callum

Oh, girl

I know

Lol RIP

29

COOPER

PENNY LETS OUT A SIGH, slumping dramatically out of her chair onto the floor.

I glance up from my dog-eared copy of *Othello*. After a moment, when it's clear she's determined to make the dusty underside of this table her new home, I put the book down and shimmy underneath too. It's a tight fit, given that this old table in the stacks isn't all that big, but it's worth it when I see her smile. I shuffle closer. When I ran into her on my way out of the gym this morning and she invited me to come to the library with her, I couldn't help but say yes. She looked so cute in her forest green sweater and pleated black skirt, her gold butterfly necklace shining in the hollow of her throat, that I couldn't have said no if I tried.

I let her lead the way, and she dragged me up three narrow flights of stairs to this little nook. I thought for half a second that she just wanted somewhere mostly private to hook up, but then she sat down and took out a gigantic textbook, so I rummaged around in my bag for *Othello* and the crappy little reporter's notebook I use to take notes. That was an hour ago. It's been torturous, even though we've been chatting, so I don't blame her for needing the break.

"This is a disaster," she whispers.

"Why are you whispering?"

"It's a library."

"We're so far into the stacks, I doubt anyone but us has been here in the past decade."

"Still. It's respectful to the books."

"Are you one of those people?" I ask, my voice as low as hers. "Never dog-eared a page in your life?"

"That copy of *Othello* is atrocious."

"I got it used."

"Still. I've been watching you."

I grin. "I'm distracting, I know."

"I really should be studying." She pouts, crossing her arms over her chest. "I just hate it so much. And I hate that I hate it, which makes it worse."

The emotion in her voice, that edge of wobbliness, makes me reach over and put my hand on her knee. I swipe my tongue over my lip. I want to kiss her, but I manage to hold off. "I'm sorry."

She kisses me instead, surprising me with the force of her lips against mine, her delicate fingers working through my hair. We haven't fucked since a couple days ago on the train, and every second of that was worth the ache in my knees. I become aware all over again of the fact we're underneath a table, tucked away in a forgotten corner of the library, but just when my dick twitches with interest, she pulls away.

"Thanks," she says, her voice as soft as a cloud.

"You should take your mind off it," I say, trying to sound normal instead of the total horndog I'd like to be right now. The way her skirt falls over her thighs is practically criminal. "Tell me about your book."

She shakes her head, but she's smiling. "You've been waiting for a chance to pull that out."

"Maybe. But tell me at the table, I'm too big for underneath here."

She snorts, but clambers back into her chair across from me. It was getting cramped under the table, but what I really needed was some separation. Another minute, and I'd have ruined another pair of her tights.

"It's a romance novel," she says.

"I figured."

She goes all squinty-eyed, like she's expecting me to laugh. I just raise my eyebrows. "What kind of romance?"

She sighs, undoing her braid and shaking out her hair. "I don't even know if it's any good."

"So? It's still cool that you're doing it."

"Thanks," she says. "I don't know, I'm trying my best. There are so many authors I admire, and the thought of making up a story that someone might like just as much..."

"It's magical."

She smiles. "Yeah, it is magical."

"I'm nowhere near that creative, so I'm fucking impressed." I nudge her boot with my sneaker underneath the table. "What's it about?"

"It's a fantasy romance. Basically, this wolf shifter has to get mated in order to take over the pack after his dad dies."

"And he doesn't want to?"

"Not really, but he knows it's important, so he's trying to find someone when this human woman crosses paths with him. She's on the run from her abusive ex and she needs a place to stay, so he lets her hide out with him."

"That sounds cool."

Flush colors her cheeks. "You don't have to pretend."

"I'm not pretending." I lean over the table, reaching out to take her hand in mine. She's wearing a ring with a little moon and stars hammered into the metal; I wonder if she got it because it reminded her of her book. "I'm guessing they're like, meant to be?"

"Basically. But he needs to mate a werewolf, so if she wants to be with him, she has to agree to be bitten."

A grin spreads over my face. "Kinky."

"Kind of," she admits, her flush deepening. "It's sexy, and really fun to write, even though I should be focused on school."

"Can I read it?"

She jerks her hand away. "No one has but Mia. And it's not like it's done."

I hold my hands up. "I don't have to critique it or anything. Besides, I'm sure it's awesome."

She's quiet for a moment, clearly considering it. "Maybe."

"Good enough for me."

She shakes her head slightly. "You're so weird."

"We're equally weird." I glance down at my book. I need to finish reading this and get started on my response paper, but instead, I flip to a blank page in my notebook and draw a hook. "Want to play hangman?"

"Really? Hangman?"

"You want to study even less than I do right now." I write out spaces for the word I'm thinking of: verisimilitude. "Bet you can't guess the word I have in mind."

"Is it incorrigible?" she asks dryly.

"Nope."

"You sound entirely too pleased with yourself."

"Because you'll never guess it."

She narrows her eyes; there's a competitive glint in them now. She crosses her arms over her chest and leans over the table. "Give me a hint."

"It's long."

She glances down at the paper. "A real one."

"It's a noun."

"I hate you."

I fill in the first letter and tap it with the pen. "There. If you win, I'll buy you whatever you want from the vending machine. But if I win, you're sending me your book."

She sighs, sounding put-upon, but I can tell she's game to play. She holds out her hand for me to shake. "Deal. Get ready to give me a candy feast, Callahan."

"Not a chance, Red."

30

COOPER

October 29th

RED PENNY

It's really cool that you're buying Ryan's equipment

I'm so glad his mom agreed to sign him up for the team

He deserves the best

That's sweet

My uncle bought me my first pair of skates

I was wondering how you got into hockey, given your dad and all

Yeah, it was my Uncle Blake. Haven't seen him in a while, but he taught me how to skate, took me to my first game

Why haven't you seen him?

It's a long story, but basically, he's struggled with addiction. He's out in California, has been most of my life

:(I'm sorry

Have you gotten in touch with him yourself?

My dad would lose his shit if I did

I guess skating was always in the cards for you

Between the hockey coach father and the professional figure skater mother? Yes, there was some inevitability

October 31st

I can't believe that I have to be at UMass for Halloween. The universe is punishing me

RED PENNY

You specifically?

It must be cosmic payback for last season

That's awful philosophical of you

I can't even drink after the game b/c my room is next to your dad's

LMAO that's hilarious

The real tragedy is it means we can't have phone ?!

What's that favorite word of yours?

Oh, yes. Incorrigible

You're incorrigible

But you're right, that sucks. Guess you'll just have to imagine me using my new toy ;)

November 3rd

LUCKY PENNY

Thanks for convincing me to go to office hours... I think I finally understand pathogenesis

That's great

Do you want to hang out later? Your dad cancelled practice?

I'm home right now, he's sick so I brought him some soup

Oh, okay

I hope he feels better soon

But I'll see you tomorrow?

Ryan is so pumped we're coming to his game

I still can't get over how excited he was when you taught him how to skate backwards

November 8th

LUCKY PENNY

All I'm saying is that they could have made the orcs a little less disgusting

I'm going to have nightmares, Coop!

You never call me Coop

Also, your words were "why aren't the orcs sexy" PENELOPE

You never call me Penelope

If you saw a romance novel orc, you would understand

Mmm, overbite ;P

You're a freak

You are too. A wet dream where I had elf ears? Callahan, please.

Excuse you, I thought we agreed to drop that

...

We agreed to drop that, right? Right, Red?

November 11th

PENNY

Mia is hooking up with some guy she met on Tinder... pray for my ears

?! instead?

Three days too long for you?

I have a game tomorrow...

You need to pick me up

And I'm bringing Mark Antony

I still can't believe you let Mia name your new friend

See you in fifteen

_____

31

COOPER

THE MOMENT I see Penny shove open the door and run down the stairs to my truck, I know she's planning something.

One, I've never seen her wear a coat that long before; it's cold, but not *that* cold. Two, her hair is soaking wet, and she told me just last week that she hates to go out without blow-drying her hair.

Oh, and third, she has a huge pink dildo in her hand. The present I got her at Dark Allure, to be exact, which her roommate has named Mark Antony for reasons neither has managed to explain without dissolving into giggles. I'm so distracted by the fact she didn't put it in a bag or anything that I forget to unlock the passenger door. She knocks on the window with the dildo as she does a little dance to stay warm.

I roll the window down instead of unlocking the door. "You look deranged."

"I'm freezing my tits off! Open the door!"

When I do, she hops in and kisses me without a second thought. That's been happening a lot recently; kissing with our clothes on and everything. It's like our kiss underneath the table in the library opened that possibility. I don't hate it—I love it way more than I should, in fact—but it surprises me every time. She rips open her coat.

"Holy fuck," I say.

Did I get into a car accident on the way here and this is my brain's last-ditch effort to wake me from a coma? There's no fucking way that Penny's wearing those thigh-high boots I love along with a black lace bodysuit. I pinch myself on the arm, and it hurts like a bitch, so I guess I'm not dreaming.

She's wearing dark lipstick. Her mouth curves into a delectable smile as she takes in my expression. "You like it?"

"Like it?" I say. My voice cracks like I'm a teenager again. "Red, are you trying to kill me?"

The bodysuit is practically painted on; it pushes her tiny breasts together in a sticky-sweet curve, and the ribs of the suit accentuate her shape in a way that makes me want to haul her into my lap and mold my hands to her hips. The bikini cut shows off her thighs to delicious perfection. My cock throbs. I want to be inside her so badly I can't think straight.

"You said you need to relax," she says. I did say that, not in so many words, but she got the drift and went above and fucking beyond. "Now hurry up, I didn't take this shower for nothing."

"Why did you?" I ask, reluctantly tearing away my gaze so I can focus on getting us back to my place in one piece.

"So you can fuck my ass, obviously," she says.

I hit the brakes and practically throw the truck into park. Her eyes widen, like she really has no fucking clue what she's giving me right now. I want to fuck her pussy, of course I do, but after her reaction to the suggestion, I haven't pushed it again. If we get to the end of the list, that will be the last hurrah. Fucking her sweet bottom, though? I can't stop fantasizing about it. I fingered her ass the other day, licked her there too after a spanking, and she came so hard she nearly cried.

I lean over and kiss her. I'm probably messing up her lipstick, but I don't give a shit. She smells clean, like lavender and mint, and she licks right into my mouth like she's just dying to get a taste of me. We make out for what must be a couple of minutes; my hands tangle in her wet hair and hers come around to clutch at my back. Eventually, though, I make myself pull away. If we go any further, I'm either going to be too distracted to drive or come in my pants, and neither sound all that appealing when I can finally be in Penny somewhere other than her soft mouth within the hour.

When we get to the house, I thank the universe that Izzy is out with friends and Sebastian is... wherever he is, I don't know and don't care now that he's not the only one getting action, and carry Penny straight from the truck to my room. She's laughing, breathless, squirming in my arms with the dildo still clutched in her hand. I toss her onto the bed, drinking in the sight of her. The coat's open, her chest is heaving, and she looks good enough to eat.

"Callahan," she says, sitting up on her elbows. "I'd have pushed for this sooner if I knew it would turn you into a werewolf."

"Is that what your werewolves do?" I say as I tear off my jacket and fling it aside. I take off my shirt next, then work on my pants. She takes off her coat and throws it onto the floor, but thankfully doesn't touch the rest. "Kidnap unsuspecting women and carry them away to their dens?"

"Sometimes," she says cheekily.

I join her on the bed, pulling her into my arms and kissing her neck. I scrape my teeth down the column of her throat just to feel her shiver. "What about this?" I murmur.

Her breath stutters. "Always," she says. Her nails scratch at my bare back. "You know a monster likes to bite."

I do bite her then, lightly, drawing out a hitched moan. "Is that what you want, sweetheart? A bite?"

"As long as it comes with your cock."

"There's my girl." I sit up, running my hand down her bare thigh. Her skin is smooth, pale and dotted with those freckles I can't get enough of. "You really want me to fuck your ass?"

She nods, the words tumbling from her in a rush. "Please, it's all I've been able to think about."

I kiss her again. "Turn around."

"Don't rip this," she warns.

"I'll be a perfect gentleman," I say, although really, even if I ripped it, I'd just buy her five more in whatever colors she wanted. A baby doll blue would look beautiful on her, although the black is striking against her complexion.

I start with her boots, unzipping them one at a time and letting them drop to the floor. I run my hands up the backs of her legs, cupping that lace-clad ass with my palms and squeezing. There's a zipper on the side of the bodysuit. I tug it down slowly, an inch at a time, kissing and nibbling at the back of her neck as I do. Then I ease it away, reaching around to cup her tits and rub my thumbs over her nipples. She moans, reaching back to grab my arm as she looks over her shoulder.

"Let me know how you're doing, okay?" I say, kissing her forehead. "We can stop anytime."

She nods. "I'm ready."

I don't hear any hesitation in her voice, so I reach over to get lube and a condom from the nightstand. I run a hand down her back. "Hands and knees, sweetheart."

She gets into position, trembling already, her head hanging low against the pillows on my bed. I give myself a moment to look at her perfect ass before smacking it lightly. Her soft cry makes my balls tighten; I want to get inside her immediately. I can't, though—our arrangement means giving her the experiences she wants, and this is her first time trying anal. I need to go slowly. This is about her, not me, even though I'm the one who asked for the hookup.

I slick up my fingers and press a kiss to the cold nape of her neck. She shivers. I stroke my free hand down her side as I rub her asshole with my finger. "Relax, Red. I've got you. Just like last time."

She does, taking a deep breath and letting it out slowly as I press my finger inside her. "I've fingered myself here before, too," she says.

The mental image of that is so hot I need to stop for a second, but then I shake my head and force myself to focus. I've watched her touch herself before; several weeks ago, we had a memorable evening in her room where she used her old toy while I stroked myself. I came on her tits and licked them clean, and afterward, I stayed and watched *The Bachelor* with her and Mia. The thought of her slim fingers doing something so dirty makes my grip on her hip tighten.

I work the next couple fingers into her slowly, stretching a bit at a time. She's trembling, moaning, her head turned to the side and her pretty mouth wide open as she submits to the dirty ways I'm touching her. When she's pressing back against me every time I pull back, dying for more contact, I roll the condom onto my cock and stroke myself a couple of times with a slick hand.

"Breathe. Let me in."

She nods, gasping as I spread her cheeks. The first press of the head of my cock against her asshole makes her pant, curling her hands in the sheets. She's on her knees and elbows now; I hook my hand around her to splay over her belly, anchoring her at the angle I want.

When I'm in her all the way, relishing in her tight warmth, I press my lips to the nape of her neck. It's tough to stay still, but I need to let her adjust. I rub her clit as I mouth at her shoulder, hoping to spark pleasure against any discomfort she's feeling.

"Tell me how it feels."

She just moans. I smile against her skin. "Use your words. Is this okay?"

"Yes," she gasps out. "Fuck, you're big."

I let out a low laugh. "I know. You're taking me so well."

"Yeah?"

"Yeah, sweetheart." I thrust shallowly; the motion makes both of us moan. "You're being so good. It's like your body was made just for me."

The words are catnip to her. I can practically feel her smile, how she relaxes. Fondness fills up my chest and spills through fucking everywhere—my heart, my lungs, in between every rib, settling in my stomach like a huge gulp of hot chocolate on a wintry morning. I can't stop grinning. She's the sweetest girl I've ever had, and if I'm being honest, she's ruining me for anyone else.

"Move," she begs. "Please, I need it."

She needs it like I need it. I roll my hips as I fuck into her with more energy, building up a rhythm between my long thrusts and the strokes against her clit. She's going to come just like this, I can feel it, stuffed full of my cock with her breath hitching. My balls are aching; I have to clench my ass to keep from blowing my load too early. She's moaning loudly enough that I'm glad we're the only ones in the house.

"Penny," I groan. "Penelope. Gorgeous girl."

"Put the dildo in my cunt," she gasps out. "Please, I can take it. It's on the list."

I stutter, losing my rhythm. "What, Mark Antony?"

"*Cooper*," she whines.

I reach across the bed and grab it. "That's his name, right?"

She giggles, and the sound is like pure sunshine. "Don't even, Callahan. Are you going to put it in or not?"

I'm distracted by the way she's furrowing her brow, her lower lip jutting out in a pout. I wish I could kiss her from this angle, but I have to settle for pressing the dildo against her hole. She drops her forehead to the bed, shaking now like she's about to fall to pieces; she must be close. I push it in without ceremony since she's slick enough she's dripping, and she fucking *sighs* when she's stuffed full in both holes, like she's been waiting for this moment and now she's finally able to enjoy herself. I barely manage another two full thrusts before she comes, and her pleasure, the way her body grips me tight and doesn't let me go, sends me over the edge.

It's a long time before either of us move. She's boneless, whining when I pull out, taking the toy with me. I pull on a pair of boxers, so I won't accidentally flash my siblings if either comes home, then head to the bathroom down the hall for a washcloth. Penny's in the same position when I come back. I gather her into my arms, and she kisses me tiredly, resting her head on my shoulder as I wipe her clean.

"Pretty girl," I breathe. I kiss her again, long and slow, enjoying the weight of her against my chest.

"Feeling more relaxed?" she asks.

"I feel like I could go out on the ice tomorrow and get a hat trick."

"Good. I've wanted that for ages, so thank you." She snuggles even closer. "Is it okay if I..."

I wrap my arm over her middle. "You're not leaving right now."

"Oh, no?" she says teasingly.

"Not when we have *The Return of the King* to get to,

finally." I slide off the bed again and rummage around in my dresser for a sweater that Penny can wear, since she came over in basically nothing, and toss it to her before going over to my gear bag.

She pulls the sweater over her head. "Please tell me that Aragorn gets even hotter."

"He does," I say, mostly to hear more of her sweet laughter. "Heads up."

I pull the bag of gummy bears out of a side pocket and toss it to her. She catches it, her eyes lighting up when she realizes what it is. "Gummy bears?"

I scratch the back of my neck. "Just remembered that you like them."

Her smile makes my breath stick in my throat.

"That's sweet of you." She rips the bag open and pops one into her mouth. "Is anyone home? Can I use the bathroom first?"

A couple minutes later, we get settled in bed with my laptop balanced atop a pillow in front of us. Penny climbed into my lap when she came back from the bathroom, so we're a tangle of limbs, but I don't mind. As far as viewings of *Lord of the Rings* go, this has been my favorite, and I've seen these movies nearly a dozen times.

Penny puts a couple of gummy bears in my palm. When she turns to kiss me, her breath smells like sugar. "Thank you," she says. "Even though they're smelly. Why were they in your gear bag? I doubt my dad wants you guys eating candy on the bench."

"I always like having a snack around." The truth is I bought them and put them in my gear bag for a moment just like this. I knew she'd smile, and I wanted to see that smile happen because of me. I got exactly that, and while I'm glad we fucked —I really do feel more relaxed, ready to buckle down and focus on beating Merrimack—it's that smile I'll be thinking about as I take the ice tomorrow.

I press play on the movie. "I forbid you from screaming when the orcs are onscreen."

"But they're just so gross!"

32

PENNY

I DON'T PLAN on going to the game against Merrimack, but Dani, Allison, and Will invite me and Mia, and it sounds like a better Friday night than staying at the library late, so I pull my coach's daughter privileges to get us seats in the front row, right behind one of the goals. On the way into the Markley Center, we bump into Sebastian and Izzy, who are going to the game with Izzy's friend from the night of the Haverhill party, Victoria—apparently Victoria hooked up with the goalie, Aaron Rembeau, and they might be dating, but she's not sure and wants to stake her claim—and two friends of Sebastian's from the baseball team, Rafael and Hunter.

In a weird twist of fate that I'm almost—but not quite certain—Cooper has nothing to do with, we all have seats in the same row, so by the time the game begins, we've morphed from two groups into one large one, ready to party. Rafael and Hunter are twenty-one, so they bring back beers for us to share, and Mia smuggled in not one, but *two* flasks. As McKee skates out in royal purple, sticks raised to acknowledge the cheers and shouting, I take a big gulp of whiskey. It burns going down, but

I'm holding my own... at least until I see the 'C' on Cooper's sweater.

It's a bad idea, a terrible one, but I jump to my feet all the same and pound on the glass, shouting his name. He sees me—all of us, really—and skates over.

Sebastian gets the question out before I do. "He made you captain?"

Cooper looks dazed, honestly. His hockey sweater is crisp, not a thread out of place. My father had to have just given it to him in the locker room. Cooper and I are friends now. If he knew about this already, he would have said something. He glances down at his sweater, like he's just noticing the 'C' for the first time.

"Yeah," he says. "Didn't say much. Just said I earned it and handed it to me."

"Congrats, man," Sebastian says, thumping on the glass with his palm. Mia and the rest chorus their congratulations.

"This is amazing!" Izzy says. "Mom and Dad are going to flip!"

"Sounds like my dad," I say. I'm busy drinking in the sight of him—with his pads on, he looks formidable as fuck, and I want to climb him like a tree and knock the helmet right off his head so I can pull his hair—but then the referee blows the whistle, ruining the moment.

"Enjoy the game," he says, knocking at the glass with his glove. "Party with you all later, yeah? Don't have too much fun without me. And Izzy, wait, I want to tell them myself."

He skates off. I stand at the glass for a moment too long, my hand pressed flat against it. If my dad glances over, he'll wonder what I'm doing, acting like a lovesick WAG. I need to sit down, to clear my mind and enjoy the game, but I'm stuck in place. I'm ecstatic for Cooper, I know how much this means to him—

but when we first agreed to our arrangement, we said we'd keep it going until he made captain.

Now that's happened, and if his game wasn't back before, it definitely is now. He'll be able to have any girl he wants—because who wouldn't want to sleep with the captain of the hockey team? Combine his status with his reputation, which I know firsthand is worth every word, and he won't have to worry about relaxing before games for the rest of the season or the next one, and certainly not when he graduates and scoops up the splashy rookie deal he wants so badly. Why would he want to keep up a thing with a girl who hasn't even let him fuck her pussy yet when he could have that and more, all in one night, from any number of girls who will mob him the moment he walks out of the locker room post-game?

"I'm sorry for what I said the night of the party," Sebastian says.

I shake my head slightly as I look over at him. "What?"

"I was too harsh to you. I know you care about him."

I swallow. "Yeah, he's a good guy. A good friend."

Sebastian just nods. Pathetically, I want to ask him what Cooper has said about me. I want—need—the answer to be what I just said. *She's a good friend.*

Even though I desperately want to keep going through The List with him and him alone, this is the out we both need. And since I can't bear to hear it from him, I need to be the one to say it first.

MCKEE CRUSHES MERRIMACK 7-0. It's such a high score for hockey that it's hard to believe, but the whole team brought incredible pressure in the first period, and just never let up. To Victoria's delight, Aaron Rembeau made several spectacular saves. I watch as she meets him outside the locker room, and if she had any worry about their status before, the way his eyes light up as he goes to kiss her hello puts that all to rest.

"Great, let's hit up Red's first," Sebastian is saying to Mia. The two of them have taken it upon themselves to arrange the afterparty. I'm petrified of trying to use my fake ID at a bar my dad could stroll into at any moment, so I'll be drinking a soda there, but it'll be worth it to celebrate the win with the team.

Cooper walks out of the locker room with Evan, freshly showered and still looking a little stunned.

When he spots us lingering, he smiles. "How'd you all get back here?"

"Penny sweet-talked her way in," Sebastian says. He claps Cooper on the back. "How's the captain?"

"Exhausted," he says. He played a clean game, no penalties, and showed off his skill set beautifully. I hope an NHL scout was in the stands, or will at least get the tape of this game, because it showed him at his best. Some hockey players, defensemen especially, rely on their physicality to keep the puck away from their guy's net, but Cooper is a true skill player. When he goes pro, I'd be willing to bet he leads the league in points as a rookie. It's one reason my father was so insistent that he clean up his act—a player like him needs to stay on the ice, not rack up time in the box, even if he's ready at a moment's notice to go fisticuffs.

"You clocked over half an hour of ice time," Evan says dryly. "Coach couldn't keep you off."

"Keeping track now, huh?" Cooper says, play-punching Evan in the stomach. They wrestle for a moment, both laughing; even if Cooper is exhausted, he has more than enough energy for the night ahead. I ignore the flicker of desire that pokes its head up hopefully. It's time to squash it.

"Hey, when you play, I play," Evan says. "I was dragging by the end."

"Great game," one of the other players, a guy I don't recognize, says as he passes. Another guy claps Cooper on the shoulder, giving him a nod, but his buddy, who I vaguely recognize as Brandon Finau, scowls. Clearly not everyone is thrilled about the decision to name Cooper the captain.

I can see Dad at the other end of the hallway, talking to his coaching staff, so I tug on Cooper's sleeve. I'm sure that he noticed me at the game, but I'll just text him congratulations later; I don't want to get drawn into a conversation with him right now. Not to mention that he'd flip if he smelled the alcohol on my breath. "Let's head out."

Since everyone is a little sloshed already, we just start walking toward downtown. The cold stings less with whiskey in my belly, but I still stick close to Cooper. He's like a furnace, and it's magical. He took my hand the moment we left the building, and I know I should pull away—more accurately, I should ask if we can talk—but it's too nice to steal the warmth radiating from him to want to ruin it out here in the cold. The group, Victoria and Aaron, Dani and Will and Allison, Izzy and Mia, Sebastian, Rafael, and Hunter, and Evan and Jean too, breaks away from us as we turn onto Main Street. I realize this is by design the moment Cooper pulls me behind a bush and kisses me hard on the lips.

Sneaky bastard.

I wrap my arms around his neck, standing on my tiptoes for better leverage as I kiss back. It's automatic, as natural as breathing. We make out for what must be five minutes at least, his hands underneath my sweater all the while. I shiver, but not from the cold; his fingertips feel like little candle flames. When he eventually steps back, it's a reluctant unwinding, pulling out one hand and then the other, licking into my mouth one more time before taking a breath.

"Cooper," I say. My voice feels thick. I'm nowhere near drunk, but for a moment I wish I was. Drunk me would forget what she needs to do. "You made captain."

"All thanks to you, Red," he says.

Fuck, his voice sounds tender. I shake my head. "No. This was all you. You're so fucking talented, you would have gone first round in the draft if you'd entered."

That makes his mouth twist. "Doesn't matter," he says. "What matters is now."

"Yes," I say, seizing upon that like a life raft in shark-infested waters. Only the sharks aren't sharks, they're feelings, and I really, really don't want to be devoured by them. Not when I know the way out, in the end, is filled with pain. "You got what you wanted. We don't... have to continue doing this. Don't feel obligated when I'm sure there are like, half a dozen girls at Red's right now, just waiting for you to come in."

He's quiet so long I almost repeat myself, but then he shoves his hands into his jacket pockets and looks at the frosted-over ground.

"Is that what you want?"

33

PENNY

I STARE at him for a long, frozen moment.

Yes.

No.

No, it's not what I want, but I can't fall for him, and he can't fall for me, and somewhere in between banter about books and stupid texting conversations and gummy bears and sex so good I cry, I think that's what might be happening, and if I give in and the whole thing shatters, if my life shatters for a third fucking time—

"Yes," I manage to say, even though my chest is aching like someone just struck it with an anvil. "It's what I want."

"But we didn't finish your list."

"It's... it's fine. It's whatever."

"Bullshit," he says, his gaze searching mine. He swipes his hand through his damp hair. "Penny, why are you lying? What happened?"

I open my mouth—to say what, I don't know—but before I can muddle through my thoughts, a plaintive little meow breaks the silence.

"Was that a cat?" he says, looking around.

I drop to my knees, wiping furtively at my cheeks to get rid of the stubborn tears, and peer underneath the bush. "Oh my God, there's a kitten."

Cooper gets to his knees too, putting his hand on my arm to stop me from reaching into the bush. "Wait, it might bite. Let me do it."

He carefully pokes around the underside of the bush. There's another meow, louder this time, and then he pulls out a skinny orange cat with big, amber-colored eyes. I'm not sure how old it is, but if I had to guess, only a couple of months. It hisses, showing Cooper its teeth. I reach out for it, and Cooper gingerly deposits it in my arms. It curls up in the crook of my elbow, giving him a look that clearly says it thinks I'm the superior option here.

"Does it know I've never interacted with a cat before?" Cooper says.

"Never?"

"Never. Be careful, it could have rabies."

"I doubt it." I stroke my finger between its ears, and it meows again, sounding a lot less annoyed. It must have been freezing underneath that bush. "I wonder what it's doing here, it's cold."

"There's no tag?"

"Nothing."

"Weird," he says, brushing his hands on his knees before straightening up. "Should we like... bring it to the firehouse or something?"

I raise an eyebrow as I stand. "Isn't that for babies?"

"Probably." He eyes the thing like he expects it to start howling like a banshee. "Be careful, Pen. It could hurt you."

I laugh. "Cooper, it's a three-pound kitten. Hardly threatening."

"I don't trust it."

"Stop being such a baby. Look, it's cute." I hold it up. It meows again, batting at the air with a tiny paw. "I had a cat when I was little, they're perfectly adorable animals."

"Dogs are perfectly adorable animals," he says. "Cats are magical beings with malicious intent."

I hug the kitten closer to my chest. It needs a bath for sure, and some food. I can't even keep a cat in my dorm room, but I'm already hoping that when we bring it to a vet, they don't find a microchip. If anything, I can try to convince my dad to take it in. "Can it stay at your place tonight?"

He wrinkles his nose. "Fine. Let's take it back to the house. It's not like we can bring it to the bar."

I bundle the kitten inside my coat, which it must appreciate because it rewards me with a purr. "I think it's a her."

We each send a text—to Mia and Sebastian, respectively—and head toward his house. It's cowardly, but having something immediate to focus on makes it easy to ignore our unfinished conversation. It doesn't even feel awkward as we walk together, and I can't decide if that's a positive or a negative.

When we get to the house, Cooper heads straight for the kitchen. He grabs a bowl and fills it with water, then takes a can of tuna out of the pantry. "This is probably fine to give her, right?"

I settle on the floor, sitting with my legs crossed, and pull out the cat, holding on so she won't bolt. "Yeah. Just a little. She might just want the water for now."

He spoons a bit of the tuna into another bowl, then sets both down on the floor. He sits with his back to the refrigerator, looking at the kitten with a dubious expression one might usually reserve for slightly expired cheese, but I catch a flash of relief when she goes for the water and takes a couple of sips.

I stroke a hand down her back. "Can I give her a bath in your sink?"

"Sure, sweetheart."

I swallow. "Callahan."

"I don't want to change things, Penny." He reaches out tentatively and rubs the kitten's ear. She looks at him, but doesn't back away or anything. Even though she's not a newborn, fortunately, she's still tiny, and his hand looks so big in comparison. "We started something, and I want to finish it. I don't want to sleep with anyone else right now."

I bite my lip. "What happened to one-time hookups?"

"I changed the rules for you." He reaches over, cupping my chin with his hand and tilting my head up, so we're looking each other in the eyes. I swallow; he looks as intense as he did when a hit slammed him into the boards right in front of our faces late in the second period. "Tell me you really want to stop, and I'll respect that, but if you're asking, I want to keep going."

It would be smart to put distance between us. To try to just be friends. But he could tell I was lying, and I can't bring myself to try it twice. Not when my heart is hammering and I'm dying to kiss him so badly, I'm having trouble thinking straight.

"Fine, but we're not dating," I manage to say.

"I know." He rubs his thumb across my cheek. "There's so much more I want to do with you."

"Show me," I whisper.

He leans in, kissing me firmly on the lips, but the kitten meows loudly. We both succumb to laughter, breaking away as the kitten leaps into Cooper's lap; the initial distrust seems to be fading quickly. He picks her up, looking her in the eyes, and she reaches out to bat at his nose.

"Besides," he says, "I need us to be good. We're cat parents now."

When he stands, I follow. He hands the kitten off to me, clearing away the sink and running the water.

"I thought you didn't even like cats," I say.

"I don't," he says. "I like this cat. We're going to take it to the vet tomorrow, and if it doesn't belong to anyone, we're keeping her. So buckle up, because you're Mommy and I'm Daddy."

"If we're her parents," I say, trying to keep my voice even although I'd really like to let out a happy scream, "she needs a name. The cat I had when I was little was named Lady."

For some reason, that makes him snort. "Sorry," he says, checking the water temperature with his finger. "Just makes me think of *Game of Thrones*. Which we're watching next, by the way."

"Um, no. I was going to suggest *Twilight*."

"We'll watch both." He looks back at me and the cat. "Tangerine."

"What?"

"Her name. It should be Tangerine."

I hold her up. She doesn't seem to mind the name, necessarily, but that might just be because she's eyeing the sink like she knows she's about to suffer the indignity of a bath. "Tangy?"

He kisses me. "Yeah, like you. Your taste, anyway."

"*Cooper.*"

He grins. "What?"

"You're the worst."

"Sure," he says, his eyes practically sparkling with amusement. "Get over here, Mother of Cats."

34

PENNY

I'VE NEVER HAD baby fever, aside from the occasional reaction to a well-written breeding kink scene, but if I become a parent, I think it's going to go something like this. In the past week, Cooper and I have texted about nothing but Tangerine. Tangerine's feeding schedule. Tangerine's shots at the vet. Tangerine's progress with the litter box. He snuck her into my dorm room last night, and she made biscuits with her little paws on his chest while we watched *Eclipse*. He keeps saying that he's still warming up to her, but I've seen the pictures he sends. He's obsessed with her, and so am I, and that couple with the tiny baby we saw at Target a couple of days ago while we were buying Tangerine a proper cat bed has nothing on us.

Currently, though, Tangerine is staring at Cooper as he tries—again—and fails—again—to teach her how to play fetch. I finish scribbling an answer in my lab notebook and peer down at them. I'm on my stomach on his bed, homework spread out around me. He had been working on a paper, but boredom eventually won out, and now he's on the floor, sitting cross-legged while Tangerine stares at him.

"She's not going to do it," I say.

"She will," Cooper insists. "She was interested in it earlier. Tangy, show Penny what we've been working on."

Tangerine just flicks her tail, blinking her bright eyes. Her collar, which is hot pink and covered in rhinestones since Izzy came with us to Petsmart to buy it, stands out against her now-shining fur. She looks nothing like she did a week ago, all muddied and half-frozen; I swear she's gained a pound already.

He tosses the toy mouse again, and again she watches it sail over her head with only mild interest. He sighs, scratching her between the ears. "All right," he says. "If it's just between you and Daddy, that's cool."

I sort through the papers in my binder. The lab report I've been working on for the past hour is, to put it kindly, a mess. I had to redo the math in step one approximately seventeen times. And now I can't find the data collection sheet I need to move on to the next section. "Shit."

"Something wrong?"

"I left something I need at my dad's house." I sit up, biting my lip as I check the time on my phone. "This is due tomorrow; I need to go get it."

"I can drive you."

"It's only like three blocks over."

"I'll walk with you, then. You said he went out, right?"

I sigh as I slide off the bed and grab my boots. "Yeah. He wouldn't say, but I think he's on a date."

He grins, snatching up Tangerine for a kiss before depositing her on the bed. "Go Coach."

I roll my eyes. "I wouldn't even mind. It's not like I want him to be alone. But he's so secretive about it, like he thinks I'll die if I hear he has a girlfriend."

"Do you know who she is?"

"I have an idea, but I'm not sure." I open the door, and

Tangerine jumps off the bed rather athletically, running out into the hallway. She adores sleeping on Izzy's bed.

"Iz, we're heading out for a few minutes," Cooper calls.

Instead of answering, we hear Izzy shriek, "Tangy! You can't jump on my computer!"

He snorts as he leads the way down the stairs. "Do I know her?"

"Yes."

He raises his eyebrows. "Tell me."

We bundle into our coats and head out into the cold. I wouldn't mind driving, actually, but in case Dad is around, I wouldn't want him to see Cooper's truck. "I think it's Nikki."

"Our boss Nikki?"

"Yep. They've known each other for a long time. She trained with my mother. She's the one who told him about the coaching position at McKee."

"Huh. Like I said, go Coach. She's pretty hot."

I roll my eyes again, but he's right, she's beautiful. That's about as far down that road as I'm willing to get, so I'm relieved when we reach the house. As I unlock the door, Cooper peers around like he's standing in front of a haunted house, not one of the many perfectly pleasant colonials on this block.

"This is kind of weird," he says. "I've never been to Coach's house before."

"I keep trying to get him to host a team dinner here," I say as I jiggle the doorknob. This is an old house, like most of the ones in this part of town; the front door always sticks because it's not quite centered in the frame anymore. I don't mind this house, but I still miss the one we had in Tempe, even if it felt a lot smaller and sadder after Mom wasn't around anymore.

"Yeah, we always have the winter banquet at Vesuvio's." Cooper follows me to the kitchen in the back. On the table, which as usual is covered in binders and stat sheets and the big sketch pad Dad uses to plan out his playbook, I find the data collection sheet I filled out in the lab earlier this week. Somewhere in between shoving around all the crap on the table so we could eat our takeout and grabbing my stuff so I could head to Cooper's, I totally missed it.

"Okay, let's go," I say. I wheel around, practically smacking into Cooper; he's looking down at the sketchbook.

"That would never work," he says, frowning as he traces Dad's messy handwriting. "Jean's not good at feinting."

I hold up the sheet. "We're good. Let's go."

"And deny me the pleasure of seeing your bedroom, Red?"

"Trust me, it's nothing to write home about."

"What if I told you it came with a make out session?"

I bite back my smile. "Fine. But you're not allowed to make fun of my Robert Pattinson poster."

"Like that's news, sweetheart. I've seen the way you look at Edward."

I reach over to pinch him, but he steps out of the way in time. I sigh, leading the way upstairs.

We moved to Moorbridge before my senior year of high school, so I spent an entire year living here full time before starting at McKee. Cooper was a freshman during my dad's first year of coaching at McKee. For whatever reason, it's weirder to think about me going to Moorbridge High School while Cooper was only ten minutes away than to think of last year, when we were both on campus and didn't cross paths. If we had, though, I doubt we'd be doing what we're doing now.

I flick the switch for the overhead light. Cooper has a thoughtful expression on his face. It's one thing, seeing my dorm room, and something else entirely to see a version of my teenage bedroom. Yellow paint on the walls, a blue area rug on the floor. A tiny twin bed settled against the wall and books everywhere. My *Twilight* poster, which I pinned over my bed and never took down, and of course an entire shelf full of trophies and medals, relics of a time in my life that's long gone. I reach down, rubbing at my knee. Phantom pain always crops up whenever I ponder the cost of those awards.

"You made first place a lot," Cooper says.

I smile wryly. "I had a good coach."

"Was it your mom?"

"Yeah. Someone else took over when she got sick, but before that, she was my coach." I sit on the bed, swallowing down the wave of emotion that always accompanies talking about her. I know I could stop, and Cooper wouldn't push, but something about seeing him here makes me want to continue. He sits down next to me on the bed, taking my hand in both of his. "I know that the stereotype is like, the mean mom forcing her daughter to do the same thing she did, reclaim her glory, whatever, but she wasn't like that."

"What was she like?" he asks softly.

I trace over his palm. "She was wonderful. She made it fun. I did all my routines to upbeat songs. At my ballet lessons, she danced alongside me. We kept scrapbooks of all my competitions, the program notes and ribbons. She always kept gummy bears and sour worms in her purse in case I needed cheering up. I know her career ended because she got pregnant with me, but she never made it seem like I ruined her life. I was a surprise, but my parents wanted me."

I smile, remembering a time she told off another mom for yelling at her daughter after a disastrous program. "She never yelled. When I made mistakes, we went over them in a way that somehow made me feel better, even though I messed up, you know? She made me feel grateful that I had the opportunity to make the mistake in the first place and learn from it."

My voice sounds thick, the way it always does when I talk

about her. It's almost been a decade, and yet I can't reminisce without crying. I wonder sometimes if that's how it'll be for the rest of my life; if I'll tell my kid about her one day and sob the whole time. It's like the pain becomes fresh all over again, like I'm experiencing every moment in that hospital all at once.

Cooper pulls me into a hug, and I melt against his chest gratefully. "I'm sorry," he says. He winces. "And I'm sorry for saying that. I know those words aren't helpful."

I shake my head. "It's fine."

"What happened? If you want to share."

"She had ovarian cancer. It was really aggressive." I wipe at my eyes, looking at him. "She had the same hair as me, you know. This pretty ginger color. It all fell out the moment she started chemo. I was thirteen. Fourteen when she passed."

He hugs me so tightly it knocks the breath from my chest. "I remember from the picture on your nightstand in the dorm. Should I stop calling you Red? Does it bring up bad memories?"

"No." I sit up, sniffling as I try to manage a smile. "I really like it. Don't stop."

He brushes his lips over my forehead. "Thank you for telling me."

"I don't talk about her often enough." My smile goes wobbly again. "Dad doesn't like to. I think it still hurts too much."

"You know, it would feel weird to make out under the gaze of Edward Cullen," he quips.

I laugh wetly. Three times in a row now, his thoughtfulness has taken me aback. Asking about my mom. Checking that I still want to be called 'Red.' And now this—knowing exactly when I need humor to keep from spiraling.

"We go way back," I say. "I started reading *Twilight* in the hospital. It was the series that made me fall in love with reading."

"Well, that settles it," he says. "We need to do a book swap. I'll read *Twilight*, and you can check out *Lord of the Rings*."

I reach over to the bookshelf next to my bed; my well-worn copies sit right in the middle of the top shelf. I take out the first one and flip through it. If he reads it, he'll see all the passages I highlighted. I've read hundreds of books since, and I know the series isn't perfect, but I still adore every single word. "You probably won't like them. The books are nothing like what you usually read."

"I like the movies," he says. "And you'll like *The Fellowship of the Ring*."

"Fine," I say. "But if I bail because there isn't enough romance, don't—"

"Bug?" Dad calls. "Are you home?"

My heart drops straight through to the floor.

"Closet," I mutter, shoving at Cooper. "Go."

He shuts himself in my closet at the exact moment Dad knocks on my door.

35

COOPER

SINCE I STARTED HOOKING UP, I've been shoved unceremoniously into closets twice—once because the girl I was hooking up with had a boyfriend she neglected to tell me about, and once because her strict parents would have flipped if they saw she had a boy in her room. I've hidden underneath the bed, underneath the covers, and on one memorable occasion, clung to the terrace like Romeo fucking Montague. And those are just the times I didn't get caught. I still wince whenever I remember getting hit on the ass with a well-aimed slipper while I ran out of a house in nothing but my underwear. That grandmother had some arm.

But until now, I've never taken hiding so seriously. I'm barely even breathing in case Coach hears it. I'm not that worried about what will happen to me if I get caught—I just want to save Penny the embarrassment, especially after she was so honest with me about her mother.

"Penelope," he's saying, "I thought you went back to the dorms."

"I did," she says. I watch through the slats in the door—it's a shutter-style wooden door, which means I have a sliver of a view, but that makes it even more likely Coach will notice that something is up—as she holds up the lab report data sheet. "I forgot this, I had to come back for it."

"I hope you didn't walk all the way from campus," he says. "Mia still picked you up, right?"

"Yeah." I watch as she runs her hand through her hair. "I took a cab here. I need this for something due tomorrow and I didn't want to cut your date short. How did it go, by the way?"

As if in reply, a woman calls, "Larry? Is everything okay?"

"Be down in a moment, Nikki," Coach says. He's blushing, which I've never seen him do. I didn't realize he was even capable of it.

"Oh," Penny says. She's also blushing furiously. "That's, um, great, Dad. I'll grab an Uber back to campus."

"I can drive you," he says.

"No, it's cool," she says quickly. "You should enjoy yourself."

"I hope you're still focusing on school," Coach says, gesturing down to the book in her hands. "I don't want you reading too much of that stuff, Pen."

Indignation erupts through me. Penny crosses her arms over her chest, hugging the book. "I'm still doing everything I need to do for school."

"You won't become a physical therapist unless you buckle down. You know that."

A physical therapist? I didn't even know that was Penny's plan; she's never mentioned it. I've been wondering why she's putting herself through a biology degree when her passions so obviously lie elsewhere. Now I see why, and unfortunately, I get it. She wants to make her dad happy, even if that means studying something she's not interested in. Wanting to make my dad happy is why I'm at McKee right now instead of possibly in the league already.

"I know," she says. "I'm working on it, I promise. I'm going to office hours all the time."

"You've seemed distracted recently," he says. He takes a step closer, concern written all over his face. "You'd tell me if something's going on, right? It's not something like Preston?"

"No," she snaps. She grabs the rest of the books from the shelf and tucks her data sheet into one of them. "It's nothing like that."

"Because you could always go back to weekly visits with Dr. Faber. You're still taking your pills, right?"

If possible, the blush on her face gets darker. She glances back at the closet. I wince, wishing I could put my hands over my ears, because this has stumbled into territory that is obviously not my business, but I don't want to risk making noise and ruining things even worse.

"Dad," she says. "Seriously, I'm fine. I'm taking my meds. And rereading a series I like doesn't mean I'm about to go off the deep end again. It's not like that was even why I... whatever. I'll talk to you later."

She flees the room. Coach Ryder stays there for a moment, arms crossed over his chest. I don't realize it until he takes in a broken breath, but he's tearing up. He pulls a tissue out of his pocket and carefully wipes his eyes, then clears his throat.

"Sorry about that, honey," he says to Nikki as he leaves the room. "Can I get you that nightcap now?"

BY THE TIME I wriggle out the window, brave the jump to the ground, and sneak around the house, Penny is halfway down the block. I run to catch up to her. She's crying, big gulping sobs that hurt my heart to hear. When I put my arm around her shoulders, she shrugs it away.

"Red."

"When we get to your house, can you drive me home?"

I swallow back the protests I want to make. "Sure."

"Thanks."

"I'm sorry," I blurt.

She looks over. "For what? For hearing all that? It's not your fault you were there."

I latch onto the safest topic to bring up, even though I can't stop wondering who Preston is and why she sees a psychiatrist. "You don't want to become a physical therapist."

She sniffles. "No," she says thickly. "But you know how sometimes you latch onto something and can't let it go? After my injury, I got kind of interested in my physical therapy, and he suggested I should do that as a career. It's not like I have any better ideas, so whatever. It's whatever."

"It's not whatever. It's your life. What about your writing?"

"You don't know the whole story."

"So tell me."

She stops on the sidewalk, looking up at me with tears on her cheeks; her breath crystalizes in the air as she sighs. "I can't," she says, her voice cracking. "Don't worry about it."

I can't stop worrying about it, though. I can't stop when we get to the house and she gathers up her things. I can't stop when she takes my copy of *The Fellowship of the Ring* off my shelf and cradles it to her chest like she's holding a prize. I can't stop when she hugs Tangy goodbye, or when we drive to campus in silence, or when she dodges my kiss on the way out of the truck. I worry about it in bed, Tangerine tucked against my side and snoring daintily as I read the first couple chapters of *Twilight*. My worry is taking on a shape I know it's not supposed to, but it's not like I can just make it go away. I told her last week we're not dating, and I'm going to hold onto that as long as I can, but with every second that passes, my feelings march into territory I've never felt before.

She told me about her mother, and I've got her favorite book in my hands, and I can see her thirteen-year-old handwriting in the margins, and doesn't it mean something that she offered it up to me? When she reads *The Fellowship of the Ring*, she'll see where I dog-eared the pages, where I broke the spine, where I penciled in thoughts during re-reads where things felt particularly magical. I know I'm not supposed to feel this way for her, and maybe I'm reading this whole situation wrong, but she can't be feeling nothing.

It's in my chest like a breathing, palpable thing. Not friendship. Something deeper. Eventually, I won't be able to contain it, and I'm terrified that the moment that happens, I'll lose Penny for good.

36

COOPER

"ISN'T IT WONDERFUL THAT JAMES' bye week lined up with this?" Mom says the moment she hugs me.

I've been at Markley Center for hours, preparing for the game, but I snuck out once I heard that my family arrived. I'm not in my gear yet, just workout clothes, but after I say hello, I need to get into uniform.

"Definitely." I squeeze her tightly; I haven't seen my parents since the semester began, and I've missed her especially. When Mom lets go of me, Dad steps forward and pulls me into a hug of his own. I relax for the tiniest of moments, because even though I'm taller than he is now, it doesn't feel like it, and it's rare that I wrangle a hug out of Richard Callahan. Hopefully, I'll get another one after the game. I told my siblings to keep the news about making captain a secret so I can share it with him in person.

"It's too bad we can't stay the whole weekend," James says as we clap each other on the back. "Coach wants us to get to Texas ahead of time."

"And I still can't believe you won't be here for Thanksgiving," Mom says with a sigh.

"Someone has to play Dallas," Dad says. "And it's a divisional game."

"Yes, yes," Mom says, waving her hand. "At least we'll have Bex. And the cat, right? I can't wait to meet the cat."

"The cat is so cute," Izzy says. "Mom, you're going to flip."

Bex smiles as she steps forward to hug me too. "I broke out my McKee hat for this," she says, kissing me on the cheek. "It's weird, going back to purple."

"I got you seats in the front row," I say as I lead the way across the parking lot. It's a midafternoon game, the one McKee hockey fans have been waiting for all season—the first home game against UMass. Someone started calling it the Turkey Freeze ages ago, and the name stuck, since it takes place right before Thanksgiving break. There's even a trophy, a bronze turkey in full hockey gear that we pass back and forth based on who wins. It's one of the biggest regular season games we play in Hockey East. CBS is broadcasting, and Coach already told me that I'm likely to get an interview at some point, so I need to think about how I want to present myself. My stats have been strong all season, but excellent play during this game will help show that I can buckle down even in big moments. It's going to be my first time seeing Nikolai on home ice since last season, but I'm not worried about him anymore. I'm locked in, and that means not paying him any mind, no matter what he chirps at me or what cheap shots he tries to get away with. "It's right across from the benches."

"Fantastic," says Mom. "We're so excited to see you play, sweetie."

"Wait until you see him in all his gear," Izzy says slyly. I poke her in the ribs. She squeals, dancing away from me. "Cooper!"

"Not a word," I warn.

"What?" Dad asks.

"Nothing," I blurt. "I need to head into the locker room, but I left the tickets at the box office. Evan's dad and little sister are going to be near you guys, and my friend Penny."

James gives me a look, which I studiously ignore. Ill-timed realizations aside, it's not like anything has changed since the day we had lunch with him and Bex. Penny is still just my friend, and if anything, things have been tense between us since the night her father nearly caught me in her room. When I tried to bring up what happened the other day, she looked at me like I'd just stepped on Tangy's tail. I haven't tried since.

In the locker room, the energy is high. I've always tried to hype up the guys before games—part of the reason I wanted to be captain in the first place, it comes naturally—but now, with the 'C' on my chest, I feel the pressure more keenly. Coach Ryder, looking extra-crisp today in a light purple shirt and navy suit, nods at me as I put fresh tape on my stick.

Does he know how much pressure he's putting on his daughter? Does he know how much she's still hurting? Something tells me he doesn't even know she's writing a book.

"See your parents yet?" Evan asks as he laces up his skates.

I shake myself out of my train of thought. Nothing but the game matters right now, even if whenever I look at Coach Ryder, I just think of his daughter. She'll be wearing McKee purple, but it won't be my sweater. "Yeah, I just walked them in. They're going to sit near your dad and sister."

"Sweet. Maybe after we can get dinner together."

"Callahan," Coach says. "I'd like you to say a few words before we get out there."

I give him a nod. I expected as much. Across the room, Brandon scowls. When Coach announced he was naming me captain, I worried about him giving me shit, but he's been quiet, sticking to his crew while I stick to mine. Part of me feels like I should watch my back, in case he tries to trip me up somehow, but that's just paranoia talking. As long as his feelings don't impact his play on the ice, I don't care what they are. He can hate me all he wants, but I earned this.

When we're suited up, we huddle in the center of the room. There's a cameraman man in the corner; I didn't notice him until this moment. He's probably filming a live look into the locker room. I swallow down the rush of nerves and tap my stick against the floor to quiet everyone.

"Guys," I say. "I know that when we visited UMass a couple weeks ago, we lost. That was tough."

Murmurs of agreement. That loss sucked. 1-0 is a tough pill to swallow, especially up at UMass. Nikolai jeered at me when the buzzer went off and the student band trumpeted out a victory song; I had to take a deep breath and skate off the ice before I took things in a direction I didn't want. Something about that asshole's face is just so *punchable*.

"But now we have them here, and since then, we've been on a winning streak. The Merrimack game was a fucking gem." I look around the group. Evan's looking at the floor, rocking back and forth. Remmy looks locked the fuck in, which I love to see. Jean gives me a nod, and so does Mickey. Even Brandon is listening. "We know our strengths. We're faster than they are. Our passing game is stronger. We have Remmy, who is a fucking wizard in the net. We're coming back in here after three hard periods of play with a victory."

"McFucking McKee!" Jean cries. Everyone laughs, banging their sticks on the floor as we repeat his words. Hopefully, the live broadcast has a delay so they can bleep out all the cursing. I wait by the door and tap everyone on the helmet as they pass, a good luck gesture that our captain last year did before every game.

We skate out for introductions. Someone from the school choir is singing the national anthem as the student band plays. It's a little awkward, honestly. I'm not used to all the pomp and circumstance. James is, I'm sure; he went to the national championship game for college football last season. I hook my stick over my shoulders and bow my head as the UMass guys skate onto the ice next.

When I lift my head, I almost let out an ill-timed curse. Nikolai is standing right across from me... with a 'C' on his jersey as well. That hadn't been there on Halloween.

You've got to be fucking kidding me.

His mouth twists into a smile. "Looks like we both got upgrades, Callahan."

"Go back to the KHL, Volkov."

He just chews on his mouth guard. He'd better have upgraded that too if he doesn't want to swallow a tooth.

No. I shake my head minutely. I need to focus, no matter how he tries to push my buttons. I glance over to where my family is—and Penny—and relax when I see her red hair hanging loose around her shoulders. It's like a beacon of fire, grounding me. My father has his elbows on his knees, fingers steepled together. He's not a hockey expert, but he is an ex-athlete, and he'll have plenty to critique at the end of the game. I search for a scrap of pride in his expression, something that shows he noticed the change in uniform, but there's nothing.

Penny meets my gaze. She smiles, and it knocks the fucking air from my lungs. She's goddam perfection. The only thing that would make it better would be if she was wearing my sweater. I want everyone in the whole arena—even her father—to know she's mine.

I can only hope that one day she lets me have her. Not just in bed, and not just as friends. I want all of her, every bit—the ones I know and adore already, and the ones I don't, but hope to one day. I'm earning her trust one little puzzle piece at a time, and while I don't have the whole picture, I know that when I do, I'll love it.

As McKee's athletic director steps up to the microphone to introduce the game, Nikolai leans in. "Where have you been hiding that sister of yours, Callahan? You'll need to introduce me."

I shove my mouth guard into place. "Suck my dick."

He grins, his gaze dark. He has a scar down the side of his face, like he's actually *trying* to be a Soviet-era Bond villain, and a fading bruise on his jaw that I wish I'd been the one to give him. "What about the ginger? She looks like she gives good head."

"Thank you," the athletic director says. There's applause, but it sounds subdued, like it's coming from underwater. Fucking prick. The referee gestures for Brandon and the UMass center to get into place for the faceoff.

"Watch your fucking mouth," I say quietly. "Don't talk about my sister or my girl."

Nikolai holds my gaze, but we're forced to break it when the referee says, "Gentlemen. Positions."

I skate to my spot, tapping my stick twice against the ice. I have to fight the urge to look over at Penny again. The puck drops. Brandon lunges forward, gaining possession and passing to Mickey as he skates to the blue line, and we're off.

I'm playing for my family. My father.

But most of all, I'm playing for my Lucky Penny.

37

COOPER

AS IT TURNS OUT, CBS does want an interview. The reporter catches up to me in the tunnel right when the game ends. We won in overtime, thanks to a beauty of a goal by Mickey, and I'm still sucking wind, sweat dripping from me like I've just climbed out of a pool. I had to literally throw myself in front of a couple of shots on the net, which means I'm sure to have a bunch of fancy new aches and pains once the adrenaline wears off.

"Hi Cooper, I'm Kacey Green from CBS Sports. Mind if we chat for a few minutes?" she says with a camera-ready smile. She's wearing a pine-green dress that complements her deep brown complexion, and even though she has heels on, she barely comes up to my chest. I feel like a huge, sweaty monster compared to her, but she must be used to it, because if she thinks I smell, she doesn't show it.

I lean on my stick. "Of course."

"Fantastic game," she says. "Do you feel like it showcased what you're hoping to bring to the league?"

I try my best to ignore the cameraman standing next to her

as I bend down to speak into the microphone. It would be weird to talk about myself after such a great group effort, so I say, "Thanks, Kacey. The whole team played great. We had a tough loss to UMass earlier in the season, so it's exciting to keep the Turkey Freeze trophy here for another year."

"But you really put it all out there today."

"Yeah." I laugh a bit, wincing when that makes my gut ache. "Pressed well on the forecheck, blocked some shots. It was a good effort."

"You were recently named captain."

"Yes. I'm honored that Coach and the team chose me."

"You and Nikolai Abney-Volkov are the highest ranked defensemen in Division I men's hockey," she says. "Your stats are nearly identical this season. The Sharks drafted Volkov in the first round of the first year you were both eligible, but you chose to remain undrafted."

I wait for a question, but she pauses, so I just nod. Fucking Nikolai.

"Do you have any regrets about holding out for a deal after graduation?"

"I..." Before the season started, I would have said yes, I'd rather be at the pro level, putting all my energy into the one thing I care about most in the world. Let me scrap and enforce our zone and fight for my ice time like everyone else. But now? I'm not so sure. If I was in the league already, I wouldn't have met Penny. If someone gave me the choice between sticking out the rest of college or entering the league tomorrow, I don't know what I'd say.

Out of the corner of my eye, I see my father. He's leaning against the wall as he talks to someone on the phone, half in shadow, but I can feel him looking at me. Maybe other dads wouldn't wear slacks, a collared shirt, and a cashmere sweater to see their sons play hockey, but he still gets recognized everywhere he goes, so his standards aren't the same as most. Technically, he's not even allowed back here, but I'm sure someone recognized him and waved him through.

We fought about whether I would enter the draft for most of my senior year of high school. The resentment ran so deep that we hardly spoke to each other for months. It's mostly faded now, a part of the past I have no interest in reliving, but as Kacey's question echoes in my mind, and as I look at my father, no doubt able to hear our conversation, I feel the sting. He's never understood how the world of professional hockey differs from football, and he's never cared to learn, either.

"No," I say. "I've been improving with every game I play, and Coach Ryder is a big part of that. I'm where I need to be right now, even though I'm excited about what comes next."

"Congratulations again," she says. "Thanks for your time."

I thank her and wait until the camera stops rolling before crossing the hallway to my father. "Dad," I say, wiping at my forehead with the sleeve of my sweater. I can't contain my smile. "Did you hear that?"

He ends his call, a frown on his face. "What?"

"The interview."

"Is there something I should have noticed?"

I bounce on my toes, nearly lurching forward for a hug but stopping myself at the last moment. I'm drenched in sweat; he won't want me to ruin his clothes. "What about the change in uniform? Pretty cool, right?"

He looks me up and down. I straighten, years of being told to watch my posture kicking in, and smooth down the front of my sweater, just in case he hasn't gotten a good look at the new addition.

"You didn't want to tell us in advance?" he says, still studying me like I'm a complex route in a playbook.

"I wanted it to be a surprise."

"It's good that your coach saw sufficient improvements in your play and behavior."

"I've been working really hard this season."

"Which is what I expect from you," he says. "I raised you and James to become captains."

"Yes, sir."

Why did I think we'd get through this conversation without him mentioning James? No matter what I do, no matter what I achieve, even in a different sport, James will do it first. And Dad will like it better because he did it in football.

"That sloppy turnover at the start of the third period could have been a disaster," he continues.

He's right, of course; that was the biggest mistake I made during the game, and I'm not surprised he caught it. I nod, biting the inside of my cheek. It's a fair critique, even if it's not what I want to hear right now. When we go over the tape of this game, Coach will say the same thing. The remedy to turnovers is not making them in the first place. "Right, sir. But aren't you —isn't it great? And I've scored four goals already this season."

The phone in his hand buzzes. He glances down at it, and his mouth tightens. "I need to take this, son. I'll talk to you later."

"Wait, Dad—"

He claps me on the shoulder again as he passes. "Don't make sloppy plays."

I watch as he hurries down the hallway, his phone pressed to his ear. I don't catch what he says, but judging by the look on his face, it's not very pleasant.

I feel stupid, all of a sudden; I'm going home for Thanksgiving in less than a week, it's not like I won't see him there. We can talk more then. But even though I know that, part of me wishes I could've talked to him for just a little longer right now. To actually hear the words that I'm craving come out of his mouth. He tells James—and Izzy, and Seb—how proud he is all the time, so why don't the words come for me? Whenever I try to connect with him, something gets lost in translation. If he looks at James and sees himself, then I'm Uncle Blake, and he's just waiting to see when I'm going to fuck everything up.

I'm about to open the door to the locker room when I see that McKee hat with the pom-pom on top.

It's Penny, looking like she just saw a ghost.

38

PENNY

BEING the coach's daughter comes with its own set of privileges—such as access to pretty much anywhere in Markley Center. When the guard posted in front of the player area sees me, he just nods and says, "Go right ahead, Miss Ryder." Of course, he thinks I'm going to talk to my dad, but my real mission involves a certain newly-minted captain.

As I approach the locker room, I'm hit with a wave of Déjà vu. Things were never at this level when I was with Preston—a high school travel team, no matter how talented, has nothing on Division I hockey—but I can feel the memory pressing at the edges of my mind. The frigid air conditioner, the rush of humid air whenever the door opened. The wooden benches in the locker room, the raucous laughter of the team as the girlfriends snuck in. Preston spinning me around in his arms, still in pads and skates, whispering in my ear about the party at Jordan's. *His parents are in Salt Lake. He's inviting everyone. We can watch the sunset and smoke, please, it'll be out of my system by the next game, and you're not back on the competition circuit for weeks.*

I brace myself against the wall as my breath quickens. I shake my head and remind myself: I'm not in Tempe, about to sneak to a party in Alta Mira. I'm in Moorbridge, at Markley Center. I just watched the Royals play, not the Nighthawks. Cooper was on the ice, not Preston. Cooper is who I'm about to kiss.

I tuck myself into an alcove, balling my hands into the sleeves of my jacket, and take a couple of deep breaths.

"Red? You okay?"

I look up and meet Cooper's gaze. His deep blue eyes are full of concern. I bite the inside of my cheek, focusing on the bead of sweat running down the side of his face, and manage what I hope is a semi-normal smile. "I wanted to see you," I say. "Real quick."

He glances around the hallway. "Your dad is around here somewhere. Is everything good with you two? I don't want to make things worse."

"It's whatever."

"You sure?"

It's not, but I don't want to think about that right now. I resist the urge to stomp my foot, settling for crossing my arms over my chest. "Shut up and get over here."

He grins, and it knocks the air from my lungs. This is what I was looking for. Not Preston, not a tower of memories that I've fought to blast to pieces. Dr. Faber has had a lot of advice for me since she became my therapist, but one of my favorites has always been that making good memories helps make the old ones hurt less. I'll never sneak into that locker room to see Preston again, and I can make the memory fade just a little more with one good kiss from Cooper.

When he has me in his arms, he cups my face with both hands and kisses me tenderly. I can smell the sweat on his skin mixing with his deodorant, and I love it as much as I loved finishing my routine right on beat, listening to the last strain of music fading as I froze like a perfect statue. We can't go further than this, not here, but that doesn't mean my body doesn't respond, waking up thanks to his touch. When he pulls away, I make a soft noise.

He tucks my hair behind my ear. "You sure you're good, gummy bear?"

He says it to make me smile, I'm sure, and it works. He looks pleased, like it took him a while to think up that one, and it's cuter than it has any right to be.

I clear my throat. "Great game. And no penalties."

"Yeah." He shakes his head, a wondering sort of expression on his face. He must still be dazed that he made captain. I reach out and tug on the laces at the collar of his sweater. I just want to keep touching him, and if I can't get to my knees right here in the hallway to mouth at his cock, I suppose this will have to do. "I feel so clear-headed right now. It's... well, not to bring up your dad again, but it's like he said. Getting back to basics, reminding myself why I do it..."

I nod. "You have pure love for what you just did."

"Do you miss it?" he asks. "Competing?"

"Sometimes." I move on to tracing the stitching. "But sometimes I think what I really miss is my mom."

He nods. "I wish I could've met her."

My breath sticks in my throat. Only Cooper could say something like that so casually and make it sound so heartfelt. "Did you talk to your dad yet? Was he excited?"

I expect to see his smile again, so the frown is disconcerting. He glances around, but we're alone. "Something's going on."

"What do you mean?"

"I don't know. It was weird. He was all distracted and left to take a phone call before we got to talk much."

I squeeze his arm. We spent an hour on the phone last

night, just chatting, and he brought up his excitement about his family coming to see the game at least three times. He didn't say it outright, but I could tell how much his dad's approval means to him. I'm just as familiar with it, but for completely different reasons. "I'm sure he's thrilled for you."

"Maybe."

"Of course he is."

He worries his front teeth over his lip. "It always seems so easy for him when it comes to James. Izzy and Sebastian, too. They get everything, and I can't always manage a measly hug. Because apparently, it's such a hardship to be my father. Even when I do something cool, it doesn't matter, because James did it first."

I frown. "But that's football. It's not even the same sport."

"Doesn't matter."

"I doubt—"

"He's always been like this," he interrupts. "It's like... James is the son he wanted, and I'm the extra one he has to put up with."

His voice cracks at the end of the sentence. I can see in the slump of his shoulders how much that cost him to admit. He played an entire hockey game, a beautiful one, and he ought to be celebrating with his teammates right now, not worrying about what his father thinks. Even when my relationship with my dad was fractured, I never doubted his love.

"That can't be what he thinks." I wrap my arms around his middle, swaying us back and forth. I don't care that he stinks. I nuzzle my face against his chest anyway. "It's not like it's a competition."

"No offense, but you don't get it," he says, pulling out of my grasp. "You don't have siblings. You don't know what it's like to always be behind."

"But you're not behind. You're just a bit younger. And doing something totally different, anyway."

"It's not about—" He stops, working his jaw. "It's whatever. I'll see you later."

I resist the urge to reach out; something tells me he's going to pull away again, and I don't want to experience his rejection. I've never seen him like this, so defeated. It makes my heart hurt. "Cooper, wait. I'm sorry."

He just shakes his head as he strides down the hallway to the locker room.

39

PENNY

November 23rd

You're right

I don't understand. But I am sorry

CALLAHAN

Not like it's your fault

No, but you deserve better

What you've done so far this season is incredible. If he can't see that, then that's his loss

Thanks, Red

<3

November 24th

CALLAHAN

Dad decided that we all needed to go to
Dallas to see James' Thanksgiving game

> I can take Tangy. It'll just be me and Dad and
> takeout

November 26th

> Happy Thanksgiving, Callahan

CALLAHAN

How are things with Coach?

> It's fine. Aside from the fact he keeps asking
> about school

> He doesn't know how bad I suck at science

Bit ironic for the girl who just shoved Ice
Planet Barbarians at me

> Shhh it's all a fantasy anyway

> No math required

Plus, you finished Twilight. What was I
supposed to do?

> Also... I have Tangerine pics

Gimme

I've been stuck listening to football talk
all day

November 28th

I know I liked him best in the movies too but GOSH

SAM

WISE

I love him

CALLAHAN

Hobbit feet and all?

Don't get me started

Dad is asking why the cat is named Tangy

I hate that you did that to me

She's named that because of the Led Zeppelin song

You so did not mention that

Listen to it

"Tangerine"

It reminds me of you

And the cat?

December 2nd

I'm fucked

CALLAHAN

Not in a few days

No, seriously. I'm going to fail chemistry

Shit

I'm sorry, Pen

> I just failed my re-take of the last test. The prof can't help me anymore

Can I do anything? I'm getting a massage right now, but I can come over after

> Ugh, I wish I could have a massage

I'll give you one later. It'll be okay, I promise.

> I'm supposed to declare my major next semester. AND it's supposed to be biology with a pre-med track

Your novel is awesome

CALLAHAN

Pen?

> Ugh, don't remind me. It was a waste of time, I should have been studying

COOPER

Not a waste of time. You're really good at writing, I could totally tell it was your work

> Because it was cringey

Because it was funny, and sort of weird, and you're both

In a good way

The Callum character is me, right? I've always wanted to be a billionaire werewolf who gives really good head

At least the last part is already true

........I regret everything

December 8th

I'm coming to the Vermont game

COOPER

Fuck

Red, it's going to be so fucking hard to keep my hands off you

So don't

But I'm not wearing your sweater

But you're wearing someone's

How else will Vermont know I'm rooting against them?

40

COOPER

I TIP MY HEAD BACK, letting the water wash over my face. While Vermont's visitor locker room isn't anything to write home about, the water pressure is decent, and right now, that's good enough to keep my mood from going totally sour.

Penny came to the Vermont game.

I saw her out of the corner of my eye the whole time, the only dot of purple in a crowd of green. She sat a couple rows back from the boards behind one goal, her hair pulled into a braid, chewing on her lip as she watched.

When she texted to tell me that she planned to tag along to the last game before the break in the season, I was thrilled—and then she hit me with some shit about wearing someone else's sweater. We've teased each other plenty, but seeing her show up to the game in Brandon's sweater—of all the players on the team—stung like a shot to the face. She doesn't know about the trouble I've had with him, but still.

She's my girl. Maybe it's not official, but it's the truth. She's mine, and the second she admits that to herself, I'm going to shout it from the fucking rooftops.

Until then, though, I have to put up with shit like this. Watching her cheer on the team while she's wearing Brandon's #19 instead of my #24. Knowing that when I see her, if there's anyone around, I can't kiss her. I'm planning to sneak into her room later, but that's not the same as kissing her in the lobby and watching her sleep on my shoulder on the team bus. I don't know when, exactly, I became the sort of guy who daydreams about getting to watch a girl sleep, but with Penny, it seems natural. Inevitable. It's like I never dated anyone else because I was waiting for her to come into my life. Why would I have wasted time with someone who isn't her?

Not that we're actually dating.

That reminder makes me scowl. I grab the shampoo and lather up my hair. My side is aching from a hard hit that ought to have resulted in a penalty but somehow didn't—Coach yelled at the referees about it—and despite the warm water, I have a chill that won't go away. I pick up the body wash, but before I can uncap it, the shower curtain rustles.

My teammates are so fucking impatient sometimes. "Can't you hear the water, asshole?" I call to whoever is out there. There are a bunch of stalls, so it's not like I'm hogging the bathroom.

"Is that how you talk to the guys?"

I peer around the curtain. Penny is standing there, still in that patently offensive sweater, one eyebrow raised like she's about to scold me. I glance around, but none of my teammates are out and about. Someone is singing, though, horribly off-key; I'd bet, considering the karaoke night at Red's a couple weeks ago, that it's Remmy. "How did you get in here?"

She shrugs. "Not important."

"You interested in seeing another dude's junk, Red?"

She just rolls her eyes. "Even if I did, it's just a dick. Dicks, generally speaking, are not that special."

I put on a wounded face. "And here I thought you liked my disco stick."

Her snort is loud enough for the guy in the next stall to hear, so I shut off the water, shaking out my hair before reaching for my towel. Penny gulps, her gaze darting down to my crotch as blush colors her cheeks. Whatever bravado she came in here with is fading, and good thing, too—she might be cheeky enough to get away with wearing the sweater in the first place, but there's no way I'm letting her flaunt it around post-game. I wrap the towel around my hips and pull her close. She muffles a shriek against my bare shoulder as she wriggles against me, but I hold on tight. "You thought you could get away with wearing someone else's sweater, babe? Think again."

She shudders as I cup her jaw, pressing my thumb against her mouth. This is reckless; anyone could finish up in a second and see the two of us standing here, but I don't move away. Not now, when I have her caught and looking at me like she wants nothing more than to be devoured. She recovers the smirk she came in with, biting down on my thumb.

"It's just a sweater," she says. "And I told you in advance."

"To torture me." I lean in, letting her feel my breath against her ear. Even though it's cold in this room without clothes on and she's wearing the wrong sweater, I'm halfway to hard, my cock straining for attention. "Such a fucking brat, Red. Take it off before I rip it right off your body."

Her breath hitches. I press against her, knowing she can feel the outline of my dick through the towel. "You wouldn't."

I stretch the hem taut. "Watch me."

"What is it with you and destroying my clothes?"

"This isn't yours. If it was my number, it would be yours."

Her eyes widen slightly at the rough edge to my voice. Wrapping up the semester, preparing for this last game before the break, holding back the part of me that wants to beg Penny to just tell me if I have a chance at being her boyfriend—it's all been grinding on me, and the sweater is the last straw. She swallows hard, those gorgeous blue eyes searching my face. I'm about two seconds from getting onto my knees in this locker room and begging for a chance—just a chance—to show her how things have changed for me, and to ask if they're changing for her too, when the shower shuts off in one of the stalls. I whip my head around, but apparently the universe has decided to spare me at least some embarrassment, because it's Evan who reaches for his towel.

Penny scrambles away from me anyway, her face so red I can hardly see the lighter freckles. Evan freezes, water dripping everywhere; at least he has a towel wrapped around his waist. He raises his eyebrows so high they nearly hit his hairline. "I'm gonna—um—"

"I'll see you," Penny squeaks. She darts out of the room.

I scrub my hand over my face. It's a good thing she left, because if we'd had another moment alone, I'd either have spilled my guts to her or tried to fuck her against the wall, and I don't know which would have been worse for someone to walk in on.

"Man, you have it bad," Evan says. He crosses the room to where I'm still rooted in place, clapping a hand onto my shoulder and squeezing. "I didn't even realize."

"I don't," I snap.

"Dude, you were looking at her like she—what do they say? Hung the moon? You were looking at her like that. Like she climbed up on a ladder and put it in the sky just for you."

I practically bare my teeth at Evan, who just grins, clearly delighted by this entire situation. "Don't worry," he adds. "It happens to the best of us. What was she doing in Finau's sweater, though?"

SCREW WAITING until everyone settles down for the night to see her again. As soon as we wrap up at the arena, I grab an Uber to the hotel and head straight for her floor. She's on the same one as the coaching staff, which means I could run into anyone from the equipment manager to Coach himself, but at the moment, I don't give a shit. I'll lie my way through it if I need to. I'm desperate to finish what we started in the locker room.

She slipped me her room key earlier, but I knock anyway. She peers through the peephole first, good girl, and then unlocks the door.

Before she can say a word, I crowd the doorway, pulling her into my arms and kissing her hard. I kick the door closed, then spin her around, pressing her against it as I devour her mouth. She tastes like mint, and there's something sweet mixed in with the lavender of her perfume, and when I finally break away, gasping, she whines and tugs me back.

"Callahan," she murmurs against my mouth. "What's gotten into you?"

I pull away, even though it's torture; I'm rock hard in my jeans. Every particle of me is dying to kiss her, to taste her, to swallow down her moans, but instead, I tilt up her chin. She gulps as we lock eyes, her tongue darting out to wet her lips. I bite back a curse. "You know my name."

"But—"

I push my thigh between her legs, effectively shutting her up, and drag my hand down from her chin to her throat. Not squeezing, not hurting her—just holding it there like it's a necklace. There's a blue-hot fire in her eyes, passion crackling in the air between us like a live wire. I can tell she's three seconds from launching herself into my arms, so I press my thumb against her pulse to still her. It jumps just underneath her skin.

"You're calling me Callahan because it helps you pretend there's nothing deeper going on here," I say in a low voice. "Cut the shit, Penny. You know my name. Say it."

She stares at me for a long moment, defiance in her eyes and the upturn of her nose, but then she pushes me away—and pulls the sweater off her head.

She lets it crumple to the floor.

"Cooper," she whispers. "I'm scared."

"Is that why you wore his sweater?"

She wraps her arms around herself. Without the sweater, she's just in a tank top with a bralette underneath; both are canary yellow. The sight of the freckles clustered on her shoulders like so many constellations make my ribs ache. I want to pull her into my arms, but the energy in the room has shifted; one false step and she might shove me back into the hallway.

"Maybe you're right," she admits. "Maybe it was another layer of distance."

"I don't want distance." I reach out, taking one of her hands in mine and squeezing. "I just want you. Not as friends. Not as the person you fuck. I want to be with you in all those ways and more."

She shakes her head. "You don't know the whole story."

"I don't need it to know I want to be with you."

"Cooper, it's not—" She stops herself. Her eyes are swimming in tears. "You heard my dad. There's a reason I wanted to go through a list in the first place."

"And I don't care what it is."

"You say that now, but you don't know."

"So tell me." I brush away the tears on her cheeks. My heart is breaking for her, but I don't even know why, and that doesn't sit well with me. How can I help her—truly help her—if I don't know the whole story? "Tell me, Red."

She shakes her head, pulling me into a bruising kiss instead of answering. Her hands tug at my shirt until I go along with letting her pull it over my head; she takes off her tank top, too, and then her bra. She presses in for another kiss. I can feel her trembling against me. I bite her lip gently. I don't want to stop talking, but if she needs this, I'm more than willing to give it to her first.

I'm just about to pull her over to the bed when someone knocks on the door.

"Penelope? You in there?"

It's Coach's voice.

41

PENNY

I FREEZE at the sound of my father's voice. I can feel that Cooper is frozen too, but he breaks first, bending to pick up my tank top and pulling it over my head. I wipe at my face furiously as I smooth down my hair.

"Dad," I say, my voice wobbly. "I'm just doing some homework. I'll see you later."

"Penelope, open the door," he says. There's a hard edge to his voice that some would mistake for anger, but I know it's something worse: worry.

"I saw her go inside with someone," another voice says. "I just want to make sure she's okay, you know?"

That sounds like Brandon Finau. I glance at Cooper, who suddenly looks like he wants to commit murder. Before I can shove him in the direction of the bathroom, he leans over and opens the door.

Dad is standing there with Brandon, apprehension etched into every line of his face. He takes in the scene in an instant, in only the way someone used to assessing situations in mere seconds can do, and his mouth twists.

Before he can say anything, Cooper says, "Sir, we need to talk."

"Cooper," I say urgently.

He glances over at me briefly before settling his gaze on my father once more. "It's not what it looks like."

"I think I know exactly what it looks like," Dad says. He looks at Brandon, who has a smug edge to his smile, arms crossed over his chest as he surveys the scene. What an asshole. I don't know what he did, exactly, but somehow, he convinced Dad I needed checking up on. By the way Cooper is glaring at him, it's plain that Brandon wanted my dad to find *him* here. His reaction to me wearing Brandon's sweater makes a lot more sense now. It wasn't just that I wore someone else's, it's that I chose Finau's.

Whatever the beef is, I don't care. What I *do* care about is my dad seeing a shirtless Cooper Callahan in my hotel room, and the fact Cooper's bright idea to all of this is to ask him to *talk*. Cooper might've helped me back into the tank top, but I'm still feeling exposed. My stomach churns.

"Thank you, Brandon," Dad says. "I'll take it from here."

It's a dismissal, but Brandon stays put. Cooper raises an eyebrow, somehow looking cool and collected even though he's under a microscope like me, and says, "I don't know about you, but I'm pretty sure Coach told you to get lost."

"And miss the show?" Brandon drawls. "I can't believe you'd be such an idiot, Callahan. The coach's daughter?"

"This is how you get back at me for earning captain?" Cooper takes a step in his direction, his gaze dark. "Screw you for dragging Penny into this."

"Callahan," Dad says warningly. He turns to Brandon. "Finau. Leave before I sit you out of the next game."

Brandon's mouth drops open. "Why? I'm helping you!"

"And now you're done. Go."

Brandon glares at Cooper for half a second longer before taking his sorry ass to the elevator. I shrink back against the wall, hugging my arms to my stomach tightly. There's a dull ringing in my ears. I had nightmares about situations like this for a long time after the incident with Preston; I'd imagine Dad walking in on the moment everything fell to pieces. Sometimes he'd save me, but more often, he'd let me suffer the humiliation of his presence. Cooper wraps his arm around my shoulders. I turn into his chest, unable to look at my father.

"Sir," Cooper says, "Give us a minute to get more presentable, and then come in and we'll talk."

I peek at Dad. He has a funny expression on his face, like he's not sure what to think about this side of Cooper, but eventually he nods. Cooper shuts the door most of the way, then picks up his shirt, throwing it back on. He walks over to my suitcase and pulls out the sweatshirt I'd planned to sleep in.

"Thanks," I say as he holds it out to me. My voice sounds rusty, like I haven't used it in a while. "Can't believe I wore that fucking guy's sweater."

Once I get the sweatshirt on, I curl my hands into the floppy sleeves. Cooper smiles, like that's as adorable as the way Tangerine sits on the windowsill to watch for the mailman, and kisses me on the lips, feather-light. He tucks my hair behind my ear.

"It's going to be okay," he whispers.

I wish I could believe him, but I honestly don't know what Dad will think about this. Does the fact it's Cooper make it better or worse? Is he looking at this and feeling like I'm heading down the same road as before?

"I meant what I said," he adds. He kisses my forehead. "Come in, Coach."

Dad pushes open the door cautiously. "Bug. Are you okay?"

I untangle myself from Cooper. I don't want to sit on the bed—thankfully still made—so I back into a corner instead. "Yes. What did he tell you?"

Dad shuts the door behind us with a firm click. "He made it seem like you were up here with someone random. I'm sorry, honey. I just—I panicked." He frowns. "Although now I'm worried for an entirely different reason. What's going on here?"

"I'm trying to convince your daughter to date me," Cooper says. There's a hint of a challenge in his voice, like he's daring Dad to protest. If you didn't know him, you'd think he's relaxed right now, but I can see the tightness around his mouth. "I've been having a hell of a time of it."

"Penny doesn't date."

"I won't lie to you; we've had a thing going." I flush at the matter-of-fact note in his voice. That's one way to put our arrangement. "And if you don't like that, I don't care if you demote me from captain or bench me." He glances over at me, his gaze softening. "I just want a chance with her."

I bite my lip. I'm hot all over; I'm sure the blush I've been failing to contain over the past several minutes has taken on an even darker shade. Almost seeing Evan Bell naked has nothing on this. Cooper keeps looking at me, clearly wanting an answer, but I have no idea what to say. My feelings for him run deeper than anything I've ever experienced. I know where they're heading. But to put a label on this? To call Cooper Callahan my boyfriend? He'd only want it until he hears the truth about me, how broken I still am.

I open my mouth, but I don't know what I'm about to say. And then I'm saved from answering anyway, because I realize Dad is *crying*.

"Dad?" I hurry over, hovering anxiously. "Are you okay?"

"Goddamnit," he says, wiping at his eyes impatiently. "Goddamnit, Penelope."

I shrink away. My heart sinks to my belly. "This isn't like before. I promise."

He shakes his head. "After all this time, bug? You're still keeping things from me?"

"I didn't—"

"You still think I wouldn't support you?" He pinches the bridge of his nose, shuddering in another breath. "Did you really think I wouldn't support this?"

I've seen my dad cry more often than other daughters, I'm sure; between my mother and Preston, we've had a lot to cry about. But this feels different. Maybe it's because Cooper is in the room, looking between the two of us with concern. Whatever he thought was going to happen, it clearly wasn't this. My lip wobbles, but I swallow down the sob that threatens to escape. "I thought... I thought you wouldn't... respect me. That you'd think I'm taking a step back."

"I wouldn't think that."

"I didn't want things to fall apart again," I whisper.

Dad wipes at his eyes roughly. "Honey," he says, "I thought you trusted me. I thought we'd moved on."

"We did! And I didn't want to ruin that!"

"And yet you're keeping things from me again. Big things."

I bite down on the inside of my cheek. Maybe he's right. After his initial reaction to the situation with Preston, we had to work hard to get back to a place where we felt comfortable with each other. Despite the drama, he wasn't mad about the video; he was disappointed that I kept it from him until I had a breakdown and injured myself on the ice in my panic. And now, in trying to avoid making another mess, I did the same thing. Cooper reaches out his hand, and I take it gratefully, squeezing so hard I'm sure I'm cutting off his blood flow.

"You want me to go wait outside, sweetheart?" he asks. He has a fiercely protective look on his face, like he'd do anything to keep me safe. How did I ignore the real feelings brewing between us for so long? I'm sure if he thought I was in the slightest bit of danger, he'd defend me, even if it meant losing his spot on the team. I can't pretend that there's anything casual about that.

I shake my head. Maybe I still need to work up to where I'm ready for Cooper to hear the whole story—and when that happens, I'll be hoping the whole time that it's not the thing that drives him away—but he can stay for this. His support is a lifeline, made real by the way he's holding onto my hand.

"You're right," I tell Dad. I take in a shaky breath. "And I'm sorry."

"I just want you to be happy, bug." He glances down at our entwined hands, and I think I see a hint of a smile on his face. "Whatever that looks like, as long as you're safe."

"I am happy," I say quietly.

It shouldn't be, but it feels like a revelation. I'm happier than I've been in a long, long time—and Cooper is the reason. Ever since I asked him to hook up with me at the ice rink, he's been chipping away at the wards I put up around my heart long ago.

Once I put it like that, it's obvious. I have to take the leap, no matter how scared I am of falling onto the cold, slick ice. Cooper wants me to be his, and I want him to be mine. This isn't like before. He's been earning my trust, piece by piece, and even better, I *want* him to have it. Just like I want Dad to have mine, and to have his.

I lurch forward and hug my father. He hugs back, squeezing me so tightly I can barely breathe. He hasn't hugged me like this in such a long time, I'd nearly forgotten what it feels like.

"I am happy," I say again, and I'm crying harder now, but they're necessary tears. The tears that feel like a dose of medicine, not poison. "I'm sorry I didn't tell you. Cooper's right, we weren't really... dating, officially."

I look back at him. He's still standing there, entirely unselfconscious, a look in his eyes that I can't quite identify. When I smile tentatively, he gives me one of those lopsided grins that makes me want to kiss him senseless.

"But we are now."

42

PENNY

"YOU PROMISED YOU WOULDN'T LAUGH!"

"I'm not laughing at *you*."

"Oh, because it's so much better to laugh at my book." I flop down on my bed. Tangerine follows gracefully, settling atop my chest. With the dorms closed for the semester, I'm back at my dad's house. Thanks to an evening right before break that started out innocently—making out with our clothes mostly on counts as innocent where Cooper is concerned—but quickly turned filthier than a taboo romance, whenever I'm on this bed, I just think about beard burn and the rasp in his voice when he told me to come *one more time*. Case in point: we've spent half an hour talking about nothing, and my panties are damp.

"I'm not laughing at it either! I'm laughing with it. Because it's funny."

"Sure."

"You called the evil rival werewolf dude an impotent worm, Pen. Am I not supposed to laugh at that?"

I dangle a toy mouse in front of Tangy, one of the many toys of hers scattered across my room, but she just flicks her tail.

I don't regret giving Cooper my book to read, but it's still a little weird to know that Callum and Twyla, two characters who have existed almost entirely in my head and nowhere else, now belong to him too, on some level. When I finally added to it, now that we're on break, he demanded that I send him the new chapters immediately. "No, you were."

"Case in point."

I stick out my tongue, even though we're just talking on the phone and can't, unfortunately, see each other. "How has your break been so far?"

"The usual. Early morning runs with everyone minus Mom and Bex. Workout sessions to stay in shape. Watching hockey tape. Reading more of the romance novels you recommended, so I know how your twisted little mind works."

Now I'm glad that he can't see my blush. "You don't have to, you know."

"Oh, I do. I'm still your sex coach, Pen. I need to keep improving my technique." I can hear the amusement in his voice, and because apparently even that's enough to make a wave of desire wash over me, I press my legs together.

"I don't just read them for the sex," I protest.

"No, I know." He pauses, and I hear a rustling noise, like he's flipping through a paperback. "You read them because they make you happy. And that's sweet. They make me happy too. Who doesn't enjoy hearing about love?"

"Who knew you could be such a romantic?"

"I have to admit, it's a learning curve."

"You're a faster learner." I blush a little as I add, "I mean, you've been better than any book boyfriend so far."

After the Vermont game, we spent the last two weeks of the semester wrapped up in each other. *Dating.* Cooper took me to dinner as soon as we got back to McKee, and afterward, he made me sit on his face and called that his dessert. I studied for my finals on his bed while he wrote his papers at his desk, switching off between playing my music and his. We spent a memorable afternoon at an outdoor ice rink, showing off for the tourists, and another at Galactic Games, where he worked hard to win me the little stuffed bunny that's currently resting atop my pillow. We took turns sleeping over at each other's places, and because of the mini break in the season, my dad gave the guys leeway on the early morning practices, so more often than not, I woke up better rested than in literal years, wrapped up in the warm cocoon of Cooper's embrace.

Now it's almost Christmas, and while I love the holiday, I do *not* love the fact that he's on Long Island and I'm still in the Hudson Valley. Dad and I are planning to have our usual quiet Christmas—although now Tangerine is included in that, since I won custody of her for the break—and while it'll be nice, I'd rather be with Cooper. I even miss Sebastian and Izzy, too, since I've been seeing a lot of them. The day after classes ended, Mia and I came over for a dinner that Sebastian insisted upon cooking, completely with slightly burnt brownies courtesy of Izzy, and we kicked off the Christmas season with *Elf*.

"I miss you," I say, unable to keep the whine out of my voice. If we were in the same place right now, we'd be doing the horizontal tango. Preferably while trying out one of the new techniques he keeps reading about. We haven't had vaginal sex yet; that step still feels gigantic, but he's been supportive and not at all pushy, and we've had a lot of fun with anal. He stares at my ass so much, you'd think it was a freakin' Monet.

"I miss you too," he says. "Want to have phone sex?"

"God, I thought you'd never ask," I say breathlessly. "What should I be wearing this time?"

"Hmm, let's see."

"Penny," my dad calls. "Ready to go to dinner?"

Shoot. "Wait, sorry. I forgot I'm going out to dinner with my dad tonight."

Cooper groans over the line, and the sound is so fucking sexy it's torturous to say goodbye, but somehow, I manage. I change out of my sweatpants into jeans and a sweater, fresh panties included, plus these cute ankle boots Izzy convinced me to get at the mall the other day. We were supposed to be shopping for Christmas presents, but apparently Izzy's shopping philosophy is that you should always get something for yourself too, and I couldn't argue with that.

In the car, Dad glances at me, watching as I fiddle with the heater. It's freezing in the car, even wearing a thick pullover sweatshirt of Cooper's with the Rangers logo stitched on the front. I wish I brought a pair of gloves with me.

"How's Cooper doing?" he asks.

"He's good." I push past the slight awkwardness that's been hanging in the air between us since the Vermont game and add, "He's been watching that tape like you asked him to."

"Good, good." He drums his fingers on the steering wheel. "That sweatshirt his?"

"What gave it away?"

"I know my daughter, and she doesn't root for the Rangers."

I look down at my lap as I smile. "Fair point."

"Your mother used to steal my clothes." His voice sounds a little thick, the way it always does when he talks about Mom. "That Harvard sweatshirt looked better on her, anyway."

"I remember that sweatshirt."

"Eventually it got so frayed she only wore it when we cleaned the house on Saturday mornings. It was covered in so many bleach stains, the crimson washed out." He clears his throat. "Cooper... he's been good to you, bug?"

I bunch my hands up in the sleeves of the sweater. It smells like Cooper, that spicy masculine scent I love so much. "Yes."

"Thought he would be. He's a good kid." He pulls into one of the town's lots and finds a space for the car. Moorbridge is decorated for the holidays, lights hanging from the lampposts and elaborate displays in the shop windows. I bought Dad's Christmas present, a hand-stitched leather wallet, from a shop right around the corner. "But if anything happens, you'll tell me, right? I won't be mad."

I swallow; my throat feels thick suddenly. "I'll try."

Even though we're parked, he doesn't turn off the car. He turns to me instead, scrubbing a hand over his face. "I know it's different now," he says. "I know you're an adult, you can choose who you want to be with. But you're still my little girl, and I'll always be there for you."

"Dad?"

"Yeah?"

My heart is hammering in my chest. I've been avoiding this conversation as long as possible, but with grades coming out soon, there's nowhere to hide. "I know I didn't get my grades back yet, but... I'm going to fail chemistry. And probably microbiology, too."

He blinks. There's a long pause, and I shrink away, but eventually, he says, "That's okay, Pen. Let's talk about it over dinner."

43

COOPER

"FUCKING HELL, BABY." I fist my cock, giving it a slow stroke. Even over the phone, Penny's sweet little moans are driving me wild. I'm about to burst with need. "Tell me how many fingers you've got stuffed up that pretty pussy."

"Three," she says with a little gasp. "It's not enough."

There's actual pain in her voice, like she's beyond frustrated. I wish I could see her face, but she's skittish about sex over video, so we've been doing our catching up over the break via phone calls. I close my eyes, imagining her spread legs, her thin fingers shoved right up her tight cunt, aching for more. For a toy to fill her up, or even me, when we get to that number on her list. "Put your pinky in."

Her moan lets me know she did it, but she reports back to me breathlessly.

"Good girl," I praise her. "One day I'm going to fill up your cunt so perfectly, Red, I promise you'll feel it everywhere. Touch your clit for me."

She surprises me with laughter that shoots straight to my cock. "I can't get it like I want."

"Too bad, baby, because that's what you're getting right now. Come for me and I'll consider letting you use a toy."

"Letting me?" she teases. Her voice is high and breathy, but the challenge in it comes through loud and clear. "I could turn one on right now and you couldn't do a thing."

"Maybe not now," I agree, "but you know what I do to brats who don't listen."

"I don't know," she says. I can imagine her smirk. "Maybe I need you to remind me."

I still my hand, squeezing the base of my cock to keep from shooting my load too soon. I want to drag this out as long as possible; hear her have a few orgasms before I surrender to my own.

"Oh yeah?" I say. "You want it spelled out?"

"I need it," she whines.

Fucking hell, this girl is going to be the death of me. If we were in the same place right now, I'd be kissing her until I stole all the breath from her lungs.

"First, I'd take your clothes off," I say. My voice is rough now, low in volume, my eyes shut as I talk into the phone. I'm hiding away in my room; it's Christmas morning and we already did family presents, so no one should come looking unless they're trying to be obnoxious. James and Sebastian have teased me about my new girlfriend six ways to Sunday, but they know I need the catch-up time with my girl. I lick my lips, imagining pulling off Penny's clothes piece by piece, getting to see her beautiful body. Her sweet little tits, her round bottom, the soft stretch of her belly that I adore kissing. All the fucking freckles, the sea of them spread out over her fair skin. "Piece by fucking piece, so slow you're begging me to rip them. Then I'd put you over my lap because that's where brats belong, and just look."

"W-why?" she stutters.

"Because you're beautiful." I give my cock another stroke. The words stick in my throat, emotional without me trying, sweetness tempering the dirty talk. "Squirming in my lap, trying to give yourself relief—I love seeing you needy for me."

"What next?"

"You know what would be next, sweetheart. My palm, your bottom, and a work of art so fucking gorgeous I couldn't look away."

Her ragged breathing sounds like a sob. "Cooper."

"Yeah, gummy bear. That's my name. You still touching your clit like I said?"

"Yes."

"Good fucking girl. Crook your fingers, find your g-spot. Come for me as quick as you can." I swipe my thumb over the head of my cock, hissing; it's oversensitive and leaking pre-come all over my fingers. I won't push her for a picture, but I wish I could have one. She sobs for real, and my stomach clenches; I nearly climax, but manage to control myself. She sobs again, and I know she's coming by the way she's murmuring my name. My needy girl. Even in different parts of the fucking state, I can feel her need radiating like a physical presence.

I swallow back another funny rush of emotion. Even more than seeing her body right now, I want to see her face. Are her blue eyes glossy with tears? Is her brow furrowed? Is she wearing the little butterfly necklace that I like to suck on while my fingers work her deep?

"Use the toy, Pen. Any of them. Give me another."

"I'm so sensitive."

"You can do it," I murmur. I jerk myself faster now, building up a rhythm. Using a toy right after she just came will make her next orgasm quick, and I want to come when I hear those sweet cries in my ear again. "You were asking for something bigger, baby, this is it."

I hear a rustling sound, and then a buzz as the toy turns on. "I'm using Mark Antony," she says.

I can't help my laughter. "Aw, babe, and here I thought you were alone."

"Shut it," she says. She gasps like the breath was just punched out of her. I'd bet anything that she just pushed the dildo right into her sopping wet cunt. "Fuck, that feels good."

"Fuck yourself with it."

"Goddamn angle." There's more rustling, and then she says, "Okay, I'm on my hands and knees. It's easier like this."

I groan. "Now you're just torturing me."

"It's all the way in," she whispers. "I can feel it so deep, pulsing into me. But I don't want the vibrations when I know I can have you. One day, you'll be so warm and thick inside me, pressing me open. Making me take every inch of you. I won't even want to use a condom. I'll go on the pill so you can come inside me bare."

I turn my head to the side and bite down on my pillow to muffle my cry as I come into my fist. She's crying out too, no doubt climaxing again herself. I can't stop imagining the picture she just painted. I've never fucked a girl bare, never wanted to risk it, but it's different with Penny. When we take this step, I want it however she wants it, and if she wants me to spear her on my cock and come deep inside her, then that's what we'll do. I'm a goddamn lucky bastard.

"And I'll watch it drip out of you," I whisper back. "I'll eat it out of your soaked pussy and kiss you so you can taste us all mixed up. I'll be so fucking good to you, Red."

"I know, babe." The emotion in her voice makes my heart swell.

We stay on the phone, panting, for a few minutes, and

slowly, I feel myself come out of the orgasmic haze. My hand's a mess, so I grab a tissue from my nightstand and wipe it down. When my heart rate is back where it should be, I sit up against the pillows. "Make sure you go pee."

"I am now. I'll be back in a second."

"There's my girl."

In the meantime, I grab the present Penny sent to my house, still wrapped messily in paper with little ice-skating penguins on it, and take it to my bed. We decided to swap presents on Christmas Day instead of in advance, and I didn't want to take her away from her dad first thing in the morning, so we planned to do it later in the day, alone. That's why I hid in my room in the first place; we just got distracted by the phone sex. No regrets there.

When she comes back on the line, I say, "Want to FaceTime while we unwrap each other's presents?"

"Ooh, yes. Wait, give me a second. I have a surprise for you."

After a moment, she calls me. When I pick up, she's sitting on her bed, her hair hanging loose around her shoulders. She is wearing the butterfly necklace, but I only register that for half a second before I get distracted by the hockey sweater she's wearing.

Mine.

A fucking tsunami of possessiveness rushes through me. I've imagined what she'd look like in my sweater, but this is even better; she looks good enough to devour. She looks down at her chest, smiling as she plucks at the laces. "Dad got it for me. Had it wrapped under the tree and everything."

"Seriously?"

She looks at me. Even through the tiny phone screen, I'm taken away by her smile. "He really loves that we're together. I can't believe I was so worried about his reaction."

"I know I don't know the whole story, but I'm sure you had a good reason."

"Yeah, well." She turns around, showing off the back; my name is stitched above the #24. It's our home jersey, deep purple with white lettering. It looks incredible on her, but I'm already itchy for the moment we're back together and I can take it off. This one I won't rip, even if I'm dying to get a glimpse of her tits. Coach might've done it to show his support, but I'm sure when he bought it, he didn't think about me fantasizing about Penny wearing it as she straddles my lap. "Just so you know, I'm not wearing anything else right now."

I groan. Even though the orgasm wrung me out, I feel a flicker of heat in my lower belly. "There you go again. Torturing me. On *Christmas*."

"I know, I know." She grins. "It's just so easy, babe."

"Penny, it looks like a kindergartener wrapped this present."

"I was going to say, did you have this professionally done?" She holds up my present to her. The edges are crisp, the red bow still tied to perfection atop the silver wrapping paper.

"I'm just a beast at wrapping presents."

"I wouldn't have guessed this about you."

"I've been wrapping my siblings' presents since I was in middle school." I shake Penny's gift, but it doesn't rattle or anything. The shape would indicate a book, but I can't remember if I mentioned wanting to read anything specific before we left for break. "It's my most useless skill."

"No way, that's not useless. You're going to have the best time playing Santa for your kids."

I snap my head up. Penny is still looking into the camera, but a blush has erupted over her face like wildfire.

"I mean, your eventual kids," she rambles. "If you even want kids. God, I mean... yeah."

"Hell yeah, I want kids." I wet my bottom lip; now I can't stop thinking about Penny with a little red-haired baby in her arms. I haven't given much thought to children beyond knowing that one day I'd like to have a family, but that doesn't mean the fantasy isn't appealing. I'm not planning on giving up Penny unless I'm physically forced to, so maybe that's in our future. "Not anytime soon, though."

"Definitely not. Breeding kink is hot, but being pregnant? Horrifying."

I snort out a laugh. "Want to open the presents at the same time?"

"Totally." She unties the bow on hers while I tear at the wrapping paper on mine. "I hope you like it. But if you don't, I won't be offended."

"Same here." I scrub my hand over my beard, freshly trimmed because Mom insisted upon it for the family Christmas photo. "And if you've read it already, tell me and I'll take you to the bookstore as soon as I get back to Moorbridge. Hell, I'll take you anyway. Make it a date."

She smiles as she tears off the rest of the wrapping paper. "I'd like that." Then she gasps, holding up the book. "Cooper! I love this series!"

"Aw, shit, you've read it?"

"No, this is amazing! I've never seen this version before." She flips through the pages. "And it's signed? With swag? Holy crap."

She sets the first one aside carefully and picks up the next. When I saw the special edition covers of this fantasy romance series, I figured it would be her thing. She doesn't like hardcovers, so I was able to get all four books in paperback. When the author heard I was buying them for my girlfriend, she threw in some stickers and a candle that apparently smells like the scent of the love interest, a demon prince guy.

"Cooper, I love special editions." She hugs the books to her chest, breathing in the smell. "And this series is so fun. I didn't have paperbacks of it, so it's perfect! I'm going to reread them all. Maybe it'll help me get out of my writer's block with the thing I'm working on."

I smile. I love hitting the nail on the head with gifts. "Good, I'm glad. I'll need to read them."

"I think you'd like it. There's a whole war in this series, plus lots of magical creatures." She bounces on the bed. "You haven't opened yours yet."

I tear off the rest of the wrapping paper. The lumpiness makes sense when I see she grouped two books with a couple rolls of grip tape for my stick. "Oh, wow."

"I checked with Dad to make sure the tape was a good brand," she says. "But I thought it was so cool."

The tape is red, with the Targaryen House seal printed on it in black. "This is awesome. Thanks, Red." I set it aside and look at the books. One is *The Simarillion*, which I haven't read yet, and a Brandon Sanderson novel that I have, but not since I was in high school. "And these look awesome. You totally killed it. I needed something new to read, I finished all the books you recommended."

"That might've been the sexiest thing you've ever said to me."

"Clearly I need to up my game," I say dryly.

She curls against her pillows, balancing the phone so I'm seeing only half of her face. "Tell me how Christmas has been for you. Did you win the Monopoly game?"

I scowl. "Sebastian cheated. I don't know how yet, but when I do, he's a dead man."

As if I summoned him, there's a knock on my door. "Bro," Seb says, "we're starting *Christmas Vacation*. I thought you wouldn't want to miss it."

"Ooh, I love that one," says Penny. "Young Chevy Chase could get it."

"I'm going to ignore that," I say. "Come in, dude. Say hi to Penny."

Sebastian walks inside. He's still in his pajamas—Mom got us all matching Christmas pajamas and insisted upon taking the portrait in front of the tree in the den, which Bex was only too happy to facilitate—and his hair looks messy, like he just woke up from a nap. He yawns, scratching at his shirt. "All finished doing the nasty?"

"We were opening our Christmas presents, asshole."

"After a long-distance hookup, I'm sure." He flops onto my bed, waving at Penny. "Hey, Pen. That jersey looks good on you."

"It's a sweater," I mutter.

"Thanks," she says, waving back. "Cooper thinks you cheated at Monopoly."

He raises an eyebrow. "If anyone cheated, it was Bex."

My mouth drops open. "No way."

"James and Bex totally teamed up to sabotage us."

"*What?* James doesn't accept alliances when it comes to games."

"She has him wrapped around her finger." Sebastian shakes his head. "And now you. When Izzy gets a boyfriend, I'll be toast."

"Aw, someone will be able to stand looking at your ugly mug eventually."

Seb flips me the bird, yawning again. "Jesus, I'm hungover. The second bottle of Bailey's was a bad idea. Izzy's still tuckered out on the couch."

"She'll perk up once the movie starts." I stifle a yawn. I'm not all that hungover, but I could use a nap at some point. "I'll be down in a few."

"Sounds good. Merry Christmas, Penny."

"Merry Christmas, Seb. Tell Izzy I said hi."

When he's gone, I turn back to my phone. "What have you got planned for the rest of the day? Want to watch *Christmas Vacation* with us? We can text each other reactions. I cry every time he's in the attic watching the home movies and I'm not ashamed to admit it."

Her smile widens. "That sounds perfect. Let me just grab some hot chocolate and see if Dad wants to watch it too."

44

COOPER

ON MY WAY DOWNSTAIRS, I run into my father. It's petty, but I've mostly ignored him over the break. He hasn't tried to explain why he left the UMass game early—because he never came back after he took that call, Mom just said he had business to take care of—and I haven't asked for one. I figured that after he acted like nothing had happened over Thanksgiving, I wasn't about to get more answers at Christmas. I eye him warily as he claps his hand on my shoulder.

"There you are," he says. "Come into my office for a few."

"We're about to watch a movie."

"I know. This'll only take a moment."

I text Penny not to start the movie without me and follow Dad to his office. The room is a certain brand of oppressiveness; the football-related memorabilia, especially the locked case with the Super Bowl rings, dominates the space. I half expect him to sit down at his mahogany desk, but he remains standing, frowning as he looks at his bookcases. Even in tapered sweatpants and a sweater with a Christmas tree on the front, he looks formidable. I stand up straight and resist the urge to flee for the safety of the den, where I'm sure Izzy is complaining about being woken up from her nap and James is doing something adorable with Bex, like feed her a sugar cookie in little nibbles. I'd rather that than this awkwardness.

He looks at me. "Feeling good about your grades?"

I just nod. It took a lot of all-nighters to finish my final essays, but I managed. Penny, not so much. I resist the urge to wince as I think about it. She finally talked to her dad about switching up what she's studying, and at least the way she tells it, he's supportive, but that doesn't mean she feels good about failing half her classes.

"Good, good." He rubs at his chin. "Has anything been going on?"

"What do you mean?"

"Not—the girlfriend," he says. "Although I was surprised to hear about that from your sister."

"Her name is Penny. You met her at the game. If you paid attention."

"Yes, Cooper, I remember her," he says dryly. "Ryder's daughter, huh?"

"He knows."

He nods, quiet for a moment, apparently needing time to digest the fact I'm dating someone. The news surprised Mom too, but she got over that quickly and bombarded me with a million questions about her. She's already made me promise to bring Penny along as my date to her and Dad's foundation gala in March. Dad, meanwhile, looks like I just told him I eloped with a girl I met five seconds ago.

"Your uncle hasn't been in touch, has he?" he asks.

Uncle Blake. My heart leaps into my throat. "Should he have been?"

"No." He sighs as he walks to the desk. As he picks up one photograph atop it—I know just the one, it's of him and Uncle

Blake as children at Robert Moses, a beach on the south shore of Long Island—he shakes his head. "But has he been?"

"No."

He takes in a breath. "That's good. If he does, tell me, Coop, okay?"

"Is he back in town?"

"Possibly." He sets the photograph down and turns his gaze on me. "I know you miss him, but the situation is complicated."

"Complicated how?"

"I don't know all the details yet. But I don't want you to get hurt."

I take a step back. It's no secret that my dad has never handled Uncle Blake's problems well, but the thought that he'd hurt me is laughable. Having issues staying sober doesn't mean you're violent, or whatever he thinks. "He wouldn't do that."

"Son—"

"No, screw that." I stride to the door. "I don't know why you can't just accept that he has problems. It's not like he's an axe murderer."

"I never said that."

"But you implied it. You're refusing to help him—"

"You don't know what I've done for my brother." He takes a step closer. "You don't know the whole story."

"I know enough. You're the one who drove him away to California. Don't you want him back?"

"Yes," he snaps. "I want my brother back in my life. But you're my son, and my responsibility, and until I figure things out, if he tries to get in touch, you're going to tell me right away."

I bite back the harsh words I want to hurl in his direction and pull open the door, making sure it slams behind me. I've slammed this door so many times, I feel like a seventeen-year-old again, done being shouted at for sneaking out, for buying my truck without Dad's permission, for getting suspended from school because of a fight, for dozens of reasons. Before today, the last time I slammed it, we'd just finished arguing about whether I'd enter the draft. I'm the one who always breaks first, the one who slams the door shut. He always gets his way. He always wins.

I pull out my phone, not to text Penny—although I have one waiting from her—but to call my uncle.

I'm an adult. If he's back in town, Dad can't stop me from seeing him. And after that, I'm sure as hell not going to tell him we're in touch. If he has his way, he'll send him to another continent this time, and then I'd never see him again.

The number goes to voicemail. I push past the disappointment and start talking the second the record button beeps. "Hey, Uncle Blake. It's Cooper. I heard that you're back in town. I'm still at McKee. If you want to meet up or anything, just call me back. Thanks."

45

PENNY

"ALL RIGHT, Ms. Ryder. You're all set."

I smile at Nicole, one of the women who works at the registrar's office at McKee. She's about the age my mother would have been now, her bleach-blonde hair pulled back into a bun. Her blouse is a seriously bright shade of pink, and her long nails match. I'm not sure how she types with them, but she was way faster than I am on my laptop. "Thanks so much."

"Congratulations. It's a big deal, declaring your major. And you should have enough time to make up everything you need even without getting those credits from last semester, but if not, we can always discuss options for continuation. It's always easier to work on the one you declared from the start instead of switching."

I nod, holding the sheet of paper—official approval of a major in English—close to my chest.

"Hockey fan?" She gestures to the sweater I'm wearing, giving me a smile.

It's a good thing it's January, because all I want to do is wear Cooper's hockey sweater. Lately, whenever I'm wearing it at The Purple Kettle or one of the other communal spaces on campus, a girl who must have the hots for Cooper gives me a dirty look. The best times are when we're together and he kisses me; I can't deny I get satisfaction out of setting the record straight. He might've been one of the biggest players on campus, but now he's mine.

"It's my boyfriend's." My heart skips a beat at my own words. I don't think I'll ever get tired of calling Cooper that. "He's on the team."

"I should have recognized the last name," she says. "You're Coach Ryder's daughter."

I tuck my hair behind my ear. "Yep."

"My husband loves hockey. He plays in a beer league in Pine Ridge." She laughs a little, leaning over the desk. "He's terrible, but I go to see him anyway. Good luck with everything, hon. Let me know if you need help."

On the way out of the building, freezing air smacks me in the face, but I don't care. I fold the piece of paper, carefully tuck it in my bag, and text Dad that I'm all squared away. Admitting to him I failed two of my classes—despite trying my best, which is the especially depressing part—was awful, but he ended up being supportive. Maybe he's just relieved that I'm trying hard not to keep anything important from him, but he's even been excited, if bemused, about the romance novel I'm kind-of-sort-of writing. Aside from him, Cooper and Mia are the only ones who know, and I intend to keep it that way until it's finished.

I send Cooper a text as well. He's in a nonfiction seminar all afternoon, but judging by his recap of the first meeting last week, it's fall-asleep-on-the-desk boring, so I'm sure he's checking his phone from time to time. I'm right; before I make it to the building for American Literature I, he sends back a row of exclamation marks.

COOPER

!!!!!!!!!!!!!!!!!

I'm really excited

I mean, I have no idea what to do with an English degree

But right now I don't care

I know what you're going to do. You're going to be a kick-ass author

I chose English as my major because I like to read and it sounded pretty impractical to me, which was perfect, since my dad wouldn't budge on the whole college thing

But it's really not. It helps you learn how to think, and how to communicate, and how to appreciate art

It helps build empathy

Even for the loser sitting next to you in class eating the most disgusting sandwich ever

Help me, Red

It might be entirely onions

You know, that was beautiful up until it wasn't

I have to go to American Lit I

You're taking it with Stanwick, right?

Yeah

Sweet, enjoy

I have my period so fingers crossed I don't have a cramp attack

I CURL into the smallest ball I can manage and let out a moan.

My period did me the favor of not being a bitch while I was in class—and it was a super interesting class, all about colonial period literature—but now, it feels like someone is stapling me with a nail gun from inside my uterus. Cooper will be here any moment, and I'm in an ugly old pair of sweatpants, a long-sleeved shirt that says, 'Holy Salchow' on it—a Christmas present from Mia—and fuzzy socks. A distant part of me thinks I should at least brush my hair before he gets here, but that would require moving, and nothing sounds worse.

"You okay in there?" Mia calls.

"I think I'm dying."

She pokes her head into my room. "You're not dying."

"I don't know, I think I might be bleeding out." Another cramp hits me; it feels like someone has my lower back caught in a vise. "If this is the end, make sure Tangerine remembers me as the one who gave her more snacks."

"Is she okay?" I hear Cooper ask.

"No," says Mia. "But at least it's physical pain. My periods turn me into a raging bitch."

Cooper comes into the room, a plastic bag dangling from one hand. His gear bag is slung over his shoulder; he texted to say he was coming from practice. By now, I'm used to seeing his beard just a touch longer because it's winter, but it makes desire jolt through me. I press my legs together; even with the cramps, my body is aching with need. He glances over his shoulder, brow furrowed.

"Was she making a joke?" he asks. "I sort of assumed that bitchiness was her default state."

"I heard that!" Mia shouts from her room.

"Like you're not proud of that!" Cooper calls back.

I snort out a laugh, burying my head in my pillow. "Be grateful my anti-anxiety meds keep things steady."

"I'm grateful for anything that helps you." He sits down next to me on the bed, his hand settling on my shoulder, and rummages around in the plastic bag. "I brought some reinforcements."

He pulls out a heating pad, the tampons and pads I asked him to pick up on the way over, and best of all, gummy bears. I rip open the package and breathe in the sugary scent. "Is the package new because I complained that your gear bag was too smelly to store my precious gummy bears in?"

He rolls his eyes. "It's not too bad."

"It smells like an armpit. A gigantic one." I wrinkle my nose as I chew.

"Well, it's not too bad now. I got a gym bag deodorizer, and it's working." He leans down and unzips the little side pocket he keeps snacks in—AKA gummy bears for me and protein bars for him—and pulls out a plastic bag. "Also, I've been putting them in here. A double layer of stink protection."

I'm about to think of a snarky comeback, even if it is adorable that he's trying to make the bag less gross just for me, when a cramp makes me grit my teeth, doubling over. Cooper is there right away, pulling me into his arms. He sets the gummy bear package on my nightstand and smooths my hair away from my forehead. "Oh, sweetheart."

"It's just... fuck. It hurts."

"Yeah. It's okay, I've got you. Want the heating pad?"

I shake my head. "Could you maybe..." I trail off, flushing. He's done enough already. There's a difference between gingerly fingering myself because it helps with the cramps and asking *him* to ride the red tide.

He works his hand underneath my shirt and rubs my belly. I groan, turning my face into his neck. He smells clean, with hints of cinnamon—his masculine, almost spicy cologne. I bite down gently, and he huffs out a little laugh. He keeps on massaging my skin as he kisses the top of my head. "Could I do what, Red?"

"I'm too gross."

"You're never too gross."

I squint at him. "You know, I poop and everything."

He laughs. "You know, I heard something about girls doing that. So weird."

"Okay, if I'm not gross, what I want to ask you is."

He traces around the birth mark next to my belly button. "You want me to give you an orgasm."

I bury my face against his chest. "You don't have to."

"Fuck, have to? I want to. It helps, doesn't it? With the cramps?"

"Usually, yes."

He pats my belly. "Give me a second. I'll find a towel, so we don't have to wash the sheets."

As he sits up, I give him another squinty look. I'm not even sure how this happened, but I have Cooper's devotion, and I think if I asked him to do just about anything, he'd at least consider it. But this doesn't fall under the umbrella of normal boyfriend duties, as far as I know, and I don't want him to get grossed out and then decide he's not attracted to me anymore.

All of which tumbles out of my mouth in a big jumble. He just raises an eyebrow when I finish rambling. "Sweetheart, there's literally nothing that could make me stop being attracted to you." He flashes me a grin and adds, "You know I like when things get messy."

46

PENNY

I FLOP AGAINST THE BED. This is going to be the best period orgasm ever or a total disaster, and while I hope it's the former, the latter seems more likely.

Cooper comes back with a towel and spreads it over the bed. Then he coaxes me out of the ball I've curled into once more, with gummy bears as a bribe. "Do you want all your clothes off?" he asks as I shove a couple into my mouth.

"Just my bottoms, I think," I say when I've swallowed.

He pulls off his sweatshirt and jeans, so he's just in a t-shirt and underwear, then settles on his side next to me in the bed. It's a tight fit, given the fact it's just a twin, but we've made it work plenty of times already. He leans over and kisses me.

"Lift your hips for me, sweetheart."

My face feels like it's literally aflame as he pulls down my sweatpants and panties. I press my legs together, but he just curls his hand over my thigh. "Let me see. Want me to just touch your clit and keep the tampon in? Or should we take it out so I can finger you?"

"I want your fingers," I admit. "I can always run to the bathroom and take it out."

He kisses me again, softly, and reaches between my legs. "I've got it."

I tense as he pulls on the tampon string. He goes slowly, kissing me all the while, and I've never given much thought to whether this would be sexy or just plain awkward, but somehow, he manages to make it the former. Maybe it's the fact he's man enough not to be embarrassed or grossed out, or maybe it's the way he strokes my hair as he looks down at me. I'd swear there's love in his eyes, but I'm probably imagining it. He replaces the tampon with two fingers; I gasp against his mouth. He bites down on my lip, as gentle as the way he's fingering me, and gives my clit a long, sensual stroke.

"Talk to me," he murmurs. "Is this good?"

I nod, then remember my voice. "Yeah. I feel really... full."

"Good." He curls his fingers, making me cry out. I swear, his fingers are like magic; he knows exactly how to hit my g-spot. He keeps working my clit with his thumb, and soon I'm trembling, unable to hold back the whimpers.

"Shh," he says. "I've got you. You're such a good girl, Penny, letting me take care of you."

I sniffle. I don't deserve this, but I'm going to ride it as long as he's willing to give it.

"Cooper." I reach my arms up around his neck, pulling him into another kiss. "Babe, I need..."

"Tell me, gorgeous girl. Tell me and I'll give it to you."

Tears leak out of the corners of my eyes. Maybe my period is making me more emotional than usual, but how can I not react to words like that, said so quietly they couldn't be for anyone but me if they tried? I kiss him so hard our teeth scrape together, but he gives as good as he gets—and understands what I wanted anyway, a third finger, stretching me in the most delicious of ways. I buck my hips, seeking just a little more contact, a little more friction, and he rewards me by rubbing my clit faster. Orgasms always come quickly when I'm on my period, and it doesn't take long at all before I bite down on his shoulder, riding out a climax that has me shaking. He jerks when I bite him, laughing against my hair, and the sound goes straight to my core.

"Fucking hell, Red." He keeps moving his fingers inside me, pressing his lips to my temple. "Can you give me one more?"

"Not sure," I say with another gasp.

"I think you can." He looks down at me; from this angle and the low lighting, his eyes look like the sky before nightfall. I blink, holding his gaze. There's an almost feral glint in his eyes, like he's looking at the sexiest woman he's ever seen, and his voice has that rough edge to it that I've noticed when he's about to come. "Relax and let go for me."

I break apart while looking at him, while tears slip down my cheeks, while my heart races in my chest. The orgasm roars through me, stronger than the first, and I think I shout his name, but I can't hear myself over the buzzing in my ears. I think, distantly, that Mia better be wearing headphones, and that makes me giggle.

He pinches my thigh. "What's got you laughing so hard?"

"Just Mia. I hope her music is loud."

He pulls his fingers out carefully, like with the tampon, and wipes them on the towel. The embarrassment rushes back when I see how messy I made him, but he shakes his head at my blush. "None of that. I came, you know that? Came in my pants like I'm fourteen again and watching porn on my phone under the covers."

I choke on my laughter. "No fucking way."

We clean up together; not for the first time, I'm grateful for the private bathroom. The cramps haven't gone away entirely, but they're less vicious than before. Cooper insists on carrying me from the bathroom back to bed. He settles me underneath the covers, turns on the heating pad, gives me the gummy bears and my water bottle, and finally climbs in beside me, balancing his laptop on his stomach.

"Something weird happened earlier," he says as he queues up the comfort movie I requested, *The Princess Bride*. He's never seen it, and I just know he's going to get a kick out of Wallace Shawn's character's exclamations of 'inconceivable!'

"Weird how?"

"Remember how I left my uncle that voicemail?"

"Yeah."

"I think I saw him."

I pause with a gummy bear halfway to my mouth. "What do you mean, you saw him? He didn't call you back?"

"No, he hasn't said anything, but he was sitting in the stands during practice. Left before I could get a closer look." He shakes his head. "At least, I thought it was him. I don't get why he'd just drop by suddenly without saying a word."

"Maybe your dad knows he was there?"

He snorts. "Hell, if he does, he's actively plotting how to get him back across the country."

I cuddle against him, and he puts his arm around me. "I hope it is him. I know you miss him."

He just nods, pressing play on the movie. "I'd rather have him around than my father, I'll tell you that."

47

COOPER

I CHECK my phone for the time before sliding it into my pocket. Penny and I are both in the English building on Thursday afternoons, but my seminar ends half an hour before her creative writing class. Even though the end of January has been wet and miserable so far and I stepped in a puddle of half-melted ice earlier, I can't stop smiling. As soon as she comes out of the building, I'm going to surprise her with a trip to the bookstore.

Maybe for other girls, you get her flowers or chocolate or trips to the spa. I know what my girl likes, though, and that's books instead of flowers, gummy bears instead of chocolate, and semi-public orgasms instead of spa treatments.

Fuck, I'm grinning like an absolute asshole. I used to tease James about it, but now I get it. You have the girl you need in your life, and it feels like anything is possible. We're deep into the season now, where every game counts just a little bit more, but I'm relaxed. Aside from the fact that UMass is ahead of us by a game and Dad and I haven't spoken since Christmas, life is good. Penny's my redheaded angel, and if not for the fact I know I wouldn't want a relationship with anyone but her, I can't believe I went almost twenty-one years before experiencing what it feels like to be able to call a girl mine.

She's practically skipping on her way out of the building as she chats with a classmate, but as soon as she sees me, she runs into my arms and jumps. I catch her weight easily, making her laugh against my lips as she graces me with a kiss. She's warm from being inside a toasty classroom for over an hour. I kiss her back for a couple of seconds before setting her down.

"What are you doing here?" she says. "Thought you had practice."

"I've got about two hours before I need to be at the rink." I clap a gloved hand atop her head. "Figured that's enough time for the surprise I have planned."

Her grin lights up her entire face. "A surprise?"

"You have the time?"

"For you, always." She takes my hand as we start down the sidewalk. "What is it?"

"Don't you know how surprises work?"

She keeps begging me for hints the whole walk over. One of the nice things about McKee is that Moorbridge is entwined with the campus, so you can hop around both without always needing to get in the car. We could have taken the bus; it's chilly out, with piles of snow on either side of the sidewalk and ice melt crunching underneath our shoes, but it feels pleasant with her by my side.

She realizes I'm heading for Book Magic when we turn the corner onto Main Street, and she starts skipping for real, practically dragging me to the entrance. I stop her just before she runs inside, though, and say, "Here are the rules."

She pouts, those big blue eyes fluttering. "Rules?"

"Well, one rule," I amend. I'm going to enjoy the fuck out of this. "Whatever you want, I'm buying."

A slow smile works its way over her face. "Whatever I want?"

"Anything."

"Wow," she breathes. "This is better than sex."

"Well," I say, "not better, but—"

"Bye!" She pushes open the door and runs inside before I can finish my sentence.

I follow, shaking my head, but I can't stop smiling. She might think that a trip to the indie bookstore in town is better than getting down to business, but I'll change her mind later. I've been dying to come on her tits again, and I know my dirty girl won't say no to that.

I find her in the romance section, which I was expecting; she already has three books tucked under her arm. She beams at me in a way that makes my chest hurt, and I can't help but cup her face with both my hands and tilt it up for a kiss. Her lips are just a little chapped and cold, and I have this unstoppable urge to look around the store until I see someone and introduce Penny as my girl.

When we break apart, the mischievous look on her face is gone. She just looks happy. I still don't know what happened in her past that sometimes makes her shy away from me, but I hope she's realizing that whatever it is, I'm not going anywhere.

And then I do spot someone, a woman a couple years older than us, wearing a Book Magic t-shirt. Her black-framed glasses, plus the curly brown hair, give her an owlish look. She nods at the book at the top of Penny's stack. "That one is great."

"Oh, awesome," she says. "I don't read that much historical romance, but it's been on my list for a while."

The woman nods as she straightens a display. "When you finish it, come in and tell me what you thought. It's my favorite in the series—Miles is such a wonderful hero."

"She's writing a book," I say, gesturing to Penny. "My girlfriend. It's seriously good."

"Cooper," she says, blushing.

"What?" I say. "It is, and I read so you know I'm not lying. It's a romance novel."

The woman gives us an interested look. "We have a creative writing group that meets here twice a month," she says. "Do you go to McKee? You could join us."

"Um, I'd..." Penny gives me a wild-eyed look.

"She'd love to," I finish.

She blushes deeper, but says, "That sounds amazing, I really would love to. When's the next meeting?"

I leave Penny to chat with Monica—the woman introduces herself as we keep talking—and wander to the fantasy section. I pick out a couple books for myself, then snag a copy of *Daisy Miller*, which I need for my Modernism class. By the time I meet Penny at the register, she has ten books in her arms and is chatting with Monica like they're old friends.

"I'll email you the first chapter tonight," Penny says as I take the books out of her arms. She reaches up to kiss my cheek. "Thanks, babe."

Monica steps around the counter to do the checkout. "He supports your writing *and* he's buying? Make sure you keep this one."

48

PENNY

January 28th

> She loved it

COOP

Red!!

That's awesome

> I know! I can't believe it

Well, I can. It's a damn good book

> I'm excited to go to the writing group

Want me to meet you in town when you're finished? We could go out for a late dinner

> That sounds nice

You still need to come to my dad's for dinner. He keeps asking me about it, like you don't see him more than I do

What about this weekend? We can bring
Tangy over

> He loves her so much. It's convincing him to
> get another cat

You should go to the shelter with him to pick
one out

February 1st

COOP

When I suggested the shelter thing, I didn't
mean literally

> I know, it's wild

> I barely got the sentence out of my mouth
> before he grabbed his car keys

What's its name?

> His name is Gretzky

Adorable

> I like our daughter better <3

> But he's sweet

> Apparently Nikki likes cats too

Still going strong?

> I guess?

Still cool with it?

> I want him to be happy

February 3rd

COOP

?!

We're in the same room, babe

I know, but you look so peaceful with your headphones on

So you thought this was the perfect time to drag me out of the zone?

I know you're writing about very important fictional smutty goodness

But I'm just saying, if you need someone to act out scenes with, I'm right here

And super bored

Actually, I'm writing a battle scene

Oh???

Of course /that's/ what gets you excited

I literally have a sword tattooed on my body

Just get over here and kiss me

49

COOPER

THERE HE IS AGAIN.

He's sitting in the stands, watching the practice from the shadows. I've made a couple mistakes during our drills because I can't stop staring. Black leather jacket, Yankees cap pulled low over his face, plenty of scruff—it's my Uncle Blake.

But what the hell is he doing here? Watching me skate like I'm five again and on my first pee wee team, all without even a text to let me know he's in town?

Evan squints at him when I point him out. "Are you sure?" he says. "He's your uncle?"

"Yeah. Don't know why he couldn't just text." I clap Evan on the shoulder. "I'm going to go ask Coach if I can take a break to talk to him."

"Whatever Cooper wants, Cooper gets," Brandon mocks as I skate by. "I guess that's how it is when you've put your dick in—"

I skate back around to him. "You want to finish that sentence?" I lean in, glancing over at Coach deliberately before settling my gaze on Brandon. "Because if I need to kick your ass, I will. And then I'll tell Coach exactly who dared disrespect his daughter."

Brandon swallows but doesn't say another word.

"That's what I thought." I shake my head. "Watch your fucking mouth. And next time you see Penny, you're going to apologize for that stunt you pulled in Vermont. You understand?"

His expression wavers, like he's considering telling me to fuck off. I just raise an eyebrow.

"Fine," he snaps.

Coach gives me permission to talk to Uncle Blake—at least I hope it's him, because if not, this will be awkward—so I head up the stairs. When I get to the row he's sitting in, he raises his hand into a little wave.

If I wasn't sure before, I am now: it's my uncle. A little older, a little more worn looking, but definitely him.

"Hey, Cooper," he says as I sit down next to him on the bench. It's casual as anything, like I just saw him last week for Sunday dinner.

"Uncle Blake." I accept his sideways hug. He smells like cigarette smoke and cheap soap, but that's familiar when it comes to him. "What are you doing here? I called you."

"Business brought me back to New York," he says. "Thought I'd see my nephews, and Eagles tickets are too damn expensive."

My face falls. Of course, he's hoping to see James. Everyone always does. "You can just ask him for tickets," I say coldly. "I've got practice."

He reaches out and punches me in the arm before I can get up. "Just kidding, Coop. Thought you knew how to take a joke. Sorry I didn't respond to your message, I thought this would be easier."

I bite the inside of my cheek. "What's going on? Are you okay?"

"I just want to catch up, like you. Maybe I could take you out for dinner? When you're finished, of course."

I raise my eyebrows. "Um, sure?"

"Birthday's soon, right?" he says. "Call it a gift."

It's been so long since I've seen him, I'm almost surprised he remembers. He hasn't been in town since I was seventeen, and that was only for a short time before he went away to rehab again. I wonder if he's clean, then feel guilty for thinking it. He's doing his best, I'm sure, and he mentioned getting dinner, not a drink. Dad is the one who's judgmental about him and his struggles, and if there's anyone I *don't* want to be like, it's him.

"Thanks." I look down at the ice, where the team is still practicing. Coach Ryder blows his whistle, and the boys stop, giving him their attention. "I'll get changed."

"Atta boy." He slaps me on the back before he gets up. "I'm excited to see what my favorite nephew has been up to."

When practice ends, I change as quickly as I can, say goodbye to the guys and Coach Ryder, and book it. Part of me, a tiny little irrational part, wonders if Uncle Blake will be gone, but he's leaning against the building, having a smoke. Wintertime means the sun has already slipped below the horizon, but an overhead light illuminates him, making the black leather of his jacket shine.

When he sees me, his eyes light up. They're like mine—like Dad's—that deep blue. Callahan blue, my mother used to tease. She's always been nicer when she talks about Uncle Blake, even though she's not the one related to him.

"Know anywhere good around here to grab a bite?" he asks.

"Pizza okay?"

"Come on, kid. I can do better for your twenty-first birthday."

"There's a good burger place not too far away." I hitch my bag onto my shoulder. "Did you drive here?"

He scrubs his hand through his hair. "Had a buddy drop me off."

"No problem," I say, rummaging around in my pocket for my keys as we cross the parking lot. "Remember that truck I bought after saving all summer? Last time you were in town? I've been working on it this whole time."

"Really?"

"Yeah. It runs great now." I run my hand over the glossy black hood before hopping inside. "Sweet, right?"

Uncle Blake settles into the passenger seat. "I'm sure Rich loves this."

"It's been a sore spot," I say cheerfully. "He wanted to get me a Range Rover like James, but I prefer this."

"See, you and me, we're the same," he says. "There are Richards and Jameses. Blakes and Coopers."

I glance at him. "That's one way to put it."

He gives me a half-smile. "Tell me what's up with you, kid. I know I haven't exactly been around. But I'm clean and sober."

My heart swells in my chest. "I'm glad."

"Took a while to get back on my feet and make it stick, but I'm here."

I make a left; I know how to get to this restaurant in my sleep. I've lost count of the amount of times Sebastian and I have made late-night burger runs through the drive-through window. The shakes are the perfect consistency. I probably shouldn't have one, but it's not like I can try to use my fake ID one more time to order a beer in front of Uncle Blake.

"I'm good," I say. "Season's been going well. I'm... I'm team captain."

"There's the Cooper I remember." He smacks his palms together. "I suppose it makes up for missing out on the draft."

My breath sticks in my throat. "Yeah. Mostly." I pull into the parking lot. On a random weeknight in February, it's not too crowded, just a couple of other cars in the lot. "It's fine, I love my team and I'm really improving."

"There's no need to be so modest. You'd have gone first round, and you know like I do." Uncle Blake leads the way to the door and holds it open for me; the blessedly warm air blasts us in the face. "If you were my son, I'd have pushed you to do it."

"It's not that I didn't want to."

He waves his hand. "Right. Rich."

I huff out a laugh. "No one calls him that, you know."

"I'm his brother, it's allowed."

We order burgers and fries and a chocolate shake each. I need to take Penny here sometime; I know she'd prefer the strawberry milkshake and I love the little happy dance she does when she's tasting something good. Maybe when McKee does one of its film screenings on the quad in the spring, we'll make it dinner and a movie.

Uncle Blake picks out a booth in the corner. The neon of the sign on the wall above washes over his face in shades of pink and purple. When I sit across from him, he leans in, elbows on the sticky tabletop. "Scouts been in touch?"

"Some," I say. "They know I'm staying for the duration. Dad and James' agent is going to work on an offer after graduation."

"Fuck that," he says, fiddling with his watch. It's an expensive one, a gold and silver Rolex. My dad has a Rolex too, and judging by his graduation present to James, I'll have one coming my way after next year. "Teams are going to be lining up around the block. You won't need an agent. Save your money."

I shake my head. "No way. Contracts are complicated."

"You have something they want. I've watched your highlights this season. You're a fucking superstar. You could be the next Makar."

I let out a disbelieving laugh. It's flattering that he's seen the tape, but it's a big leap to go from 'Hockey East top defenseman' to 'Norris Memorial Award winner.' Even if that's the thing I fantasize about, it's not the kind of the dream I'd admit aloud. "Sure."

"Don't let anyone tell you otherwise. You have the fucking talent; you should be in the league already. Not playing for some college team and writing papers."

"I'm fine where I am," I say, a touch sharp. "And McKee isn't some college team. We're good enough to win the Frozen Four this year."

He settles back against the booth, hands held up in surrender. "I'm serious, kid. But we don't have to talk about it."

"Sorry." I take off my cap and scrub my hand through my hair as I breathe in. "But I'm fine where I am. Really."

"Well, go on, tell me more." He gives the server a flirty grin as she sets down our meals, and she blushes as she walks away. I resist the urge to roll my eyes; apparently my uncle's charm is alive and well. "I'm here now. For good this time."

"Seriously?"

"Serious as a heart attack." He picks up his shake and knocks his glass against mine in cheers. "I've stayed away too long. It's time that changed."

50

PENNY

I SETTLE against the couch cushions, breathing in the familiar smell of ylang-ylang and orange blossom. Dr. Faber sits across from me in her leather armchair, her notebook open to a fresh page. She crosses one leg over the other and entwines her fingers, each adorned with at least one ring. I've sat in this exact place more times than I can count, but whenever I arrive, I remember the very first appointment.

I wore a pair of ripped jeans, which exasperated Dad; he'd somehow gotten it into his head that Dr. Faber was ancient and would be offended by her teenage patient showing too much skin. He walked me all the way to her office, tutting about it, and then Dr. Faber opened the door, and she wasn't ancient at all, but instead in her early thirties and wearing a sundress and clogs, tattoos winding around both of her arms, pink hair cut into an asymmetrical bob. I loved her immediately. I don't see her as often as I used to, but her office, with its blue walls and abstract art, its collection of throw pillows and creaky old radiator, feels comforting. I don't have any aunts of my own, but that's what Dr. Faber has always felt like to me; a relative I can be honest with without fear of being judged. I can't wait to tell her that the guy I'd been hooking up with is now my boyfriend.

"Did your dad drive you?" she asks.

I tuck my hair behind my ear, unable to hold back my smile. "My boyfriend did, actually."

She smiles too. "Boyfriend? Penny, that's wonderful. Is he the young man you mentioned at our last session?" She flips through her notes. "Just before Christmas, you mentioned you'd been experimenting with a guy named Cooper."

"Yes. That's him."

She scribbles a note. "How did this happen?"

"We kind of... developed feelings, I guess, while we were working through the list I had. You know the one."

She nods, still smiling. When I explained The List to her, back when we first started doing sessions, I expected concern, but she was all for me trying it one day, provided I was crossing off the items with someone I could truly see myself trusting. That's why I like Dr. Faber; she's always understood where I'm coming from and has never made me feel like my desires are wrong. "Does your dad know you're dating?"

"Yeah. And he likes him. He already knew Cooper, you know? Because of the team."

"Right, of course." She settles back, recrossing her legs. "You sound good, Penny. Do you feel good?"

"Yeah." I take a deep breath. "Really good. I... I really like him. He's so different from Preston. I have fun with him, and I really think I'm starting to trust him."

"That's great." She makes another note, giving me a gentle smile. "Let's get into that in a moment, because I know what time of year it is, and I'm sure you haven't forgotten either."

The warmth running through me cools down. "No."

"But I want to hear more about Cooper and your list. Did you cross off every item?"

"Almost." I huff out a laugh. "I'm sure you know what's left."

"Vaginal sex?" Her voice is frank. That's another thing I've always appreciated about her; she tells it like it is while still staying kind. It reminds me of Mom. She never met Dr. Faber, of course, but I think she would approve.

"I want to do it. I want to have that experience with him."

"Has he expressed any feelings on the topic?"

"I'm sure he wants to." I drag my teeth over my lower lip, considering it. "He's never tried to pressure me or anything. And we have fun doing other things. But this would be really special, you know? Or at least I hope it would be, unlike last time."

"Don't rush, but I think that allowing yourself to have this experience could be an empowering one. Even more so than the other acts of control and reclamation of agency that you've engaged in with him."

"You make it sound better than my roommate."

She laughs. "That's what it is, at its core, right? Taking back power. You're powerful, Penny. The fact that you've given yourself so much space to explore your sexuality on your own terms is something you shouldn't take lightly. The Penny I first met wouldn't have done this."

My throat feels blocked up suddenly, but I squeak out, "Thanks. I know. Sometimes I feel the same as I did back then, but then I remember that I'm not. I'm growing."

She gives me a warm look, subtly nudging the tissues in my direction. She knows by now that I'm as likely to cry because I'm happy as I am because I'm sad.

"It's almost February 18th," she says, a careful note in her voice.

"Yeah." I take a tissue, even though I'm not crying, and fold it into a little square. The first anniversary of the party, I was a mess; I could barely talk through my anger and panic. I'm better now, but that doesn't mean I'm looking forward to it—even if that date is Cooper's birthday. If I can manage to get through it without having a panic attack, I'll consider it a successful day. "I've been trying not to think about it."

"Out of avoidance?"

"More like... out of stubbornness." I shrug one shoulder. "It's Cooper's birthday, the 18th. I want to celebrate with him. I'm helping his siblings plan a surprise party for him. I don't want to be a wreck, you know? And I haven't had a true anxiety attack in ages. So, every time my mind brings it up, I try to redirect."

"What coping strategies are you using?"

"Reminding myself that I can control my thoughts. Doing a breathing exercise. Taking a time out and reading for a few minutes instead. The stuff we've talked about."

"That's excellent," she says. "But I also want you to give yourself grace if it ends up being hard. I fully support you wanting to make new memories—it's been working well for you—but this day still has baggage."

"It's not fair," I say fiercely.

"I never said it was," she says. She leans in, clasping her hands together again. "Penny, does Cooper know anything about Preston?"

"No," I admit.

"Why do you think you've been holding back?"

I shred the tissue into little strips, then realize I'm making a mess, so I ball it into my fist instead. I force myself to meet Dr. Faber's eyes. "What if he finds out and decides it's too much to handle?"

"Has he done anything that makes you feel like that's a possibility?"

"It's always a possibility." I fiddle with my moon ring; it's that or grab another tissue to destroy. "What if he thinks…"

I can't even say it aloud, but Dr. Faber catches my drift.

"Only you know the right time to tell him," she says. "But I would encourage you to try to be open about it. Go with your instincts on this one. You just told me that you're starting to trust him. If you trust him with your past, it could bring you even closer."

"Or send him away."

"Maybe," she says. She reaches forward, covering my hand with her own. "But love is almost always worth the risk."

51

PENNY

All good at the therapist

Finished now

COOP

Good girl. I'm out front

I STUFF my phone into my bag and pull up my collar before heading out of the building. Cooper's truck is right by the curb. I hide my smile—the echo of praise bouncing around in my mind—as I pull open the door. I'm grateful that he isn't making me walk all the way across the parking lot, because the wind is miserable.

The first year I lived in New York, I thought the change in weather would help me. When I lived in Tempe, February meant nice, mild weather. A nice night is what led to that house party, after all. I wanted the bitter air and messy slush to remind me I wasn't anywhere near Preston.

It hasn't exactly worked out like that, but maybe this year—

with Cooper's birthday to celebrate—I'll finally move on. I ended my session with Dr. Faber on a hopeful note, especially since my meds are still working well and I've been able to successfully use my coping mechanisms. Plus, I haven't had a full-blown panic attack since I met Cooper, and that must count for something.

He leans over to kiss me as I buckle in. It's toasty warm in the truck cab, and his beard scratches against my skin pleasantly. I deepen the kiss before he can pull away, and somehow, that makes him lean his elbow on the horn. The honk startles us both into laughter.

Love. Dr. Faber mentioned love. I wasn't sure that I'd ever tell anyone those words ever again. I'm still not sure, but the possibility sparkles in the distance like a far-off sun shower.

"Whoops," he says, darting in for one last kiss before putting the truck in drive. "Sure everything's okay?"

"I'm good," I say firmly. I take out my phone to text the same thing to my dad. "It was mostly a checkup for my next prescription."

"Good." He cranes his neck around to make sure no one is coming before he pulls out of the lot. "Good girl. I'm proud of you."

I flush. "It was just a therapy session."

"And that's hard fucking work. There are gummy bears for you in the glove compartment."

My heart does the staccato as I pull them out. When Dad used to take me to therapy, back when I needed it more often, he always had a pick-me-up for after, ice cream or a trip to Barnes and Noble or even gummy bears. The fact that Cooper thought of the same gesture is sweeter than he knows.

"You're still cool with going to this game?" he asks.

"Totally. I want to meet your uncle."

"Cool." He settles his hand on my thigh, driving one-handed. Heat fills my belly. The casually possessive nature, combined with the fact he didn't draw any attention to it, is hot enough to make me want to ask him to pull over. I haven't blown him in his truck since we first got together, so we're due for it. Maybe after the game. The other day, he joked about me fingering him, and since then, I've been unable to stop thinking about how hot it would be to give him a taste of his own medicine—especially if I had his cock stuffed down my throat at the same time. It's something I've always been into, but I didn't even put it on The List; I didn't think that I'd ever be able to find a guy that in-tune with my fantasies.

He glances over. "What are you thinking about?"

"Dirty things."

He shakes his head. "You're hornier than I am."

"Only sometimes." I play with his fingers, biting my lip as I look at him. He glances over again, swallowing, and I almost ask him to ditch the game so we can go fuck instead, but I know how important all of this is to him. The relationship he's been building with Ryan, which his mother is grateful for because she doesn't know the first thing about hockey, and the one he's rekindling with his uncle now that he's two years sober and back in his life.

So, I bite my tongue and tamp down the desire running through me on the way to the rink in Pine Ridge, where Ryan's team is playing. They're the Moorbridge Ducks, and the uniforms are so tiny and adorable I nearly cry whenever I see them. Too freaking cute.

Cooper kisses me as soon as he parks the truck in the lot. "Fucking hell, Penny. Bedroom eyes are called that for a reason."

I just blink innocently at him. "Can I put my fingers up your ass after the game?"

He growls, practically yanking me across the seat, and it's a good thing he just turned the truck off, because my knee hits the gear shift. I end up in his lap, a tangle of limbs, and he kisses my face everywhere he can reach; his hands are on my ass, massaging it through my jeans. I shiver, even though I'm not cold anymore. He's so fucking *big* that he makes me feel tiny.

"Dirty fucking girl," he murmurs. He noses past my jacket collar, kissing and sucking on my neck. I shudder, my hands finding their way to his hair. I can feel his dick through his jeans. If we don't tear ourselves away, he's going to have a hard-on—and I won't be far behind; already I can feel my panties getting damp. I grind against him, unable to help myself, and he groans, tilting his head back.

I take advantage of his exposed neck to give him a matching hickey, right by the scar underneath his ear. When I asked about it, he told me it was from an old car accident that he barely remembers. He hisses, tugging at my hair when I bite down on his shoulder next. I lean back to look at my handiwork, but he just pulls me close again, his mouth against my ear.

"'Course you fucking can," he whispers, his voice low and rough and *delicious*. "But I'm coming on your face and leaving you messy, because only brats torture their boyfriends right before going somewhere public."

I mash our teeth together as we kiss, smiling all the while. "Only if you spit on it after to clean me up."

"AND THEN HE tore off his gloves and challenged the kid to a fight. Six years old." Blake beams at Cooper, clapping him on the shoulder. "Pee wee league and already determined to defend his teammates."

Cooper ducks his head, but I catch sight of his smile. Throughout the game, we've been cheering on Ryan—who is becoming quite the confident skater, and even scored a goal earlier—and Blake Callahan has been happily telling me every story from Cooper's childhood that he can think of.

"Ryan is scrappy like that," Cooper says. "When he started in the class I taught with Penny, he was timid, but he's totally different now."

We watch Ryan take a shot and cheer, but the goalie swallows it up. I sip my soda. "You're coming back, right?"

"Soon as we win the Frozen Four," Cooper promises.

"Good. I miss you over there." I give Blake a sideways look, but he doesn't seem bothered by the mushiness. Apparently, he remembers Cooper as the player he used to be—high school Cooper was even more wild than college Cooper, not that I'm sure I believe it—and he couldn't believe when Cooper told him he was going to meet his girlfriend. Blake has been witty, hilarious without trying to be, and quite the flirter as well; he shamelessly chatted up a woman at the concession stand and winked when her husband came to collect her. It's no wonder that Cooper missed his presence in his life, especially with how strait-laced his dad is. Sebastian told me the other day that he approves of our relationship, but Cooper hasn't been in the mood to talk about his father, so I haven't mentioned it. His family's foundation is having a gala—that's the word he used, gala, like we were suddenly in a royal fantasy court—next month, and I'm already bracing myself for the awkwardness.

"Penny," Blake says, "don't you agree Cooper could sign with a team tomorrow and kick half the league's asses?"

"Probably." My stomach does a somersault at the thought of Cooper leaving me to go play in the NHL. I've already thought about the fact he is going to graduate a year ahead of me. Long distance for a year while he's off in some city, possibly across the country or even in Canada, is going to suck, however necessary it'll be. The thought of giving him up sucks even worse, after all. "But there's no rush. Right?"

"Right," Cooper says, giving his uncle a narrow-eyed look.

"Just wanted to make she knows what a stud you are," Blake says. He rubs at his beard, giving me a roguish sort of grin. I can't help but blush. "Besides, she gets it. Right, Penny? Coach for a dad and all."

"Yeah." I re-focus on the game, where Ryan is on the ice again and showing off his ever-growing skills. Cooper was like that once, tiny but fierce. I was too. It's silly to think about, because he was in New York while I was in Arizona when we were around Ryan's age, but what if we met as kids? Would we have liked each other? I have the sudden image of a little Cooper challenging me to a race on skates. He'd be in a hockey sweater and pads, his blue eyes shining, and I'd be in leg warmers and a leotard, my hair in a bun instead of loose around my shoulders. I was shy when I was little, and something tells me I'd have had a little-kid crush on Cooper so huge I wouldn't have been able to talk around him.

Now he's the man I'm dangerously close to falling for, and while his future is in the NHL, there's no part of me that wants it to come early, even if he could technically try.

"If his own father isn't going to brag about him, someone has to," Blake adds. He nudges Cooper's side. "One day, that little buddy of yours down on the ice will be wearing your sweater."

Cooper's smile isn't his usual one—no wide grin, no bravado. Just softness. My heart melts, and things don't get much better on that front when Ryan runs off the ice at the end of the game a couple minutes later and throws his arms around Cooper's waist.

"Did you see the whole thing?" he asks excitedly. "Even my goal?"

"Every moment, buddy," Cooper says. He takes Ryan's helmet off and ruffles his sweaty hair. "Where's your mom? Let's talk to her about me finding a time to help you work on stick handling."

52

COOPER

IT'S POURING by the time we get back from Pine Ridge, and somehow, in the dash from my truck to the door, we manage to get soaked to the bone. I'm shivering uncontrollably. The moment we get inside my house, I push Penny against the door, kissing her so deeply I taste the sugar on her tongue. She's chilly like me, but at least there are sparks in the way our breath washes over each other. She wraps her arms around my neck, tugging me even closer; I've been with her long enough to know that means she wants my full weight on her. My cock is responding. It stirred when she whispered those filthy things in my ear right before we went to Ryan's game, and now that's all rushing back. I oblige her, pressing her right up against the door, my leg between hers. I push her coat off her shoulders and unwind the scarf from her neck, and I'm just about to tug down her sweater for a glimpse of her tits when someone coughs.

Penny's eyes widen. "Cooper!" she whispers, hitting my arm.

I groan, turning around. Sebastian, Rafael, and Hunter are

on the couch, jostling each other as they play a video game. Victoria is sitting on the loveseat; Remmy's stretched out on it, his head in her lap. Izzy is on the floor with Tangy, reading a book—or at least she was, until she spotted us.

"You couldn't do that in the car?" she drawls. "Or, I don't know, your room?"

"Why are all of you here?"

"Believe it or not, we have lives that don't always involve you," Sebastian says. He glances over for half a second. "You hungry? I made stew."

"It was fucking great stew," Hunter says. He doesn't take his eyes off the game; he's concentrating so hard his tongue is poking out of the corner of his mouth.

"The way he toasted the sourdough? Perfection," Rafael chimes in.

Remmy waves. "Hey, Coop," he says. "I'm guessing Pen's there somewhere behind the wall of muscle, so hi, Penny."

"Hey," Penny says as she runs her fingers through her wet hair. "Stew sounds, um, great, Sebastian, thanks."

"Later," I add. "We have something to take care of first."

"Sure," Izzy says exaggeratedly. "Don't be too loud."

Penny pouts. "I really would like stew," she says. "At least stew is hot."

I tug her upstairs. "I have a better idea for warming you up."

When she sees that I'm taking her to the bathroom, not my room, the lingering hesitation on her face slips away. She grins, kissing me as soon as we click the door shut.

"Can it even fit us both?"

I turn on the shower spray, then tug off my clothes. "We'll see."

"Always thinking of ways to get me naked," she teases. I

watch hungrily as she slips out of her clothes, baring all that smooth, freckled skin.

I raise my eyebrows. "You were the brat first."

She crosses her arms over her chest, cocking her hip. My mouth goes dry at the sight of her; she's in nothing but a cotton thong and socks. Her blue eyes blink at me, soft as a spring morning, as she licks her lips. A raindrop rolls down her cheek, a tantalizing preview of what she'll look like once she's soaked in the shower. "And you made me promises, Cooper."

"Let's not make a liar out of me."

She slides the thong down her long legs along with the socks, then steps past me to push open the glass door. It's fogged up already, warming the whole bathroom. She sighs with pleasure as the water washes over her. My cock, already growing heavy, unencumbered by anything as silly as a pair of boxers, twitches at the noise. It's like when she made that fucking interrobang our code for sex; one glance at it and I was halfway stiff.

I join her in the swirl of steam, pulling her back against my chest and pressing a fast kiss to the place her shoulder meets her neck. She moans, tilting her head back. I splay my hand over her belly, pressing my fingertips against her slick skin. She sways slightly, not a dance but as close as it comes in a shower stall, and I move with her, relishing in the heat that chases the damp from my bones. There's something contemplative about her right now. A deliberateness in the way she looks up at me through her lashes. My belly tightens at the sight of her parted lips, her flushed cheeks, the pale pink buds of her nipples gone stiff.

"You okay?" I murmur. Maybe she's thinking about her therapy session. I've never been to therapy, but I have no doubt that it's hard. It sounds like writing, honestly—holding a piece of yourself out to someone else willingly and hoping that they understand it. She's my brave girl for doing both. "What's on your mind?"

She shakes her head slightly as she turns in my arms, so we're facing each other. "Just something Dr. Faber said earlier."

"Did you tell her about me?" I cup her jaw. "Not that you need to talk about it, if it's hard."

"No, it's okay," she says. "I told her. She approves."

"I'm glad."

She smiles. I love the way she smiles at me when we're alone. It's like she's giving me part of herself, a little slice of the sunshine that lives inside her soul. I run my thumb over her lower lip, then groan, as I always do, when she bites down.

"Did you really mean what you said earlier?" she asks.

"I'm no liar." Hell, this girl could tell me she wants to fuck me, and I'd take her to Dark Allure to pick out a strap-on. We've mostly finished her list, so maybe it's time to make a new one together. I've never been scared when it comes to sex, and I'm not scared now. "That massage oil I like is in the corner next to the shampoo."

Her smile turns sly. She tosses her wet hair, made several shades darker by the water, over her shoulder—and then sinks to her knees. "Sebastian must love that."

"He thinks it's beard oil."

She bursts into laughter as she reaches back and grabs it. "Why is it here?"

"Because I can't get you off my goddamn mind, and at least in the shower, I have some privacy." I steady her as she works to get the cap off the bottle. "Tell me if the tile hurts your knee too much."

She just waves her hand. "I'm fine."

"It hurts worse when you're cold."

She looks up at me, dragging her teeth over her lip as she

pumps my cock with one delicate hand. "I'm not cold anymore."

I brace one hand flat against the shower wall, then sink the other into her hair. The water pounds on my back, making me groan as much as the first touch of Penny's lips to my cock. She kisses me all over, then mouths at the head, doing that swirling thing with her tongue that makes my balls tighten.

"Fucking hell."

She pulls off deliberately. "Don't you mean heaven?"

The cheesiness makes me snort. She laughs before going back to work, taking me deep into her throat. I'm so focused on the sensations, how warm, wet, and tight she feels, that I'm not expecting the press of her finger against my asshole. It's slick with oil, rubbing in a way that adds a new level to the sensations already running through me. I choke out a groan, bracing myself more firmly against the tile.

She pulls off. "Is this okay?" she asks, pressing the tip of her finger up into me just slightly.

I tug at her hair sharply. It feels odd, but not in a bad way. "Yeah, sweetheart. Keep going."

She works her finger in the rest of the way, torturously slow, lavishing my cock with attention all the while. When she crooks it, she brushes against my prostate, and I grunt, just barely resisting the urge to shove down her throat. She gets the hint anyway, taking me all the way as she explores that spot inside me. She even adds a second finger; there's a moment of discomfort, but then it washes into everything else. I've only massaged myself here from the outside, and I thought that felt good, but this is on a completely different level. It sparks deep waves of pleasure that leave me near panting, on the verge of coming right down her throat. She doesn't let up, either, on a mission to fucking torture the one of the best orgasms of my life right out of me.

I shut my eyes; I'm tense all over, nearly shaking again, this time from heat and pleasure instead of cold rain. She drags the nails of her free hand down my stomach. I gasp, pressing against her more firmly, unable to keep from forcing the rest of my cock down her throat.

I open my eyes, gazing down at her. She takes me beautifully, my good girl, as she continues to tease my prostate. I feel like I'm coming already, full of so much pleasure I'm bursting. The moment she presses the tips of both her fingers against that little nub, massaging firmly, I come for real.

She swallows it all, looking like a goddamn dream as she does. She eases her fingers out of me as I pull away. Her mouth isn't just wet from the shower water; there's spit all over her lips and her chin. I help her up, and she winces, but she's smiling as she kisses me.

"Holy fuck," I say right against her mouth.

"Good?"

"I must be in heaven, like you said." I rub my hand down her side. "Does your knee hurt?"

She presses another kiss to my lips, softer this time. "Worth it."

"So that's a yes." I reach over and turn off the shower. I help her out of the stall and wrap her in a towel, then pull one around my waist. "Let's finish this in my bedroom."

She protests when I pick her up, but I don't want her falling if she's feeling unsteady. "Meaning I'm gonna come?"

"Yeah, baby. You're gonna come."

I ignore the whoops coming from downstairs as I ease my bedroom door open. I set Penny down on the bed, then unwrap the towel. Water dots her body, flushed grapefruit-pink from the heat. She sits up on her elbows, meeting my gaze as she spreads her legs.

"Now I'm wishing I came on your face," I murmur. Even though I'm spent from the orgasm, my cock stirs with interest.

She smiles cheekily. "You know I love when you're inside me."

Possessiveness unfurls like a sail, sending warmth from my scalp to my toes. I take a step forward and press my hand against her belly. "Here."

She shudders as she puts her hand over mine. "There, babe."

I sink to my knees, kissing her on the lips before dragging my mouth lower, to her perfect tits. I cup her pussy, warm and wet, and grind the heel of my hand against her clit. She whimpers, pressing against me, seeking as much contact as possible. I'd planned on kneeling, massaging her knee while using my mouth to get her off, but instead I stretch out on the bed and tug her so we're spooning.

My softened cock fits into the crease of her ass snugly. I hook my chin over her shoulder as I work her with my fingers. She's such a mess already, it's easy; I get two fingers into her and find her g-spot as I continue to rub her clit. She's shaking, letting out a string of little sighs and moans. My come is in her belly. She's all fucking mine. The thought makes me choke out another moan.

I wring one orgasm out of her, then keep going until she gives me a second. I don't want to stop touching her, even for a moment, but eventually she twists in my arms. Her pupils are blown wide, her bottom lip bitten. She cups my face on either side and kisses me like it's the last thing she'll ever do. She's shaking even worse than when we got home, but at least she's warm.

"Fuck my ass later," she murmurs. "I wanna feel you deep."

Then she slides off the bed and uses the towel to dry off the rest of the way.

I don't move for a moment, caught up in her words—words she apparently means for me to sit with for the rest of the evening—and in watching the way she moves as she walks around. She raids my dresser for a t-shirt, then peeks into the hallway. Apparently, the coast is clear, because she darts out, coming back a moment later with our discarded clothes.

"Cooper?" she asks as she tosses me my clothes. "Did I break you?"

"In a good way." I shake my head slightly. "You sure you want to go back downstairs?"

She wavers, but then her stomach growls loudly. "Gummy bears aren't dinner," she says, somewhat sadly. "I've learned that the hard way."

When we head downstairs, Penny settles on the loveseat with Victoria—the guys pulled Remmy into the game—and takes out her notebook. I detour to the kitchen and heat two bowls of stew, then bring them out with bread and iced tea.

"That was way too long," Izzy says, glancing over at me. She's still on the floor, a couple cat toys spread out around her. Tangy is sitting a foot away, flicking her tail. She doesn't look very impressed by the display. It takes my daughter a lot to get excited. A simple toy won't do; you need to break out the tuna or the catnip or, on special occasions, the bird videos, for that.

"Agreed," Sebastian says dryly. He pumps his fist as he makes a kill. Hunter high-fives him. "We were about to send a search party."

Penny laughs, thanking me as she takes her bowl of stew. "Don't go searching if you're not sure you'll like the answer."

Izzy cups her hands over Tangy's ears. "Excuse you, there are innocents here."

"What're you playing?" I ask pointedly. I join Izzy on the floor, but scoot so I'm leaning against Penny's legs. Instead of changing into the clothes she'd been wearing, she opted to stay in my shirt, adding a pair of sweatpants that she had to roll up half a dozen times before they'd stay on her slim hips. I set my bowl aside to let it cool, massaging Penny's knee through the fabric. She rests her hand on my shoulder and squeezes, a subtle thank you.

"Halo," Rafael says. "Wanna join in?"

"Maybe after I eat."

Tangy slinks past Izzy and settles in my lap. I cuddle the warm weight of her against my stomach as I work my fingers over Penny's knee. Outside, lightning flashes, followed a few moments later by the rumble of thunder. Penny sinks her hand into my hair, half-dry now, and scratches her nails over my scalp. My eyes slide shut.

People talk about love like it's a given, but until now, I didn't know if that included me. Yet every moment like this? Penny by my side, working her way into my life just as thoroughly as Tangerine? I thank the universe that I'm lucky enough to experience them.

53

COOPER

February 14th

PENNY

I FINISHED

Aw, without me?

Shut up, you know what I mean

Babe

I'm so fucking proud

I can't believe it

I can

You're a goddamn rockstar

I just keep staring at the document like, I don't know even

Like it's all going to disappear

It's a mess but it exists??? I'm???

Send it to me

Don't you have that big paper to write?

Eh. It'll still be big a couple hours from now

That's what she said

Walked right into that one, didn't I?

Whoops

I'll save it for the bus ride to Lowell

Let's get dinner to celebrate

Can we get ramen?

Plus cupcakes

Whatever you want, baby

K imma go nap now

I'll bring it all over

It is Valentine's Day, after all

<3

54

PENNY

"WAIT, so your birthdays literally have names?"

Izzy freezes in the middle of the aisle once again, forcing me to stop short to avoid bumping into her. We've been in this party store in a random strip mall for almost an hour already, gathering decorations for Cooper's birthday party, and I love Izzy, but she's so freaking slow when it comes to shopping. She nods. "Yeah. Izzy Day, which is the best day, obviously. But also James Day, Sebastian Day, and Cooper Day."

She dumps a bunch of neon shot glasses into the cart. I eye them dubiously. "Can we buy these if we're not twenty-one?"

She shrugs. "It's not like we're buying the alcohol. That's Seb's job."

I don't think Sebastian is twenty-one yet, but I don't bother asking about it. His fake is probably top-notch. "Is he actually making a signature cocktail?"

"The slap shot." Izzy grins. "I'm going to get so fucked up, I can't wait."

"Like at the Haverhill party?"

She pokes around the shelves with a little huff. "That was first semester Izzy. Second semester Izzy has more class."

"Is the class the talking in the third person?"

She puts three different 'Happy Birthday' banners into the cart. "God, I love that you're dating Cooper. Please tell me you rag on him just as much. He needs someone to take him down a couple hundred pegs."

"Probably more," I admit. "It's just so easy."

"You have to come with us to the Outer Banks this summer."

I tuck my hair behind my ear, smiling. It's nice to think of us being together that far into the future and being serious enough that I'm invited on the family vacation. I've never been to the Outer Banks—actually, I've never been to the beach, period—and I like the thought of a shirtless Cooper in board shorts. "I guess I'll have to hope he invites me."

"Oh, he will." Izzy reaches up on her tiptoes to grab some blue plastic tablecloths. "He's in love with you."

I freeze. I think I might shut down for a moment, because Izzy says something else, but I don't hear her. She throws the tablecloths into the cart and waves her hand in front of my face. "Earth to Penny."

I blink, shaking my head slightly. "Sorry."

"Did he not say it yet?" She cocks her head to the side. "Weird. Because he totally is."

Then she turns the corner into the next aisle like she didn't just rock my fucking world.

It's not that it's a surprise. I'm not an idiot, I know Cooper cares for me. A lot. But caring for someone you're dating and loving them are two different things entirely, and I don't know how to feel about it. Since I was sixteen, I've operated on a general principle: other girls get love, but not me. Not romantically, at least. I can have friends, and I have my dad, but a boyfriend? A boyfriend who loves me for me? I had one of those, or at least I thought I did, and then he ruined my life.

Cooper isn't anything like Preston. I know this. And yet, I'm having a hard time remembering that right now.

I look down at my hands. They're shaking. They never used to shake, but now, when it happens out of the blue like this, it means nothing good. I swallow. My mouth feels fuzzy, like I just ate a bunch of cotton balls. I struggle to remember my breathing exercises. Things have been so good. My meds have been working. My coping skills have been effective. Therapy twice a month has been enough. My life has finally felt like mine, and one I don't have to apologize for. Cooper hasn't pushed to hear about my past, even if he's within his rights to, and in the process, I convinced myself that it could fade away completely.

I should have known I can't outrun my memories. Not when they have teeth. Not when they lurk at the edges of my mind, ready to catch me when I stumble, especially every late February.

Why does Cooper's birthday have to be on February 18th? Out of every day in the month, in the entire year?

"Penny!" Izzy calls. I hear her distantly, like she's yelling at me from across a football field. I take a step forward and nearly stumble.

Every time Cooper and I have crossed something off The List, it's been a fuck-you to the memory of what happened. Now that we've done all but the last item—the big one, the one that feels like an "I love you" if there ever was one—I thought I was finally getting somewhere. That I'd live my own life on February 18th without feeling an ounce of shame or panic, and I'd enjoy my boyfriend's twenty-first birthday, and when all the guests left, I'd lead him to bed and finally erase the horrible moment when I realized Preston told me he loved me just so he could press record on his phone.

Now, pushing the cart into the next aisle feels almost impossible. The rest? Laughable.

"HE'S ON HIS WAY!" Sebastian calls. "Everyone be quiet!"

I dim the lights; across the room, he gives me a thumbs up as he turns down the music. I've never thrown a surprise party, but once I had some time to get my head on straight this afternoon, it was fun to set up. James, now finished with the football season and on vacation, took Cooper out for the day, and meanwhile, we decorated the house, set up a full bar, and welcomed all his teammates and friends from the English department to the house. Tangerine was supremely unhappy with all the commotion, so we shut her in Izzy's room with her toys and her favorite cat tower. I tried Seb's slap shot earlier, and it's exactly the sort of drink Cooper will love, a version of a whiskey smash, but with cherry and lime. I don't think it would be a good idea to drink tonight, but I hope Cooper enjoys himself. He deserves it, especially with a dwindling number of games in the regular season to stay focused on otherwise.

The front door opens, and Cooper walks through first. "Well, he's been good to me," he's saying, but the sentence dies as James turns on the lights and we all start cheering. He stands frozen for a moment—he really is surprised, which is adorable and makes my heart race in the best way—but then he laughs. "No fucking way!"

"Happy Birthday!" Sebastian shouts. "Drinks on you next time we're at Red's, you old bastard. Now let's fucking party!"

He turns up the volume on the music, sending Nirvana through the speakers. Evan put together a playlist of Cooper's favorite songs. I snuck a couple of the ones I've gotten him to enjoy lately, namely by my eternal favorites, Taylor Swift and Harry Styles.

Cooper pulls me into his arms and spins me around; he's got a hand low on my back and the other on my bottom, a possessive grip that only gets more wonderful when he kisses me hard right up against the now-shut front door. I take a deep breath, enjoying his scent and the chill of the night air hanging around him. I missed him today, and when things went sideways for a moment, I wished I could have talked to him. I wasn't about to ruin his birthday, though, and it's for the best. I just need to stay in the moment. A shitty house party at Jordan Feinstein's back when I thought sneaking a beer was scandalous has nothing on a surprise birthday party for my boyfriend.

I smile as his lips move against mine. "Happy Birthday, babe."

"Did you do all this?" he asks as he glances around the room. We moved the furniture to the walls to make room for a dance floor, and thanks to all the decorations Izzy and I got earlier, the whole thing is decked out in blue-and-silver balloons and streamers. Instead of a cake, we opted for cupcakes in different flavors from the bakery in town, frosted purple and white with little edible swords stuck down the middle. Sebastian and James are planning to man the bar in the kitchen, Bex has a film camera to take pictures, and we even have a fire pit going in the back for anyone who wants a break from the inside but doesn't want to freeze their ass off. Throw in the beer pong and darts tournaments his teammates are planning, and it ought to be Cooper's favorite type of party.

"It was Izzy's idea," I admit. "For your Cooper Day. But Sebastian and I helped plan it. Bex too, and Evan and Remmy and Mia, and James helped keep you away for the day."

He shakes his head in disbelief. "So basically everyone. This is incredible, Red. Thank you."

I beam at him. "How does it feel to get to throw out the fake IDs?"

"Like I'm a new man." He hugs me closer, putting his chin on top of my head and swaying us to the sound of Kurt Cobain's voice. I listen as he greets someone, accepting birthday wishes. I press my face against his throat and ignore whoever they are.

He strokes his hand through my hair. I have it half up, half down, specifically because the other day while we were playing *Super Smash Bros,* he glanced over mid-race and said, "You look goddam gorgeous when your hair is like that."

My mid-thigh, long-sleeved, baby doll-blue velvet dress has a plunge neckline I can get away with braless, making even my practically non-existent boob situation look enticing. I'm wearing the thigh-high boots that he loves and a scrap of lacy panties with tights that I am actively hoping he'll rip, and in my purse, I have something ridiculous that will help to cross out the only other item on the list besides vaginal sex—roleplaying —and I know he'll be into it. I've seen how he looks at Arwen enough times to get the hint that elf ears are a turn-on for him, and since he's been good-natured about a version of him starring as a werewolf in the book I'm writing, I can do this. The sillier I can keep things, the looser and more relaxed I'll feel, and I'll need all the help I can get later.

Eventually, we break away from each other. He holds onto my hand as we weave through the party. Sebastian makes him a slap shot, and I snag a hard seltzer for myself before we meld into a group of his teammates, already engrossed in a game of darts. I chat with Evan, Victoria, and Mia while Cooper plays and wins the first game, because apparently his general athleticism applies to anything he tries. It's also fucking sexy to watch, a fact that Victoria teases me about when it's clear I'm not concealing my blush all that well. While he's getting set up for another round, he tilts his head back for a kiss, and it takes every ounce of effort I have not to drag him upstairs right this second.

"Want to play?" he asks. "Next game?"

"I don't think I'll be good at it." I wrinkle my nose. "I'm not good at things that involve... whatever this involves."

"Hand-eye-coordination," Mia supplies. She quirks up her lips, matte black and as neat as her winged eyeliner, and raises her glass to me. She's wearing black skinny jeans, heels that I'd break an ankle in, and a halter top that she somehow pulls off despite the highlighter shade of green; people have been staring at her since the moment the party got going. She'll have her pick at the end of the night, and I'm sure that'll leave a trail of broken hearts. "You can do a lot more with your feet."

"That's what she said," Izzy says slyly as she glides by. She's wearing a silver mini dress with white leather boots and plenty of glittery makeup. When Sebastian saw her, he joked that she looked like a go-go dancer, and honestly, the comparison is apt. She did her hair in the bathroom while Mia helped me with my makeup, and now it hangs around her face in big, soft curls. Too bad that if any guy even thinks about staring at her, he'll get the attention—and not the good kind—of three older brothers. Compared to her and Mia, I feel like a kid playing dress-up.

I reach out and grab Izzy's hand. "Iz, this looks amazing."

She beams. "Maybe I should become a party planner."

"You really could," Mia says. She gestures at the space with her drink, already down to just the ice. It feels more crowded than before, somehow. I wonder when all these people arrived, and if Cooper knows them all, or if they just heard there was a party at the Callahans', which never happens, and swung by. It makes my skin itch, the thought of random strangers just showing up. "The thought of being in charge of arranging something like this makes me want to stab myself in the eye with a dart, but you'd be good at it."

"Mood," Victoria agrees, accepting another drink from Remmy when he comes around with a cocktail for her and a beer for him. He kisses her lightly on the lips, which makes me smile. "But you're fantastic."

"And a little terrifying," Sebastian adds, right on Remmy's heels with a beer in one hand and a cocktail in the other. "I bought the wrong salsa, and I had to go back to the store."

He hands the cocktail to Mia, who looks at it with a singular arched brow before trading him her empty glass for the full one. "You weren't kidding when you said you'd be my personal bartender."

Sebastian takes a long sip of beer before answering, "Darling, you ought to know by now that I stick to my word."

Cooper and I glance at each other. Mia and Sebastian are both flirtatious by nature, but honestly, I don't even think Mia likes him all that much. Then again, Mia doesn't like many people, so that's not generally a good way to measure her interest in someone.

"I didn't even know there was a wrong kind of salsa," Cooper says. "That sounds fake."

Izzy huffs out a breath. "I give you the best Cooper Day since the Rangers meet and greet, and these are the thanks I get?"

He laughs, ruffling her hair. "Thanks, Iz. You're the best little sister a guy could ask for."

"Don't touch the hair," she grumbles, but I catch sight of her smile. Not for the first time, I wonder what it must be like to be her. She's so glamorous, but she's willing to get down and dirty for volleyball, and growing up with three overprotective jocks for older brothers? It sounds so foreign to me I can hardly imagine it. "We're singing 'Happy Birthday' in an hour."

Cooper groans. "And leave me to stand around awkwardly while you do?"

"It'll be fun," she says. "Right, Penny?"

I shrug, blinking at Cooper innocently. "It is a birthday party."

"I should have known that you and Izzy would be an awful combination," he grouses. "I regret pushing you to be friends."

I just reach up and kiss his cheek. "Show me how to play darts."

55

PENNY

I'M TERRIBLE AT IT, as I could have predicted. I send more darts into the wall than the board despite Cooper's help, but at least it makes everyone laugh. When the game ends, I lean against the wall gratefully. Being the center of attention, even for something dumb like a terrible darts game, doesn't make me feel good.

I wrap my arms around my stomach and watch as Cooper chats with his teammates. Even Brandon is here. Evan insisted that Cooper would want the entire team, even the guys he doesn't get along with that well, to be here. I'm sure he's just trying to keep things good with the team. It's why I didn't protest, because especially now, hockey comes first—but Brandon was an asshole for what he did, and even if Cooper has moved on, I haven't.

I'm staring. Brandon makes eye contact with me, no doubt feeling my gaze, and raises his beer. I try to smile, but my face feels like plastic.

"Penny, drink?" Sebastian asks as he walks to the kitchen.

A drink can't hurt. It's a party, after all. I'll just eat a bunch of cupcakes to soak up the booze. "Sure, thanks."

He brings back a slap shot for me and another for Cooper. I gulp it down a little too fast. The whiskey burns my throat, making my eyes water, but I like it. I like the way it settles like fire in my belly. I ask for another, and down that one too.

Mia pulls me into the center of the room so we can hop along to some choice tracks from *Reputation*. Izzy and Bex join us, plus Victoria and Dani, and soon pretty much every girl in the room is dancing while the guys look on, some of them whistling and holding up their phones like they're at a concert. As one song blends into the next, I realize that the edges of the room look hazy. The music sounds distant, like I'm hearing it from a distance. James comes by with a tray of shots, and I grab two, downing one and shoving the other at Mia. She holds it up, grinning, before throwing it back.

Bex uses her camera to take a couple of Polaroids. "One of the birthday boy and his girl!" she shouts over the music.

Cooper shimmies over, wrapping his arms around my waist and hooking his chin over my shoulder. My heart thuds, but somehow, I smile as Bex takes the picture. She shakes it to help it develop, then passes it over to us. Cooper is grinning; he put up rabbit ears behind my head. I'm smiling, but I look about as comfortable as I feel. Set apart from him, even though I'm in his arms.

"Adorable," Bex says. "I'm so glad you're together."

I swallow back the onslaught of emotion and say, "Thanks. I'm glad too."

Cooper kisses me, but before we get too into it, Evan whistles and drags him away to do shots with Mickey and Jean and a bunch of other guys from the team. I weave through the crowd slowly, looking for Mia, but I don't see her; when I get to the kitchen, it's empty except for, of all people, Brandon. I try to back out quickly, but he spots me.

"Penny?" he asks.

I swallow, resisting the urge to flee to the living room.

"What?"

He gestures to me with his beer. "Can we talk?"

Part of me wants to say no, but he looks sincere enough. If Cooper had a real problem with him, he'd have told me, right? He was an asshole to both of us in Vermont, but that doesn't mean he's not capable of being nice. I take a step forward, feeling a little unsteady; the whiskey is hitting me hard.

"I just wanted to apologize," he says, walking around the counter and leaning against it. I take another wobbly step, and he reaches out to keep me on my feet. He grimaces, holding onto my forearm. "I was an utter asswipe, and I'm sorry. I respect Coach Ryder, and you and him. I was just bitter. I shouldn't have gotten involved with—"

I jerk away from him.

Tropic Blue.

"Penny?" he says, frowning. "You okay?"

Now that I've smelled his cologne, it's the only thing I can notice. It's pouring into me like smoke, an ugly plume of seawater and oak. I almost gag; I turn my head to the side to take in a clean breath, but it won't fucking leave. I glance down at my hands. They're trembling, yet I can't feel them. I can't feel anything, actually, and the music in the background has faded to a far-off tune, and two seconds ago I was warm, with whiskey in my belly, but now I feel so cold, it's like I stripped naked and walked out into the February night.

Tropic Blue. I haven't smelled that since Preston, and yet my nose remembers every note. He was wearing it that night, doused himself in it. I smelled it on him, and at the time it turned me on. Other girls' boyfriends wore Axe, but mine had already upgraded to a real cologne. He was a man, and that night I snuck upstairs with him at Jordan's party, I was determined for him to make me into a woman.

Kisses in the upstairs hallway. Finding an empty room. Taking a couple hits from his joint, even though it made my eyes water.

I shut my eyes, like that will dislodge the memory playing in my mind like a movie. I press my palms against my face. I think Brandon's still talking to me, but I can't hear past the dull ringing in my ears, and I can't focus on a fucking thing but the scent on his skin. He grabs my arms, pulling my hands away from my eyes; I shove him backwards and make a break for it. I need to get away. If I can just get away, he can't film me—

I push through the room and dash for the stairs. I can't breathe. My throat feels like someone shoved hot coals down it, and everyone's face is a big blur, a smudge of a memory. I stumble upstairs, almost falling as I miss a step. My vision blurs as I yank open the door to Cooper's room, slamming it shut behind me. I slide to the floor, taking in a big gulping sob as I bury my head in my arms. I still can't feel a thing, not my feet or my hands, but my heart is thudding like it's about to fly right out of my chest.

I'm in Cooper's house.

I'm in New York.

Cooper.

I'm with Cooper, not Preston. I don't even know where Preston is right now. I know where my boyfriend is, though. He's downstairs having a good time on his birthday. I'm his girlfriend, and I should be by his side, but instead I'm up here, alone. Stupid. *Drowning.*

Seawater and oak. Spraying it on my wrists because I wanted to smell like him. He loved that, didn't he? He had me wrapped around his finger.

The glass bottle was deep blue with a turquoise top. *Prettier than your eyes*, he'd said, the day I discovered it, in his room with him for the first time. Had he been planning it even then? What about me made him decide I was the perfect girl to betray?

I try to take a step, but fall to the floor, hitting my head on the corner of the bookcase next to the window. Pain shoots through my forehead, but I grit my teeth and crawl to the closet. I need to get the scent out of my nose. I need to shake the memory free, and I need to tear it to fucking pieces.

Somehow, I make it to the closet. I pull it open and crawl inside, curling up into a ball on top of a pile of shoes. I reach up and grab at a random sweater, pulling it from the hanger and burying my face in it. Cooper's musky scent fills my nose, and my next sob is one of relief. I can do this; I can calm myself down. Five quick minutes and I'll be back at the party.

"Red? Baby, where'd you go?" The voice sounds distant, but at least I know it's Cooper's. Preston never called me Red.

Not fast enough.

56

COOPER

"THIS IS A FUCKING GOOD DRINK," I tell Seb as I throw my arm over his shoulders, pulling him into a sideways hug. He's not expecting my weight, so we fall against the wall together, but that just makes both of us laugh. "You really designed it yourself?"

"Sharp, just like you, bro," he says, grinning at me. "Sweet, too."

"The first part sounded pretty badass."

"Yeah, well. You're so sweet on Penny, it gives me a goddamn toothache."

I don't even have a retaliation, and the worst—or possibly best—part is that I don't want to retaliate. So what, I'm sweet on my girl. She's everything to me. I'll take being whipped if it means I can get on my knees to worship her.

So instead, I just ruffle Seb's hair, pressing a quick kiss to his temple. "Thanks, brother."

I've had plenty of memorable Cooper Days, but this tops all the rest. Having everyone I care about here, all my siblings, my friends and teammates, my girlfriend, makes my heart swell bigger than I thought it ever could. The only bad part about having everyone around is that I can't drag Penny away and take off that little blue dress she's wearing. If it wouldn't be rude, I'd insist on running upstairs for a quickie.

I glance around as I sip my drink, but I don't see her. With almost everyone piled into the living room, we're way past capacity, but everywhere I look, I see a familiar face. I'm sure Izzy didn't intend it this way, but it's a nice reminder of all the connections I've made so far at McKee. Uncle Blake got me thinking about the draft again, but if I entered it and then a team called me up? I might never have developed such tight bonds with Evan or Remmy. I wouldn't have gotten to live with James one more time last year. Worst of all, there's a good chance I wouldn't have met Penny at all, and she's everything to me. Even the thought of that hurts. I rub my chest as I settle against the wall.

Bex took a Polaroid of the two of us just a couple minutes ago, and that picture is going in my wallet first thing in the morning. I shake my head, smiling into my plastic cup. When I found out that James had a picture of Bex in his wallet, I teased him mercilessly. Now, I'm going to be the one dying to pull it out and show everyone. *Hey, want to see my girlfriend? Isn't she the most beautiful woman in the world?*

"We should get some beer pong going," Evan says, nudging my side. "Try and beat last time's record."

"Definitely," says Remmy. "I call Vic for my team."

Evan groans. "That means he's going to want Penny to partner up with him."

Remmy laughs. "All my love to Pen, but if she can't throw a dart, what makes you think she can throw a ping-pong ball?"

I shrug. "Well, yeah. But I don't care."

"Because you're whipped," Jean says, thick through a

mouthful of chips. "She's got a rope of fucking fire around your throat."

"You some kind of secret poet?" Remmy says. "Got a touch of country in you?"

"They have cowboys in Canada too," Jean says, exaggerating his accent so Remmy bursts out laughing.

Evan sighs, looking around the party. "What do you think my chances with Mia are?"

Seb snorts. He claps Evan on the shoulder. "Buddy, respectfully, she'd eat you alive and spit out your jock strap."

"I could fuck with that," Mickey says, breaking away from his conversation with a chick I vaguely recognize as a friend of Izzy's. She gives him an outraged look and stalks off. I wince, but he doesn't seem to notice.

I get it, Mia's a fucking formidable force. If I was still a different sort of guy, I'd have tried to get her into bed already. I agree with Sebby, she'd walk all over Evan. Mickey could sweet-talk his way into her bed, but I doubt he'd be able to stay there if he was so inclined.

I follow Evan's gaze. Mia is grinding up against a guy I vaguely recognize from the baseball team, and he's got both hands low on her hips. No Penny, though.

"I need to find Penny if we're going to play," I tell the guys. "Be back in a second."

"No quickies!" Remmy says, snapping his fingers at me as I push off from the wall.

"Like you didn't already make out with Victoria in the bathroom," Jean says.

"For like five seconds," Remmy says mournfully. "Then she grabbed my junk and told me to watch her as she walked away."

"Hot."

"That's only hot to you because you've never gone further than second base."

I snort as their voices fade into the background. A Harry Styles song is playing—at least, that's who I think it is; even if I pretend not to care for it in front of Penny, his stuff is a good vibe—so I figure I'll find my girl on the dance floor. But I weave through the crowd twice and don't see her. Izzy's with some of her friends from the volleyball team, James and Bex are making out against the coat closet, Mia and that baseball player are totally eye-fucking, and a bunch of freshmen from the team have taken over the darts board. No Penny.

"Hey," I ask Rafael as he passes by. "You see Penny anywhere?"

"I think she went into the kitchen."

I clap his shoulder. "Thanks, man."

In the kitchen, though, there's only one person there—Brandon. Honestly, I'm surprised he showed up. Grateful, because we need as much team unity as we can get, this late in the season and this close to clinching Hockey East, but still. We haven't spoken outside of necessity since I told him to apologize to Penny, and I don't think he's done it.

I lean against the doorway, crossing my arms over my chest. "You see Penny around anywhere?"

"She was just here."

"You talk to her? I'm still waiting for that apology, you know. Call it a birthday present."

He walks around the counter, rubbing at his chin. "That's what I was trying to do."

"Trying?"

"I don't know, man. She totally freaked out, she just bolted—"

My stomach clenches. "Which way?"

He holds up his hands placatingly. "I didn't mean—"

"Which. Fucking. Way?"

"I don't know. I think maybe she went upstairs."

I shove through the crowd. At the base of the stairs, I slam into some girl I hardly recognize; she shrieks as her drink splashes on us both, but I ignore it. I take the stairs two at a time and shove open my door. My heart is smashing against my ribcage with every beat. Whatever Brandon did, whatever happened, I'll handle the moment I know my girl's okay.

"Red? Baby, where'd you go?"

I don't see her. I turn in a circle, just in case I missed her, but my room isn't all that big. My bed is still made, and no one is sitting at my desk. I peek under the bed just in case she's trying to play some weird form of hide-and-seek, but there's nothing but dust. She wouldn't have gone to Seb's room, but maybe she's in Izzy's with Tangerine? Or the upstairs bathroom?

I'm just about to leave when I see that my closet door is ajar.

I crouch down, pushing it the rest of the way open. "Penny?"

My heart thuds so hard I feel it like a bruise. Penny is curled up on the floor of my closet in the tiniest ball she can manage, her face buried in one of my knit sweaters. Her shoulders shake as she sobs, the big gulping kind that comes from deep in your chest. She's trembling so badly I can see it, even a foot away from her.

Everything freezes. I can't hear for a moment, the rage coursing through me is so strong, but I shake my head, blinking back the haze on the edges of my vision, and that helps. Forget beating hard. My heart is about to shatter. I say her name again, quieter, but either she doesn't hear me, or she ignores me, because she doesn't pick her head up.

I need to see her eyes.

I crawl into the closet with her. It's a tight fit, considering it's just a regular-sized closet and I'm twice her size, but I manage. I reach out, laying my hand on her knee, and she jerks it away.

"Red," I murmur. I have a hard time keeping my voice down, but she's clearly terrified, and if I yell—even if that's what I really want to do—I'll just scare her more. "Hey, gummy bear. Can you look at me?"

She lifts her head.

I bite back a curse. What I'd really like to do is slam my fist against the wall, but I manage not to. Barely.

Her big blue eyes are bloodshot. Her face is flushed, shiny with tears. But all that pales in comparison to the cut on her forehead. It's already bruising, a trickle of blood making its way down the side of her face.

Everything in the whole goddamn world falls away.

I work my jaw until I can talk semi-normally. "Who did this to you?"

Her voice is a raw whisper. "What?"

"Was it Brandon?" I'm shaking nearly as bad as her. "What the fuck did he do to you?"

Her brows draw together. She shakes her head. "It was the smell."

I rip a strip of fabric off the hem of my t-shirt and hold it to her bloodied temple. Is she concussed? Her eyes look clear enough. "What smell?"

"His—I didn't—" Her face twists up as she sobs again. She bats at my hand, but when she sees the blood, she shudders.

"What? Baby, breathe, tell me what's wrong."

"His cologne!" she says, her voice flayed raw. "Tropic Blue. The same. The exact fucking same as Preston's. He always wore it; he was wearing it when he…"

She trails off, shaking her head, and wraps her arms around her knees.

My blood runs cold. I haven't heard her ex's name many times, but I figured that was because of an ugly history. This doesn't sound like your usual shitty breakup. I shut my eyes briefly. I almost don't want to ask, but now that the door is open, I need to walk through. She needs me. "When he what?"

She sobs again. Her voice feels like knives piercing my skin. I gather her close, rocking her. "When he what, Penelope? Tell me."

She shakes her head. "Cooper, I can't. I can't stand to lose you."

I'm shaking my head right back before she even finishes talking. "You're not going to lose me. Whatever it is, you're not going to lose me."

She sniffles. "How can you know?"

My breath catches in my throat. I've never said these words before, but they're truer than anything else in the world, and there's no use holding back when Penny needs to know once and for all that for as long as she lets me, I'll be hers. I can't recall the moment I realized; it could have been a thousand different ones, brief moments coming together to create a constellation that's imprinted on the fabric of my soul. Every time she smiles at me, I fall in love all over again.

"Because I love you."

57

COOPER

THE MOMENT the words leave my mouth, my chest feels lighter. It's like I've been carrying around an enormous secret—although honestly, I'm sure anyone can see my feelings flash across my face in neon whenever I look at her—and now I can finally relax.

For a long moment, she just looks at me. I resist the urge to pull her back into my arms. I need her to choose this, to choose me and us. To walk through the door of memory together. No matter how ugly the story is, no matter what she'd endured, I'll be there at the end, holding her tight.

She has to know that by now. If she doesn't, then I've fucking failed as a boyfriend.

"I trust you," she says. There's something fierce in her expression, a touch more of the Penny I'm used to seeing. "I never thought I'd be able to trust anyone like this again."

I reach out then, pulling her into my arms. She tucks herself against me, making herself small. I tighten my grip around her waist as I brush my lips against her hair briefly. "You can trust me. Take your time."

She nods against me, sniffling. "I think I fell," she says. "When I came upstairs. I was panicking, I couldn't... I hit my head, I think, on your bookcase."

"I'll chop it to pieces tomorrow."

I think I get a smile. I can feel the outline against my chest. "All I could smell was Tropic Blue."

"What's Tropic Blue?"

"A cologne." She sniffles again. "A really shitty cologne. My ex used to wear it all the time."

"Preston."

She stiffens in my grip. "Yeah. Preston. But Brandon was wearing it. He was trying to apologize for what happened in Vermont, and he reached out and I smelled it, and it's like... it's like I was back there. At a different house party. A different February 18th." She laughs for real this time, bitter, shaking her head. "I just knew I needed to make it stop."

The sweater. She must've been looking for something to stop the memory, to shake herself out of her panic attack. I pick it up and hand it to her. "Here, baby."

She looks up at me. Tears still fill her eyes, but her voice is steadier. I brush a stray tear away from her cheek. She buries her nose in the sweater again. I don't even try to tamp down the rush of possessiveness that I feel.

"Thanks," she says thickly. "Take it as a compliment, I guess. You smell good."

"I'm glad." I run my hand through her hair, untangling it gently.

"Preston filmed me when we had sex."

I thought I'd braced myself for whatever she was going to say. I was wrong. Her words hit me like a fucking freight train. It's like she just punched me square in the throat; I can't breathe for a moment.

Suddenly, it all makes sense. No sexting, no pictures. No

video calls when we hook up long distance. The tripod at the sex shop... my face burns. I was an asshole to her without realizing it, mocking her pain. Fucking hell.

Her lower lip wobbles, and fresh tears leak out of her eyes. I force myself to keep looking at her, even though I want to melt into the floor. I don't know what to say. What the fuck do you say when someone you love tells you something so painful, you can feel the memory and it's not even yours?

"Sweetheart. I'm so sorry." I swallow down every curse I wish I could throw at him, an asshole I'd punch out in two seconds if I ever got the chance. "Did he... I mean, was it..."

"No, it wasn't like that." She laughs hollowly. "I wanted it so badly. I thought I loved him. I wanted to be that close to him, to share that experience with him."

"That's sweet," I manage to say.

"It was our first time." She plucks at my shirt with her fingernails. She went to the salon with Mia the other day to get them done; each midnight blue nail has a snowflake on it. "We'd been dating for a while, and it was perfect, you know? I was a figure skater. He was a hockey player. Older, which made me feel special. His team would be on the other end of the ice while I practiced with my crew, and we'd all hang out. By the time we'd been dating for six months, I felt ready to take the next step. He'd had sex before, but I hadn't, and I wanted to feel that close to him."

I'm starting to feel faintly nauseous. It makes sense to me that Penny would treat her first time as a big deal. Virginity's a social construct, sure, but that doesn't mean it doesn't carry a lot of weight for most people. No wonder she planned out a list she wanted to follow; she needed control over her own experiences since her first time was tainted. "You planned it?"

"Sort of. One night, after a big game, we had a party. His

teammate's parents were on vacation, so we had a house to ourselves. We ended up in bed, and we had sex."

She flicks her eyes up, as if to gauge my reaction. I just rub her arm soothingly. "Did you realize it then?"

"No." She shakes her head. "He hid his phone. I didn't know until a couple weeks later, when I found out he was showing it to everyone he knew. I loved every moment, and I thought it was secret and special, and meanwhile all his friends were laughing about what a slut I was. He did it on a dare."

What the actual fuck. My grip tightens on her to the point she squirms. I force myself to take a deep breath and relax. "A fucking dare?"

"Let me finish," she interrupts. Her voice wavers, but I nod. "Eventually, it wasn't just them watching it, it was our whole school. People would try to deny it, but everyone saw it, even my friends. I broke up with Preston, but then my dad wanted to know why, and I just... I couldn't tell him. After Mom died, things got distant between us, so I didn't even know *how* to tell him. It was too embarrassing. They saw everything, Cooper. The whole thing, start to finish."

She pauses. I hug her close, rubbing her back soothingly.

She takes a deep breath, then says, "He found out right before my short program at Desert West. It was the first competition of mine he went to in ages. Someone told her mom, who told him. He tried to confront me about it, but I had to go perform. I had a panic attack in the middle of my routine. That's how I tore my ACL. I fell and crashed into the boards."

She's speaking in a matter-of-fact tone, like she's explained this before and needs the distance to get through it.

"What happened? Please tell me that fucker is in jail."

She shakes her head. "We pressed charges, but nothing ended up happening except him and a couple of the guys getting kicked off the hockey team."

"Jesus Christ."

"But honestly, I didn't even... care," she says, hesitating. "About what happened to them, I mean. I just hated that everyone thought I was some... some slut, for putting myself in a position where I allowed myself to be filmed. Someone even came up to my dad in a restaurant and told him he'd never have let his daughter do that. Preston's parents talked shit about us to anyone who would listen."

"But he supported you, right?"

She takes a deep breath. "Yeah. But it wasn't the same, you know? Not that it had been in a long time, but I tried to keep it from him, and then suddenly I had this huge injury, and whenever we went somewhere in town, people stared, and I wasn't... I wasn't his little girl anymore. Everything was different. It even affected things at his job at Arizona State—one of his bosses' grandsons was on the team. They didn't renew his contract, so he got the job at McKee and moved us to Moorbridge for my senior year of high school. It took us so long to get to where we are now, and then I almost fucked it up anyway in Vermont."

I pull back so I can look her in the eyes. No wonder she was so adamant about our arrangement being a secret at first. She didn't want her dad to judge her, even if it meant keeping another secret from him. "Sweetheart, I'm so—"

She wipes her face quickly. "Don't," she says. "We should get back to the party."

"We're not going back down there." I kiss her forehead softly. "It doesn't matter."

"But it's your birthday party."

"And I don't give a fuck about the party when you're hurting." I stroke her face. "What do you need from me? How can I help you?"

"I don't want to think about it anymore." She grabs at her

dress, lifting it up. "I want to forget it. Give me the last thing on the list, Cooper, please. I need it. I need *you*."

She tries to pull the dress over her head, but it gets tangled up around her elbows. I tug it down gently. We've both been drinking, and we're in my closet, and as much as I'd love to be that close to her right now, I can't. Not when she deserves more. I shake my head.

"But I trust you," she whispers.

"I know," I say. I know how hard it was for her to admit all this; I can see it in her eyes. Telling me about her mother was hard, but this was harder, and it required a level of trust she hadn't given a guy since Preston, and now we both know how that turned out. "I know you do, baby. So let me keep showing you that you can trust me. We'll do this when we're sober and we're both ready, really ready, okay? I promise."

She plasters herself to me, hiccupping. "You said you loved me."

I squeeze her tightly in answer.

"Do you still?" Her voice is barely audible. "Did I fuck it up?"

"No, baby. You didn't fuck up anything." I rock her in my lap. Here, away from the party and the rest of the world, feels like my one shot at getting her to realize just how deep my feelings are. "I love you, and I'm not going to stop."

"I want to say it." She digs her fingernails into my back. "But every time I try, the words fall apart."

My heart thuds. I do want her to say it. I want her to say it more than I've ever wanted anything. But she just gave me a huge piece of herself, and I can't push. I need to trust that it's coming, however terrifying it is to wait.

"You take your time," I murmur. "I'll be right here."

58

PENNY

February 19th

> I want you to know that I'm ready
>
> And not just because of last night
>
> I'm ready because I want to take this step with you
>
> Because I trust you
>
> Okay?

COOP

Okay, sweetheart

Come over, I've been working on something

I thought my first time was special.

Sure, it was in someone else's house. We'd both been drinking. But it was everything I wanted it to be, everything I imagined—and it happened with the person I thought I'd be experiencing it with for the rest of my life. I wanted every single moment of it, the awkwardness and the discomfort. Before I realized what he did, I replayed every moment in my mind. I wanted that memory to be as well-worn as an old pair of skates.

Turns out, I didn't know what special even meant until this very moment.

Cooper and I didn't join the party again. Instead, he helped me out of my clothes and into some of his, for comfort, and got Tangy from his sister's bedroom. I cuddled with her while he explained the situation to Sebastian. He snagged some cupcakes while he was down there, and water bottles so we wouldn't be hungover in the morning. I fell asleep in his arms with a whiskey headache and a stuffy nose from crying, and I didn't doubt for a second that it was where he wanted to be.

But this? This is magical.

I stop in the doorway to his room and look back at him. "You did this?"

He runs his hand through his hair, ducking his head as he smiles. His hair is a touch longer now, and his beard is too, with the season coming down to the wire. Outside the window, it's snowing, the sort of fat, wet snowflakes that always make me think of Lucy from *The Peanuts*. They didn't cancel class, but I suspect that everyone who went to the party last night used their hangovers as an excuse for a snow day. We had a snowball fight earlier with his siblings, and Izzy and I made a tiny snowman that's currently hanging out on the front porch. After the heaviness of last night, the day felt as sweet as the hot chocolate Sebastian made for us.

Now, though, we're alone. He cleaned, changed the sheets, and lit candles along the windowsills. He strung fairy lights over the bed and around the windows. The sight of the low light sends a shiver of heat through me. When we fuck, it's usually dirty, but he somehow knew—like he knows a lot of things, I'm realizing—that I need sweet for this.

"Is it too cheesy?" he asks.

I lean up and kiss him on the lips. "Nope."

"Hopefully we don't set the house on fire."

"Only with our passion," I say, just so I can see him cringe. I bite my lower lip as I grin at him. "Too much?"

"Come here, you," he practically growls, pulling me into his arms and carrying me to the bed. Like usual, he throws me down. I bounce a little, watching as he takes in the sight of me on his bed. The sheets are cool and clean, and I can't wait to feel them against my bare skin.

I grab my hem to pull off my sweater, but he shakes his head and does it himself. I blink up at him as he fixes my hair after. I'm not about to cry, I did plenty of that last night, but the tender expression on his face is nearly enough to trigger the waterworks. All that quiet, almost bashful tenderness, and it's for me and me alone.

He tugs off my jeans, then runs his hands down my thighs, kneeling so we're more-or-less eye level and he can kiss me. I kiss him back, but only for a moment; I'm eager for him to strip down too, so it's his bare skin I'm feeling. It's only been a couple days since we last fucked, but it feels like a criminally long time since I've seen his tattoos. When I tug on the fabric of his navy pullover sweater, he takes it off, along with his t-shirt, and kicks down his jeans. When he joins me on the bed, we're just in our underwear, and I relish in the feel of his warm body as he pulls me close. He's like the Arizona sun at midday in July; I want to bask in his glow.

He kisses the hollow of my throat, then takes the butterfly charm on my necklace into his mouth, sucking on it for a few moments before spitting it out wet. I shiver, bringing my hand up to tangle in his hair. "I turned off my phone and computer," he says.

Tears prick my eyes. So much for not crying. "Really?"

"It's just the two of us, Red. I can show you."

I nuzzle his beard as I shake my head. "I trust you."

After holding those words to my chest for so long, giving them freely feels strange. But it's a good strange, and I hope that over time, it feels as normal as breathing instead. From our very first meeting, Cooper has been giving me reasons to trust him. He gave me the biggest one of all last night when he told me he loved me. I haven't said it back yet; it's the last step and one that feels far away still, but I can feel myself inching closer. How could I not, when he made this warm cocoon for us to retreat into?

He rolls us onto our sides, stroking a big hand through my hair. "My good, gorgeous girl," he murmurs. "Talk to me, okay? Tell me what you need."

"Just you." I roll my hips against him. He's halfway to hard, which I can feel. It sends another pleasant shiver through my body. Soon, I'll feel him deep in my core. I've loved everything we've done together, but this is what I've been craving since the very first time he dropped to his knees and spread my legs for a taste of me.

He sits us up, which is harder than it sounds because I refuse to stop kissing him, and pulls my bralette over my head too. He runs his hand down my front, fondling my breasts before settling it on the waistband of my panties. His touch might be gentle, but the fierceness in his eyes makes my breath stick in my throat.

"This is just as important to me," he says as he strokes his fingertips over the scrap of fabric. "I want to hear every moan, every whimper, and every time you say my name. You're mine, and I'm yours, and I want to fucking hear it."

He drags the panties down my legs and tosses them aside, then does the same for his boxer-briefs. He tugs on my leg until I fall against the pillows. He stares right at my tits for a long moment before taking one into his mouth, sucking on it practically whole; he plays with the other one with his callus-rough fingertips.

I buck my hips, seeking contact, and he rewards me by putting his thigh between my leg and grinding it slowly against my already-wet folds. I moan like he wants, and he rewards me by giving my other breast the same treatment, all while his leg moves with slow, delicious friction. It's nowhere near enough, but he knows that. When he finally finishes his torment, he replaces his leg with his hands, spreading me even wider. I'm exposed for him, every inch of my bare body, but under his heated gaze, I don't feel anything but desire. No worry, no panic. I feel fucking sexy thanks to Cooper's low groan and the way he licks his lips. A woman who knows exactly what she wants and is going to get it.

"Want to make sure you're nice and wet," he says as he kisses down my belly. He pays extra attention to my birthmark, which gets me blinking back tears again. Good tears. I fist my hand in his hair and tug his head lower.

The first touch of his tongue to my pussy has him moaning. He presses his tongue flat against me, simply breathing in without moving. Then he swirls the tip around my clit, getting close enough my stomach clenches, but easing back at the last moment. I pull on his hair. He huffs out a laugh before he finally sucks on the little bud.

"Brat," he says, his voice muffled. "Fuck, I'll never get over how you taste."

He works a finger into me as he sucks on my clit, and then another, scissoring them. He rubs the tips of his fingers against my g-spot, and I tilt my head back as stars dance at the edges of my vision. He takes pity on me, continuing to work that spot until I come with his name on my lips. He doesn't give me a breather, even when I tremble with oversensitivity; a third finger works me from the inside as he keeps playing with my clit.

"Cooper," I whine. "More."

"What, my fingers aren't thick enough for you?"

I dig my heel into his back. "Please, babe. I don't want to wait anymore."

He finally pulls away, his lips shiny with my slick and his pupils blown wide. He pulls out his fingers, and I feel the ache of the loss immediately. Usually, at this point, he'd grab a toy to fuck me with, but not now. Instead, he grabs a condom from the nightstand and rips it open with his teeth.

I sit up, reaching for his cock. He's all the way hard now—I'll never get over how turned on he gets when he eats me out—and groans the moment my hand wraps around his cock. A toy is nice, sure, but his cock is warm and stiff, and his skin is like velvet. He's so thick and long that he'll fill me better than any toy, even the expensive one he bought me, ever could. I'm well-practiced, but I'll feel the stretch, the same way I do when he's fucking my ass and thrusts in all the way. I rub my thumb over the tip, spreading pre-come around, and use my other hand to fondle his balls. They're hanging heavy, no doubt aching.

I help him roll the condom on. The moment we're finished, he pulls me into a deep kiss, licking into my mouth. I can still taste the remnants of hot chocolate on his tongue. His scent, thank God, is clean and cool and nothing like Tropic Blue. He strokes the side of my face tenderly as he pulls away. He blinks his beautiful blue eyes, made darker with desire, and runs his thumb over my bottom lip.

"You still good?" he asks. "Still with me?"

I just nod, arrested by the intensity in his voice. He kisses me one more time, like he can't help it, and then pushes me against the bed. I spread my legs as he settles between them. He takes his cock in hand, giving it one last stroke—and then, while looking at me, pushes in, inch by inexorable inch.

He's trembling from the effort not to go too fast. I grip his arm, arching my back as I take him. It's a tight fit, but that just makes it even more delicious; I can feel him so deep, I swear he's filling me completely.

"Fuck," he gasps. "Fuck, baby girl, it's like you were made just for me."

I hook my leg around his hip and urge him closer. I want to feel his chest against mine; I want to kiss while he fucks into me with deep thrusts. I want to have been made for him—him and no one else. He gets the hint, pressing his forehead to mine as he thrusts. We breathe into each other's mouths, temple to temple, as he pushes in deeper than before. He presses a bruising kiss to my lips as he thrusts again, faster this time. I clench around him, and he practically chokes out a moan, his hips stuttering before he regains his rhythm.

I tease him like that a couple times, and he retaliates by pulling out nearly all the way. I beg for him to press back in, and he does, but only after he digs his nails into my thigh hard enough that I cry out.

Once he starts fucking me hard, he doesn't let up. We're both laughing and kissing and grabbing at each other tightly, and the joy and relief of it feels like a balm on my soul. He comes while pressed deep inside me, his thrusts erratic and yet just as delicious. His fingers find my clit and drag me right over the edge with him. After, he flops on top of me like a big, warm, athletic blanket, and I pet his hair as he mouths at my tits lazily.

I could do this for eternity and still not have my fill of it, and judging by the way he moans my name, he feels the same way.

59

COOPER

"I DON'T LIKE IT."

I give Seb a sideways glance as I knock more snow off the windshield of my truck. "You don't have to like it."

"There's a reason he isn't—"

"Yeah," I interrupt. "That reason is Dad being a judgmental asshole. He's trying his best, and he's doing well. If Dad refuses to see that, then that's his loss."

"It just seems weird." Seb kicks at a chunk of snow, sending it across the driveway. "He's out of our lives for years, and then suddenly he's back? Why now?"

I work my jaw as I finish clearing the windshield. I know Sebastian has only met Uncle Blake a few times, and he's nowhere near as close to him as I am, but some support would be nice.

"It's hard," I say as I toss the ice scraper into the truck. "I can't imagine how fucking hard it must be to get sober and stay sober if you're an addict. He's here, and he wants to be family. If you came to lunch, you'd see that."

Seb glances at the house. "Fine. But let's take Izzy along too."

We have to wait another half an hour for Izzy to get ready, but eventually we meet Uncle Blake at a lunch place downtown. He's there already, sipping on a soda while he reads something on his phone. He stands to clap my back, then pulls Izzy into a hug.

"No way," he says. "Isabelle, you've grown up so much."

Izzy tucks her hair behind her ear. "Hey, Uncle Blake."

"You still playing volleyball?"

"Yeah," she says. "I'm on McKee's team. Season is over, though."

"Still got that wicked serve?"

She laughs. "What do you think?"

"Atta girl. What about you, Sebastian?"

"Baseball season starts up soon," Sebastian says. He leans away from Uncle Blake when he reaches out to clap a hand on his shoulder. I just barely manage to not roll my eyes. You'd think I invited him to tag along to lunch with a random stranger off the street, not our relative. "I'm good."

"Good, good."

The server comes around and we order. Uncle Blake settles back in his chair, considering the three of us.

"I can't believe how much you look like Dad," Izzy blurts.

"Handsomer, though," he says with a grin. "And with less of a stick up my ass."

"What are you doing back in New York?" Seb asks. "Coop says you're here for good."

"Yes." He scratches the back of his neck. "I'm working on finding a place."

"What about a job?"

"Sebastian," I snap.

Seb just keeps staring at Uncle Blake. "I don't even know what you do."

Uncle Blake scrubs his hand over his jaw. He shaved, so I get what Izzy means; without the beard, he looks just like Dad, except a couple years younger. "I have a few things in the works."

"Like what?"

"Sebastian, seriously, shut the fuck up."

Izzy widens her eyes at my sharp tone. I can't help myself, though. I have no idea what Uncle Blake is doing now, but I don't care. He could work as a dishwasher, and I wouldn't give a shit—the important thing is that he's here, and he's trying.

"It's fine, Cooper," he says. He leans over the table, settling his elbows on the top. "It's a fair question. I used to work in finance. In the city. When I was in California, I helped develop several businesses."

"And what? You're going back to Wall Street?"

"I'm working on it." He glances over at me. "I have... some debts, though, from rehab. A good treatment center isn't cheap, and your father refused to help."

Sebastian scowls. "He didn't have to."

"No," he agrees. "But he helped in the past, just not this time. Not the time that really stuck."

"Sounds like him," I say.

Sebastian snorts. "Sure. This time is different, right?"

Uncle Blake looks to Seb, who crosses his arms over his chest. "Maybe we should talk about this in private, Cooper."

"No," Seb says. "Whatever you're going to say to him, you can say to us, too."

I stand, sending my chair skidding backwards. "I should have known it was a fucking mistake to bring you. Let's go outside."

Sebastian stands too. "Jesus, Cooper. Use your head."

"No." I take off my baseball cap and run my hand through my hair. The people at the next table are looking at us, but I can't bring myself to care. "I would have expected this from Dad, but it's really fucking shitty to be getting it from you, too. He's family, and if he needs our help to get back into our lives, I'm going to fucking help."

I yank open the door right as the server comes around with our drinks. I don't care. I'm not hungry anymore. I step onto the slushy sidewalk, shoving my hands into my pockets, tucking my chin into the collar of my sweater. My coat is still inside, but whatever. A woman walks by me with her dog, and the dog tries to say hello; I bare my teeth at him as the woman pulls him away.

Fuck, my stomach hurts.

The bell on the door rings as Uncle Blake steps out a moment later. We're about the same height, so we stand shoulder to shoulder. I don't want to glance back and see Seb and Izzy in the restaurant, but I can't help myself. Izzy looks upset, and Seb is rubbing her back. Shit. I feel bad, but it's not my fault if they don't understand how important this is to me.

"I don't want to do this," Uncle Blake says after a long, quiet moment. "But if I could just get some help with the debts, then it'll be easier for me to get set up here. You have your trust fund now, right?"

I gained access to it the moment I turned twenty-one. "Yeah."

He nods. "Good. That's good." His face twists up as he huffs out a broken little laugh. "I'm sorry," he adds. "This is pathetic. But if I could have some help, I can pay you back. Your father isn't the only one with connections. I could find you a better agent, someone who will do what's best for you, not what's best for your father."

I blink. "But... Jessica is going to be my agent. We'll have our own relationship."

Uncle Blake raises his eyebrows. "You sure about that? Sure your father isn't going to try to control the whole thing? You told me about how he handled things with your brother. It's in his nature, Cooper. It's like I said, he's one kind of person. James, too. Then there are people like us. Don't you want to forge your own path?"

It's all I've ever wanted, and Uncle Blake is the only one to ever recognize that. Who took me to the rink for the first time? Who taught me how to hold a hockey stick? Maybe he is right, we've always been different. Not just second sons, but in a different category entirely. Maybe if I truly want the future I've always dreamed of, I need to distance myself. I've worked my ass off to get here, and nothing that I do will ever compete with James. From the moment I chose hockey, I lost my father's interest.

But I can help Uncle Blake. I can make a new relationship. He's not my dad, but he's family, and he sees the real me.

"How much do you need?"

60

PENNY

I RAISE my beer along with the rest of the group as Cooper steps into the middle of the circle. Even though there are other people at Red's, we took over the scene the moment we arrived. The whole group is buzzing with excited, relieved energy.

"Hockey fucking East champions!" he roars.

The guys explode into cheers. Evan and Remmy, Jean and Mickey, Brandon and everyone else, guys I've spent almost an entire season cheering on, start chanting "McFucking McKee!"

I join in, along with the rest of our crew, and we're so loud, we drown out the music and the televisions above the bar. By winning their conference, they have an automatic place in Regionals. I know they have a lot of hockey left to play, but I can feel in my bones that they're going all the way to the Frozen Four in Tampa Bay, and they're going to be champions. Out of every Division I hockey program in the country, they're going to be the ones holding up the trophy.

I haven't told Cooper yet, but I've started looking at flights to Florida. They'd have to lock me up to keep me from cheering him on—wearing his sweater, thank you very much. At tonight's game against Maine, I yelled so much my throat hurt. I was sitting next to some random older lady, and eventually she got so exasperated she snapped and said, "Your boyfriend isn't the only one playing."

She must've been a Black Bears fan.

"Speech!" Remmy says. The guys echo him, thumping on the tables and the bar and stomping their feet.

Cooper holds up his hand, pretending to think. "Ah, fuck," he says. "That was it."

Everyone laughs, even the bartender and the group of guys sitting at a table nearby.

"You're Cooper Callahan?" asks one of them. "Richard Callahan's other boy?"

"Yes, he is," Cooper's uncle says as he shoulders through the crowd to us. He ruffles Cooper's hair, pulling him into a hug. "That's my fucking nephew. Get his autograph now, boys, before he's in the NHL."

"Your father was a hell of a quarterback," one of the other guys says. "Good for you, kid, finding your own success."

Cooper flushes. He reaches out for me, wrapping his arm around my shoulders and squeezing. "Great fucking game, everyone. Great fucking season. It's been an honor to ride it out with you, and I know we have a lot left to give. Let's celebrate, then get back on the ice and get ready to rock and roll right into Regionals."

"Hear hear!" Brandon says. He raises his beer, giving me and Cooper a nod. I nod back. He doesn't know the details of why I bolted the night of Cooper's birthday party, but he apologized properly to the both of us for what happened in Vermont, and I really think he's proud to support Cooper. "Royals!"

"Royals!" the guys shout.

Cooper kisses me, his hands tangling in my hair. I can hear

his teammates ragging on him, and I smile against his lips. I thought I'd never let myself get close to a hockey player again, much less a whole team, and look at me now. Kissing my Hockey East champion boyfriend in a bar, already aching for a chance to get him alone. Experiencing the last item on The List opened the floodgates; I've been on him every chance I can get. Everything we did before then was incredible, sure, but now that I know what it's like, nothing beats coming with Cooper's cock pressed deep inside me. I literally made an appointment with my gynecologist to get an IUD so that he can come inside me bare. I want him to claim me from the inside out every fucking time.

"My Lucky Penny," he murmurs, clutching fistfuls of my sweater in his hands. "Couldn't have done it without you."

"I helped your focus that much?" I tease.

He pulls back, looking me in the eye, and I can tell he's not joking.

"Remember how this started?" he says. "Our arrangement? It still works for me, baby. I get a taste of you and it's off to the races."

I think Evan overhears us, because he pivots on his heel and starts talking loudly to someone about what seed in the bracket of 16 McKee will end up having, but I can't even bring myself to be too embarrassed.

"What about now?" I say coyly. I reach up so I can whisper the next part in his ear. "I've been soaked for you since the moment the game started."

He groans. "Fucking hell."

Before I can coax him into taking me to his truck or the bathrooms or even the back of the bar, his uncle claps a hand on his shoulder. "I've got some people I want you to meet," he says. "Business associates. Sorry, Penny."

"It's okay," I say. Sebastian has been difficult about Uncle

Blake, but someone needs to support Cooper, and I know this relationship is important to him. Even if it's a little weird that he's giving his uncle a lot of money—like, thousands of dollars out of his trust fund—that's his decision to make, and I'm going to support him. "I'll go dance with Mia."

Mia pulls me into a hug the moment she sees me. She's wearing a hockey sweater too—Mickey's, but she refuses to go into detail—and her black skinny jeans make her ass look fantastic. I tell her so, needing to shout the words over the noise of the bar, and she grins, grabbing both my hands and spinning me in a circle. Someone presses play on a new song on the jukebox, so Johnny Cash gets switched out for The Heavy. I down the rest of my beer, set it on a table, and dance along. I know I'm terrible at it, but I don't care right now, not while Mia and I are in sync with each other and can't stop laughing. I don't really know the words, but I try to keep up anyway. Mia smacks a kiss on my cheek as she grinds her hips against mine.

The back of my neck prickles. Someone's watching me. I shimmy a little as I turn around, expecting it to be Cooper, but instead, I lock eyes with a guy sitting at a nearby table. He's in his thirties, probably, wearing a suit, an empty beer glass by his elbow. His phone is out, propped against the napkin dispenser, and maybe I'd think he's just texting, but there's something about the way he's looking at us that makes my hands feel clammy.

He's watching, and he's recording for later.

"Mia," I say urgently. "Mia, stop."

I gesture to the guy, who raises his hand and waves. Mia's face goes from joyful to incandescent with rage in half a second. I don't even have time to register anything but the turn of my stomach before she stomps over to him, grabs his phone, and throws it against the jukebox. It doesn't stop the music, but almost everyone in the bar freezes. Cooper shoves through the crowd, Sebastian on his heels.

"Fucking bitch!" the guy snaps, staggering to his feet. He's over a foot taller than Mia, but she just crosses her arms over her chest. "You're going to fucking pay for that."

"Shut your face, pencil dick," says Mia. "We saw you."

Cooper tugs on my elbow, one eye on me, the other on Mia. "What happened?"

I swallow down the wave of revulsion I'm feeling long enough to start, "He had his phone out, I think he was—"

Cooper's already striding in his direction. "What, your pickup game is that fucking pathetic? Can't get women to look your way twice, so you need to record them, you slimy fuck?"

He gets right up in the guy's face, shoving Mia behind him. She tries to lunge at the guy, but Cooper hauls her around the waist and into Sebastian's arms. Cooper is the same height as this guy, but he must have at least thirty pounds on him. There's a dangerous glint in his eyes as he backs the guy up against the wall.

Yet this idiot grabs his beer glass and smashes it against the side of Cooper's head before Cooper can take a swing.

I scream as the glass practically explodes. Cooper's temple is a bloody gash, dark red running down his face like paint. He cocks his fist and punches the guy in the face, then kneads him in the stomach.

Sebastian sets Mia down—she's been struggling to get out of his arms this whole time like a wildcat—and says, "For fuck's sake, Mia, stay put!" before jumping into the fray right alongside Cooper.

The guy is still struggling, kicking and punching everywhere he can reach. He catches Sebastian in the throat with his fist. Sebastian stumbles back, gasping for air, and Cooper's rage hits a new level; he grabs the guy around the waist and drags him through the crowd. Evan and Remmy help shove him onto the sidewalk. Someone shuts off the music, finally, which is good because my ears are ringing, and we all hear loud and clear when Cooper shouts, "If you want to keep your eyes, scumbag, you'll get the *fuck* out of here."

I shove past everyone until I see him. His eyes are wild and dark and he's trembling. There's blood on his face, running into his eyes, his beard, the collar of his shirt. I stifle a hysterical giggle as I grab a rag off the top of the bar and press it to his temple.

Maybe another girl would be mad, but I don't feel anything but satisfaction and awe. He fought for me. He fucking fought *for* me. "Baby. Baby—"

He pulls me close, burying his face against my hair. He's getting it bloody, but I don't give a shit. "Are you okay?" he demands.

I pull back, swallowing as I nod. "Yeah. Thank you."

He laughs. "Thank you?"

"No one's ever stood up like that for me." I press a kiss to his lips, even though I can taste copper. "No one's ever fought for me."

"Since I can't beat up your ex, this is the best I could do."

Blake walks over, a grim look on his face. "Get yourself to urgent care," he says. "You're going to need stitches. I'll smooth things over here."

61

COOPER

TRYING to write a paper hungover is bad enough, but add in the stitches, and I can barely focus on my computer screen. Still, this paper is due tomorrow, and despite the upcoming playoffs, I need to keep my grades steady. I'm glancing down at *Daisy Miller* again, trying to remember the point I was trying to make about the nighttime stroll through the Roman ruins, when the doorbell rings.

Izzy is upstairs with Tangy, working on her own homework, and Sebastian is in his room too, as far as I know. We had each other's backs during the bar fight, sure, but things are still icy between us. He didn't thank Uncle Blake for convincing Red's to forget about the whole fight—in fact, he got them to agree to ban the guy who tried to take the video of Penny and Mia—and the only time we interacted today was when he tried to convince me, again, not to transfer the money to Uncle Blake's account. I did it already, but I don't plan on telling him that. Not when it makes him react like Uncle Blake asked me to give him a kidney.

Which I would do if he needed it. Especially after last

night. He even called Coach and explained the whole situation while Penny went to urgent care with me. I haven't spoken to Coach yet, because however justified I was in protecting and defending Penny, I've been keeping my temper in check, and the bar fight blew that all out of the water. Since it's not related to hockey and the other guy started it, I think I'm in the clear, but that doesn't mean it's not a loss of control with bad fucking timing.

The doorbell rings again. I heave myself to my feet from my place on the living room floor, books and my laptop spread out in front of the television, and pull open the door. I suppose it's too much to hope it's Penny. She would have texted if she was on her way over, and I think she's at her dad's house right now, anyway.

It's *my* father.

I gulp as I take a step back. The energy radiating off him feels like a bomb—sparking, smoking, right on the edge of going off. He walks in without saying a word. I shove my hands into my sweatshirt pocket as he brushes past me. He stands right in the middle of the living room, glancing around for what feels like the longest moment ever before he finally meets my eyes. The suit, the expensive peacoat, and the watch gleaming on his wrist all feel out of place in our college house. Why is he here? When I texted him to say we won Hockey East, he replied with the thumbs up emoji and a reminder not to get complacent, as well as to be quicker on the forecheck.

Maybe that sort of pressure works for James, but I'm ashamed to know I need more than that. Even an 'atta boy' would have made me smile instead of wanting to throw my phone across the room.

His face twists in disapproval as he examines me. I know I look awful; the stitches and the surrounding bruise are disgusting. I'm sure I'm pale, too, hungover and exhausted, my hair greasy and in need of a wash. With the mood I've been in today, you'd think we just learned we wouldn't be making the playoffs at all instead of winning our conference.

He sniffs as he takes off his coat and drapes it on the back of the couch. He's in a suit jacket, no tie; he takes off the jacket too, then methodically rolls his sleeves to his elbows. "Cooper."

"Sir."

He gestures to my face. "Why the fuck did I hear about this from your brother?"

I swallow down the outrage I feel as I glance at the stairs. Fucking Sebastian. Of course he had to bring Dad into this. "Why did you even come here? You could have just called."

"I was in the city finalizing a few things for the gala."

The gala. I've been so focused on hockey and Penny that I forgot about it entirely. A night in New York City at the Plaza Hotel, pretending to be on good terms with my whole family so my parents can get lots of donations for their foundation. Sounds like hell.

"Well, you can go back to whatever it was you were doing," I say, ignoring the way my stomach flips; a tiny part of me had been hoping he wanted to congratulate me in person for the conference win. "Uncle Blake and I have it handled. Everything is fine."

He laughs shortly. "Oh, is that it? You've got it handled? My son has stitches on his fucking face because of a bar fight, and my addict brother has it handled? What happened to telling me if he got in touch with you?"

"Hey," I say sharply. "He's sober. And he's actually been here for me recently, no thanks to you."

He sighs. "Cooper. You don't know the whole situation."

"I know enough. He's your brother, yet he's never been anything but a screwup to you. No matter what he does, you can't see him any other way. And it's how you've always seen me. *When* you even see me."

He blinks. "What?"

I bite down on my lip, even though it's aching. My eyes prick with tears. "Don't pretend you didn't start ignoring me once you realized I wasn't going to be a football player like James. Like you. At least Uncle Blake doesn't act like he wishes I was someone else."

"I don't wish—"

"Let's just stop pretending," I say, suddenly so tired I feel it in my bones. I wish I was anywhere but here, having this conversation, but I have no choice. The train has left the station. I can't turn back. "Stop pretending when I know the truth. James has always been your favorite, especially now that he's the next you. When you look at Sebastian, you just see your dead best friend. Izzy's your perfect little girl and can do no wrong. Me? I'm your fuckup, and I'll never stop being that, no matter how hard I try."

"Is that what you really think?"

"When I made captain, it's like you didn't even care." I press my palms to my eyes, trying to hold back the tears. I haven't cried in front of my father since I was a little kid, and I'm not about to do it now. "I worked really fucking hard to get there, and you just pointed out my mistakes."

His mouth opens, but he says nothing. I push past him, heading for the table in the entryway so I can grab my keys. Maybe it's cowardly to leave, but I need to see Penny. She's the only one who can make this situation just a bit less shitty. Besides, if I stay here any longer, I'm afraid I'll do or say something I regret. What did Dad say? Hockey brings out the worst in me? Wouldn't this be the fucking time to prove him right.

"Cooper."

I open the door.

"Goddamnit, Cooper, look at me."

I take a deep breath and shut the door. When I turn to look at him, I feel the first tears fall, but I hold my head high. I glance up the stairs and see Sebastian standing there. He looks stricken, which makes my heart thud dully. What did he think would happen if he dragged Dad into this?

"Your uncle is manipulative." Dad shakes his head, laughing bitterly. "Whatever he's been telling you is a lie."

"You just can't stand the idea of me having my own relationship with him."

"He's using you, and when he thinks you've served your purpose, he'll move on to someone else. You're not a fuckup, son, but right now you're sure as hell acting like one."

I yank open the door. "Thanks for the heads up."

He follows me onto the porch, but I ignore him. I get into my truck and start it up, and he pounds on the glass, but I just back out of the driveway.

By the time I get to Penny's house, I can barely see through my tears. I thought I cried hard the night of my birthday, after Penny fell asleep and I didn't have to be brave for her anymore, but this is worse. I manage to park the truck, and somehow, I find myself ringing the doorbell. Coach answers it. When he sees me standing there, he pulls me into a hug. He doesn't even say anything, just shuts the door behind us, letting me lean on him with all my weight. His hand rubs my back soothingly.

"Hey," he says. "Hey, son, it's okay. Take a deep breath."

62

PENNY

I TURN in a slow circle around the dressing room, watching the skirt of the dress I'm wearing rise and fall. "I'm just saying, we don't have to go."

"Which is sweet," Cooper says. "But I can't do that to my mother, no matter what's going on with my dad."

I bite my lip as I look at Cooper. He's in the corner, sitting on a ridiculously tiny poof with spindly legs. If I wasn't so worried about us breaking it, I'd slide into his lap and kiss the frown off his face.

In the week since the conference win—and all that came after it, including a fight Cooper had with his dad that he still won't tell me the details of—he's been in one of two moods: withdrawn, scowling at everyone and everything around him, or horny as hell. The latter is more fun for me, of course, if not for the fact I know he's doing it to distract himself from whatever's going on with his dad. He's been spending a lot of time with his uncle, too. I hope he never stops thanking Cooper for giving him a quarter of a million dollars. When he told me the exact amount, my stomach crumpled like a car in a wreck.

That's a lot of money to give someone, even with the best of intentions.

"Okay," I say. "But we can always bail if it ends up being too much."

"Got it."

"I just want you to have a—"

"Twirl for me." He makes the motion with his finger. "I like you in this color."

I glance down at the dress. The black is more Mia's style than mine, but I can't deny that it makes me look elegant. A bit more grown up. I could use that, attending a fancy New York City gala on Cooper's arm. Instead of twirling, though, I put my hands on my hips. "Cooper Callahan. Are you even listening to anything I'm saying?"

"With you in that dress?" He grins unrepentantly. "Not really."

I shrug out of it and drape it over the chair. "You're the worst."

"Try the green one. Emerald would look gorgeous on you, baby."

I sigh and pull that one on, then turn so he can help me with the zipper. When it's up all the way, I let the skirt fall. This is a proper formal dress, full length and sleek with a sweetheart neckline. Cooper was right. The deep green looks excellent with my complexion. As I stare at myself in the mirror, he whistles, then not-so-subtly adjusts his pants.

I raise an eyebrow at him without turning around. He can see it through the mirror. "Do you actually think that's going to work?"

"I don't know, is it?"

I throw my hands up. Fuck. Maybe it's a bad idea, but it is working; now I just want to sit on his cock. I try to shimmy out of the dress, but he stands, stopping me with a hand on my wrist.

"Don't," he murmurs. "I want to fuck you in it."

"We haven't bought it."

"Don't care."

"If you ruin it—"

He cuts me off with a kiss. "Apologize. Pay for it and whatever else you want. I know the drill. Now be a good girl and get me the rest of the way hard."

Desire swoops through my belly, settling somewhere lower. I've been wet for him the whole fucking day; it turns out that dress shopping in New York City is great for my libido. Izzy would be proud. He kisses me deeper, backing me up against the wall. I hope no one is around to hear us. This store is so fancy, the dressing room is a totally private experience with champagne if we want it, but we're not the only ones in the building. When I work my hand down his pants, he moans into my mouth, sparking another wave of desire. That sound is so goddamn sexy, I swear I could come from it alone. Until yesterday, I wouldn't have thought I could come just from him playing with my tits, and that happened with relative ease. I get one look at his eyes or feel the brush of his touch, and I swear I can't control myself.

I work his cock over as we kiss. As I trace my nail over the vein running down the length of it, he hisses, hauling me into his arms. We collapse to the floor, a big tangle of limbs and the skirt of the fancy dress. Before I have time to adjust, he rips my panties down my legs and tosses them aside, then pushes up the skirt, his hands finding the soft undersides of my thighs. He lifts me right onto his cock. I gasp as he stretches me, inch by torturous inch. You'd think I'd be used to this by now, considering how many times Cooper has fucked my pussy since the first, but I'm not over how fucking big he is. He fills me up to the brim, getting deeper than any toy, and it's all the better now that I have an IUD.

"So goddamn tight," he murmurs. "You take me so beautifully, Red."

I whimper loudly, but he covers it up with a kiss. I plant my hands on his chest to give myself leverage as I move on his dick. He watches me struggle to get the angle right for a few thrusts before taking pity on me and moving me up and down himself, hands planted on my ass. I squeeze around him, making him choke down a groan. He keeps helping me move with an arm wrapped low around my waist, but he wraps my hair around his fist, tugging until I meet his gaze.

"I love you," he says.

The words dance on the tip of my tongue. It's an invitation, an open door to a secret garden both of us could share. He found the key and unlocked it, and all I need to do is step through the entrance.

But it feels like the door is floating on the edge of a cliff. I might make it to the promised land, but just as easily, I could fall.

"I..."

Something flickers in his eyes. Disappointment. Maybe even fear. My heart turns to ice and cracks right down the middle. Why can't I say it? Why can't I just fucking say it?

"Cooper, I..." I swallow down the enormous lump threatening to choke me. "I..."

He looks to the side. "It's fine."

"It's not fine." I turn his face to mine and kiss him on the lips softly. "I do, I lo—"

"Don't," he interrupts. He sounds as serious as I've ever heard him. "Don't say it for me. Say it for us when you mean it."

I do mean it, but if I say it now, he'll just think I'm trying to placate him. I kiss him again, hoping the energy that sparks between us gives him a taste of what I feel. For a moment, he doesn't kiss back, but then he nips my bottom lip, and the playful gesture eases some of the tightness in my chest. Another guy might've made it into an ultimatum, but he didn't, and it's one of the many reasons I want to walk through that door. But patience can only go so far, especially for a guy like Cooper.

I just hope that when I turn the lock, it's not too late.

63

COOPER

March 3rd

DAD

Cooper, we need to talk.

There are things you need to know about your uncle.

Cooper, please pick up your phone

March 5th

JAMES

Coop, what Dad has to say is important

What, are you ignoring me too?

You better still be coming to the gala

March 9th

> **PENNY**
>
> Are you sure this is a good idea?

> He's more of a dad to me than my own father, Pen

> Okay
>
> Just... make sure you're being careful

> Did Seb talk to you?

> No. I'm just worried about you

The Callahan Family Foundation Annual Charity Gala—yeah, a real mouthful—is my mother's pride and joy, which means she expects all four of her children to be on their best behavior. Tuxedos and ballgowns are mandatory. Bickering is met with a swift glare. Most years, I use up my patience for small talk an hour in; there are always new friends of my parents to meet and make nice with. Last year, when Bex attended for the first time, people were so into her and James' lovebird act that Sebastian and I snuck out of the ballroom and crashed a wedding going on next door. This year, I have Penny on my arm, and while I wouldn't have it any other way, I have a feeling we're going to draw a lot of eyes. She should, looking hot as fuck in her emerald ballgown, complete with strappy gold heels and matching hoop earrings, and of course that wildfire hair hanging loose around her shoulders.

The other difference is that I have Uncle Blake with me. Fuck you, Dad. I hope you enjoy watching me bring him around to all your benefactors.

At the entrance to the Plaza, Uncle Blake stops, adjusting his bow tie. "Haven't been to this in years. Not since you were tiny."

"Yeah, well, you should've been here all along. Dad's been an asshole to you." I scuff at the sidewalk with my shoe, squeezing Penny's hand. Having her here means more than she knows, even if the past few days have been tense. I shouldn't have pushed her to say those words. "He needs to know that you're part of this family and not going away."

Uncle Blake claps his hand on my shoulder. "To new beginnings. I move into my new apartment tomorrow. You can come see me in the city anytime you want, you and Penny both."

I pull him into a hug. "And the job?"

"I'm back." He squeezes me tight. "I couldn't have done it without your support."

Before we follow him to the entrance, Penny tugs on my hand. She pulls me into a kiss. "If you need a break, let's find a closet."

I laugh against her mouth. "I lo—"

Stopping myself hurts, but I do, cutting my own words off with another kiss. If I keep pushing, and she feels backed into a corner, she might give into something she doesn't really feel—or maybe she'll bolt. I clear my throat. "Sounds good."

The person checking names at the door frowns when Uncle Blake gives his, but once I lean in and explain the situation, he waves all three of us through. My parents go all out for this event, but this year feels fancier than most; when we enter the ballroom, I can't decide where to look. A live band is playing on a stage at the other end of the room. The tables are set neatly, each with a white-and-blue flower arrangement in the center and full crystal dinnerware. There's not one, but two full bars, and servers in white shirts and dress pants walking around with trays of hors d'oeuvres. The chandeliers overhead sparkle in the low light. I asked my mother once why she always had the gala during the worst part of the year, late winter in New York, when the weather is still bitter and any snow that's left is sad and gray, and she replied she did it for that very reason; she wanted to give herself—and her friends and colleagues and benefactors—something to look forward to in the dreary days of early March. By the way Penny's breath catches, I think she hit the right note between magical and sophisticated.

"I'm going to the bar," Uncle Blake says.

I think the alarm shows on my face, because he laughs and says, "For a seltzer, kid, calm down." He weaves through the crowd with his head held high, like he knows he belongs here.

"Want a glass of wine?" I ask Penny. "They won't check IDs at this."

"Um, sure." She trails her fingers over the nearest chair. It's gold, with a blue silk bow tied around the back. "This is really... really fancy, Cooper, are you sure..."

I brush my lips against hers. "You're the prettiest girl here. Come on, I have people I want to introduce you to."

Before we get very far, though, my mother spots us. She's wearing a deep blue gown with a silk shawl tied around her shoulders. Her hair is done in some sort of complicated knot, held atop her head with a crystal-studded clip. The crow's feet at the corners of her eyes crinkle as she pulls me into a hug, then does the same for Penny.

"Darling," she says. "Izzy is still getting ready, but your brothers are around here somewhere. You both look so beautiful. Thank you for coming, Penny."

"Thanks for inviting me," Penny says. "This is really incredible, Mrs. Callahan."

"Oh, call me Sandra." She squeezes Penny's arm, flicking

her gaze to mine for a moment. My heart swells. "I've just been so thrilled about the two of you dating, you have no idea."

Then she leans in, the smile dropping right off her face. "Sweetie, you need to tell your uncle to leave."

I'm shaking my head before she even finishes her sentence. "No."

"Your father doesn't want him here." She glances over to the bar, where Uncle Blake is laughing with the bartender. "And frankly, I don't want him here."

I take a step back. I had been expecting this from Dad, but from Mom, too? "But... Mom, he's family."

She gives me a firm look, reaching out to cup my cheek with her hand. "And sometimes family is best loved from a distance."

"No. That's not fair." I shrug away from her touch. "He's clean. He's sober. He moved back to New York to be with us again."

She sighs. "Oh, Cooper. He said that when you were seven. Then he tried when you were ten, and again when you were seventeen."

"And instead of helping him, you keep driving him away."

"No," she says sharply. Her lip wobbles, a wave of heartbreak coming over her face. Fucking hell. I thought that even if Dad doesn't understand, she would, and the fact she's not even mad, just upset—upset because of something I did—hits me like a strike to the ribs. "We tried for so long, but some things can't be forgiven. Your father and I couldn't have lived with ourselves if you got hurt again. Make him leave, Cooper, please. We can talk about this later."

"Again?" Penny says. "What do you mean, again?"

"That was just an accident," I say slowly. "Mom, it wasn't his fault."

"What accident?" Penny tugs on my arm. "Cooper?"

Mom presses her lips together tightly. "I'm asking him to

leave, and if he doesn't, I'll have security escort him out." She wipes quickly at her eyes, then blinks twice, standing up straighter. She plasters a smile back on her face. "You need to trust me, honey."

"He's not some criminal!" My voice rises even though I don't mean for it to; a couple of people glance our way. Mom strides across the room, and I follow her, but Penny digs her heels in to stop me.

"Cooper," she says. "I think you should listen to her. And your dad. Something's not right."

"You too?" I grind out. "Penny, seriously?"

"It's just weird that he asked you for all that money." Her eyes search mine. "Think about it, Cooper. What grown man asks his nephew for that much money?"

"It's to pay off his rehab costs."

She shakes her head. Her voice is very soft. "No rehab is over a quarter of a million dollars."

"What, are you some expert on it?" I can't keep the venom out of my tone. I shake her off and stride after my mother.

My father beats both of us.

If I thought I knew what my father looks like when he's mad before this, I had been witnessing no worse than mild irritation. Rage practically dances across his features; his mouth is a tight slash, his gaze so dark even I'm taken aback. He snatches the glass right out of Uncle Blake's hand, sniffs it, and slams it down on the top of the bar.

"Gin," he snarls. "That was always your favorite, wasn't it?"

"Richard, honey," Mom says, glancing around. Her smile is all wobbly again. "Please don't make a scene."

"Oh, I'll make a fucking scene." He glances at me for half a second before grabbing my uncle by the shoulder and practically dragging him to the nearest door. "You've always been good at worming your way into places you don't belong, Blake, I'll give you that."

"Dad!" I shout. My voice rings through the room, and I know I'm drawing too much attention, but right now, I don't fucking care. I take a step forward, but someone grabs me around the waist.

"Don't," James says into my ear. "Let him handle it."

I elbow him hard, and I must startle him, because he breaks away with a curse. "Cooper."

"Fuck you," I say. "You don't understand."

James grabs me by the elbow and hustles me to the wall. I can see Penny hovering; she puts her hand on Mom's arm. The band is still playing, so I doubt the guests milling around can hear us, but they sure as hell can see us.

"Listen to me," he says. "Uncle Blake is using you."

I laugh. "You're just like Dad. He says jump, you ask how fucking high. I thought maybe when you fought for Bex, you were finally getting a backbone, but I was wrong."

His mouth tightens. "Don't say shit you don't mean."

I reach for the door Dad and Uncle Blake went through and yank it open. We're in some sort of dressing room; judging by the vanity in the corner, this is where a bride might get ready before she walks down the aisle. My uncle has his hands up, in the middle of a sentence. The moment he sees me, though, he stops.

"Cooper," he says. "Go back to the party. We've got this handled."

"Don't listen to him," I say, glaring at Dad. "Whatever he's saying, know I don't believe it."

Dad has a piece of paper in his hand. He thrusts it at me. "Fine. If you won't believe me, look at the proof."

It's a flight confirmation. JFK to LAX. Passenger name Blake Callahan. I stare down at it, then crumple it up and toss it aside. "What's it supposed to be proof of? So he's going back to California, whatever."

"He's not sober. He's not clean. That was a gin tonic in his fucking hand, and I'm sure he has coke on him somewhere." My dad's voice is like solid ice. "He's been using you this whole time, son. You want to know the reason I keep my own fucking brother at a distance? It's not because I hate him for being an addict. It's because he nearly killed you!"

The door clicks shut as Dad's words echo in the air.

Penny stands with her hands on her hips, a stricken but determined look on her face. "Cooper," she says. "Your mom just told me he—when you were seven—you got into a car accident."

"I told you that. It's how I got the scar by my ear." I look over my shoulder at my uncle, who drags his teeth across his lower lip. "Someone hit our car on the way to practice."

"He was drunk and high." She tries and fails to hold back a sob. "You got a concussion and broke your arm."

"I remember. But he wasn't—it wasn't—" I look at my uncle again. He meets my gaze, but there's sadness in his eyes. My stomach clenches tightly. "It was just an accident."

"Instead of pressing charges, I paid for his rehab," Dad says. "Only he took the money and ran off to California." He turns on my uncle once more. "You could have killed my fucking son, and instead of putting you in prison, where you *belonged*—"

"Stop," I interrupt. He tries to keep going, so I shout the word instead. "Just—stop! Fucking stop." I walk to my uncle. I'm trembling so hard I can practically feel my teeth chatter. "I don't care about the past."

"It's not the past," Dad says. "He manipulated us then, and he tried again when you were a teenager, but I kept him away. I tried to this time, but he knew what buttons to press, son. He knew how to turn you against me. Against the family."

"He's our fucking family!"

Dad shakes his head. "How much did you give him, Cooper?"

"I don't—"

"How much, dammnit?"

I bite back a curse. "Just—what he asked for. Right, Uncle Blake? For the rehab?"

Dad laughs shortly. "Of course. The rehab card. The money is for debts, Cooper. Gambling debt. Debt to his dealers. He doesn't give a fuck about anything but getting what he needs."

"Stop lying!"

"It's not a lie," says James. "He came to me first, last fall. He tried to get me to give him money. I guess when I refused, he moved on to you."

"He knew you'd gain access to your trust fund this year," says Dad. He doesn't even sound angry anymore. Just exhausted. "And now that he has the money, he's not coming back, not until he needs more."

I shake my head. "No. He wouldn't do that to me. Right, Uncle Blake?" He looks at me, but doesn't say anything. I swallow; there's a lump in my throat the size of a hockey puck. "You have the apartment, and the job—we're going to a Rangers game soon—even if you're off the wagon again, we can get you back on it. I'll help."

He rubs his hand over his jaw. "I'm sorry, kid."

I don't want it to be true. I'm desperate for everyone to be lying—everyone but him. Yet I see it in his eyes. He has what he wants, and he's not coming back.

I laugh. It sounds tinny. A recording of laughter instead of an actual sound I just made. My hands are clammy, and when I try to clench and unclench my fists, I can't quite manage the whole motion. The edges of this shitty little room look blurred.

I take a step back and nearly stumble over a chair. There's another door, not the one that goes into the ballroom, but somewhere else. I need to get to it. I need air before I stop fucking breathing.

I'm the biggest idiot in the world. Never Dad's first choice. My uncle's second choice of which nephew to swindle, apparently. Couldn't even be first at that. Now that Penny has heard the whole goddamn mess, she's going to run screaming in the other direction. I convinced myself that she loved me but just didn't know how to say it yet, but the truth is, it was only a matter of time before she left.

After this? I don't want her to be with me either. I'm a fool, and she can do better.

I pull open the door and run into the hallway. Someone calls after me, but I'm not sure who, and right now, I don't care. My shoes squeak on the expensive floor as I run down the hallway, right into the fancy, delicately decorated lobby. I shove the door open before the doorman can get it for me and skid out onto the sidewalk. I start shivering immediately, but it feels good. Let me feel something other than pain, even if it's nearly as unpleasant.

We're right near Central Park. I run to the nearest entrance and hurry down one of the many paths. I'm not all that familiar with this park, but there's an outdoor rink around here somewhere that should still be in season. We went last year, all of us, even Dad, who doesn't like skating.

I know I'm in the middle of one of the biggest cities in the world, but if I can just see a rink—a sliver of someone else's happiness, set under the stars and a late winter moon—then maybe the world will stop spinning.

64

PENNY

COOPER IS GONE.

I run to the door and peer out into the hallway. I don't see him, but he can't have gotten far. I swallow down the curse I want to shout. My heart is aching for him. But anger is coursing through me too, white-hot and dangerous. It's not directed at his uncle, though. I don't give a fuck about him, so long as he gives Cooper back his money.

Behind me, someone grunts. I whirl around. Richard has Blake backed up against the wall, his arm right over his windpipe. "Here's what's going to happen," he says, his voice lethally soft. "You're going to give my son back every fucking penny you took from him. And once you've done that, you're leaving and never coming back. Stay the fuck away from my children."

"Dad," James says. "Dad, don't—"

Blake shoves Richard back, making him stumble, and cocks his fist. James lunges forward, but before he can intervene, Richard dodges Blake's punch and nails him in the jaw with his own. His wedding ring cuts across Blake's cheek. Blake howls, covering his face as he stumbles. Richard just straightens up, adjusting his tuxedo jacket as he examines his knuckles.

"Penny," James says, pushing me to the door, "Go find Cooper."

I stop in the doorway. "No."

"No?"

I look around him at Richard. "You know, you've been a shitty dad to him."

He blinks. "Excuse me?"

Blake, still crumpled up on the floor, laughs. "Oh, this is funny."

"Shut up," I snap at him. "You're an impotent fucking worm and I hope I never see you again after tonight."

"Holy shit," James says. He looks a little scared of me, which would please me under other circumstances, but right now, I ignore him, taking a step closer to Richard. I'm getting the drift of how he operates, but what's the use of love if you're not open about it with the people you care about?

"All he's ever wanted is to feel like you cared."

"I do care." He winces as he rolls his shoulder. "I would do anything for him."

"So tell him! Tell him that!"

"He knows that—"

"No. He doesn't, that's the problem. Do you know how excited he was to tell you he made captain? And how upset he was when you didn't tell him how proud you were? Maybe if you weren't so shitty about telling your son that you loved him, he wouldn't feel like he needed to buy his uncle's affection." I spit out the words. Maybe I shouldn't be speaking like this to my future father-in-law—at least, who I hope will be my future father-in-law—but whatever. He needs to hear it. If he just fucking listened to Cooper, if he'd given him what he needs, none of this would have happened.

Richard looks stunned. Good. I hope he hears what I'm saying. I wipe at my eyes; I started to tear up in the middle and can't hold them back any longer. "You need to tell him how you feel—otherwise he won't trust you, and he'll just keep getting hurt. Trust me, I know."

I stride over to the door and yank it open. "Now, if you'll excuse me, I need to go find my boyfriend. Because I love him, and I'm not afraid to tell him that."

I gather my skirt and run down the hallway. In the movies, they make this look easy, but it isn't in the slightest. I almost trip over my own heels, only steadying myself thanks to whatever modicum of balance that years of figure skating has left me.

In the lobby, the woman at the reception desk says, without looking up from her computer, "Looking for a boy?"

I rub my knee, which is protesting. The cold is going to suck, but I need to catch Cooper before he gets too far away. "Yes. Which way did he go?"

"Left."

"Thank you!" I call as I run out of the building.

The air hits me like a freezing shower. This dress doesn't have straps, and my jacket is in the coat check, which means I'm a block of ice in under ten seconds. I grab a scrunchie from my clutch, throw my hair into a messy bun, and bunch up my skirt again. A man walking a tiny, sweater-clad dog whistles as I run by. I give him the finger while I'm still in motion, which makes me feel badass, but then I nearly slip on a patch of ice. My knee screams at me. I keep on hobbling. I don't see Cooper anywhere. Where are we again? Right below Central Park, I think. I've never been to this part of the city.

It would be so stupid to get lost while trying to find my boyfriend, but it's not like I can stop now. He has a heart of gold. I can't even imagine how much pain he must be feeling.

"Cooper!" I call. It's relatively quiet here, but I hear

nothing but faint honking and the echo of my voice. I take out my phone and call him. It goes to voicemail.

Fantastic.

I look up at the sky. Where would he go? He could've gotten an Uber, but we were planning to stay at the Plaza overnight, so it's not like there's anywhere else to go. I guess he could've gone to the train station, but he wouldn't leave the city without me. The nighttime sky is as smooth as a mirror, with an impressive number of stars dotting the deep blue. I know if I wanted to clear my head, I'd find the nearest ice rink, but we're in the middle of Manhattan.

Then I remember: there *is* a rink nearby.

65

PENNY

UP AHEAD, there's a park entrance. Central Park is huge, but there's outdoor ice skating there. It's at least a place to start. I hurry through the entrance, stopping short as soon as I'm on the path.

Even in early March, the trees bare, the snow on the ground half-melted, the park is beautiful. It's like I've stepped into a secret garden. Streetlamps illuminate the winding path, and for half a second, I forget that things are close to falling apart. There's a pond ahead, the water dark and glossy. The moon sits in it like a chip of silver. The sight of it steadies me. I walk forward slowly, turning my head everywhere in case he wandered off the path. The cold doesn't bother him the way it does me, so I wouldn't put it past him to go tromping through the snow in his fancy dress shoes.

Speaking of shoes, my toes are freezing. I bite my lip, wincing with each step.

I can't believe I was ever afraid to tell him about my feelings. That I thought I could give him my trust without my heart. I don't want to be anything like Richard, struggling to tell his own son how he feels. I love Cooper, and if I'm being honest with myself, I started falling for him the moment we first spoke.

Whatever I thought about him before, whatever walls I thought I could keep around my heart—none of that matters anymore. And if I need to wander around all night to find him so I can tell him that, then that's what I'll do.

I spot a sign for the Wollman Rink and start hurrying, my heels clacking against the pavement. I try his phone again, but again it goes to voicemail. I wrap my arms around myself and call his name. "Cooper!"

The path turns around a group of trees—and then I see him, staring at an ice rink. The rink is larger than I thought it would be, lit with floodlights and the light spilling out of the high-rises in the background. It's surrounded by trees, tall pines and maples stripped bare because of the season. Even though it's nighttime, there are plenty of skaters on the ice. Pop music plays from the ticket booth. The whole scene reminds me of the music box my mother used to keep on her dresser; tiny skaters going around in circles while 'Für Elise' played. Now that box belongs to me, but it's in my closet.

I'm putting it on my own dresser the second we get home.

Cooper's back is to me, but I would recognize him anywhere. His broad shoulders, the way his hair curls over his collar. My heart swells in my chest.

That's my guy.

"Cooper!" I shout as I run over.

He turns, his eyes widening when he spots me. He catches me when I slip right in front of him, steadying my shoulders. "Penny? Jesus, you're freezing."

Before I can ask, he takes off his tuxedo jacket and drapes it over my shoulders. He glances down at my feet, then back at me. He arches an eyebrow. "Risking your toes for me, Red?"

I smile, relief flooding through me. If he's okay enough to tease me, then that's a good sign. "Cooper, I'm so sorry."

His expression shutters. "I'm sorry I left you there."

"It's okay. I mean, I'm worried about you, and I'm sort of worried I am going to lose a toe, but it doesn't matter. Because I love you."

He pulls away, putting several feet of distance between us. I hate the loss of his touch; I hate it more than anything in the world.

"You don't need to say it for me," he says. His voice sounds hollow. "You don't need to say it at all."

I pull his jacket tighter around me. "I do. And this isn't for you, it's for us. It's like you said."

"I'm never anyone's first choice, Pen. You don't have to pretend I'm yours." He scrubs his hand over his face, looking at the rink.

I've never seen him sound so defeated. It terrifies me. To think I had a hand in making him feel this way—I can't bear it. "You are my first choice. That's why I'm standing here right now."

"Why did you want to get with me in the first place?" He laughs, and it's an ugly sound, nothing like his usual melodic laughter. "You wanted experiences without strings. A safe option. You wanted something from me, and I delivered it, and maybe this is where it ends."

"No." My voice sounds thin. Scared. "No, goddamnit, you're not listening to me. That's not what this is."

His eyes look flat. Nothing like the dynamic blue I'm used to. "Then tell me."

I swallow, forcing myself to keep looking into his eyes. I've been giving him pieces of myself for months, and now—faced with possibly losing it all—I know that the journey it took to get here was worth it. Every ugly piece of my past was worth it because it meant meeting Cooper. "It's like I've been falling all my life, and I finally landed somewhere safe. You're safe, and I love you. That's the truth."

"Penny," he says, his voice breaking.

"Please, Cooper. I'm choosing you first. Over everything. Choose me back."

Finally, finally, he reaches out and pulls me into his arms. I sob, burying my face in his chest. His hand strokes down my back, and he murmurs, low and rough, "I'd choose you in every universe. I took my heart out of my chest and handed it over to you, raw and red, and it's yours forever. You own it, and even if you try to give it back, if you abandon it, I won't take it."

"Will you take mine?"

He tilts my head up and kisses me. "Yes."

"Forever?"

"Forever."

I sob-laugh, wiping at my eyes. "Good. Because we need each other. And what cat parents would be if we got divorced?"

He hugs me tighter. For a long moment, we just breathe each other in. Even though I'm still shivering, I feel warm inside and out.

"Don't even say that word," he murmurs. "When we get married, that's it, Red. Tangy's just going to have to deal with us being insufferable."

Marriage. I like the sound of that. As far as I'm concerned, we belong to each other already, but one day, it would be nice to make it official. I don't care what the future looks like, so long as I get to spend it with him.

He puts his chin on top of my head, sighing like he's put upon. "You're shaking. We're not declaring our love for each other and then dying in a snowbank in the middle of Manhattan, come on."

I glance over at the rink. "You know what would warm us up?"

The dude operating the ticket booth and skate rentals seems bemused to hand us each a pair of skates, plus a pair of ugly but necessary athletic socks for me. Cooper needs the cheering up, and I need just a bit more magic from this night.

We skate onto the rink holding hands. It's awkward, holding up my skirt far enough I don't run right over it, but Cooper keeps me steady. We're not skating well—it's laughable, for a figure skater and a hockey player—but that doesn't matter. He keeps stopping, balancing us both so we can kiss. Eventually, we give up the pretense and just sway in place. Whenever I look up, I can't decide whether to stare at him—my new forever—or the glittering handfuls of stars in the sky.

I think it's the best skate I've ever had.

66

COOPER

WHEN I WAKE UP, all I know is Penny.

Her lavender perfume, still lingering on her skin. Her bright hair, spread out on the pillow. Her freckles. Her starburst birthmark. Her eyelashes, so long they nearly brush her cheeks. The lithe curve of her body, and her smooth, fair leg thrown over mine. Her pixie nose and stubborn lips. The bites I left on the insides of her thighs, her breasts. A picture of perfection, naked and beautiful and all mine.

Her snoring, too. But I'll never tell her that one.

I can't believe that I considered, even for a second, about giving her up. She's right. No matter how it started, we're it for each other. I might've been wrong about Uncle Blake, but I'm not wrong about her.

I'm half-hard already, thanks to sleeping naked and tangled with her, and I feel no qualms about waking her with a kiss. When we eventually made our way to the Plaza—after ice skating at Wollman Rink and a late-night bite at a hole-in-the-wall falafel place—we snuck upstairs without even thinking about going back to the gala. We warmed up once and for all with a shower in the enormous, luxurious stall. Fucked in it, too. And then again on the floor. And then finally in the bed. Despite all that, I'm nearly ready to go again.

She stirs when she feels my kiss and my hand stroking through her hair. "Babe," she mumbles.

"Hey, sweetheart."

She opens one gorgeous blue eye. "Is it morning already?"

"Something like that."

She stifles a yawn with the pillow. "Need coffee."

"All out of coffee, unfortunately. Can I interest you in some morning wood?"

That gets her to sit up. "Cooper!"

"Ah, there she is. My personal sleeping beauty."

"I'm going to smack you with this pillow."

I just grin at her. "And I'll say thank you."

"I'm going to pee." She slides out of bed, stretching, giving me a view of her pretty body. Those love bites look fucking fantastic on her. "And use mouthwash. If I can walk straight."

"If I have my way, you'll never walk straight again."

She rolls her eyes, but she's blushing. I love her for so many reasons that have nothing to do with the fun we have together, but I can't deny that finding my sexual soulmate means the world to me.

I lean against the pillows, giving my cock a firm stroke. It's fucking satisfying, knowing she still feels me that deeply. When she comes back a couple minutes later with minty fresh breath, she slips right into my lap. She fits against me so well. She kisses me, tangling our tongues together as she grinds down on my cock. I kiss back, running my hand down her back, squeezing her ass. She moans into my mouth softly. My balls ache, drawn up tight; like always, her mere presence has me pressed right against the edge.

"Need to be inside you, baby girl," I whisper. "Can I have you?"

She nibbles on my lip. "Always."

I flip us over, so she's underneath me, her head settled on the pillows. She curves her hand around my jaw as she pulls me into another kiss, and meanwhile, I stroke my hand down her body, cupping her pussy. She's slick already.

I smile against her mouth. "Such a good girl."

"No teasing," she murmurs. "Give it to me. I want to ache because of you."

I'm all the way hard now, thanks to the friction of our bodies, so I just spread her legs and rub my cock against her entrance. She glares at me—I guess that qualifies as teasing—so I smack her pussy with my palm instead. Her mouth drops open in surprise, but then she moans, tilting her head back. I smack her again, a little harder, and she lifts her hips, seeking more of the pain that mixes so beautifully with her pleasure. I roll us onto our sides, so I'm spooning her, and press her leg against her chest so I have access to her sweet cunt. I smack her a few more times, listening to her little gasps, watching as she shudders in my arms, and then finally, I shove in all at once. It's fucking exquisite, the way she feels; so goddamn tight I can barely move, feeling her pussy flutter around me as she tries to get used to my length. She cries out my name. Warmth rushes from my head to the tips of my toes. I nuzzle the place where her shoulder meets her neck and bite down as I rock into her. And because she's my good girl—my best girl, my fucking everything—that makes her reach back to pull more of my weight onto her.

Her voice shakes as she says my name again. Not Callahan. Cooper.

"You take me so goddamn beautifully," I whisper against her ear. Now that she has the IUD and we're monogamous, we've forgone the condoms most of the time, and the drag of my bare cock against her tight as fuck core leaves me dizzy. The fact she trusts me—loves me—enough to give me this gift astonishes me. If I have my way, I'll spend the rest of my life worshipping at the altar of her body.

I reach around to rub her clit, but she drags my hand away. "I can come from this," she says, her voice shaking. "Fuck me harder."

I pull her closer instead, using the leverage to work myself even deeper inside her. She cries out so loudly, I'm glad we're in a hotel room, not at the house. I must hit the perfect angle, because she tenses, her whole body a live wire about to explode, right before she sobs my name. Warm, slippery wetness coats my groin as she comes. The way she screams, the evidence of her pleasure marking both of us, sends me over the edge as well, and I come deep inside her, groaning as I breathe in her scent. Stars spark at the edges of my vision. She's gripped around me so tightly I couldn't move even if I wanted.

"Wow," she murmurs, sounding dazed. "A vaginal orgasm. I've never felt it that intensely."

"My ego doesn't need stroking, but I like when you do it anyway."

She giggles. I press my hand against her breastbone; her heart is racing like she just ran a sprint. My own is pounding as well. A vaginal orgasm. I wasn't even sure if those existed before now. Now that I do, though? It's going to be fun dragging them out of her.

We stay like that for a while, but eventually, she reaches for her phone.

"Oh, shit. We need to go."

"We can just take a later train."

"No," she says, looking over her shoulder at me. "You're getting breakfast with your dad."

I raise my eyebrows. "No."

"I set it up with him last night. You need to talk to him, love."

My breath catches in my throat. That's fucking unfair, hitting me with a pet name like that at a time like this. "I doubt he wants to talk to me."

"He does." She untangles us both and slips off the bed. "He just—"

I look at her slicked-up thighs. My mouth is watering. "I wasn't done, you know."

She crosses her arms over her chest, which just makes me look at her tits. As much fun as it is to come inside her, I love when I can suck my seed off those pale pink nipples. "Well, too bad," she says. "Your dad punched your uncle last night, you know."

I'm startled into laughter. "No way. Richard Callahan doesn't punch people."

"He does when he's defending his son." Penny runs her fingers through her hair, untangling the knots. "I know he's been shitty to you, but I told him that. I told him he needs to be honest with you, and that honesty starts now. Get dressed."

My eyes widen. "You did what?"

"It needed to be said, and I'm not sorry."

"Holy shit, I wish I'd be there to see that."

"I think I terrified James." She winces. "I might've called your uncle an impotent worm, too. I was just so *mad*."

"And you thought that insult was too over the top."

"He deserved it," she says, a fierce note in her voice. I can imagine the scene; Penny in her fancy dress, her arms crossed over her chest just like this, chin tilted as she stared down grown men. How could I have ever thought she wouldn't choose me first? When I ran away, she was there to take the heat—and then she found me and gave me her heart. You don't push away a girl like that, you keep her close and thank your lucky stars that she decided you're the one she wants. "He might not deserve another chance, but your dad does. Don't let things between you wither, Cooper. It takes a long time for them to grow green again."

67

COOPER

ONCE WE'RE DRESSED, we head down to the lobby to wait. After last night, I made sure Penny bundled up in thick socks, boots, jeans, an undershirt, a sweater, and then her coat, gloves, and her McKee knit cap. She looks like a puffball in her coat, and she's glaring at me like she's deeply annoyed, but I don't care. She's never risking the cold again, not after the stunt she pulled last night.

I feel like I'm waiting for a root canal. I've never had one, but this is what I imagine it's like: staring at the clock, willing it to go slow yet fast, a pit of dread in your stomach the size of the Grand Canyon. I'd prefer dental work to talking to my father. At least the dentist would be less awkward, and maybe even less painful. You get Novocain at the dentist, not for heart-to-hearts.

If this ends up being that. I can't imagine he has anything good to say. After he realized I gave over the money? The look of disappointment in his eyes was enough to make me want to crawl into the sewer and become one with the subway rats.

"Thank God he agreed," I hear my mother say. I whip my

head around; she's walking arm-in-arm with Dad out of the elevator. When she sees us, she smiles tiredly. "There they are, Richard."

Penny jumps up and kisses me on the cheek. "Have fun. I'm going to brunch with Izzy and your mom."

"I need a mimosa," Mom says. "And a bagel."

"Can we get bagels?" I ask Dad.

He looks like a wreck, dark circles underneath his eyes, a shadow of a beard on his face. When he buttons his coat, I see bruises on his knuckles. Huh. Not that I thought Penny was lying about the fight, but it just sounded so improbable that I didn't believe it. Yet here's the evidence, right in front of me.

He gives Mom a peck on the lips before gesturing to the door. "We can get whatever you want, son. But I need some fresh air."

I linger in the lobby for a moment so Mom can hug me. She kisses the side of my face, squeezing me tightly. "Listen to him, okay?" She leans back, cupping my chin with her gloved hand. "I love you both so much. I need you to be okay."

"I love you too," I say. My voice breaks, but it's still easier to say to her than to Dad.

She pats my cheek before turning to Penny. "Izzy said she was awake," she says, frowning down at her phone. "Time isn't her strong suit."

"It's not Cooper's either, if it's not hockey," I hear Penny say, a dry note in her tone. I almost turn around to stick my tongue out at her, but Dad is calling my name.

We stroll shoulder-to-shoulder down the sidewalk. At first, I think we're just wandering around, but then he says, "Maps said the bagel shop should be up ahead," and I realize he searched for the nearest one while I was saying bye to Mom. That makes my heart feel squishy. Then a beat passes and I feel silly. I asked if we could get bagels, so he found a shop.

We're in New fucking York. There's one around every corner here.

Still, we each get a toasted everything bagel with cream cheese, plus little paper cups of coffee.

"Penny and I went ice skating last night," I say. "At Wollman's. Remember last year?"

"I remember I almost broke my wrist," Dad says dryly. "That girl is a firecracker."

"Be mad at me if you want, but don't be mad at her."

"Mad?" He leads the way to a bench just inside the park. "I'm not mad at her or you, son. I'm mad at myself."

I nearly drop my bagel onto the sidewalk. "Dad? You feeling okay?"

He just stares out at the trees. "Blake is transferring the money back to you. What's left of it, anyway. I agreed to replace the rest, so he leaves that much sooner."

I swallow down a too-large bite of bagel. "Thanks."

Despite knowing it's for the best, my heart still aches. Maybe it's like Mom said, and he really is best loved from a distance, but I liked having him around. If it wasn't for him, I might never have discovered hockey, and then maybe I'd be a shitty wide receiver or something. It was nice to have an uncle, even if he fed right into the most fragile, insecure parts of myself.

Dad sighs, still looking around the park. A group of women fast-walk past us, and a dog walker comes from the opposite direction. No one looks at us twice, which I'm grateful for. James has said that he has trouble going out in public with Dad; someone always recognizes one or both.

James. I need to apologize to him, and to Sebastian. They were just trying to help, and I was shitty to them. I know that Dad and Uncle Blake's relationship is complicated for a lot of reasons, but I never want to be at odds with my brothers the way they are.

Dad carefully sets his coffee on the bench beside him and turns to me, his hands clasped together over his knees. I'm drawn again to his left hand; the swollen, bruised knuckles make my heart do a somersault.

"I can't believe you punched Uncle Blake," I blurt.

He closes his eyes briefly. "Not my finest moment, perhaps."

"Aren't you the one always telling me not to lose my temper?"

"True," he says wryly. "But when it comes to my children, there's nothing I wouldn't do." He sighs again. "Cooper, I haven't been a very good father to you. When I saw how you looked last night—my heart broke. I'm sorry that I fucked up things so badly. And I needed to hear it. I hope you're planning on keeping that girl around, because you could use her in your corner."

I duck my head, a small smile on my face. "She's the best."

"And you deserve the best. You deserve a father who doesn't make you question his love."

I look up; Dad's voice is breaking. There are tears in his eyes, and when he blinks, a few of them run down his face. I don't know if I've ever seen my father cry before. When James got drafted by the Eagles, maybe? At Granddad's funeral? I shake my head, barely comprehending what he's saying. "I mean, I know... I know you love me."

"I do love you. I've loved you since the moment your mother and I found out we were going to be lucky enough to have another son."

I bite my lip. Across the path, two squirrels chase each other. A woman walks by with a little kid in her arms. So many ordinary things are happening around us, and yet my heart is beating like I'm sprinting down the ice with a breakaway.

"Cooper, look at me."

It's hard, but I make myself. He wipes at his eyes carefully with a tissue before folding it back into a square and tucking it into his pocket.

"I've always been proud of you, even when I haven't shown it. I'm especially proud of the man you're becoming. And I'm sorry you doubted that. I'm sorry you felt like nothing you ever did was enough."

My vision blurs with tears of my own. I blink them back impatiently. "Why'd you never... just say that? Like when I made captain, why'd you act like you didn't care?"

"I did care. I was so fucking proud of you I could barely talk." He laughs bitterly. "But I'd just heard about your uncle from James. I was trying to protect you, and of course, all I did was drive you right to him."

"Dad?"

"Yes, son?"

"Do you..." I trail off. Fuck, this is hard, but I need to know the answer once and for all. If he's serious about honesty, then this is the chance to ask. "I mean, do you wish I played football instead? Did I disappoint you, choosing hockey?"

He surprises me yet again by carefully setting my coffee cup aside and pulling me into a hug. I'm frozen for a moment, my brain scrambling as I try to input what's happening; a hug from my handshake-yes-sir sort of father, but then I relax into it. It's like when I went to Coach, but better, because it's my dad giving it to me, not my girlfriend's. "Never. Not even a little bit."

"Are you sure? Because James..."

He rubs my back in long, comforting strokes. "Is James.

You're you. I've never wanted you to be anyone but yourself, and it's on me if that got lost in translation. My father—your granddad—he tried his best, you know? But he was the stoic type. There was always a next step. Somewhere else to go. And mostly, that worked as motivation for me. But I see now that your needs are different, and I'm sorry I've failed you for so long."

He takes in a deep, shuddering breath. "I'll tell you it as often as you need. I won't let my love go unsaid or unfelt. Not anymore. You're precious to me, son."

I'm pretty sure my brain short-circuits. I try to reply, but my voice is all strangled. Eventually, I manage a quiet, "Thanks."

He presses a kiss to the top of my head. I bite the inside of my cheek. He hasn't done that since I was very small. A kid in a hockey-themed bedroom, waiting for his quarterback father to come home from a game in time to kiss him goodnight. I'd stay up way later than I should have, just so I could get a couple extra seconds with him.

"I was coming to see you anyway, you know," he says. "The day after you got into that fight."

"Not to tell me off about Uncle Blake?"

"No. And I regret what I said." He pulls away as he clears his throat. "I wanted to surprise you with lunch to celebrate you winning Hockey East. But Sebastian called me on the way, and I let my worry and fear get the best of me. We should have been celebrating your accomplishment, and instead I cocked it all up. Again."

Hearing what he intended to do—even if it didn't happen—eases the pain in my soul. "We could do it now," I offer. "Make it dinner later, with Penny and her dad. I want you to really talk to Coach, and to get to know Pen better."

He nods. "Your mother will want to be there too, I'm sure.

After all, we'll be traveling with her to see Regionals. The Frozen Four, too, when you get there."

Warmth spreads through my insides. "If we get there."

"You will." He nods, like it's an indisputable fact. "I've seen the tape, son. You'll get there, and you'll win."

I run my hand through my hair. It's absurd, after the conversation we just had, but I'm still a little nervous about asking him for things. I've spent so long worrying about his rejection—yet if this relationship is really going to be different moving forward, I need to put myself out there just as much as him. "So, do you want me to set it up? Or are you too busy?"

"Never for you." He gathers up his coffee and the rest of his bagel, then claps me on the shoulder. "Let's go watch the skating for a while. And tell me more about this girl you're going to marry one day."

68

PENNY
EPILOGUE

Several Weeks Later

COOPER HAS his head buried between my thighs, eating me out like it's his last fucking meal—you'd think it was, he's been so dramatic about making sure everything is perfect before we leave for the Frozen Four—and I'm on the edge of coming again when I notice the clock. Back when I first saw his bedroom, I told him he was an old man for having an old-fashioned alarm clock by his bedside, but now? I'm grateful, because without it, I wouldn't have realized that we needed to leave for campus at least ten minutes ago. Fifteen, if we were really smart.

We're clearly not smart.

I hadn't planned on waking him with my best Arwen impression, but I saw The List while I was flipping through my notebook during a writing session yesterday, and I remembered that we technically didn't cross off every item, and I already had the ears, and well... that led to making out, which led to a vaginal orgasm that made me squirt, which led to Cooper getting that look in his eyes that means I'm about to be devoured. It's a look I'm powerless to resist, but in my defense, I think most women would agree with me. You don't get eye-fucked by Cooper Callahan and then turn him down when he gets on his knees.

I smack my palm against his shoulder. "Cooper!"

"Mm," he says.

The vibration of his voice makes me lose my focus, but then I see my phone—on the floor, half under his desk—light up with a call. I'd bet my last orgasm that's Dad calling, wondering why the hell we're not at Markley Center, ready to drive to the airport. "Cooper. Callahan. We're going to be late."

He just swirls his tongue around my clit. "I love it when you say my name like that."

"I'm serious."

"My Queen, you're not leaving without another orgasm."

I giggle at his faux-serious tone, but it turns into a gasp when he rubs right against my g-spot. "Babe..."

"We have time. Give me another one quick and then we'll leave."

"We definitely do not have time," I grumble, but I stay in place. My orgasm *is* building, anyway; a few more strokes and the tightness in my belly will ease. I grab at his hair, pulling him even closer to my cunt, and he rewards me by sucking on my clit. When I do come, muffled into my shoulder so we don't have to endure the awkwardness of explaining why we're running late to his siblings, he sighs, resting his head on my belly.

"Good girl," he murmurs. Those two brief words make happiness glow in my chest, because I fucking love being his good girl—the only thing that's better is being his brat, because he gets all growly—but then I remember that there's no time for cuddling.

I tug on his hair hard enough he looks up. "Come on," I say. "We need to get dressed."

"I wish I never gave Izzy the owner's suite," he says as he throws on his clothes. "I'm all sticky."

"Oh, shut it," I say with a scowl as I hop around, throwing on my sweater first because I'm dreading the whole panties situation. "Look what you did to me. My underwear is going to get soaked."

He just tosses me a clean t-shirt. "Wipe yourself down with that." He pokes around his desk, his hamper, the sheets. "I need my—fucking hell. I need my Yankees cap."

"Just leave it," I say. "Bring the bags downstairs."

"It's my lucky charm, Pen."

"I thought I was!"

He stops, pressing a kiss to my cheek quickly. "You are. You're my Lucky Penny. But this is a superstition. It's very important. The whole Frozen Four is—"

I watch, blinking, as he spins on his heel and runs out of the room. I roll my eyes. Athletes and their superstitions. Not that I have much of a leg to stand on. I remember when I wouldn't do a routine if I didn't have the right color scrunchie in my hair. I rub myself down, sniff at the t-shirt, and wince as I throw it into the hamper.

As I pull up my leggings, I hear someone scream.

I grab Cooper's alarm clock, the heaviest object I see, and run in the direction of the noise. "Cooper?"

He's in the hallway... with Sebastian. Who is shirtless and scowling. Standing across from them both, though, is Mia. She's dressed and everything, but her lipstick is smudged.

Wait, *Mia?*

"When were you going to tell us?" Cooper is demanding. "After the wedding?"

I lower the alarm clock. "Wait, are you guys together?"

"It's complicated," Sebastian says.

At the same time, Mia says, "Hell no."

"Oh my God." Tangy slinks out of Sebastian's room, meowing. I scoop her up and hold her close to my chest. "In front of my daughter, too?"

Sebastian squints at me. "Wait, are you wearing elf ears?"

I blush, snatching them off my ears. "No."

"Don't change the subject," Cooper says, his tone positively threatening. "Explain this."

"There's no subject," Mia hisses. She hoists her bag over her shoulder. "There was never any *subject*. And anyway, I'm leaving."

We turn and watch as she stomps to the stairs. Cooper raises his eyebrows at me, but I just shrug. Mia mentioned nothing to me—but as soon as I'm on the plane, I'm texting her obnoxious memes until she spills the details.

Before she hurries down the stairs, she flips her long, dark hair back and says, to a stunned Sebastian, "Enjoy watching me leave, Callahan."

THE LIST

1. Oral Sex (Receiving)
2. Oral Sex (Giving)
3. Spanking
4. Anal
5. Bondage
6. Semi-Public Sex
7. Orgasm Denial
8. Roleplaying
9. Double Penetration
10. Vaginal Sex

ALSO BY GRACE REILLY

Beyond the Play

First Down

Breakaway

ABOUT THE AUTHOR

Grace Reilly writes swoony, spicy contemporary romance with heart–and usually a healthy dose of sports. When she's not dreaming up stories, she can be found in the kitchen trying out a new recipe, cuddling her pack of dogs, or watching sports. Originally from New York, she now lives in Florida, which is troubling given her fear of alligators.

Follow Grace on social media and sign up for her newsletter for updates, bonus content, and more!

www.gracereillyauthor.com

Printed in Great Britain
by Amazon

19013815R00243